# Japanime

TOKYO    SAN FRANCISCO

**Moe USA**
**Volume 1: Maid in Japan**
By Atsuhisa Okura

Published by Manga University under the auspices of Japanime Co. Ltd., 3-31-18 Nishi-Kawaguchi, Kawaguchi-shi, Saitama-ken 332-0021, Japan.

www.mangauniversity.com

Copyright © 2007 Japanime Co. Ltd.

All rights reserved. Reviewers may reproduce the cover and/or a two- to four-page selection from the interior of the book. Otherwise, no part of this book may be reproduced or utilized in any form or by any means, electronic or mechanical, including photocopying, recording, or by any information or storage and retrieval system without written permission from Japanime Co. Ltd.

Manga University is a registered trademark of Japanime Co. Ltd.

Editor: Glenn Kardy
Project coordinator: Mari Oyama
Translator: Dale Rubin
Special thanks to Edward Mazza

First edition, September 2007

ISBN-13: 978-4-921205-19-5
ISBN-10: 4-921205-19-1

10 9 8 7 6 5 4 3 2 1    y 15 14 13 12 11 10 09 08 07

Printed in Canada

MANGA UNIVERSITY presents...

## volume one
## MAID IN JAPAN

By Atsuhisa Okura

PATTY IS AN ALL-AMERICAN GIRL WITH A PASSION FOR JAPAN. SHE IS SECRETARY OF HER SCHOOL'S ANIME CLUB, HAS WON SEVERAL COSPLAY COMPETITIONS, AND SPENDS ALL OF HER MONEY ON MANGA, PLUSHIES AND POCKY. THOUGH IMPULSIVE, SHE SPENT A YEAR PLANNING HER FIRST TRIP TO JAPAN.

## ★ cast of characters ★

RUBY IS PATTY'S BEST FRIEND, BUT IS MORE SENSIBLE. SHE LIKES THE SAME THINGS AS HER PERKY PAL, THOUGH SHE IS TRYING TO SAVE MONEY SO SHE CAN SOMEDAY ATTEND MANGA UNIVERSITY. SHE IS TREASURER OF THE ANIME CLUB, AND CONSIDERS THIS TRIP AN INVESTMENT IN HER FUTURE.

### ★ the meaning of "moe" ★

"MOE" (PRONOUNCED MOH-AY) IS JAPANESE SLANG FOR A EUPHORIC FEELING AKIN TO "LOVE AT FIRST SIGHT, 24 HOURS A DAY," USUALLY CAUSED BY THE PRESENCE OF AN IMPOSSIBLY CUTE GIRL — PARTICULARLY ONE WEARING A UNIFORM. JAPANESE MAID CAFE CULTURE IS THE EPITOME OF "MOE."

# ★ table of contents ★

**chapter one**
**COSPLAY CRISIS**     6

**chapter two**
**FAIR MAIDENS**     31

**chapter three**
**ONLINE IDOLS**     75

**chapter four**
**SCHOOL DAZE**     119

**index**
**SOUND FX**     151

## chapter one
## COSPLAY CRISIS

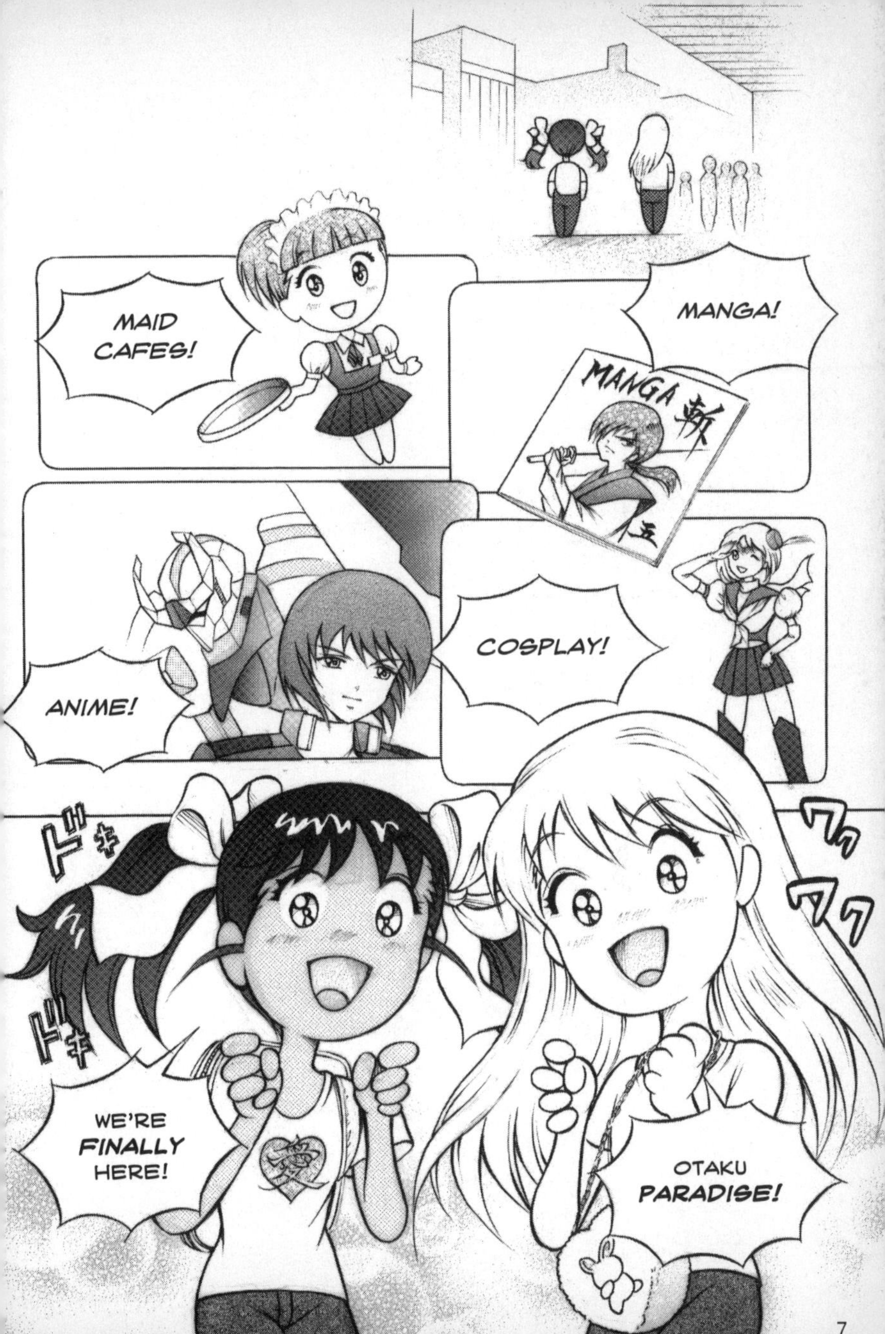
MAID CAFES!
MANGA!
MANGA 斬
ANIME!
COSPLAY!
ドキ ドキ
ワク ワク
WE'RE FINALLY HERE!
OTAKU PARADISE!

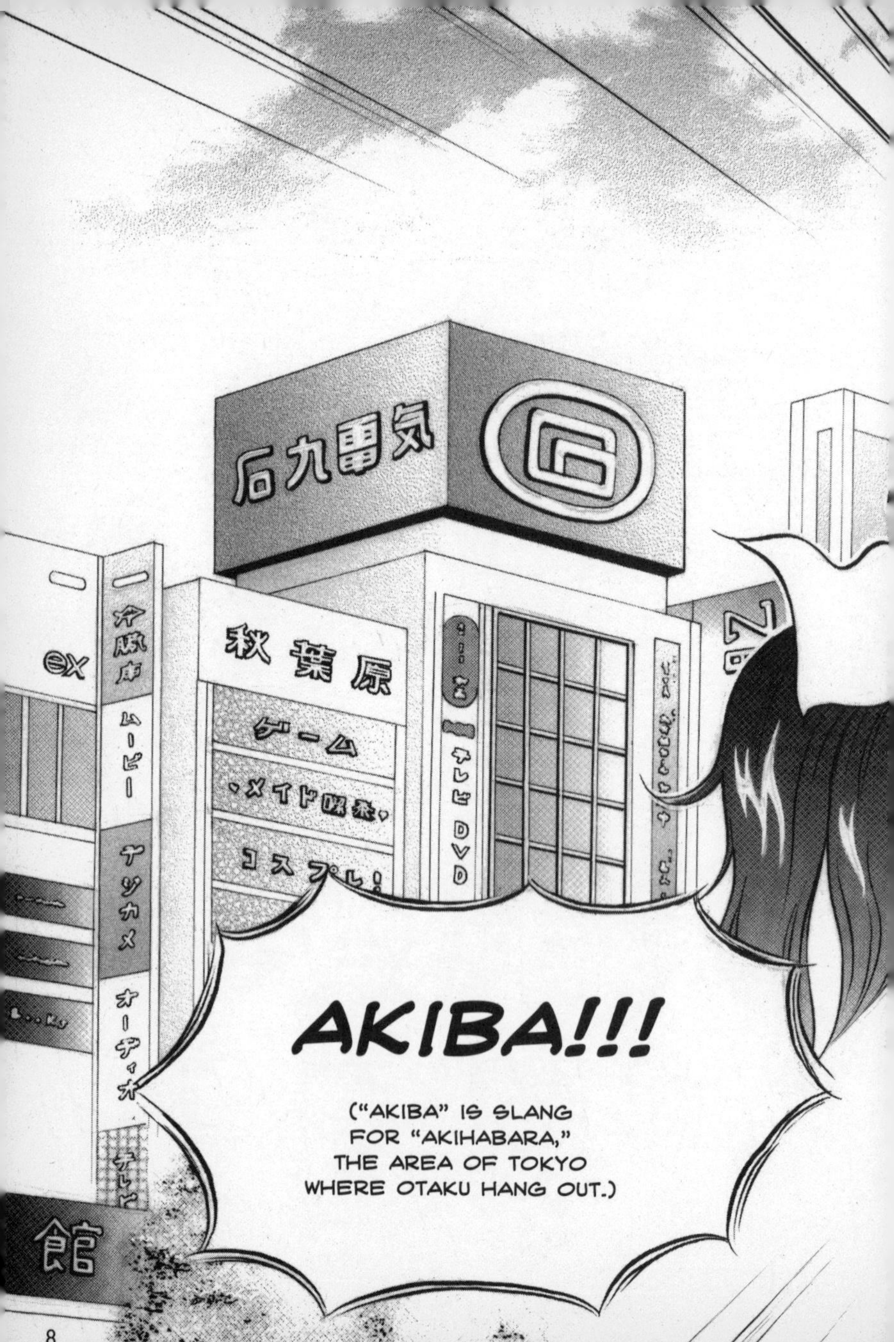
秋葉原
ゲーム
メイド喫茶
コスプレ!
テレビ DVD
ムービー
オーディオ
館
AKIBA!!!
("AKIBA" IS SLANG FOR "AKIHABARA," THE AREA OF TOKYO WHERE OTAKU HANG OUT.)

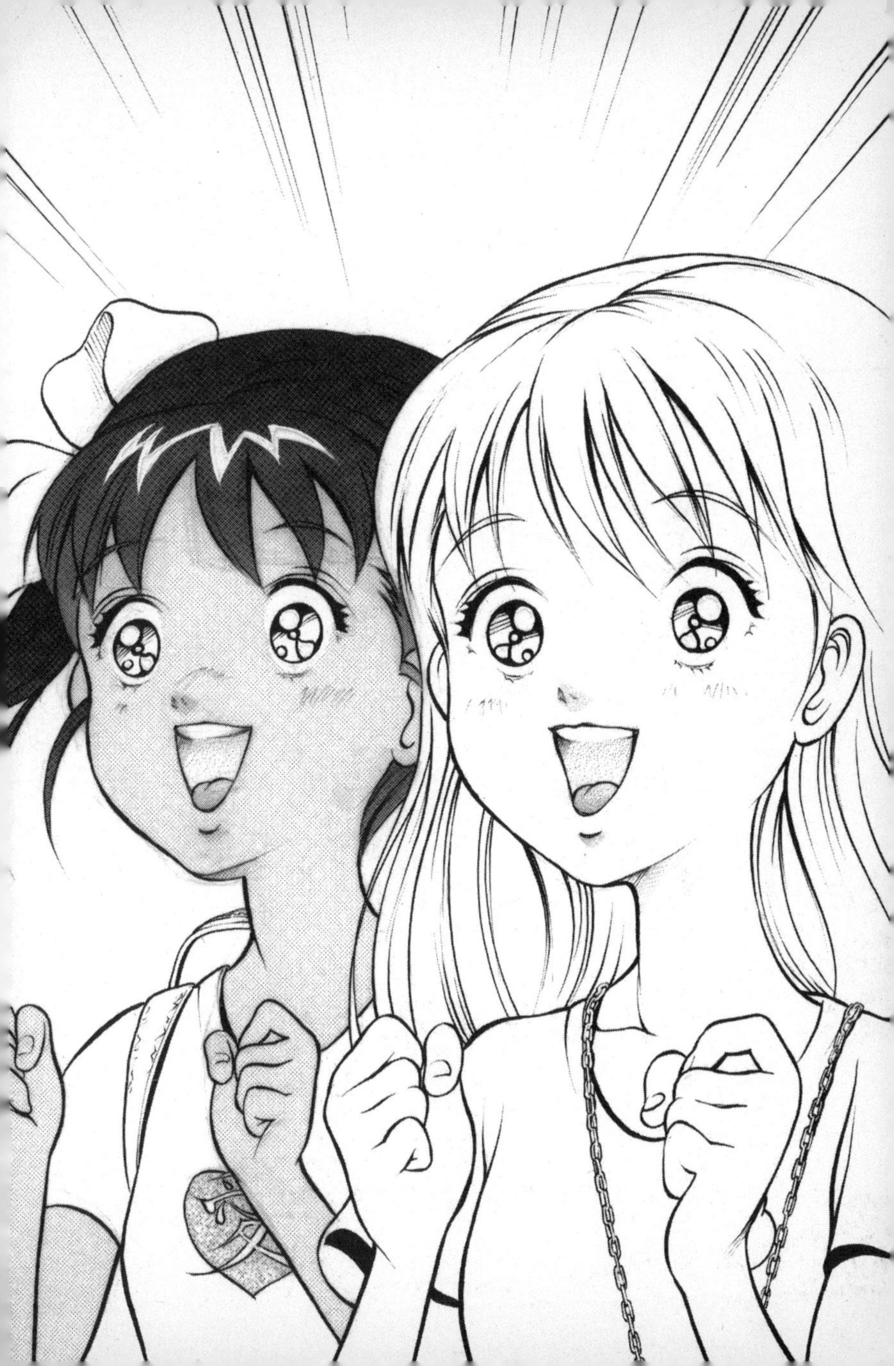

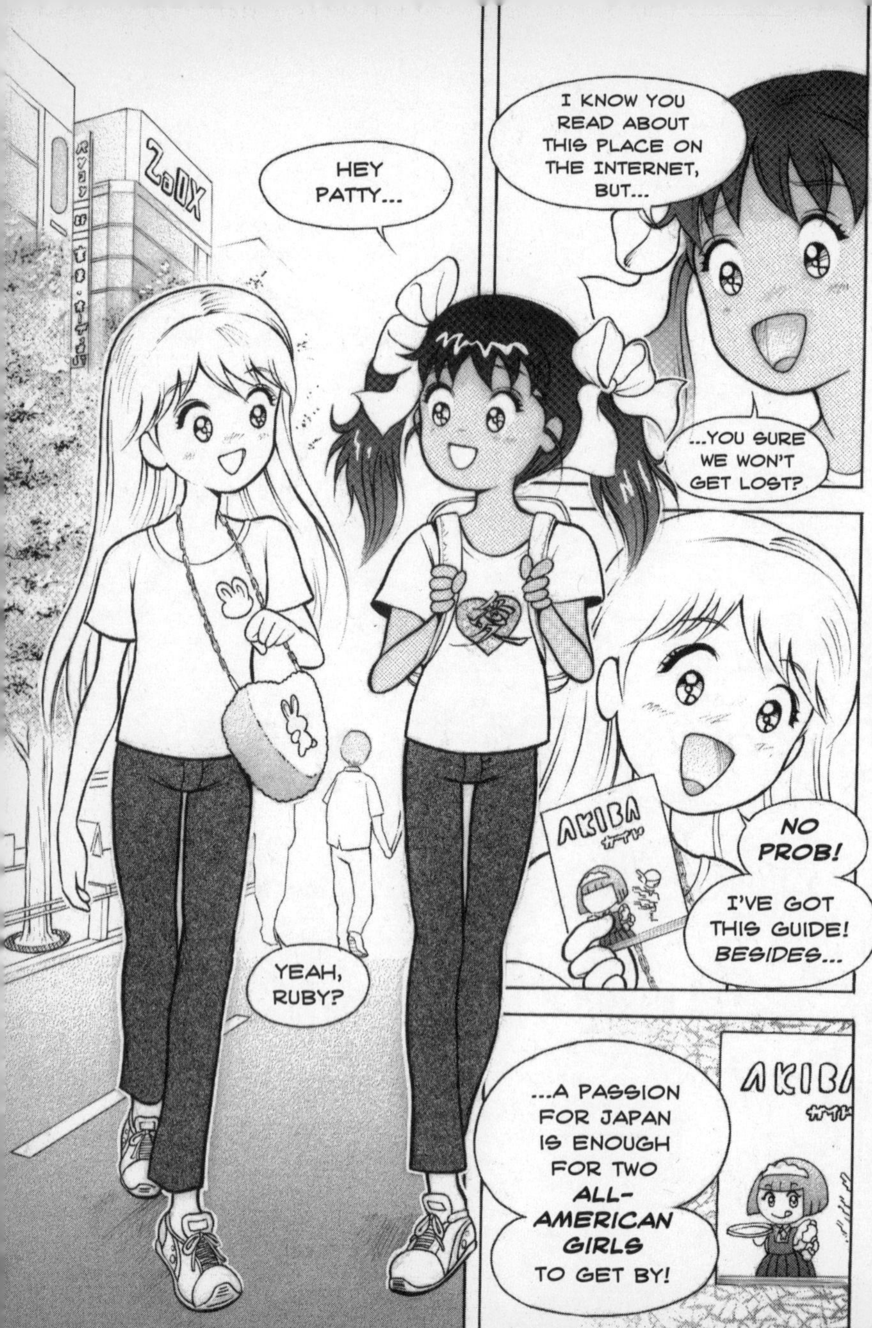
HEY PATTY...
YEAH, RUBY?
I KNOW YOU READ ABOUT THIS PLACE ON THE INTERNET, BUT...
...YOU SURE WE WON'T GET LOST?
AKIBA
NO PROB!
I'VE GOT THIS GUIDE! BESIDES...
...A PASSION FOR JAPAN IS ENOUGH FOR TWO ALL-AMERICAN GIRLS TO GET BY!
AKIBA

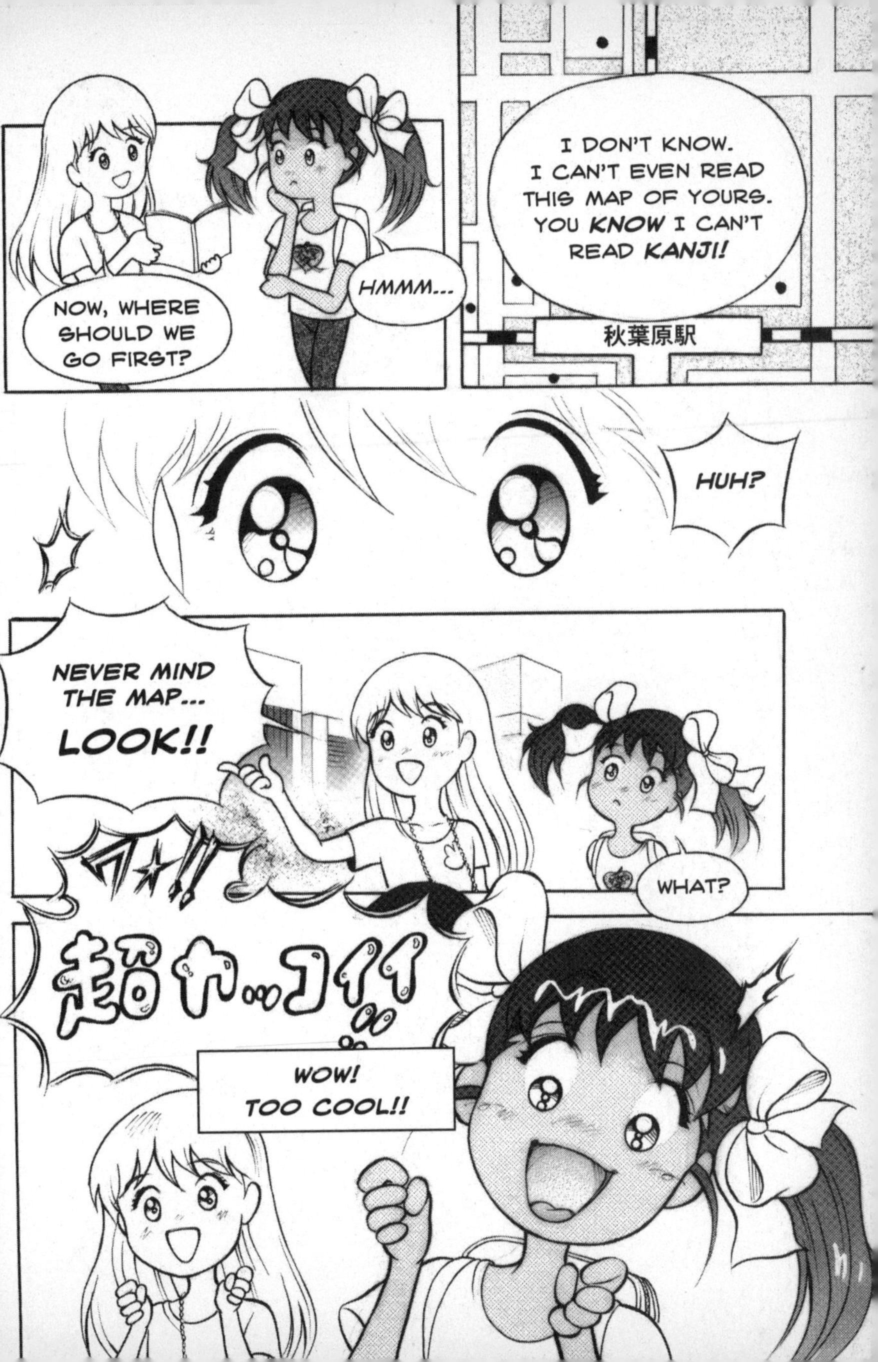
NOW, WHERE SHOULD WE GO FIRST?
HMMM...
I DON'T KNOW. I CAN'T EVEN READ THIS MAP OF YOURS. YOU KNOW I CAN'T READ KANJI!
秋葉原駅
HUH?
NEVER MIND THE MAP... LOOK!!
WHAT?
WOW! TOO COOL!!

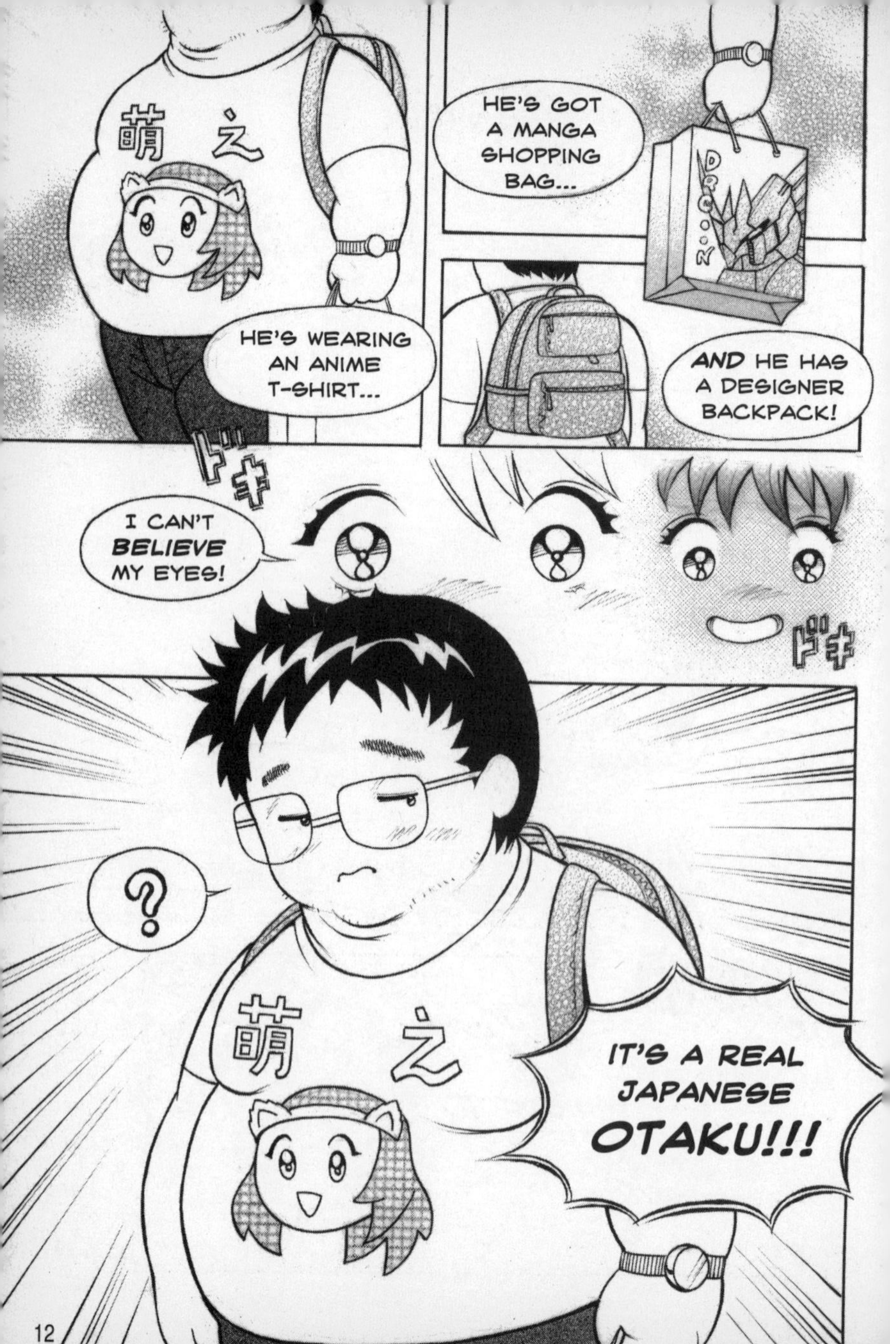
HE'S GOT A MANGA SHOPPING BAG...
HE'S WEARING AN ANIME T-SHIRT...
AND HE HAS A DESIGNER BACKPACK!
I CAN'T BELIEVE MY EYES!
?
IT'S A REAL JAPANESE OTAKU!!!

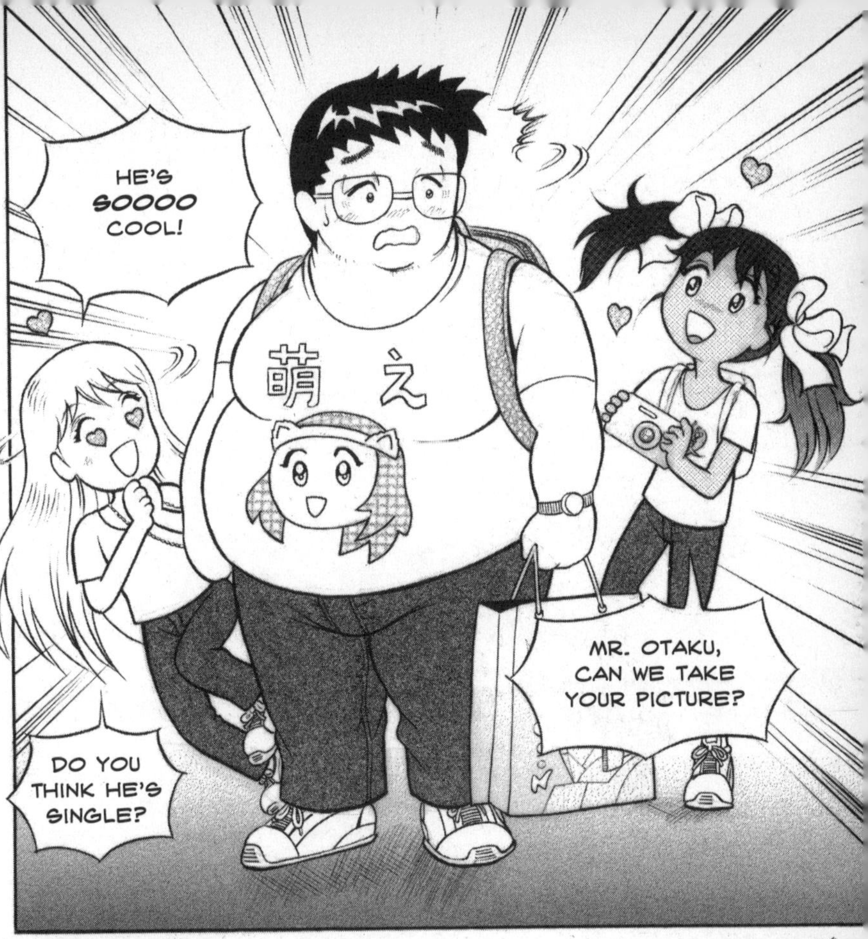
HE'S SOOOO COOL!
萌え
MR. OTAKU, CAN WE TAKE YOUR PICTURE?
DO YOU THINK HE'S SINGLE?

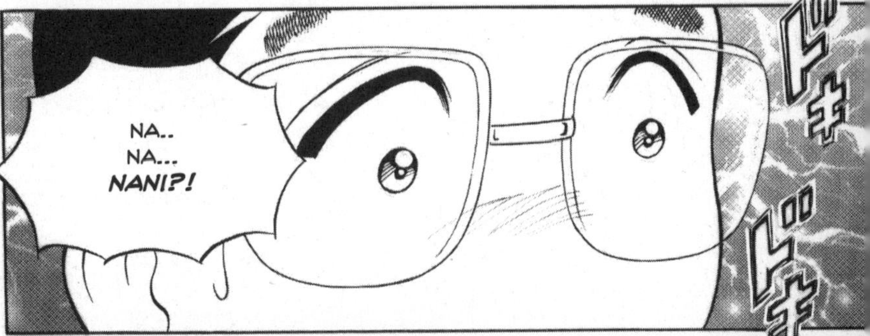
NA.. NA... NANI?!
ドキ
ドキ

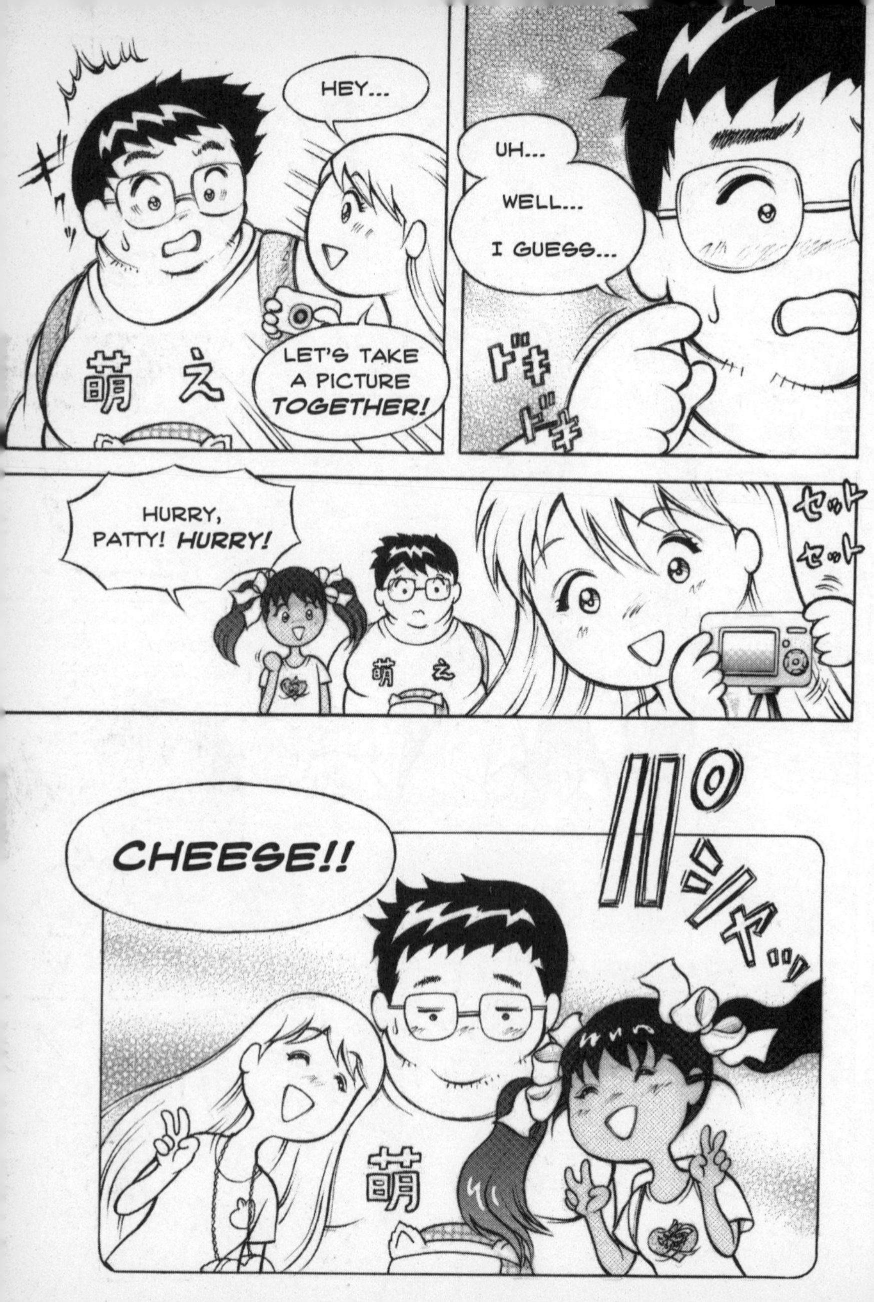
HEY...
LET'S TAKE A PICTURE *TOGETHER!*
萌え
UH... WELL... I GUESS...
ドキドキ
HURRY, PATTY! *HURRY!*
セットセット
萌え
パシャッ
*CHEESE!!*
萌

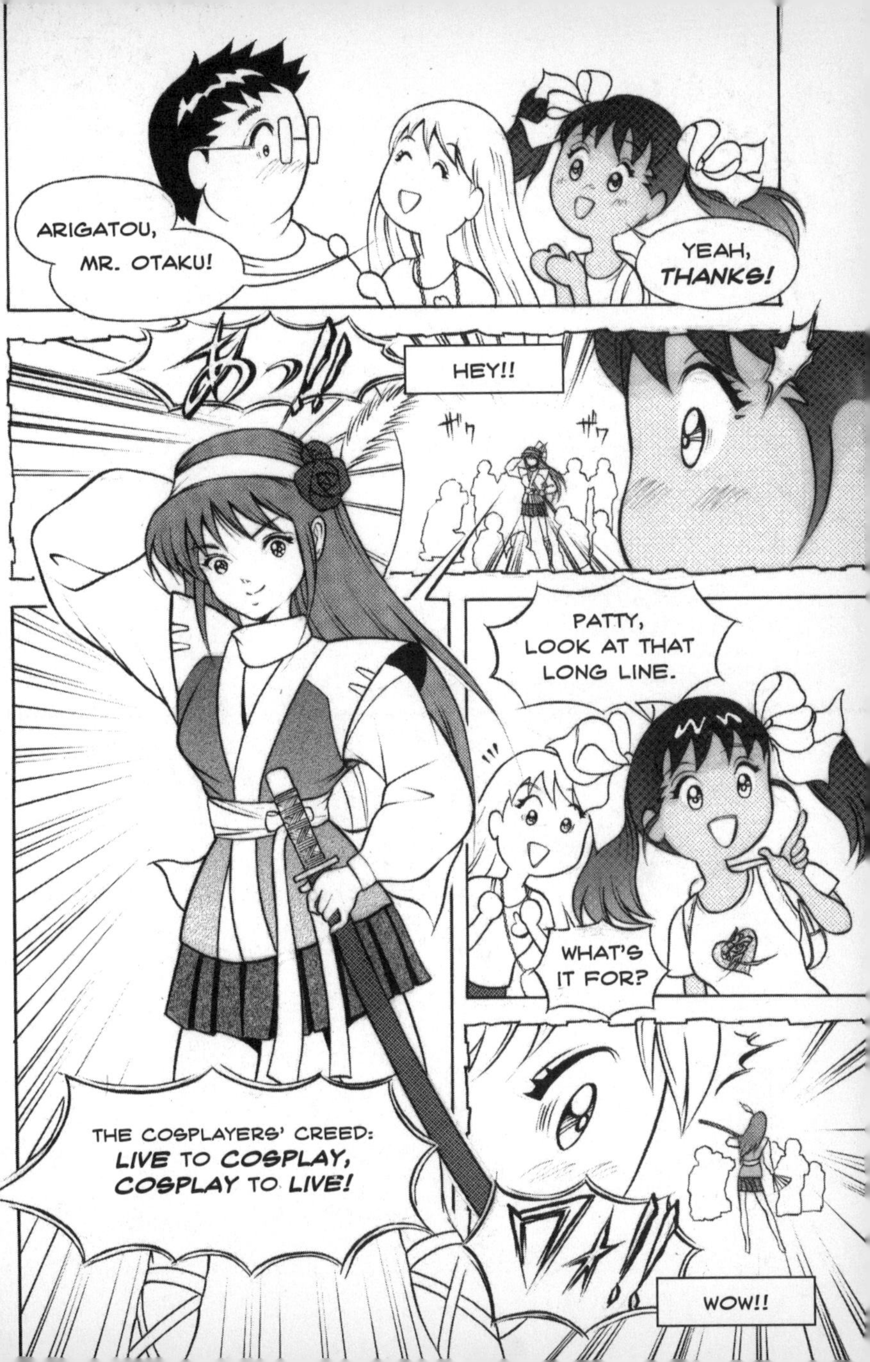
ARIGATOU, MR. OTAKU!
YEAH, THANKS!
あっ!!
HEY!!
ザワ ザワ
PATTY, LOOK AT THAT LONG LINE.
WHAT'S IT FOR?
THE COSPLAYERS' CREED: LIVE TO COSPLAY, COSPLAY TO LIVE!
ワォ!!
WOW!!

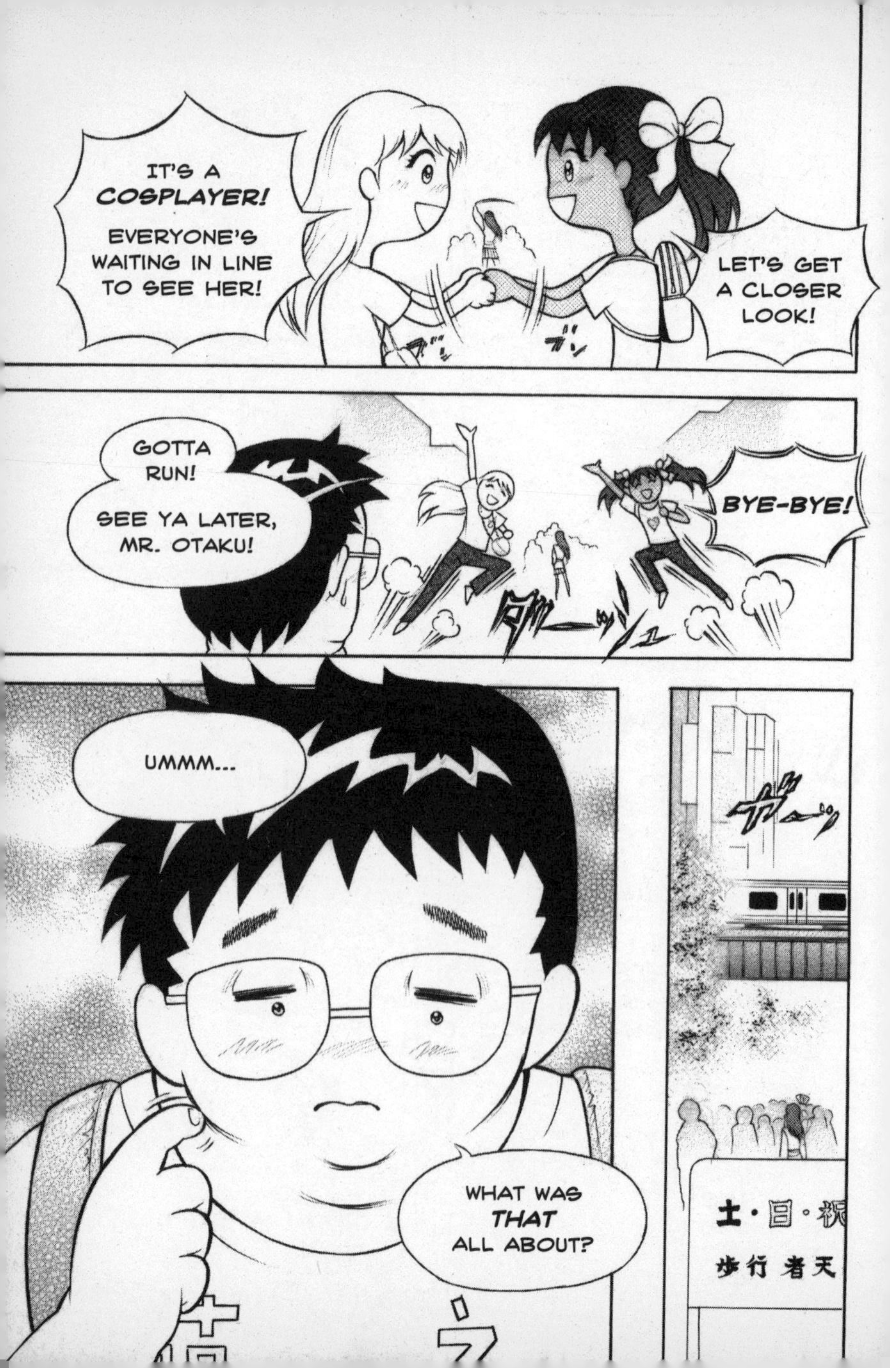
LET'S GET A CLOSER LOOK!
IT'S A COSPLAYER! EVERYONE'S WAITING IN LINE TO SEE HER!
BYE-BYE!
GOTTA RUN! SEE YA LATER, MR. OTAKU!
UMMM...
WHAT WAS THAT ALL ABOUT?
土・日・祝
歩行者天

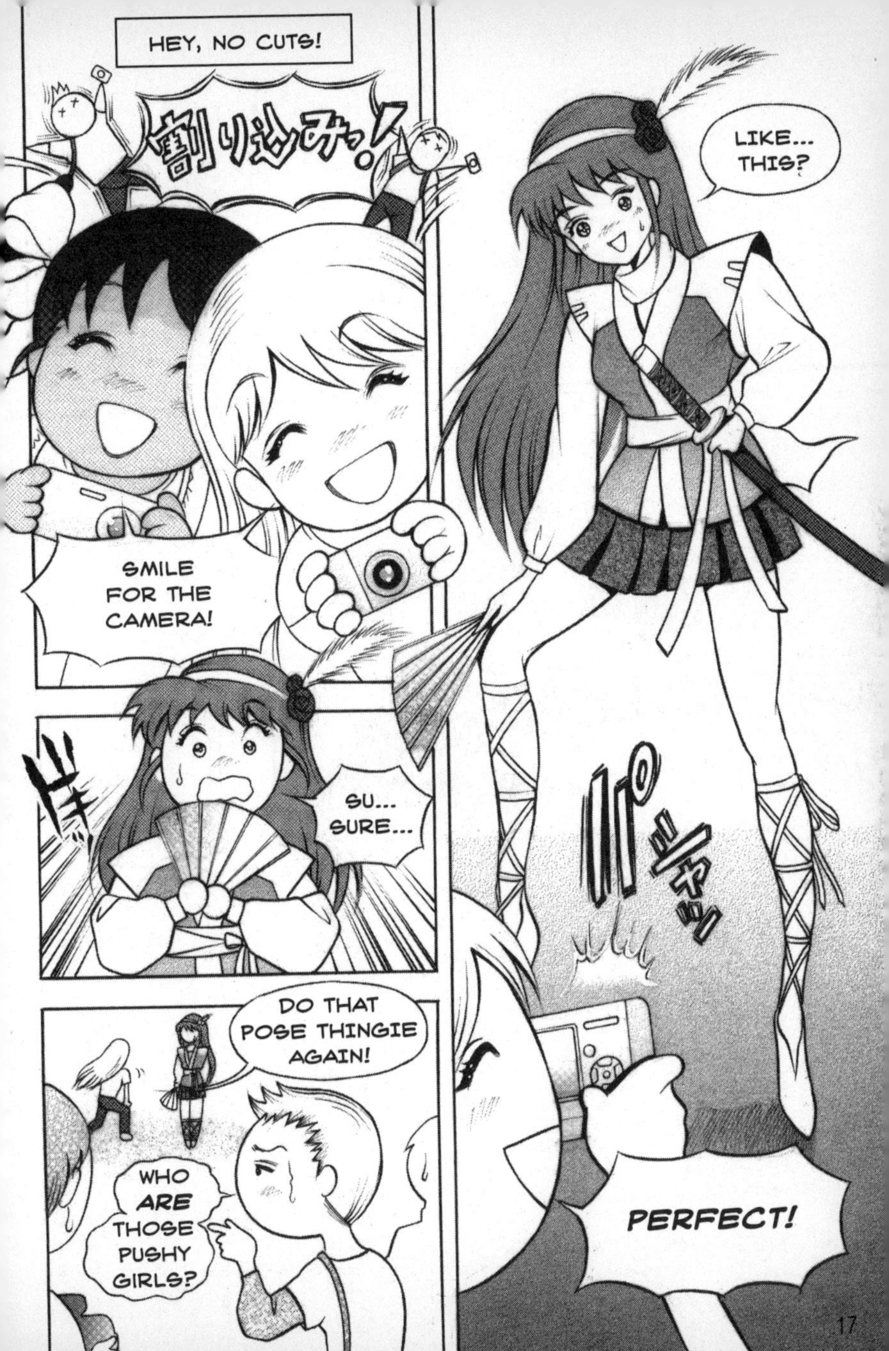
HEY, NO CUTS!
割り込みっ!
SMILE FOR THE CAMERA!
SU... SURE...
DO THAT POSE THINGIE AGAIN!
WHO ARE THOSE PUSHY GIRLS?
LIKE... THIS?
パシャッ
PERFECT!

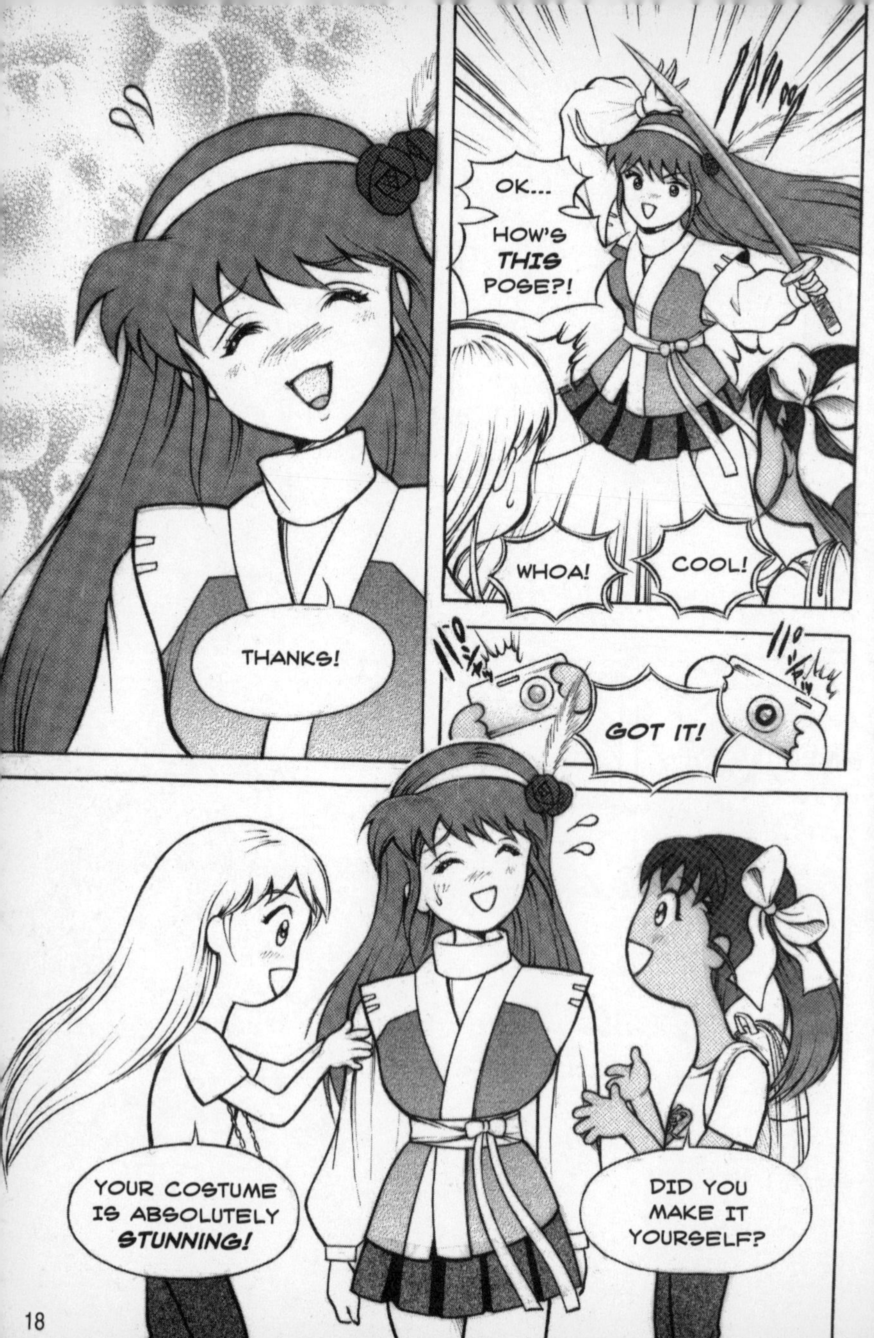
OK...
HOW'S **THIS** POSE?!
COOL!
WHOA!
GOT IT!
THANKS!
DID YOU MAKE IT YOURSELF?
YOUR COSTUME IS ABSOLUTELY **STUNNING!**

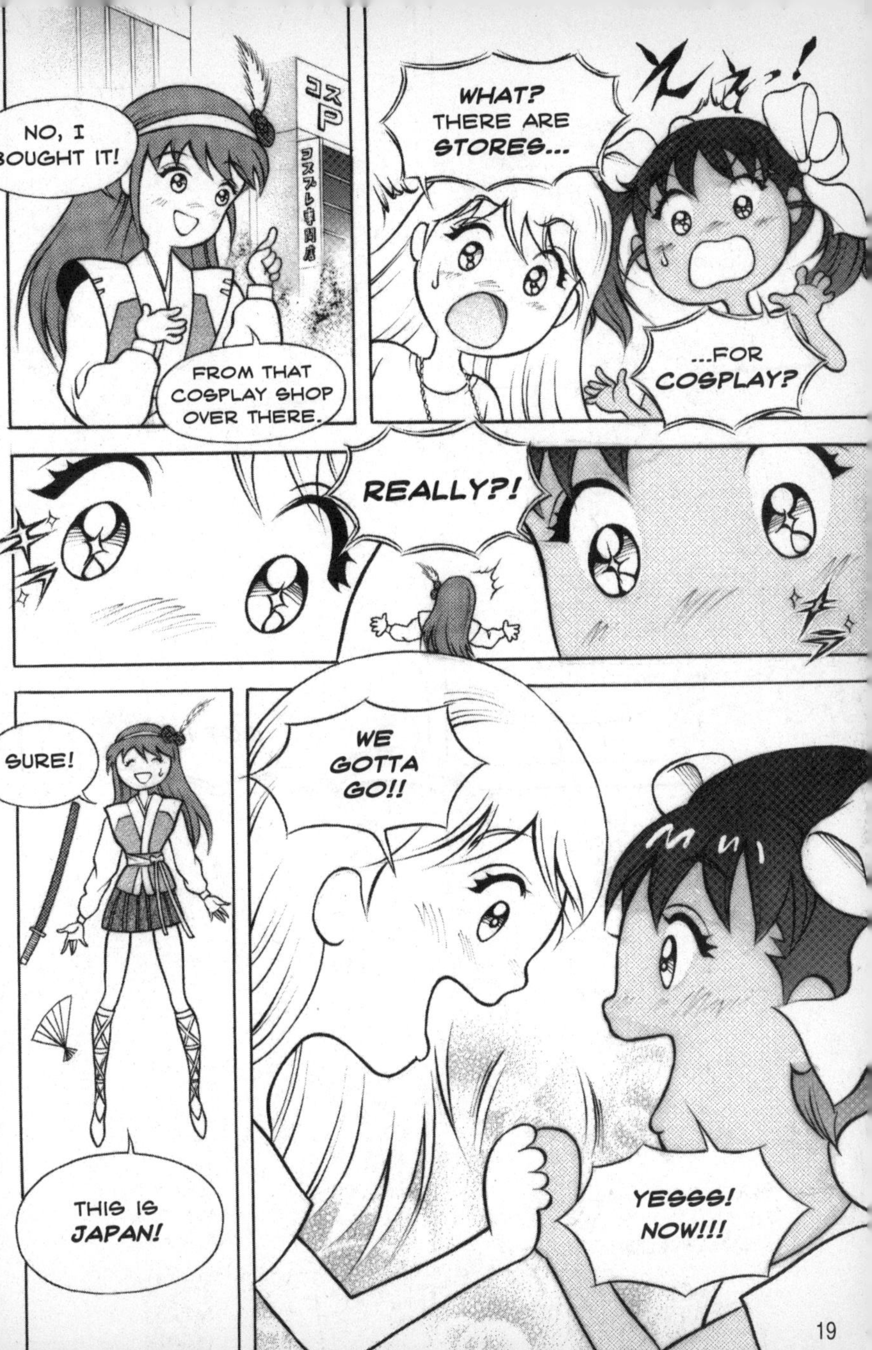
NO, I BOUGHT IT!
FROM THAT COSPLAY SHOP OVER THERE.
WHAT? THERE ARE STORES...
...FOR COSPLAY?
REALLY?!
SURE!
THIS IS JAPAN!
WE GOTTA GO!!
YESSS! NOW!!!

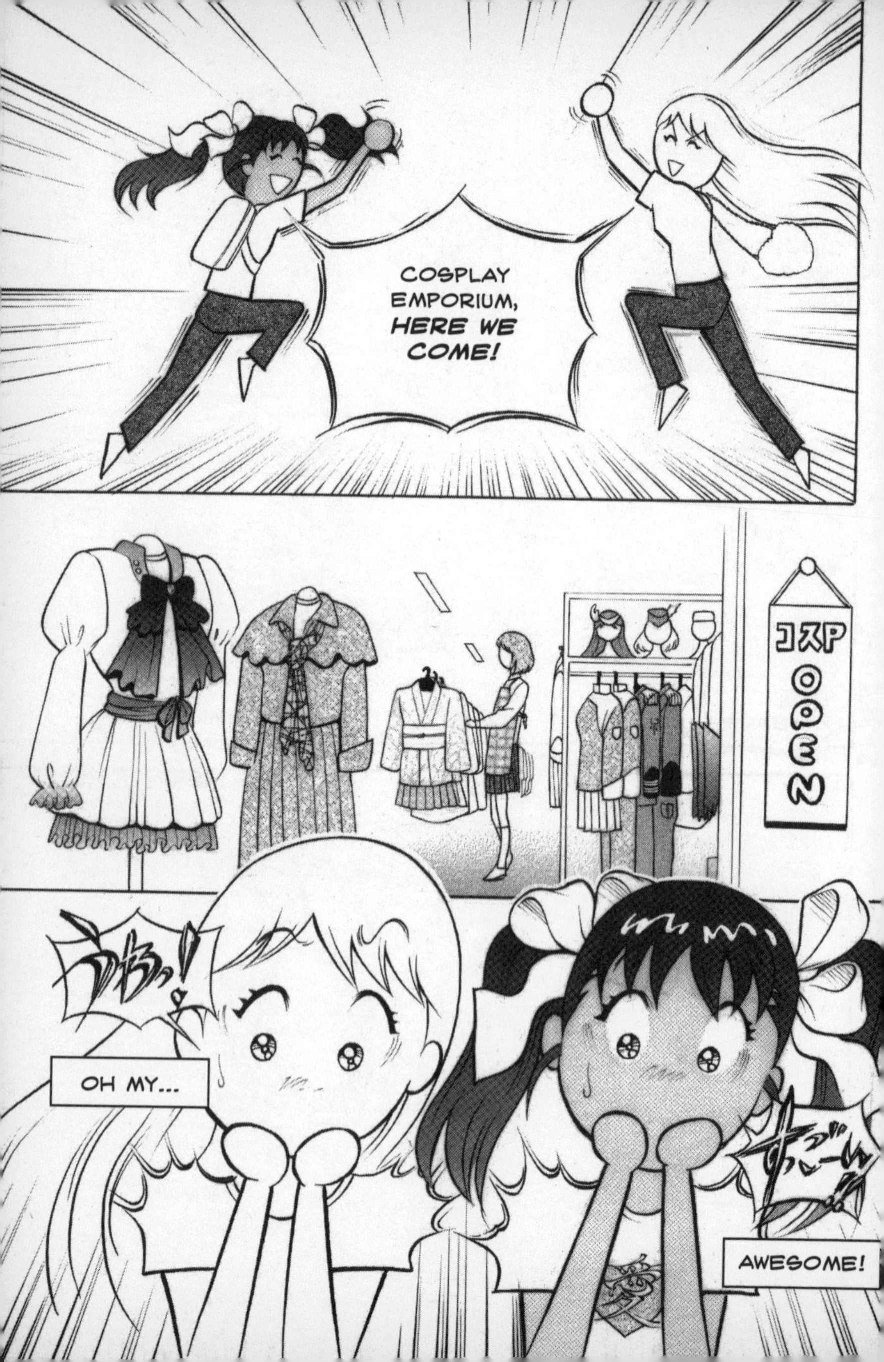
COSPLAY EMPORIUM, HERE WE COME!
コスP
OPEN
AWESOME!
OH MY...

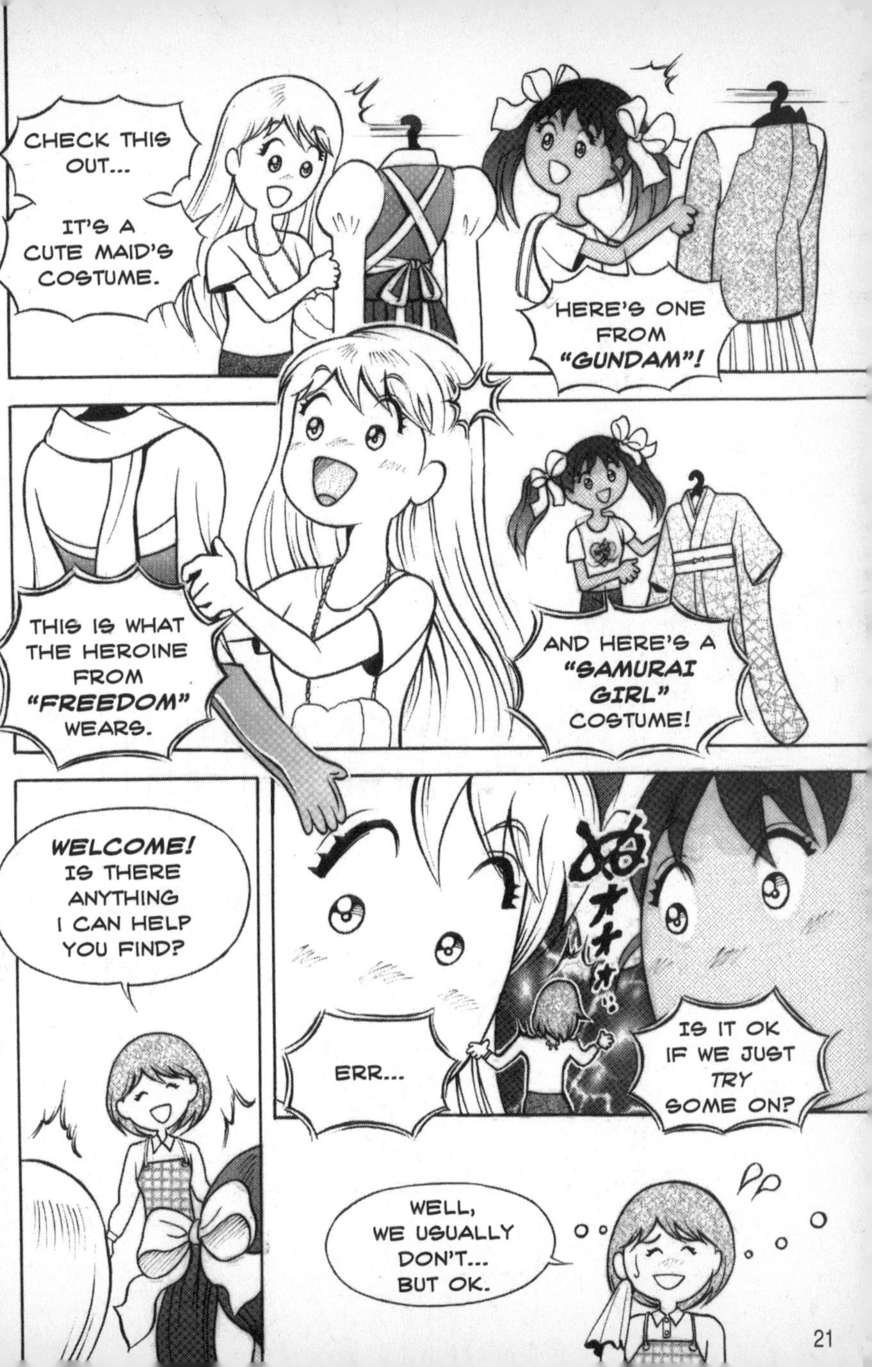
CHECK THIS OUT...
IT'S A CUTE MAID'S COSTUME.
HERE'S ONE FROM "GUNDAM"!
THIS IS WHAT THE HEROINE FROM "FREEDOM" WEARS.
AND HERE'S A "SAMURAI GIRL" COSTUME!
WELCOME! IS THERE ANYTHING I CAN HELP YOU FIND?
ERR...
IS IT OK IF WE JUST TRY SOME ON?
WELL, WE USUALLY DON'T... BUT OK.

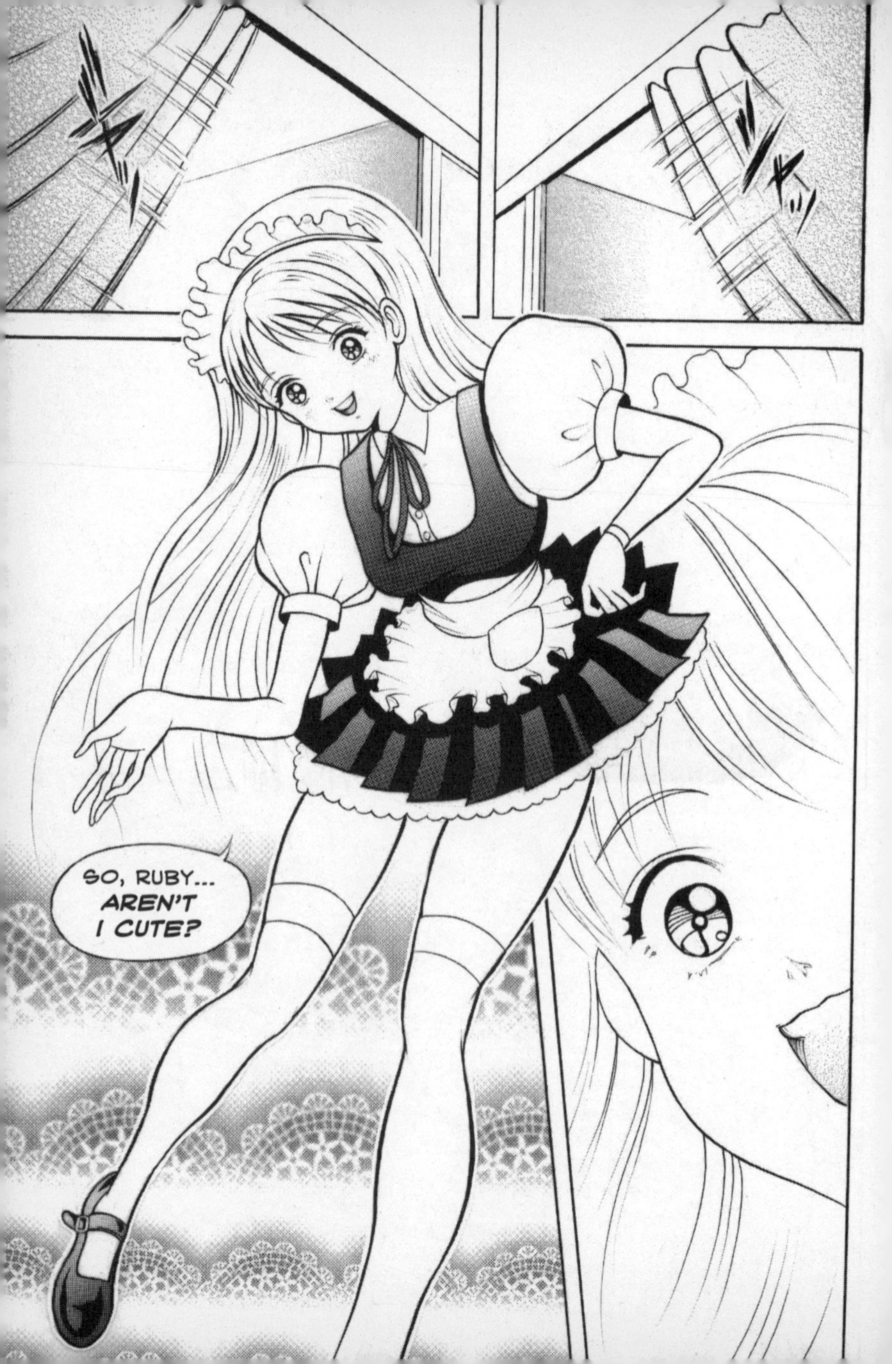
SO, RUBY...
AREN'T
I CUTE?

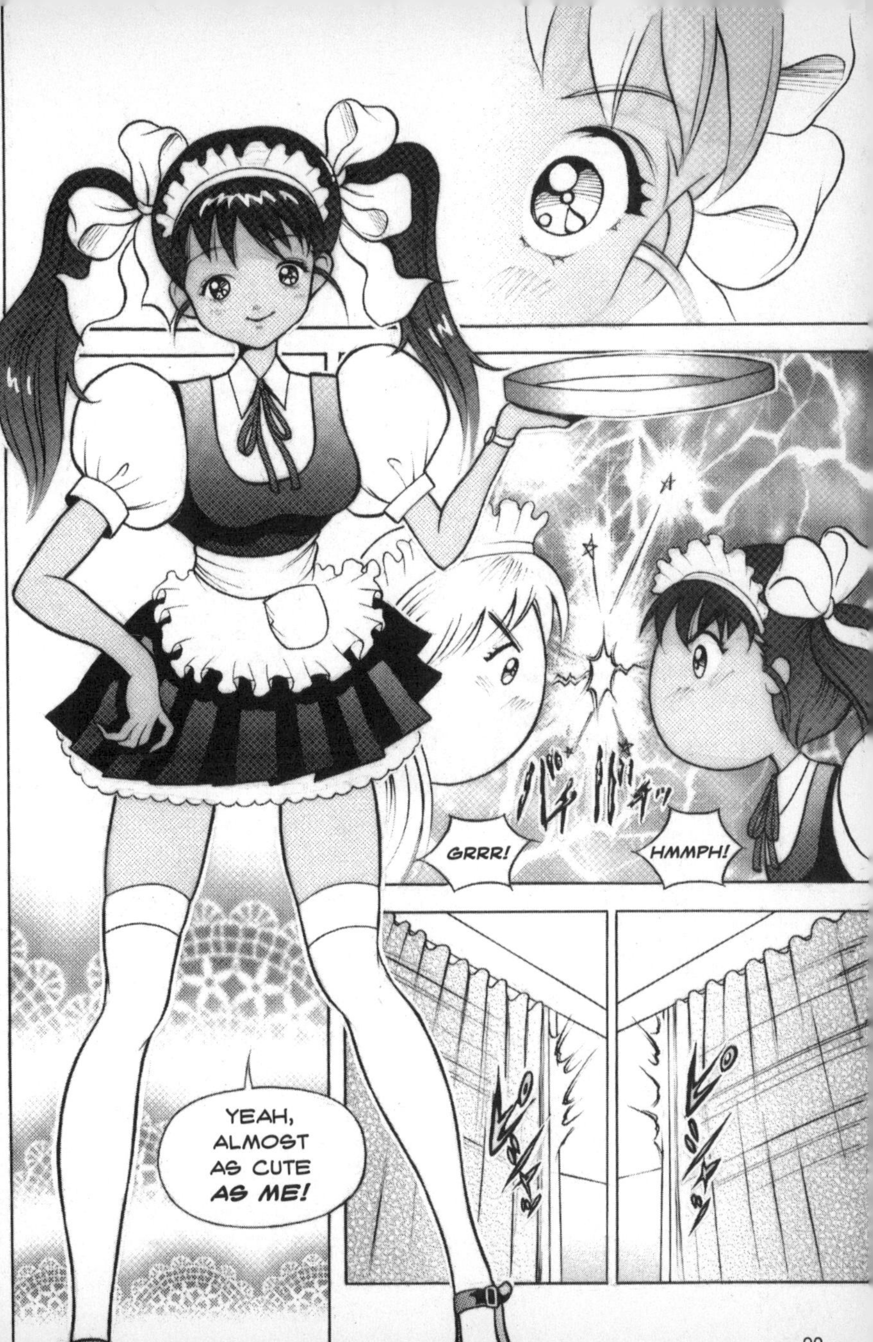
HMMPH!
GRRR!
YEAH, ALMOST AS CUTE AS ME!

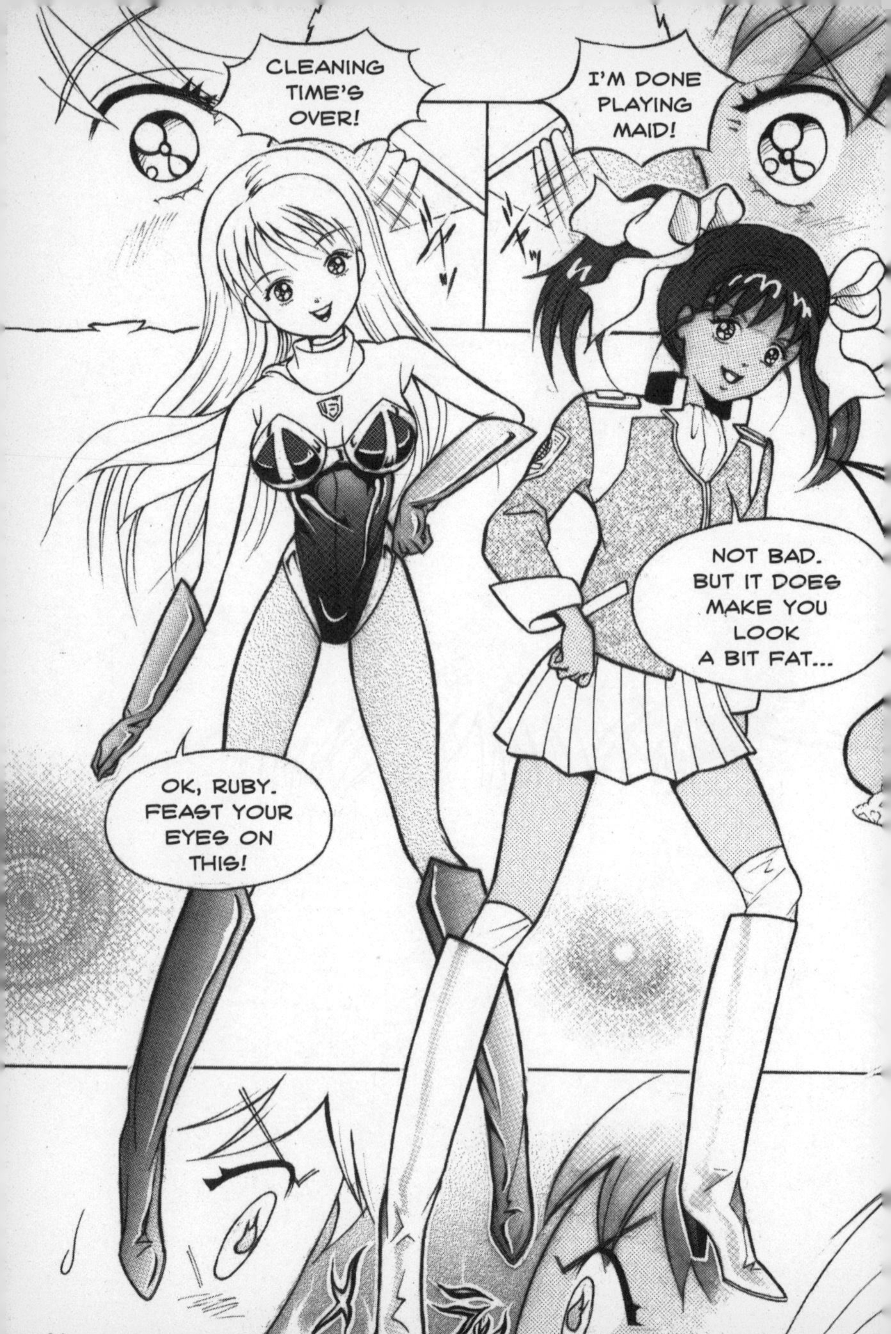
I'M DONE PLAYING MAID!
CLEANING TIME'S OVER!
NOT BAD. BUT IT DOES MAKE YOU LOOK A BIT FAT...
OK, RUBY. FEAST YOUR EYES ON THIS!

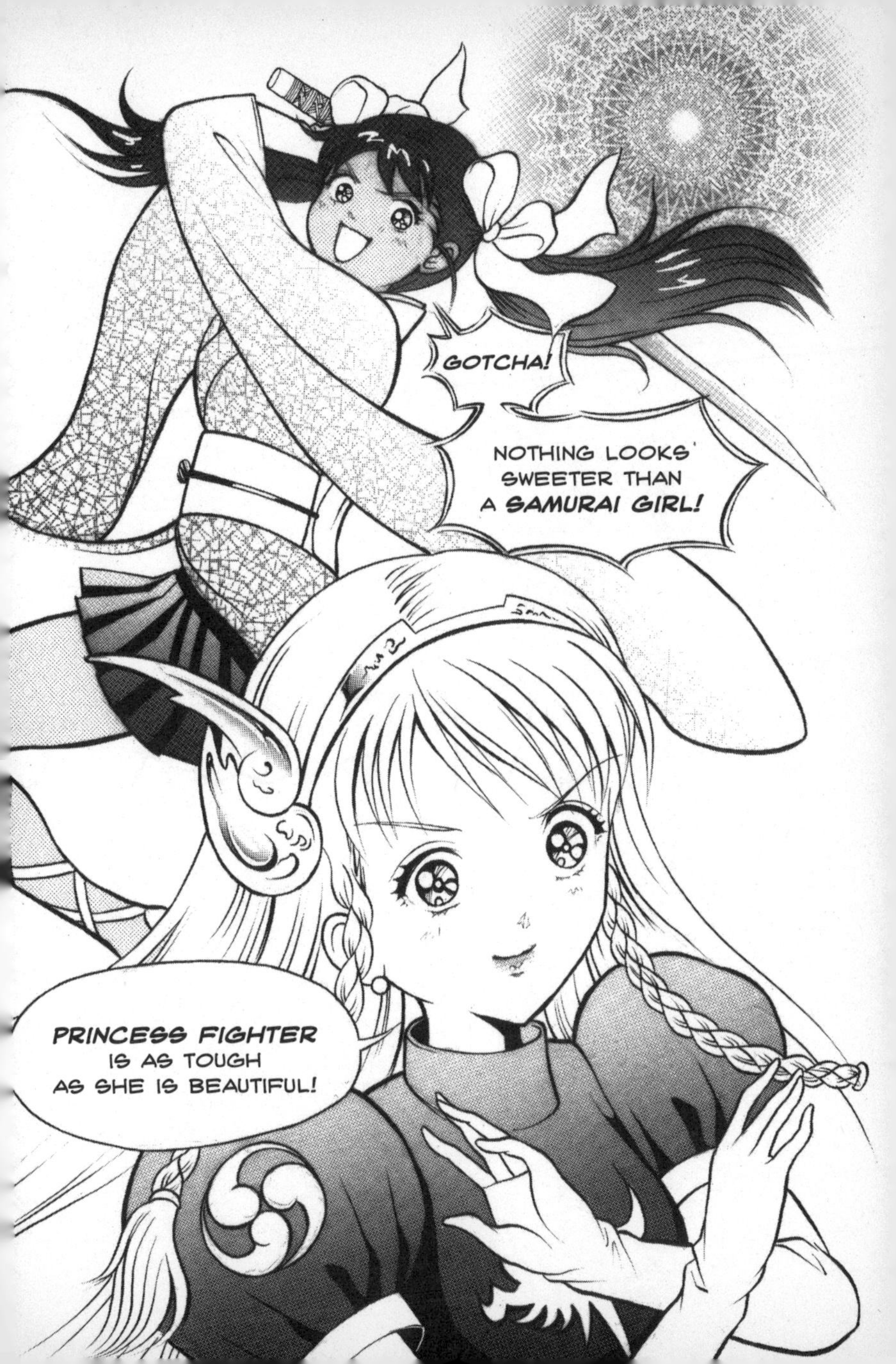
GOTCHA!
NOTHING LOOKS SWEETER THAN A SAMURAI GIRL!
PRINCESS FIGHTER IS AS TOUGH AS SHE IS BEAUTIFUL!

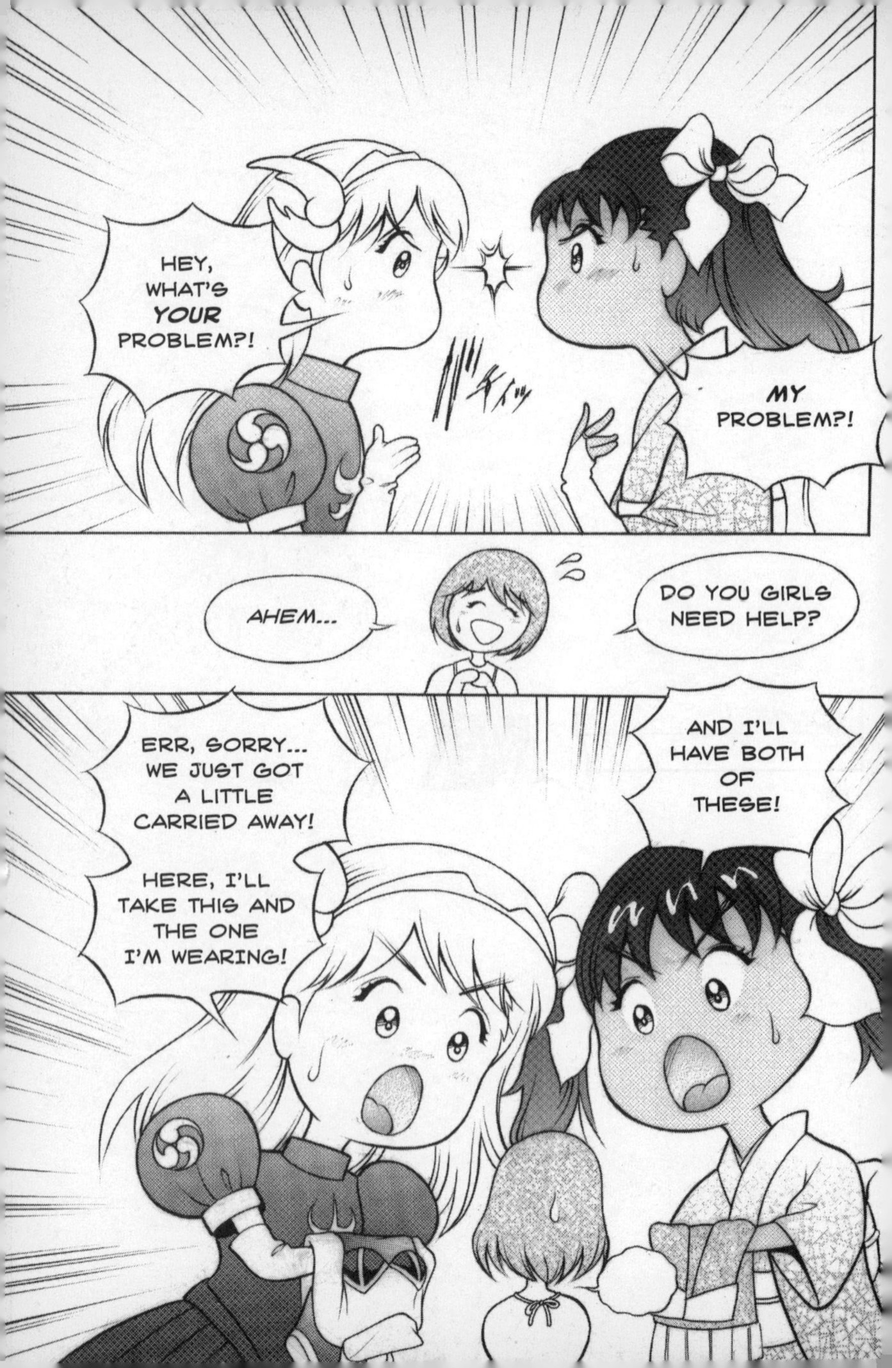
HEY, WHAT'S *YOUR* PROBLEM?!
*MY* PROBLEM?!
*AHEM...*
DO YOU GIRLS NEED HELP?
ERR, SORRY... WE JUST GOT A LITTLE CARRIED AWAY!
HERE, I'LL TAKE THIS AND THE ONE I'M WEARING!
AND I'LL HAVE BOTH OF THESE!

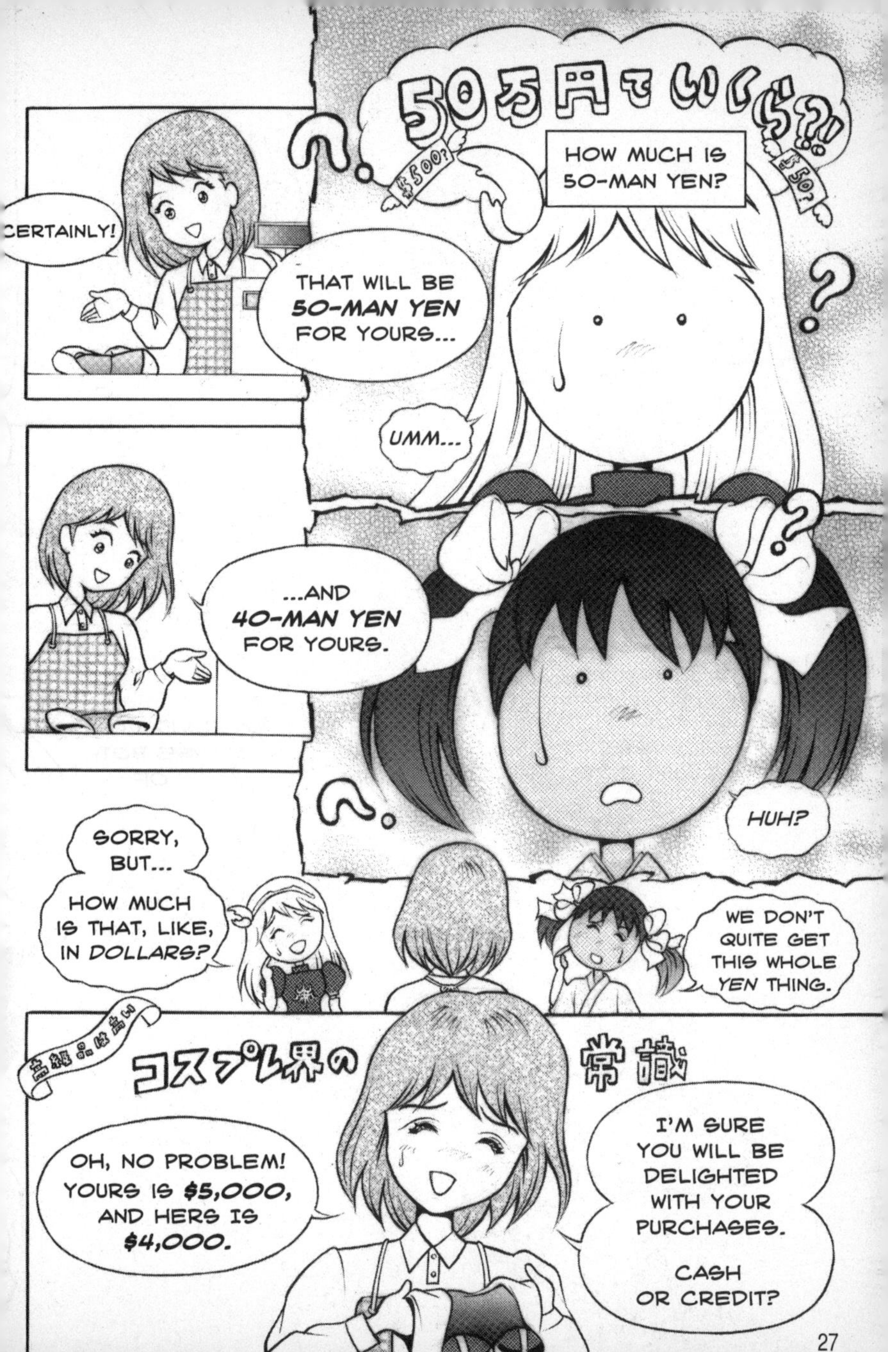

CERTAINLY!
THAT WILL BE 50-MAN YEN FOR YOURS...
...AND 40-MAN YEN FOR YOURS.
50万円でいくら?!!
$500?
$50?
HOW MUCH IS 50-MAN YEN?
UMM...
HUH?
SORRY, BUT... HOW MUCH IS THAT, LIKE, IN DOLLARS?
WE DON'T QUITE GET THIS WHOLE YEN THING.
高級品は高い
コスプレ界の常識
OH, NO PROBLEM! YOURS IS $5,000, AND HERS IS $4,000.
I'M SURE YOU WILL BE DELIGHTED WITH YOUR PURCHASES.
CASH OR CREDIT?

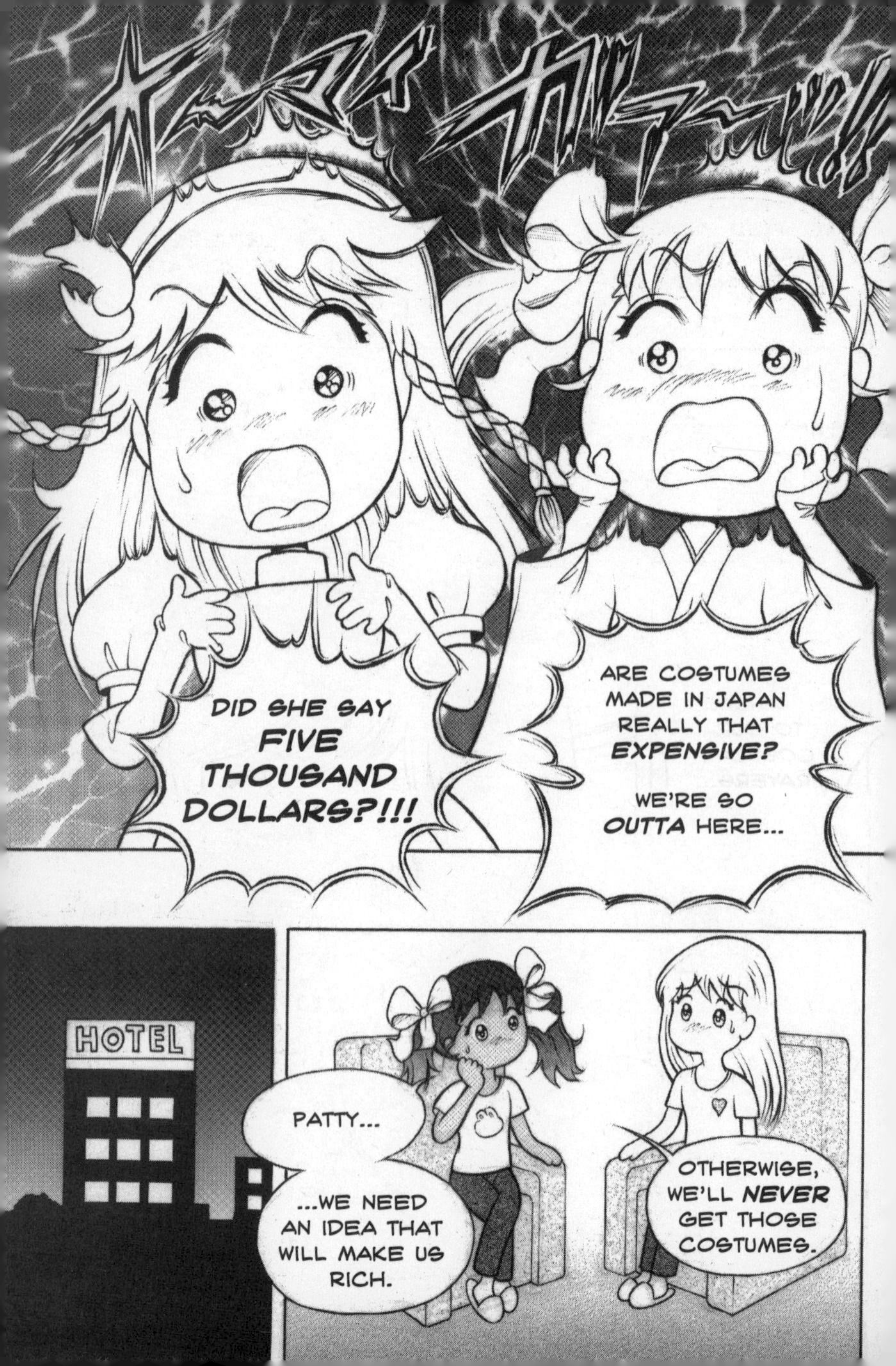
DID SHE SAY FIVE THOUSAND DOLLARS?!!!
ARE COSTUMES MADE IN JAPAN REALLY THAT EXPENSIVE?
WE'RE SO OUTTA HERE...
HOTEL
PATTY...
...WE NEED AN IDEA THAT WILL MAKE US RICH.
OTHERWISE, WE'LL NEVER GET THOSE COSTUMES.

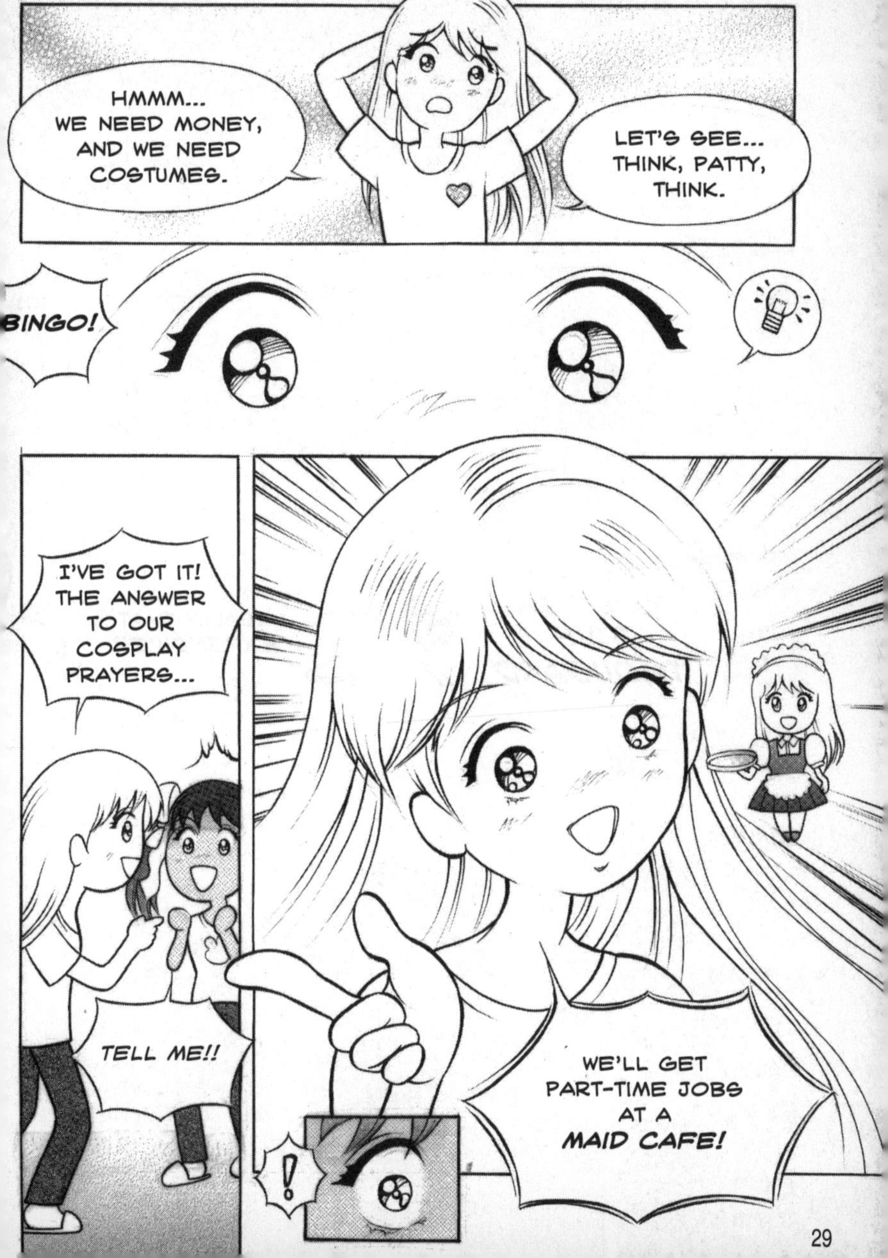
HMMM...
WE NEED MONEY,
AND WE NEED
COSTUMES.
LET'S SEE...
THINK, PATTY,
THINK.
BINGO!
I'VE GOT IT!
THE ANSWER
TO OUR
COSPLAY
PRAYERS...
TELL ME!!
!
WE'LL GET
PART-TIME JOBS
AT A
MAID CAFE!

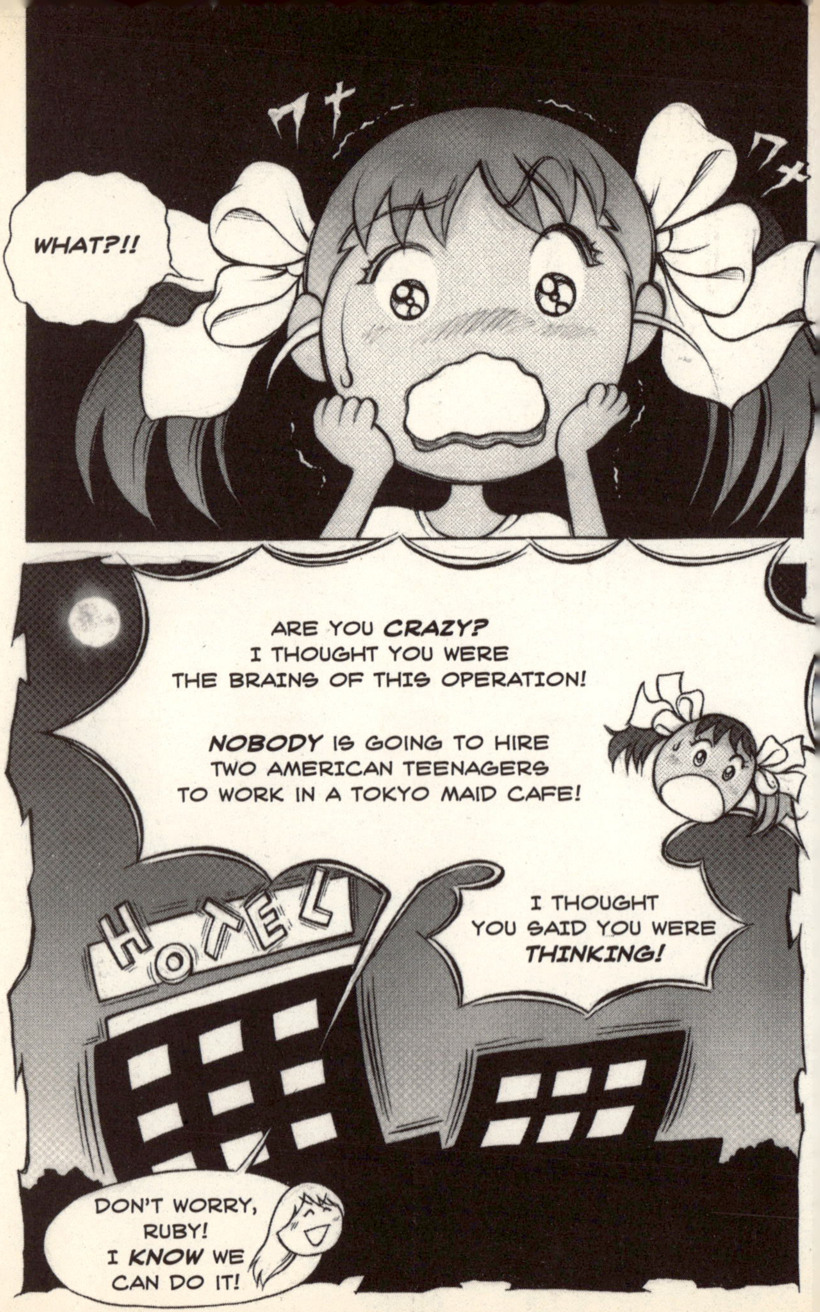
WHAT?!!
ARE YOU CRAZY? I THOUGHT YOU WERE THE BRAINS OF THIS OPERATION!
NOBODY IS GOING TO HIRE TWO AMERICAN TEENAGERS TO WORK IN A TOKYO MAID CAFE!
HOTEL
I THOUGHT YOU SAID YOU WERE THINKING!
DON'T WORRY, RUBY! I KNOW WE CAN DO IT!

## chapter two
## FAIR MAIDENS

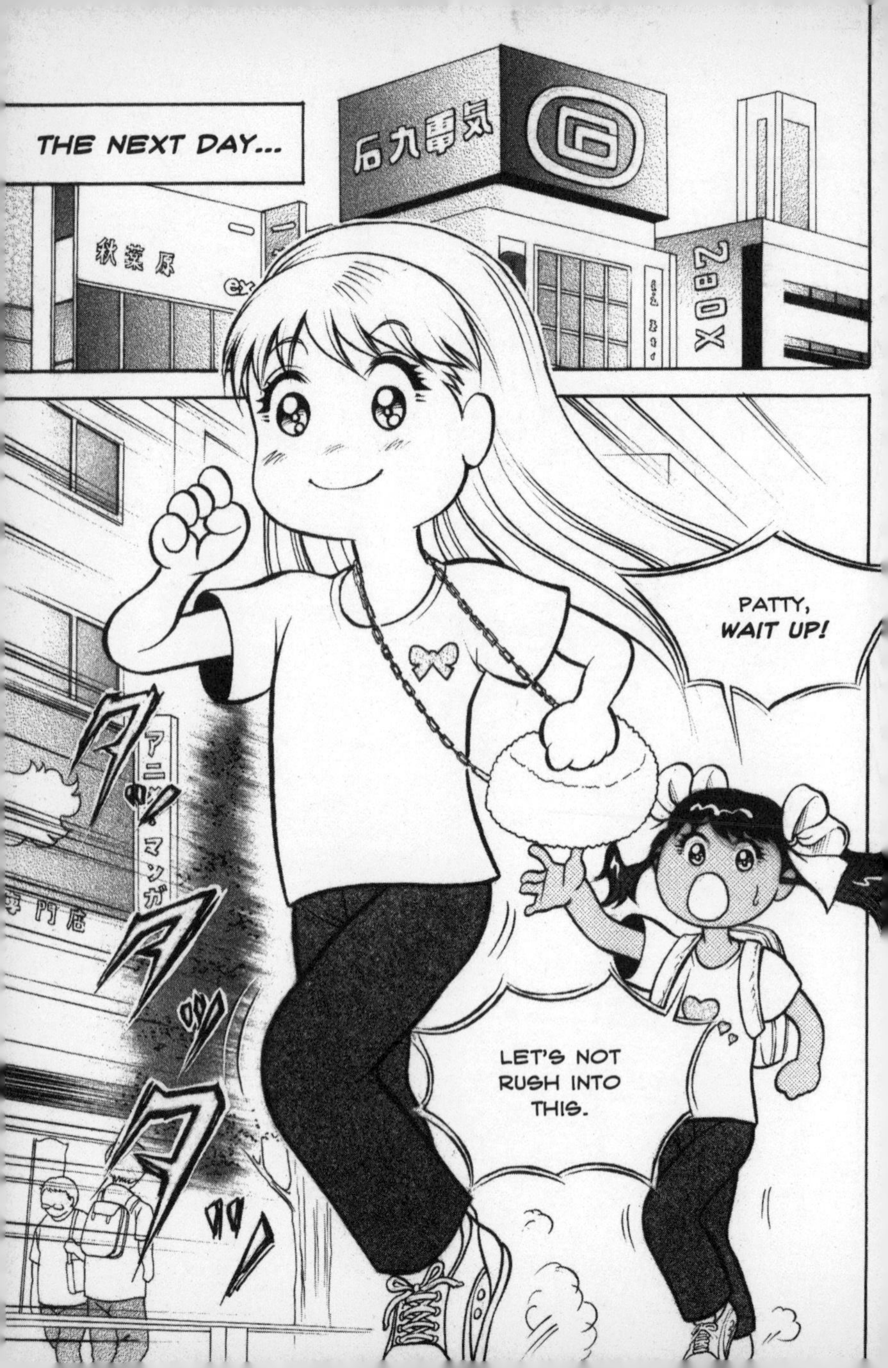
THE NEXT DAY...
秋葉原
PATTY, WAIT UP!
LET'S NOT RUSH INTO THIS.

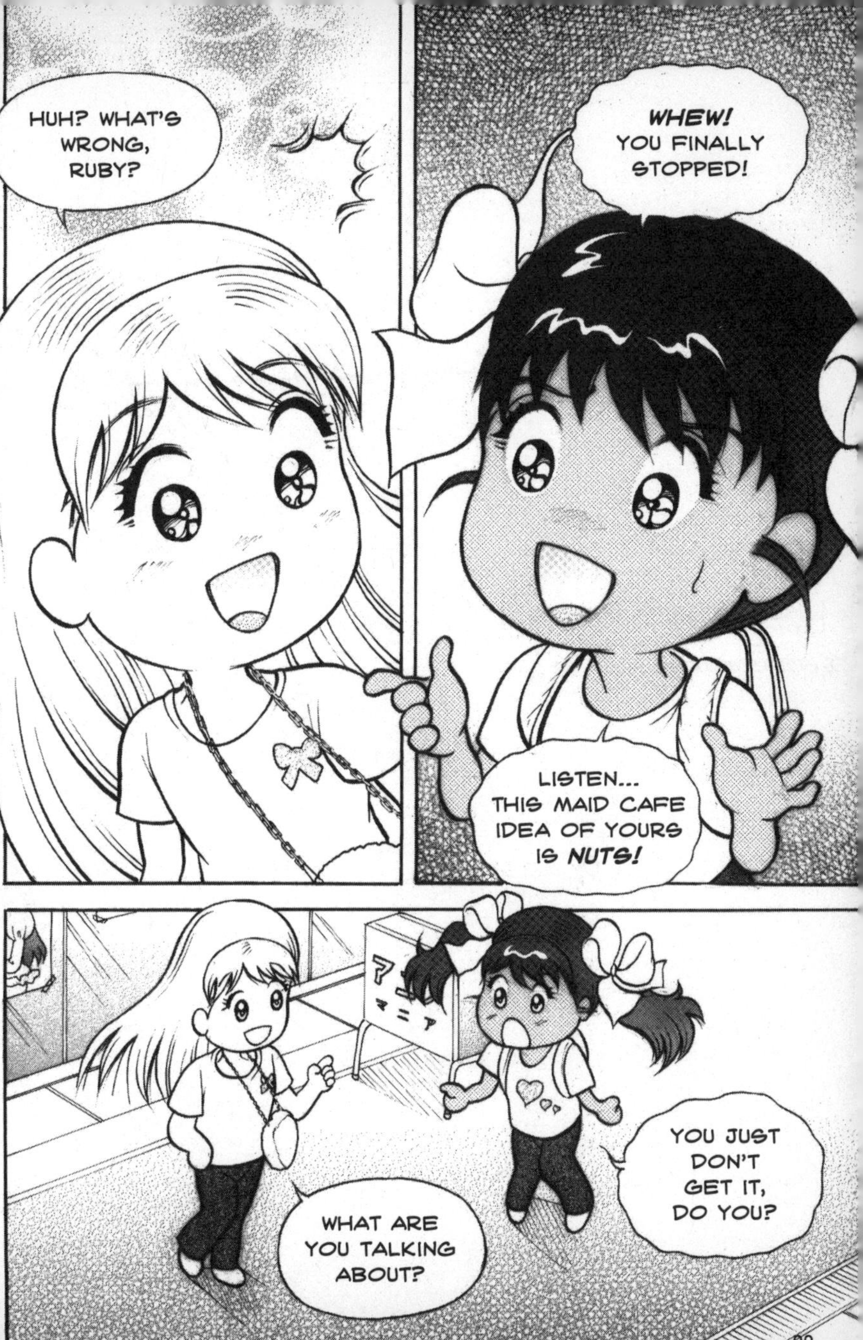
HUH? WHAT'S WRONG, RUBY?
WHEW! YOU FINALLY STOPPED!
LISTEN... THIS MAID CAFE IDEA OF YOURS IS NUTS!
WHAT ARE YOU TALKING ABOUT?
YOU JUST DON'T GET IT, DO YOU?

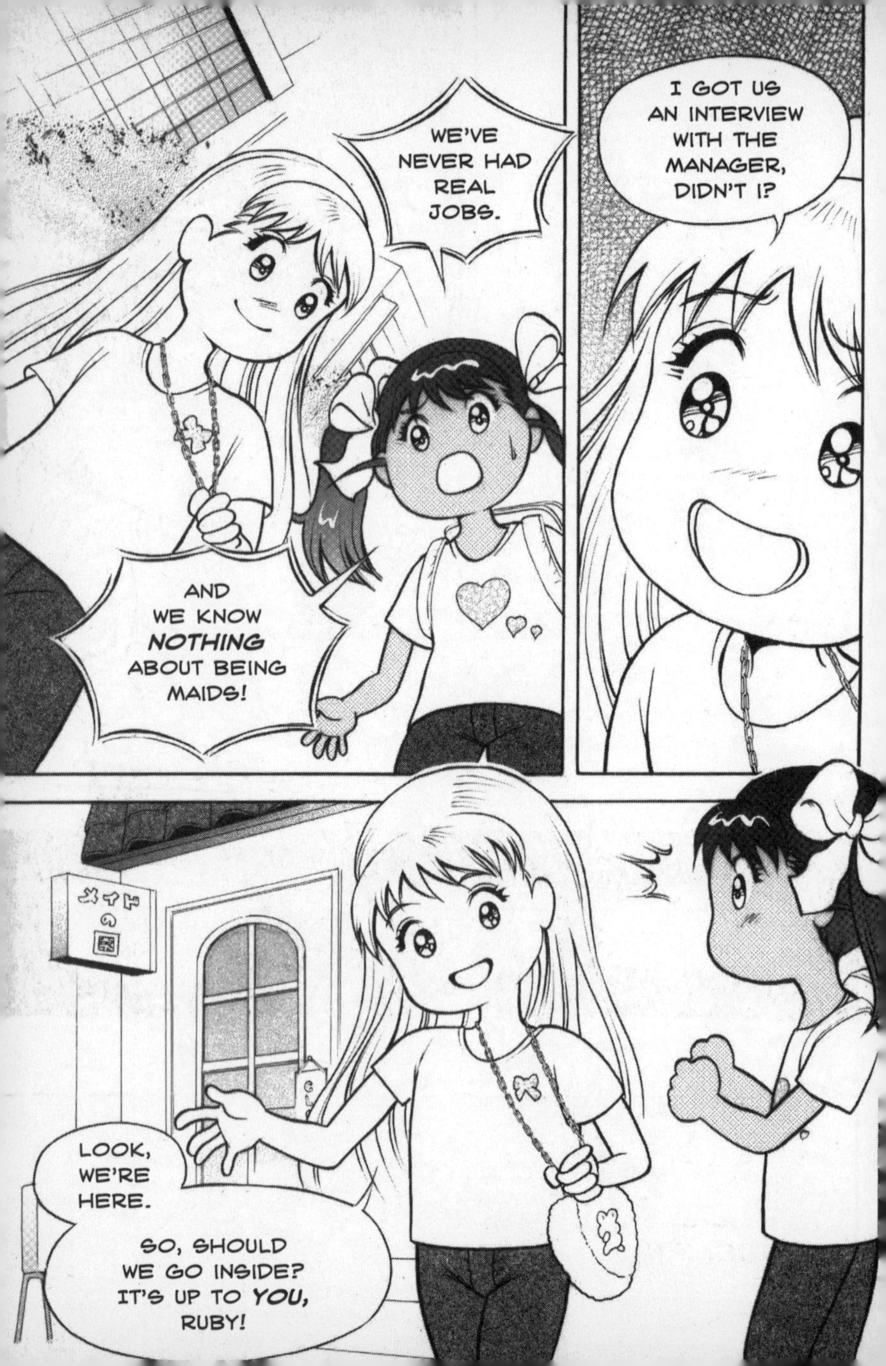
I GOT US AN INTERVIEW WITH THE MANAGER, DIDN'T I?
WE'VE NEVER HAD REAL JOBS.
AND WE KNOW *NOTHING* ABOUT BEING MAIDS!
LOOK, WE'RE HERE.
SO, SHOULD WE GO INSIDE? IT'S UP TO *YOU*, RUBY!

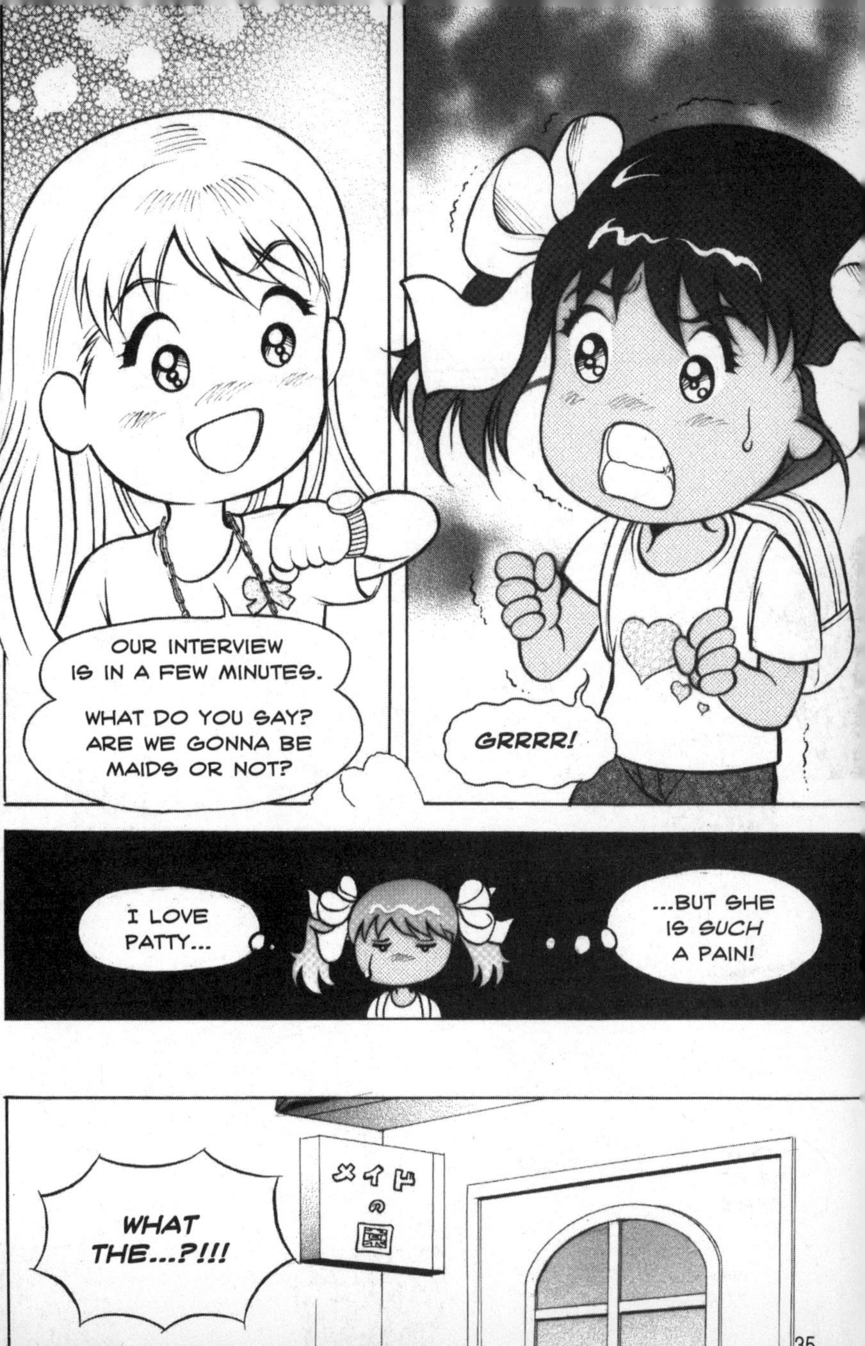
OUR INTERVIEW IS IN A FEW MINUTES.
WHAT DO YOU SAY? ARE WE GONNA BE MAIDS OR NOT?
GRRRR!
I LOVE PATTY...
...BUT SHE IS *SUCH* A PAIN!
メイドの
WHAT THE...?!!!

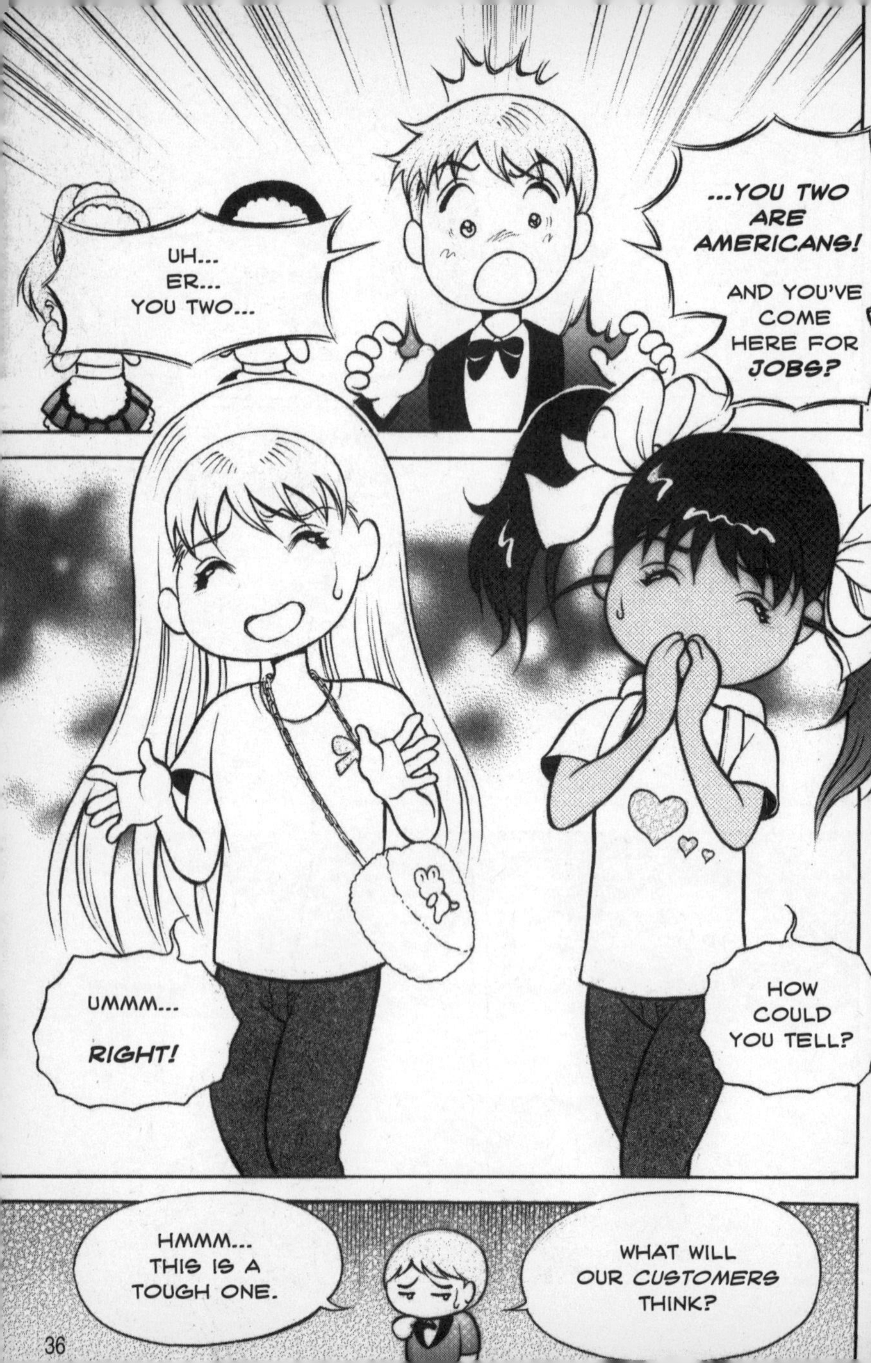

UH...
ER...
YOU TWO...
...YOU TWO ARE AMERICANS!
AND YOU'VE COME HERE FOR JOBS?
UMMM... RIGHT!
HOW COULD YOU TELL?
HMMM... THIS IS A TOUGH ONE.
WHAT WILL OUR CUSTOMERS THINK?

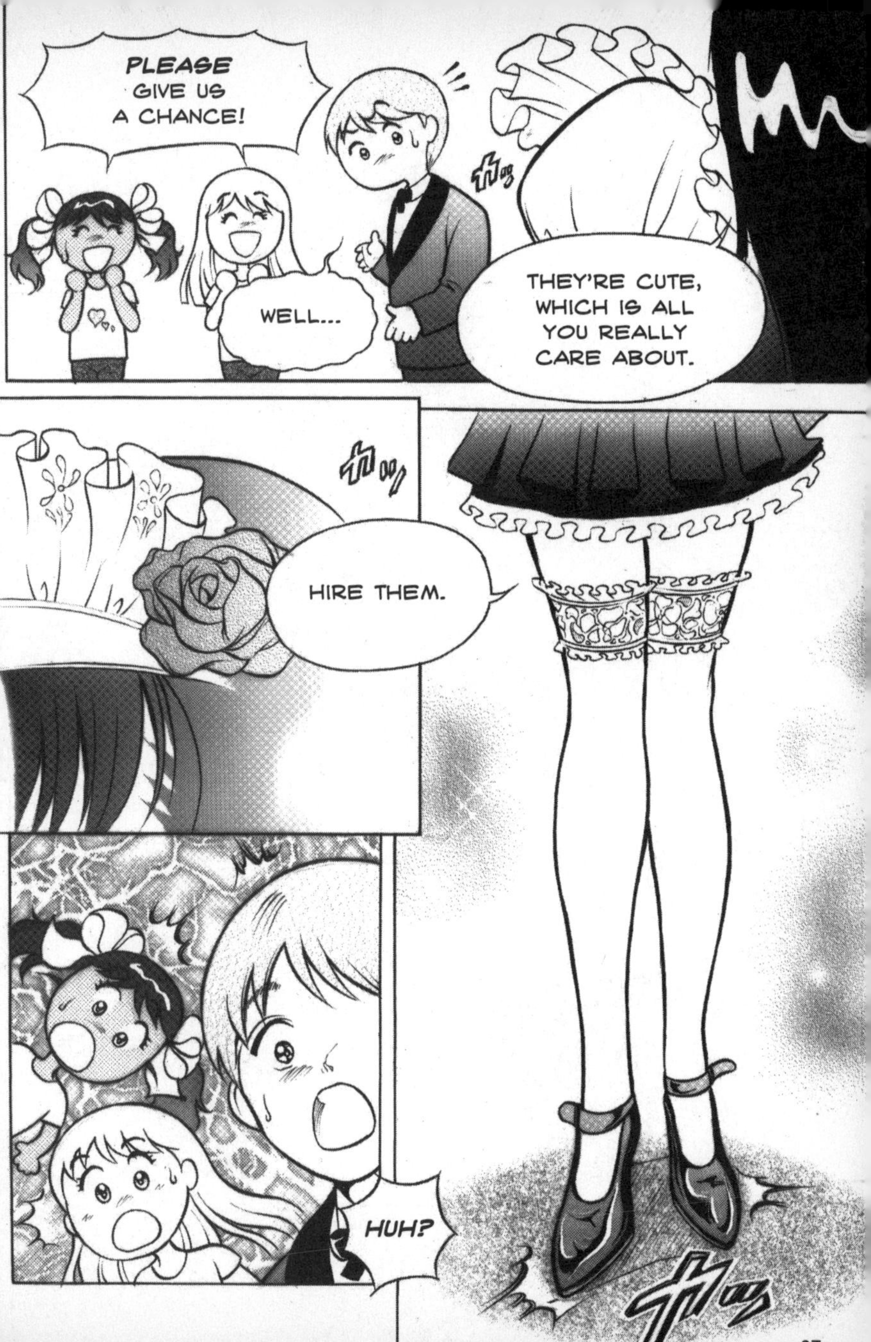

PLEASE GIVE US A CHANCE!
WELL...
THEY'RE CUTE, WHICH IS ALL YOU REALLY CARE ABOUT.
HIRE THEM.
HUH?

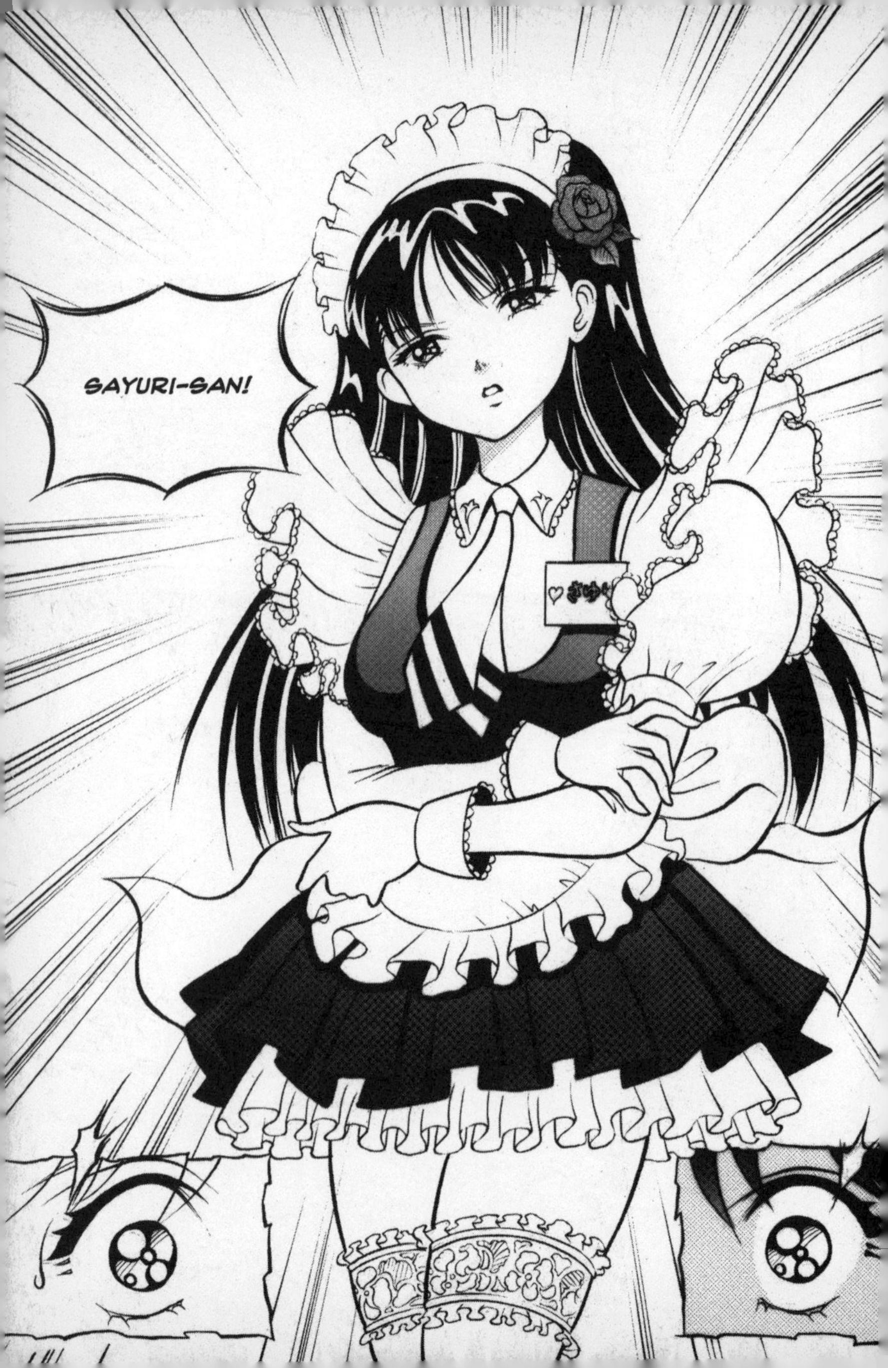
SAYURI-SAN!

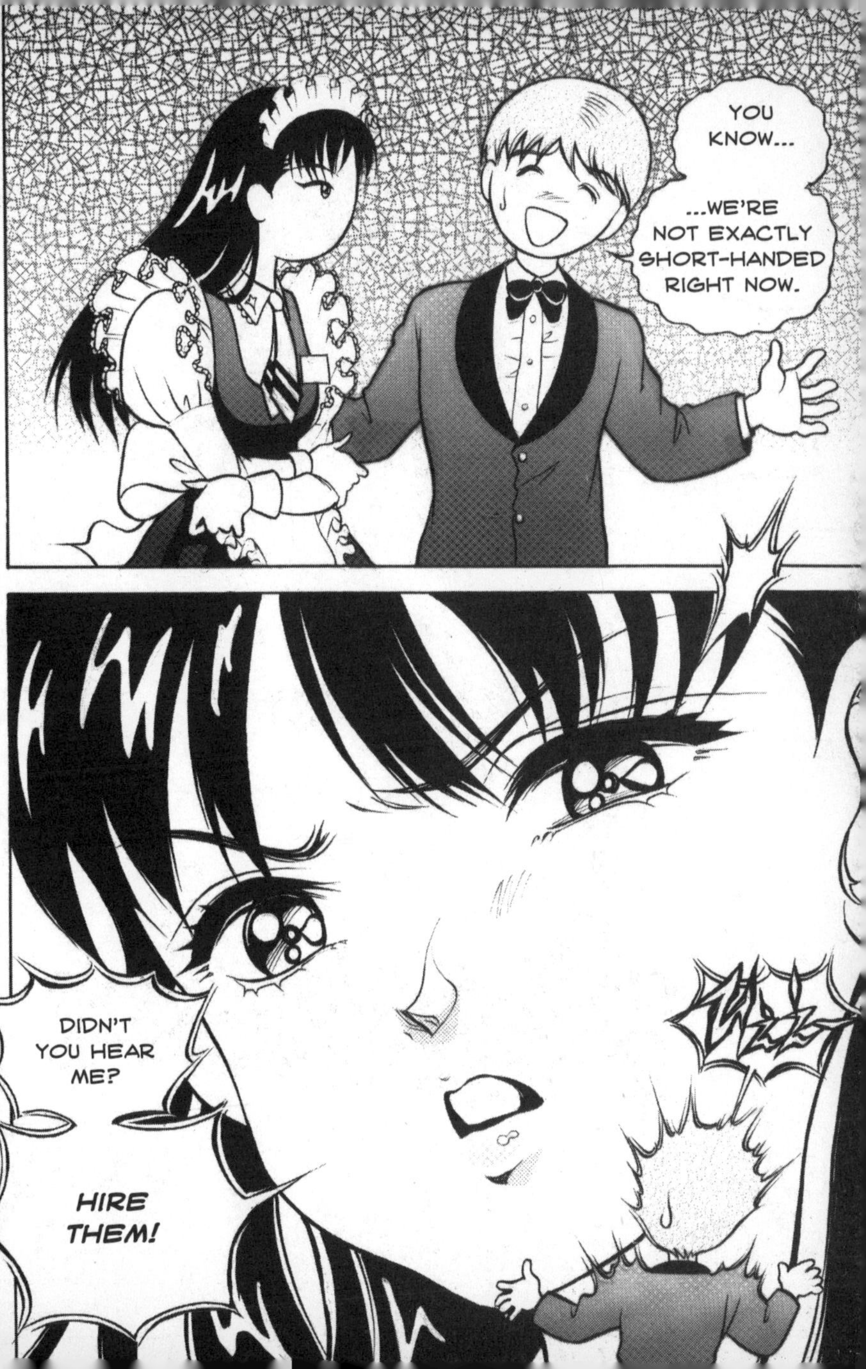
YOU KNOW...
...WE'RE NOT EXACTLY SHORT-HANDED RIGHT NOW.
DIDN'T YOU HEAR ME?
HIRE THEM!

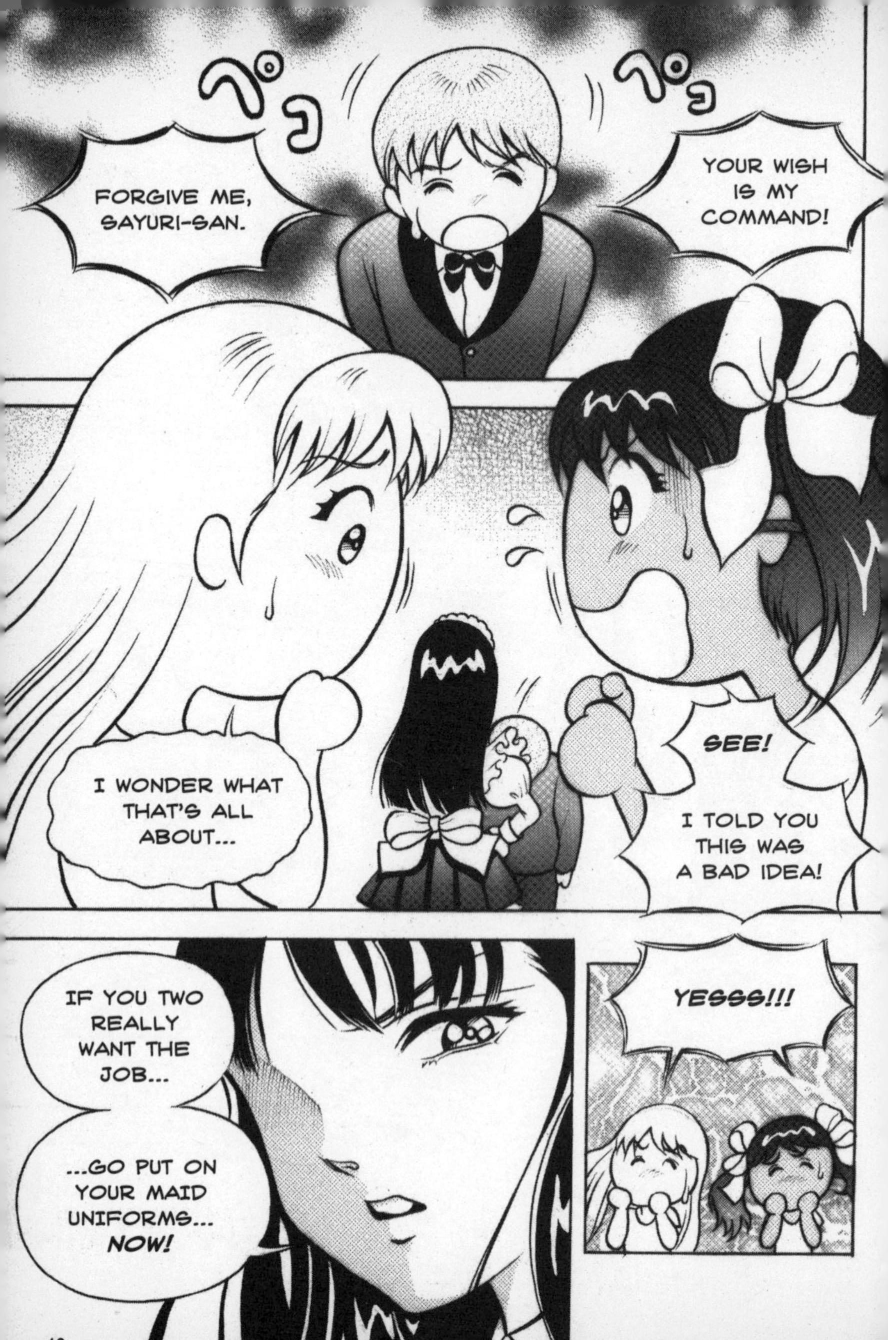
ペコ
ペコ
FORGIVE ME, SAYURI-SAN.
YOUR WISH IS MY COMMAND!
I WONDER WHAT THAT'S ALL ABOUT...
SEE!
I TOLD YOU THIS WAS A BAD IDEA!
IF YOU TWO REALLY WANT THE JOB...
...GO PUT ON YOUR MAID UNIFORMS... *NOW!*
*YESSS!!!*

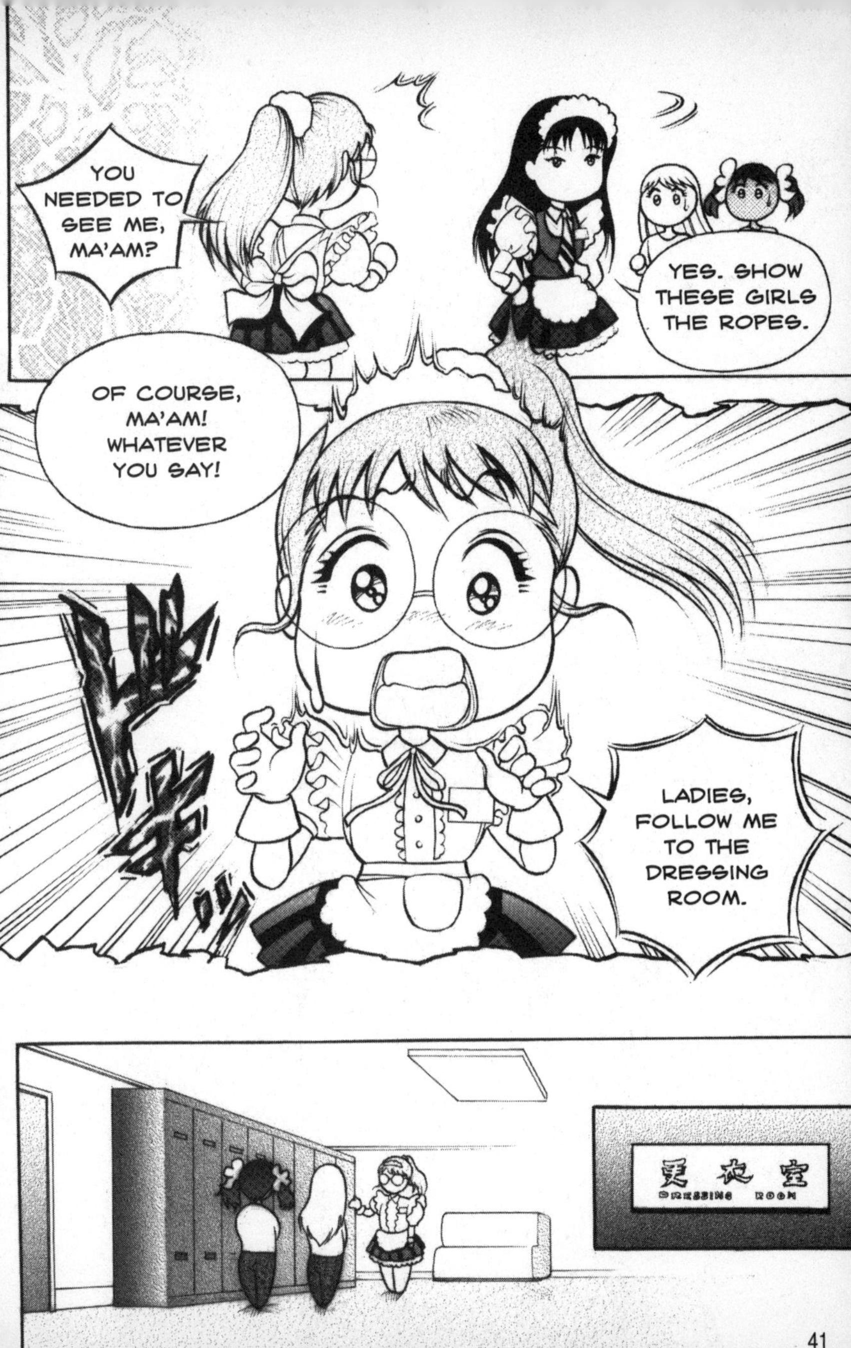
YOU NEEDED TO SEE ME, MA'AM?
YES. SHOW THESE GIRLS THE ROPES.
OF COURSE, MA'AM! WHATEVER YOU SAY!
LADIES, FOLLOW ME TO THE DRESSING ROOM.
更衣室
DRESSING ROOM

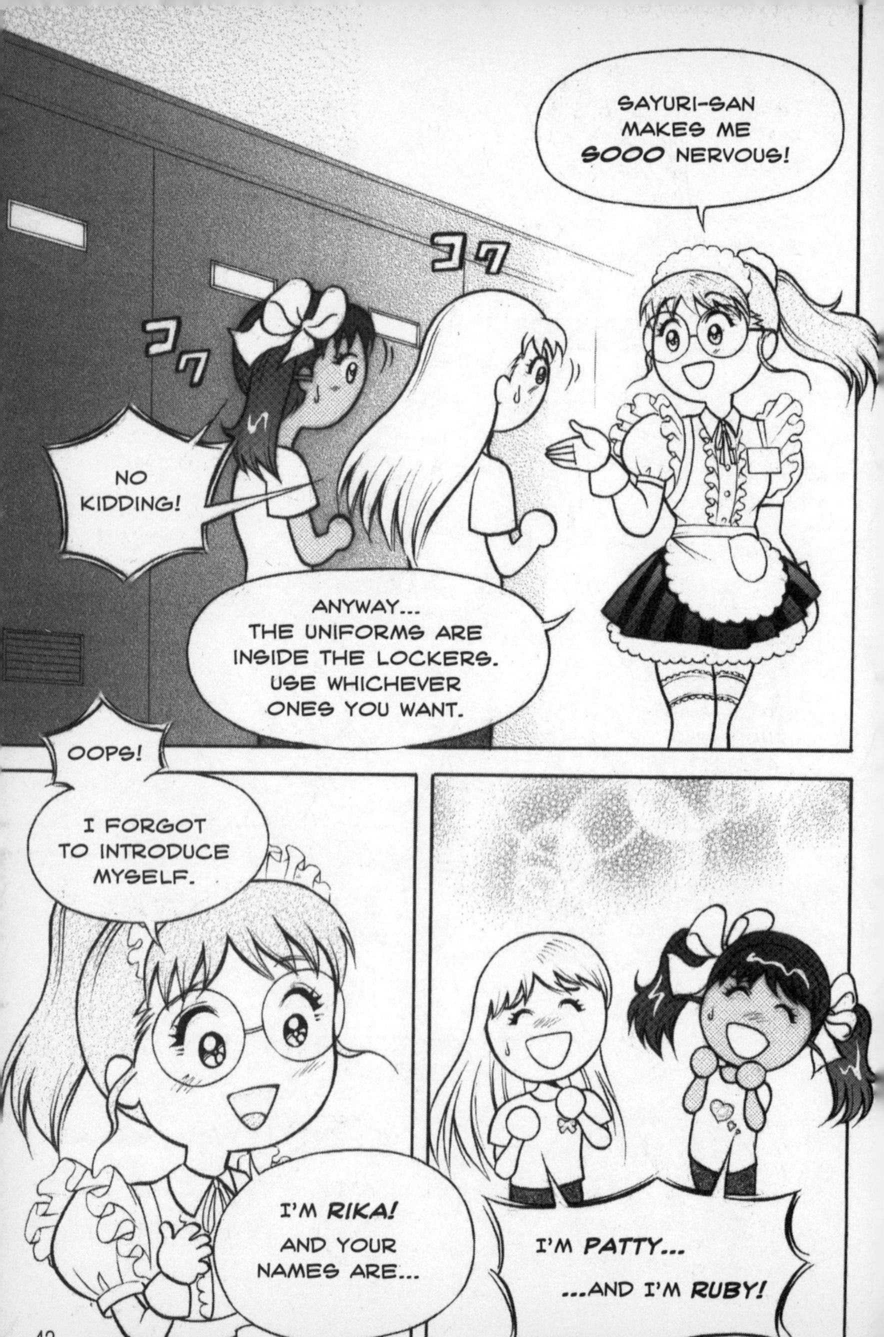
SAYURI-SAN MAKES ME SOOO NERVOUS!
コク
コク
NO KIDDING!
ANYWAY... THE UNIFORMS ARE INSIDE THE LOCKERS. USE WHICHEVER ONES YOU WANT.
OOPS!
I FORGOT TO INTRODUCE MYSELF.
I'M RIKA! AND YOUR NAMES ARE...
I'M PATTY...
...AND I'M RUBY!

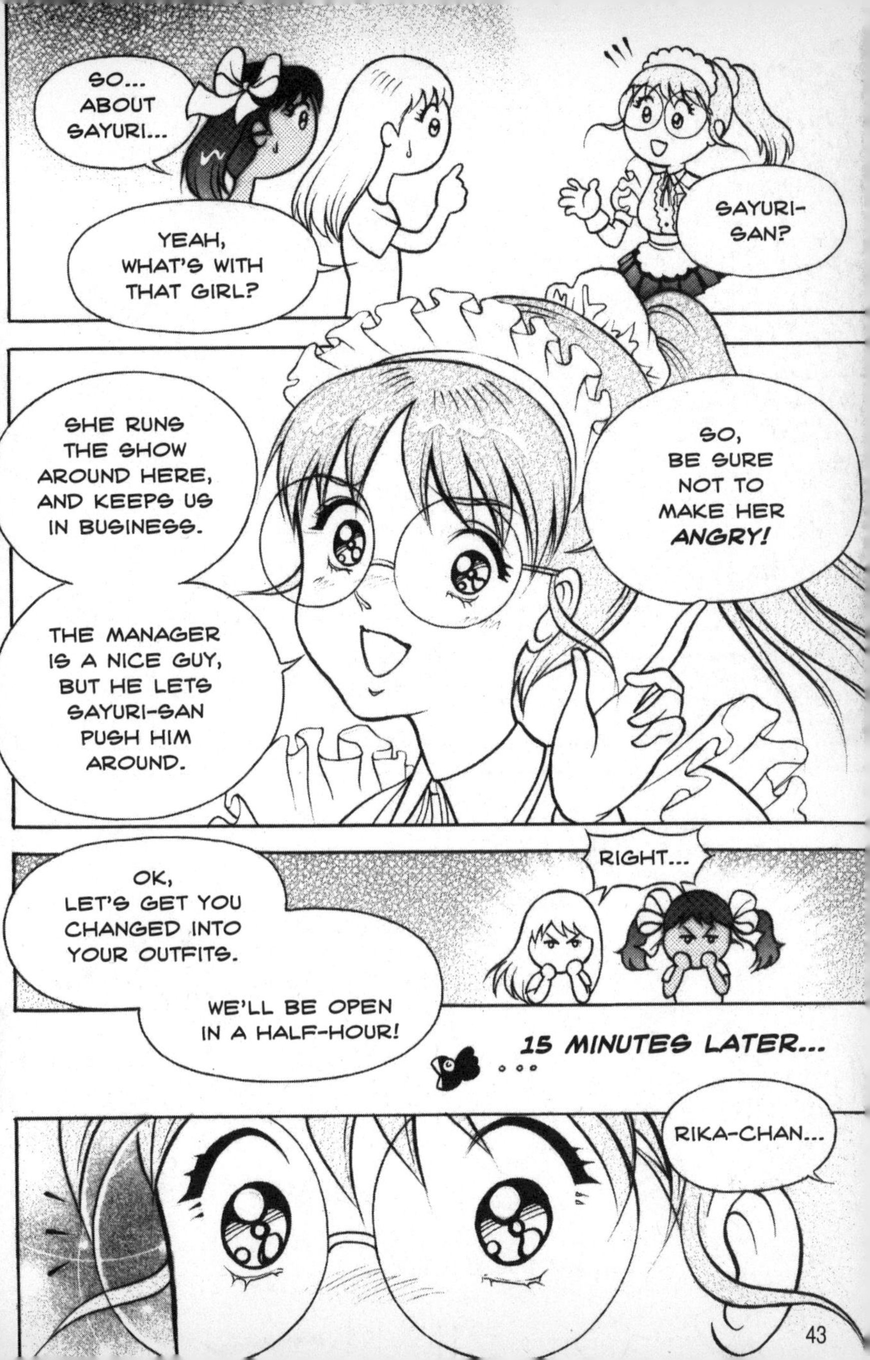
SO... ABOUT SAYURI...
YEAH, WHAT'S WITH THAT GIRL?
SAYURI-SAN?
SHE RUNS THE SHOW AROUND HERE, AND KEEPS US IN BUSINESS.
SO, BE SURE NOT TO MAKE HER ANGRY!
THE MANAGER IS A NICE GUY, BUT HE LETS SAYURI-SAN PUSH HIM AROUND.
OK, LET'S GET YOU CHANGED INTO YOUR OUTFITS.
WE'LL BE OPEN IN A HALF-HOUR!
RIGHT...
15 MINUTES LATER...
RIKA-CHAN...

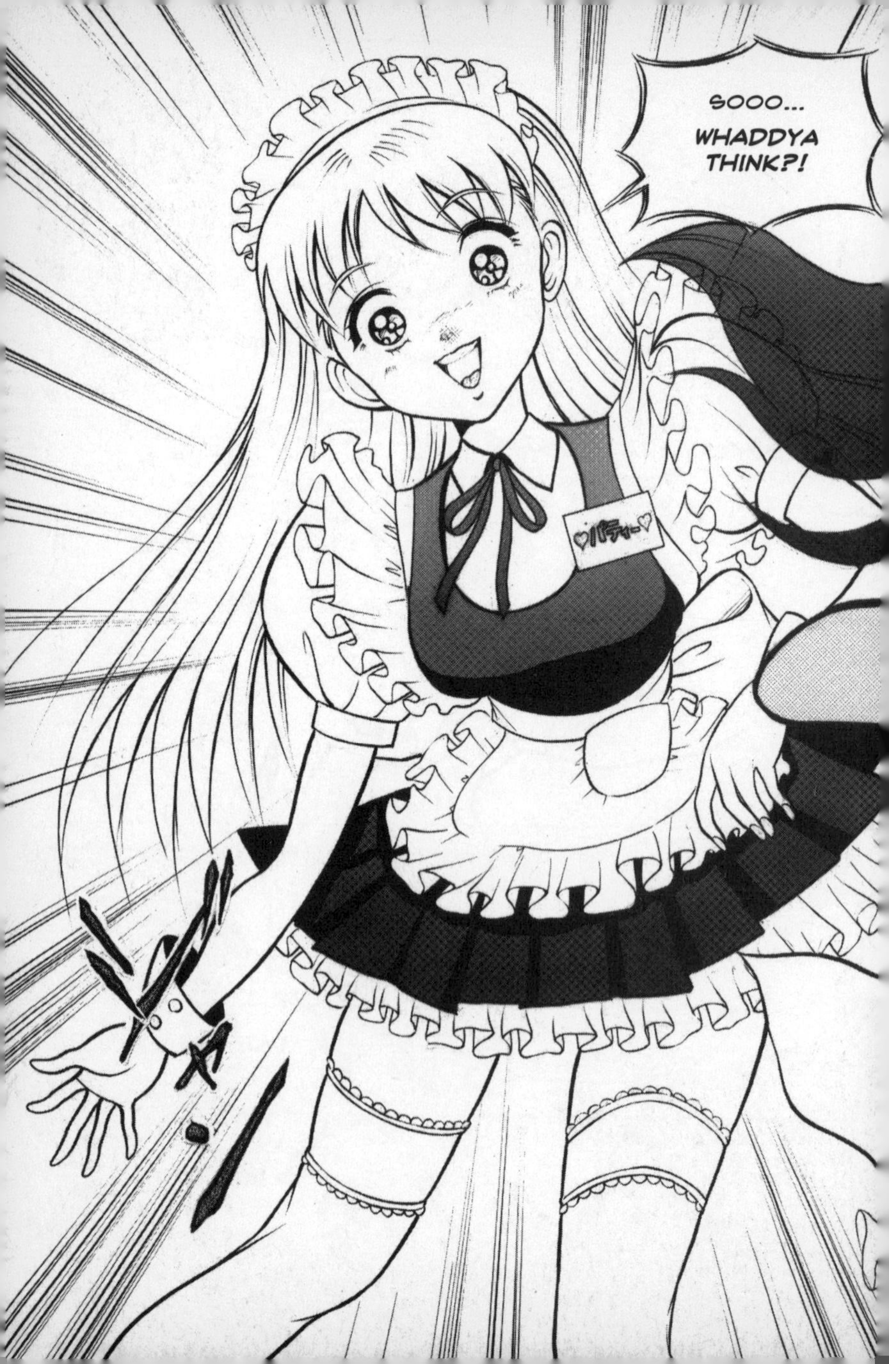
SOOO...
WHADDYA THINK?!
♡パティー♡

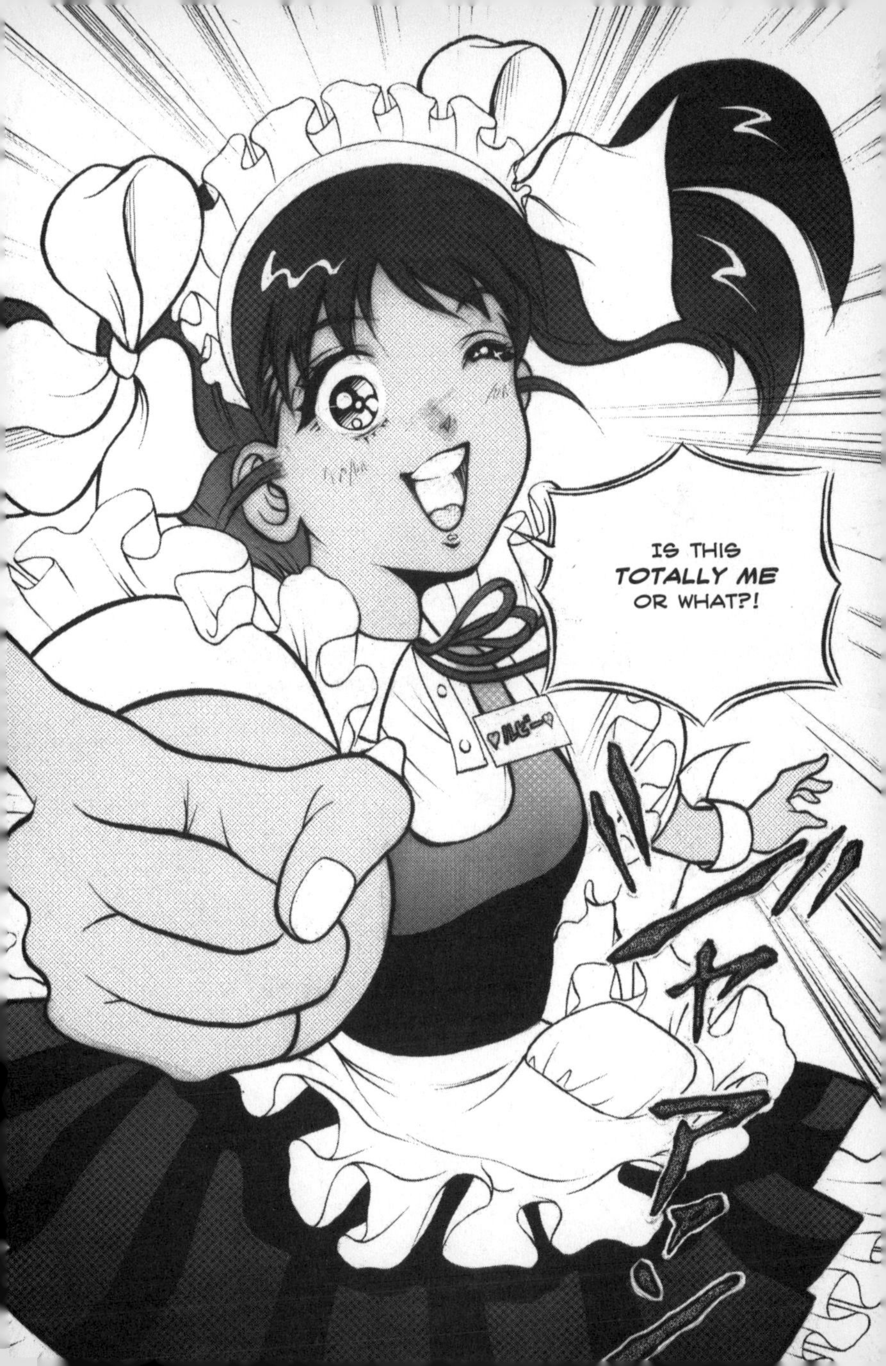
IS THIS *TOTALLY ME* OR WHAT?!

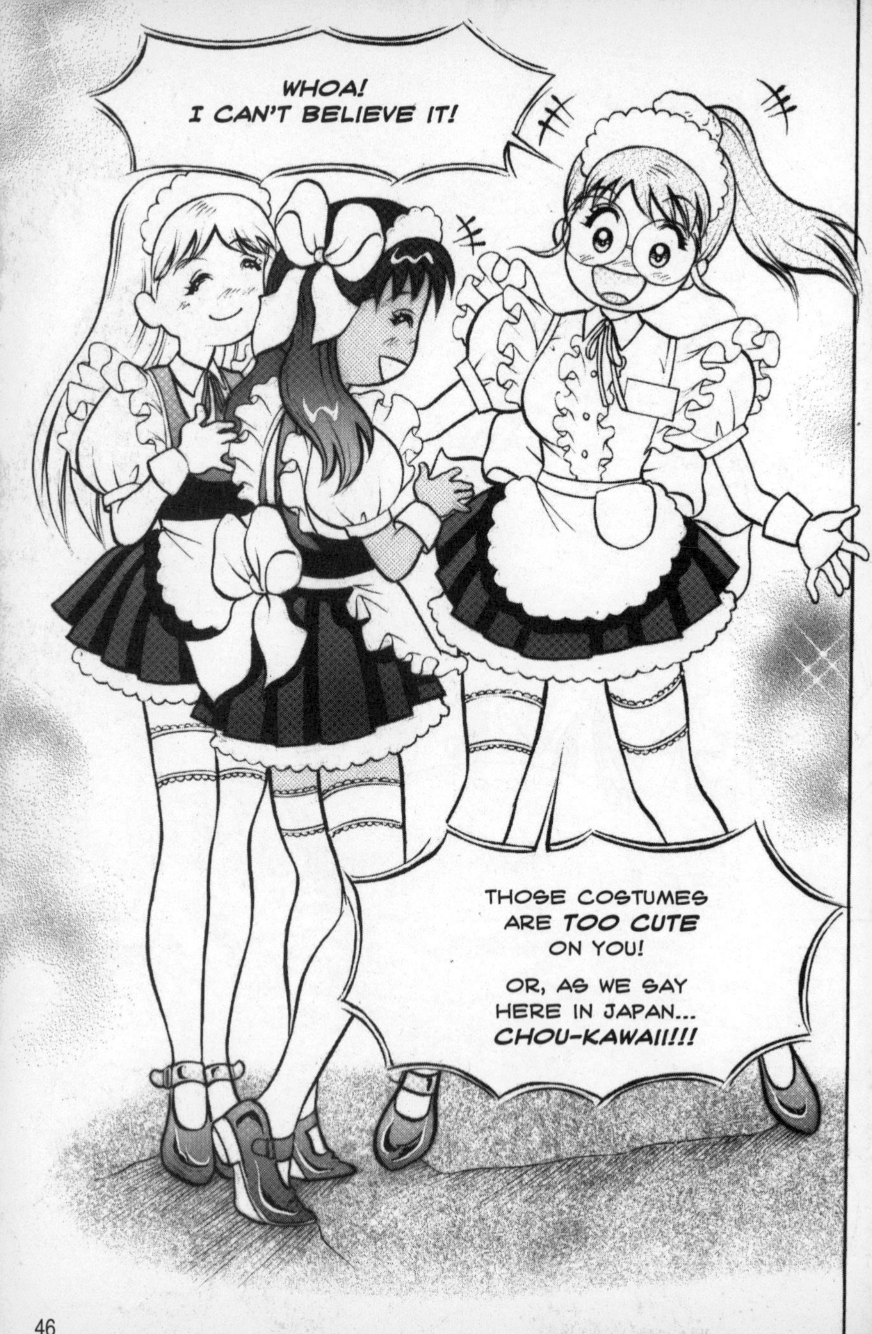
WHOA! I CAN'T BELIEVE IT!
THOSE COSTUMES ARE TOO CUTE ON YOU!
OR, AS WE SAY HERE IN JAPAN... CHOU-KAWAII!!!!

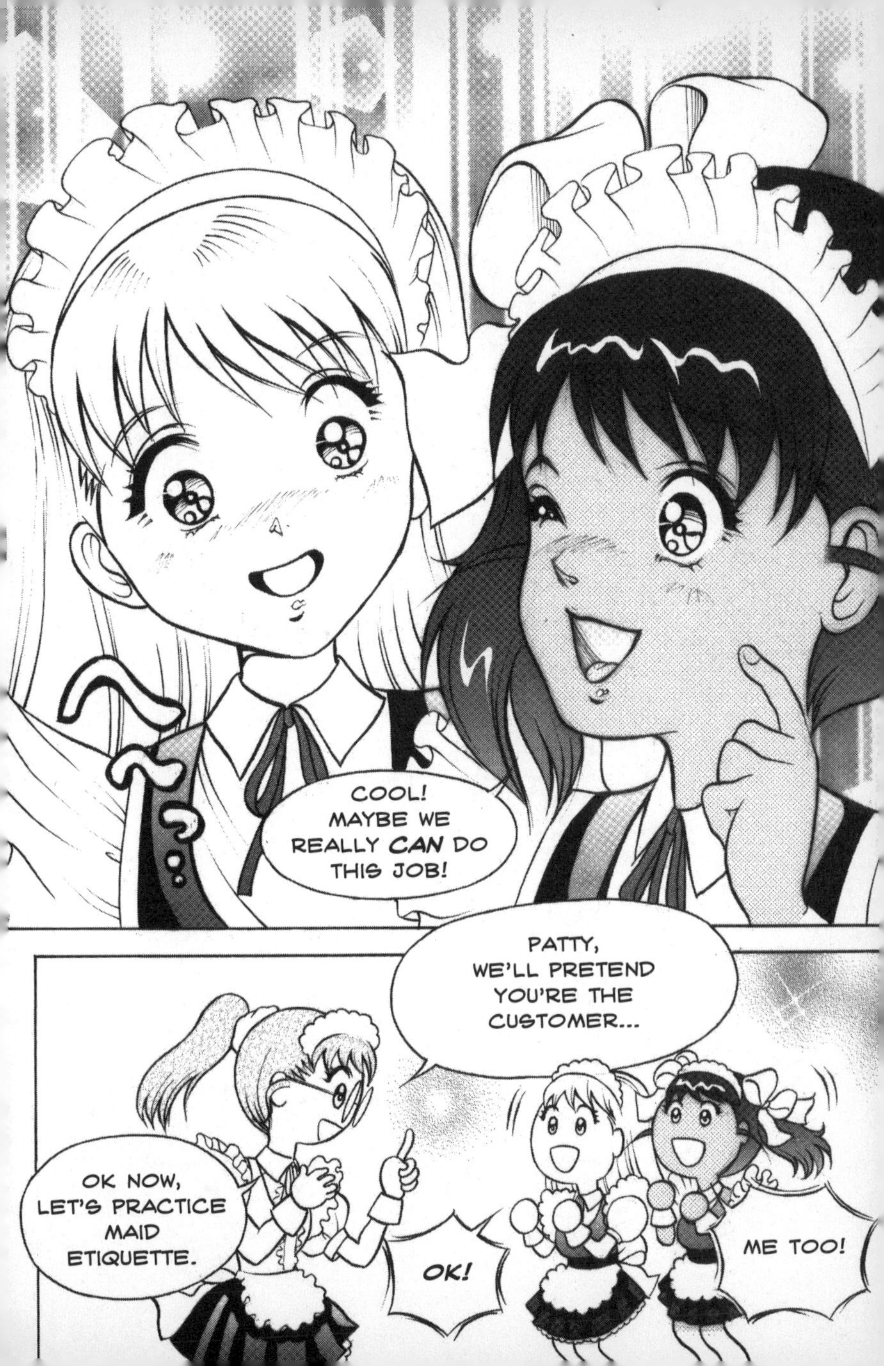
COOL! MAYBE WE REALLY **CAN** DO THIS JOB!
PATTY, WE'LL PRETEND YOU'RE THE CUSTOMER...
OK NOW, LET'S PRACTICE MAID ETIQUETTE.
OK!
ME TOO!

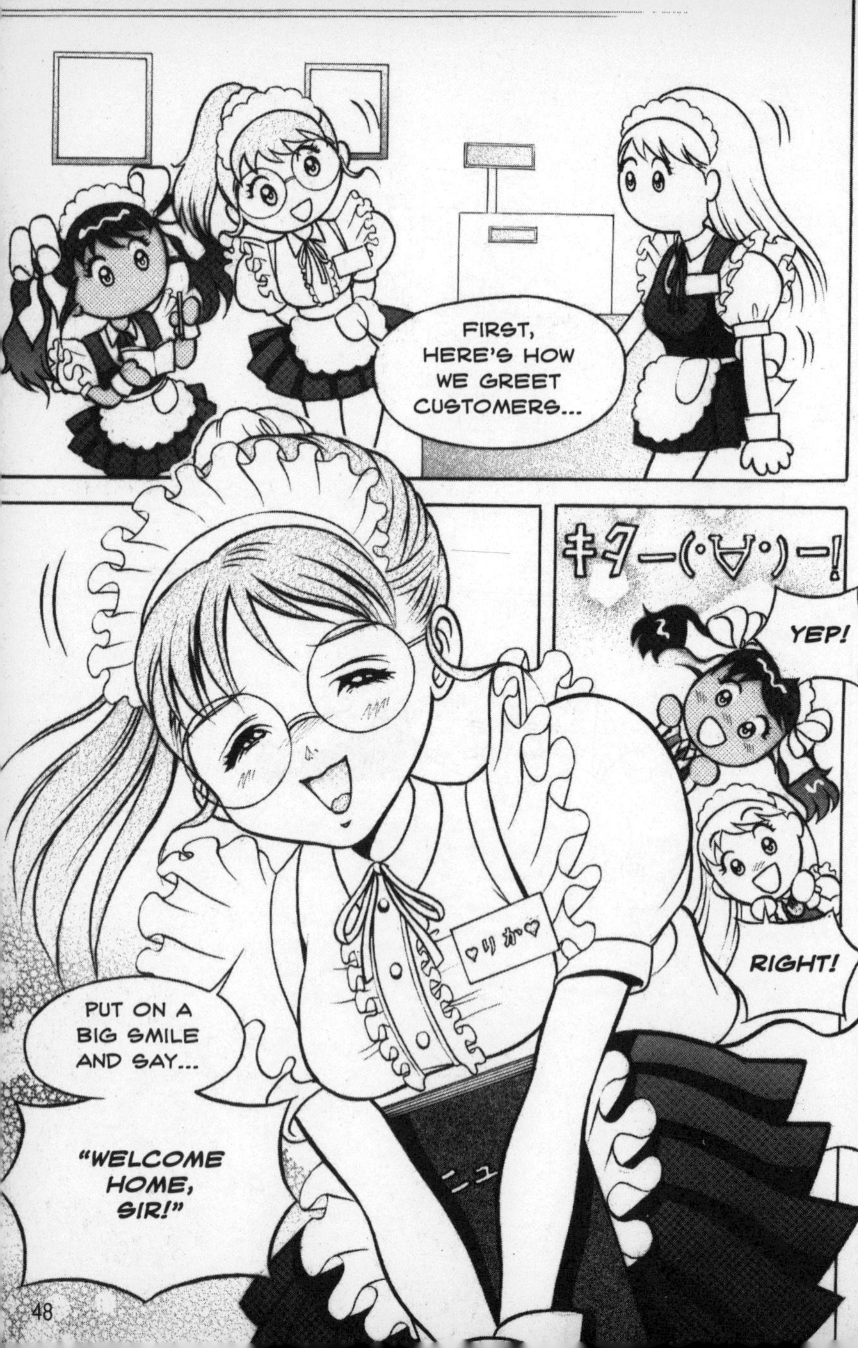
FIRST, HERE'S HOW WE GREET CUSTOMERS...
キターー(゜∀゜)ーー!
YEP!
RIGHT!
♡りか♡
PUT ON A BIG SMILE AND SAY...
"WELCOME HOME, SIR!"

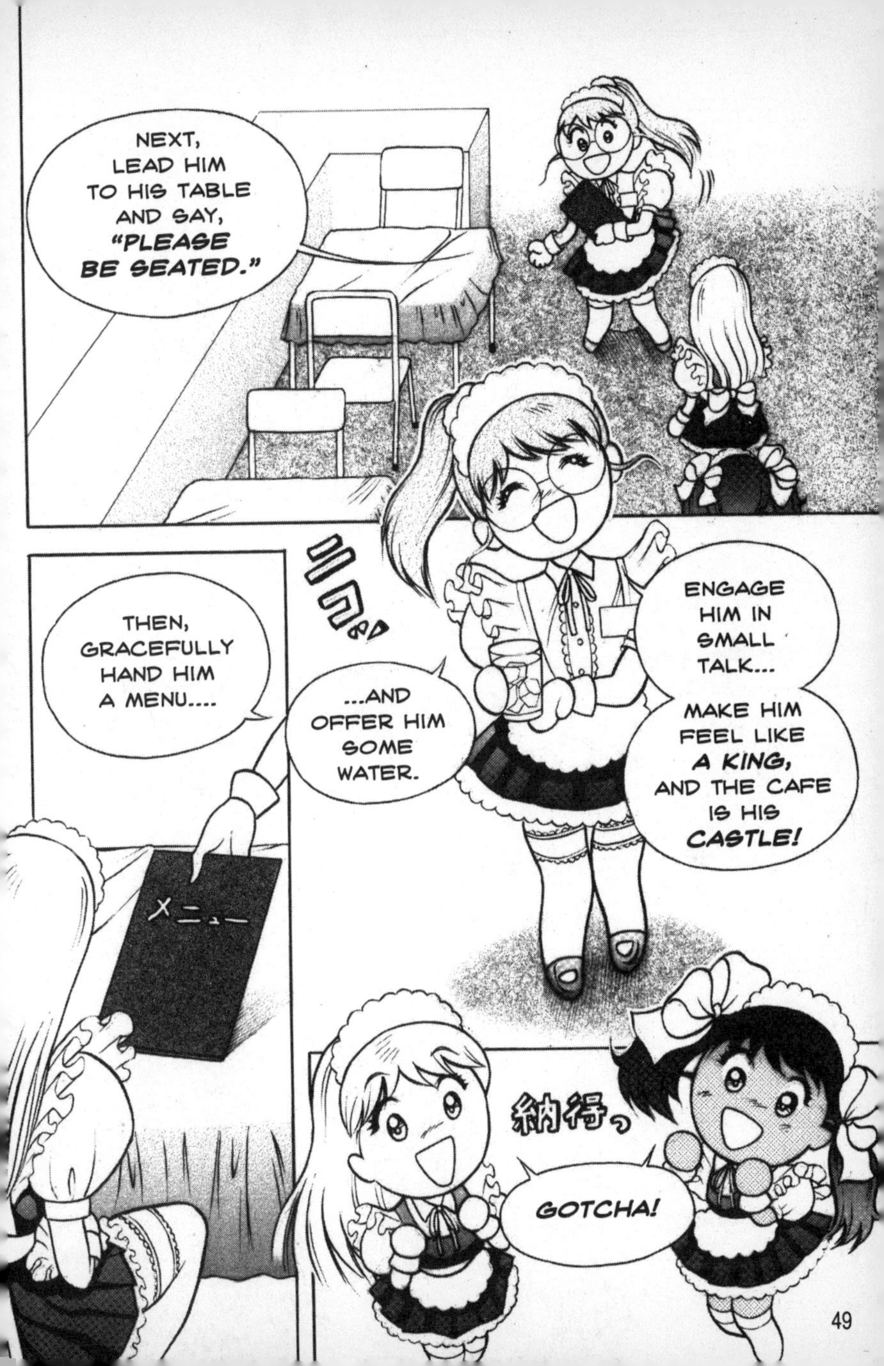
NEXT, LEAD HIM TO HIS TABLE AND SAY, "PLEASE BE SEATED."
THEN, GRACEFULLY HAND HIM A MENU....
メニュー
...AND OFFER HIM SOME WATER.
ニコッ
ENGAGE HIM IN SMALL TALK...
MAKE HIM FEEL LIKE A KING, AND THE CAFE IS HIS CASTLE!
納得っ
GOTCHA!

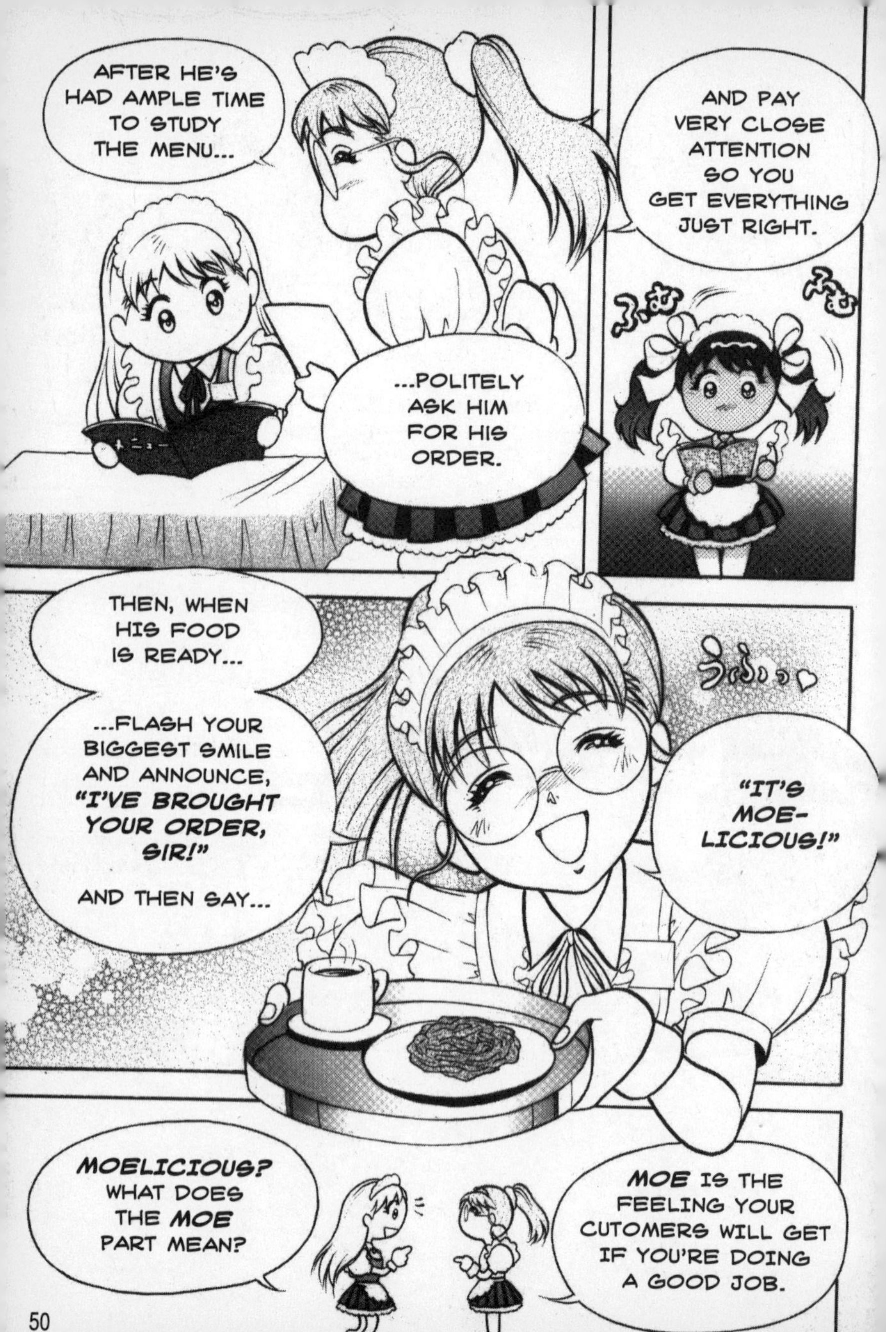
AFTER HE'S HAD AMPLE TIME TO STUDY THE MENU...
...POLITELY ASK HIM FOR HIS ORDER.
AND PAY VERY CLOSE ATTENTION SO YOU GET EVERYTHING JUST RIGHT.
ふむ ふむ
THEN, WHEN HIS FOOD IS READY...
...FLASH YOUR BIGGEST SMILE AND ANNOUNCE, *"I'VE BROUGHT YOUR ORDER, SIR!"*
AND THEN SAY...
うふっ♡
"IT'S MOE-LICIOUS!"
*MOELICIOUS?* WHAT DOES THE *MOE* PART MEAN?
*MOE* IS THE FEELING YOUR CUTOMERS WILL GET IF YOU'RE DOING A GOOD JOB.

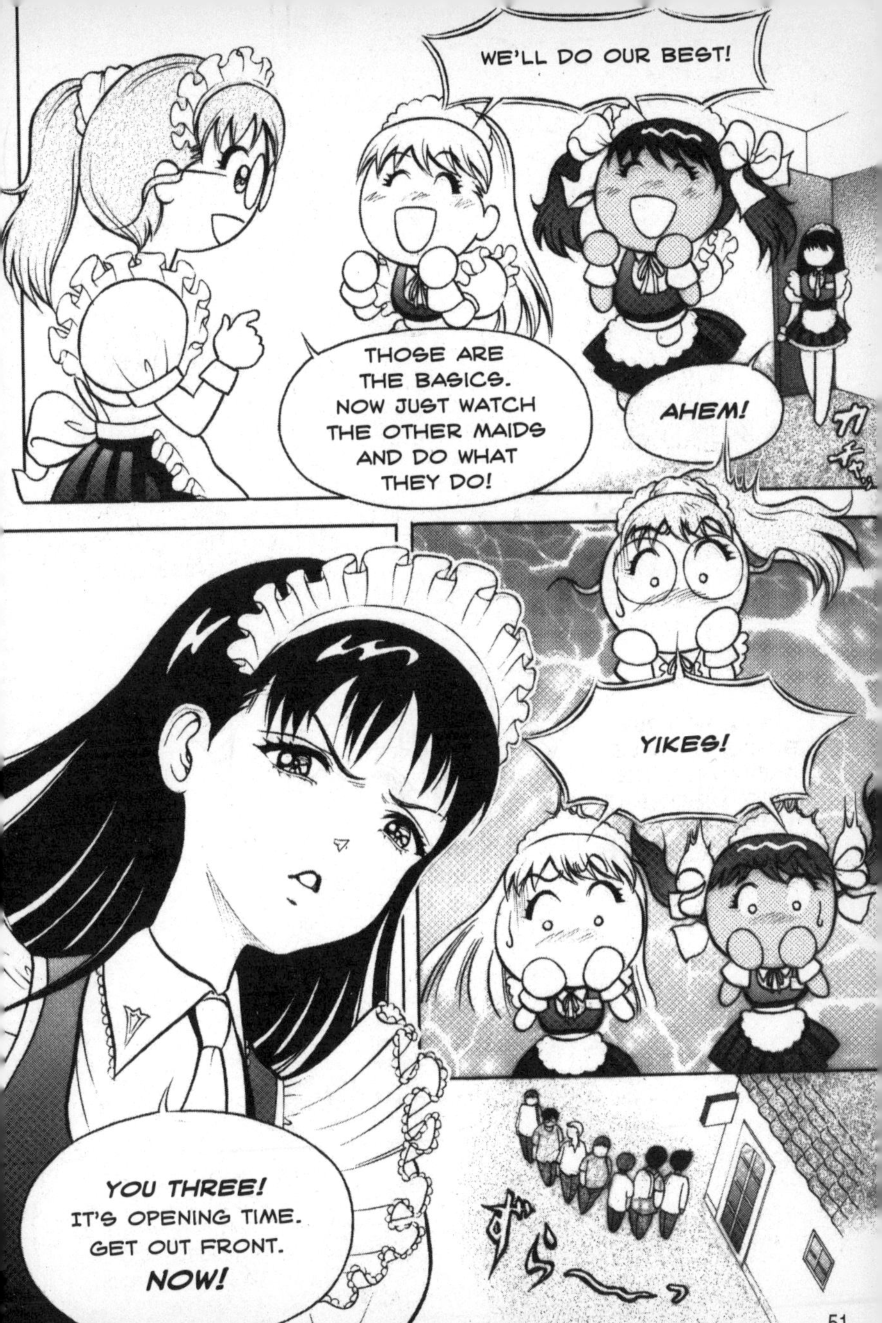
WE'LL DO OUR BEST!
THOSE ARE THE BASICS. NOW JUST WATCH THE OTHER MAIDS AND DO WHAT THEY DO!
AHEM!
YIKES!
YOU THREE! IT'S OPENING TIME. GET OUT FRONT. NOW!

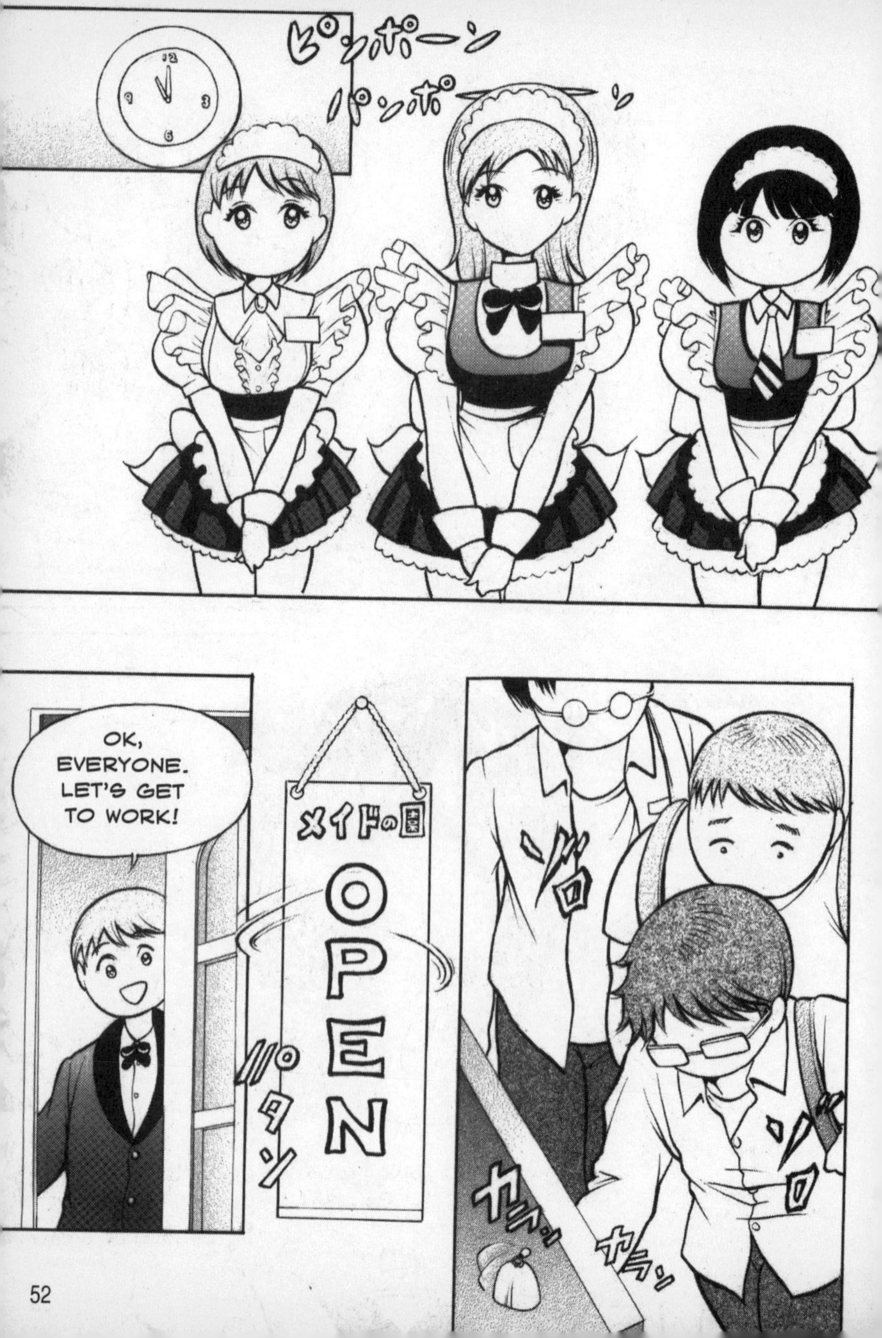
ピンポーン
パンポーン
メイドの園
OPEN
パタン
OK, EVERYONE. LET'S GET TO WORK!
ドロ
ドロ
カランカラン

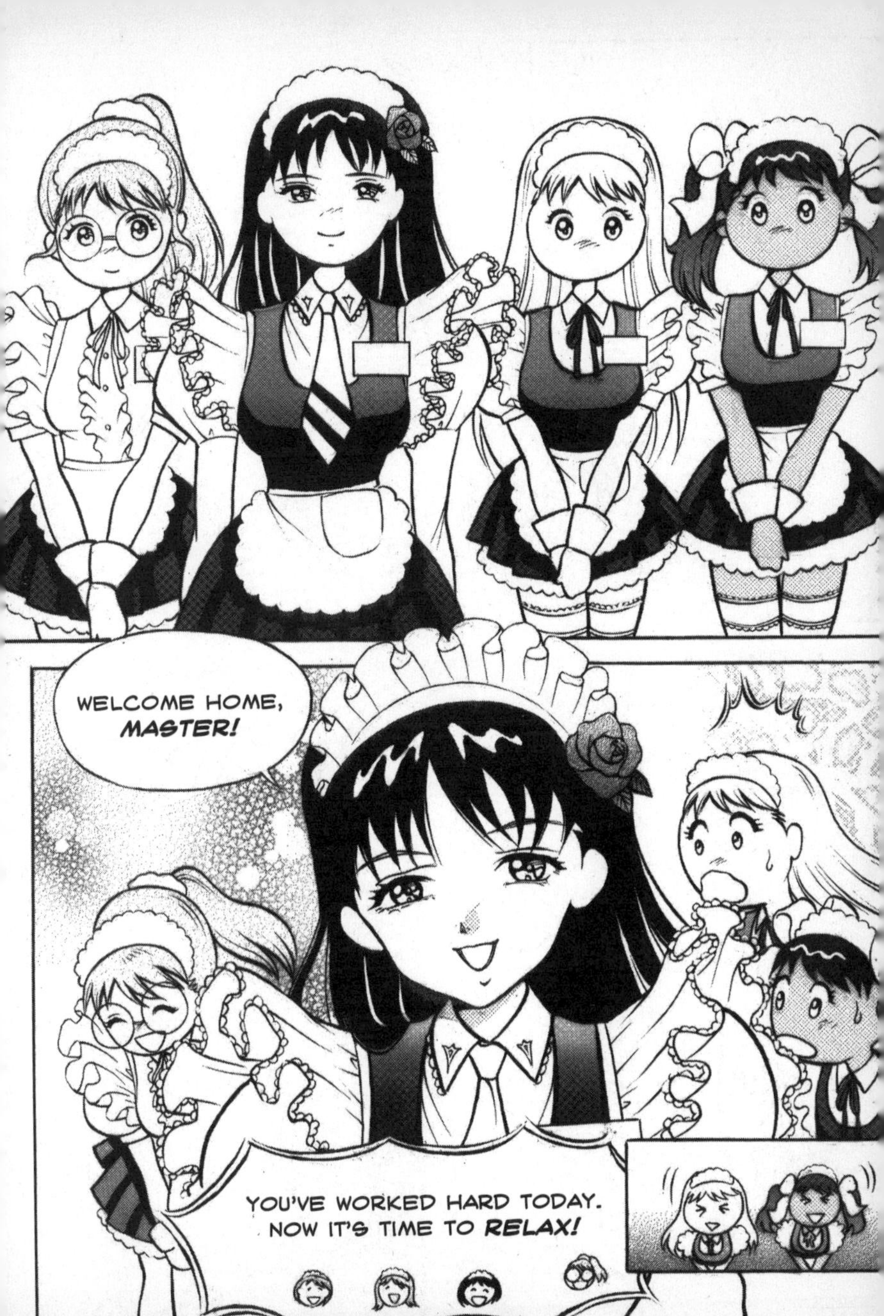
WELCOME HOME, MASTER!
YOU'VE WORKED HARD TODAY. NOW IT'S TIME TO RELAX!

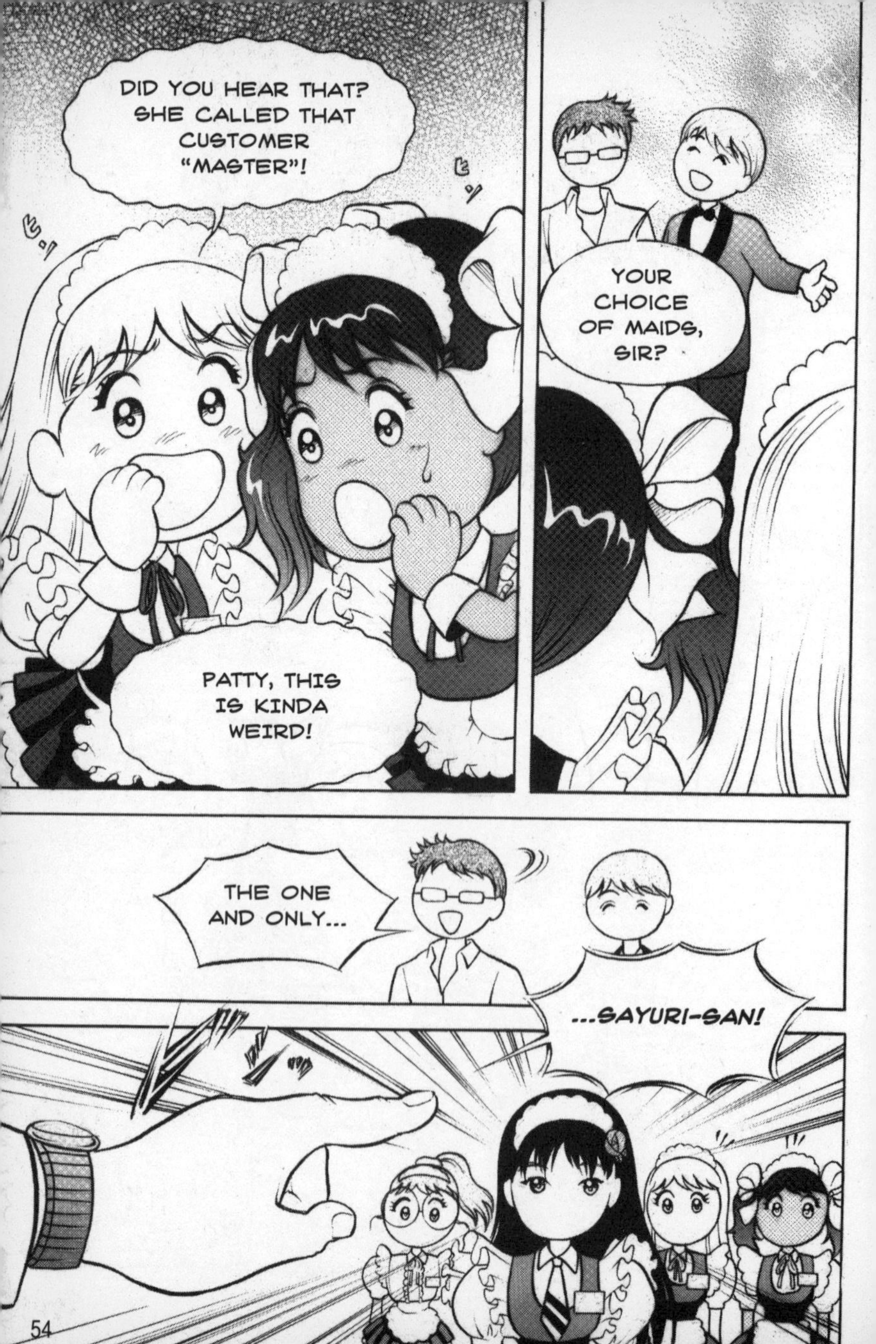
DID YOU HEAR THAT? SHE CALLED THAT CUSTOMER "MASTER"!
PATTY, THIS IS KINDA WEIRD!
YOUR CHOICE OF MAIDS, SIR?
THE ONE AND ONLY...
...SAYURI-SAN!

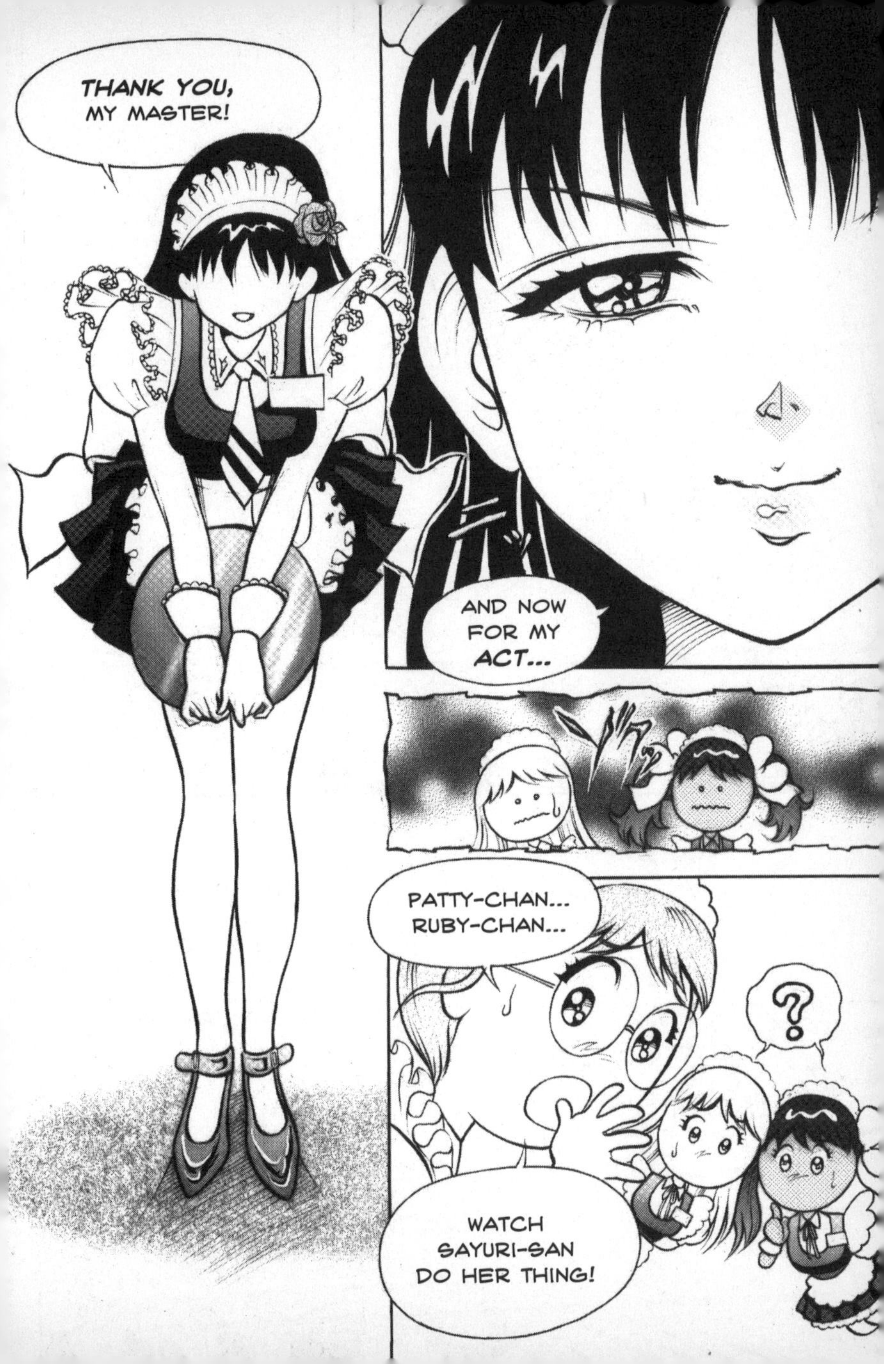
THANK YOU, MY MASTER!
AND NOW FOR MY ACT...
PATTY-CHAN... RUBY-CHAN...
WATCH SAYURI-SAN DO HER THING!
?

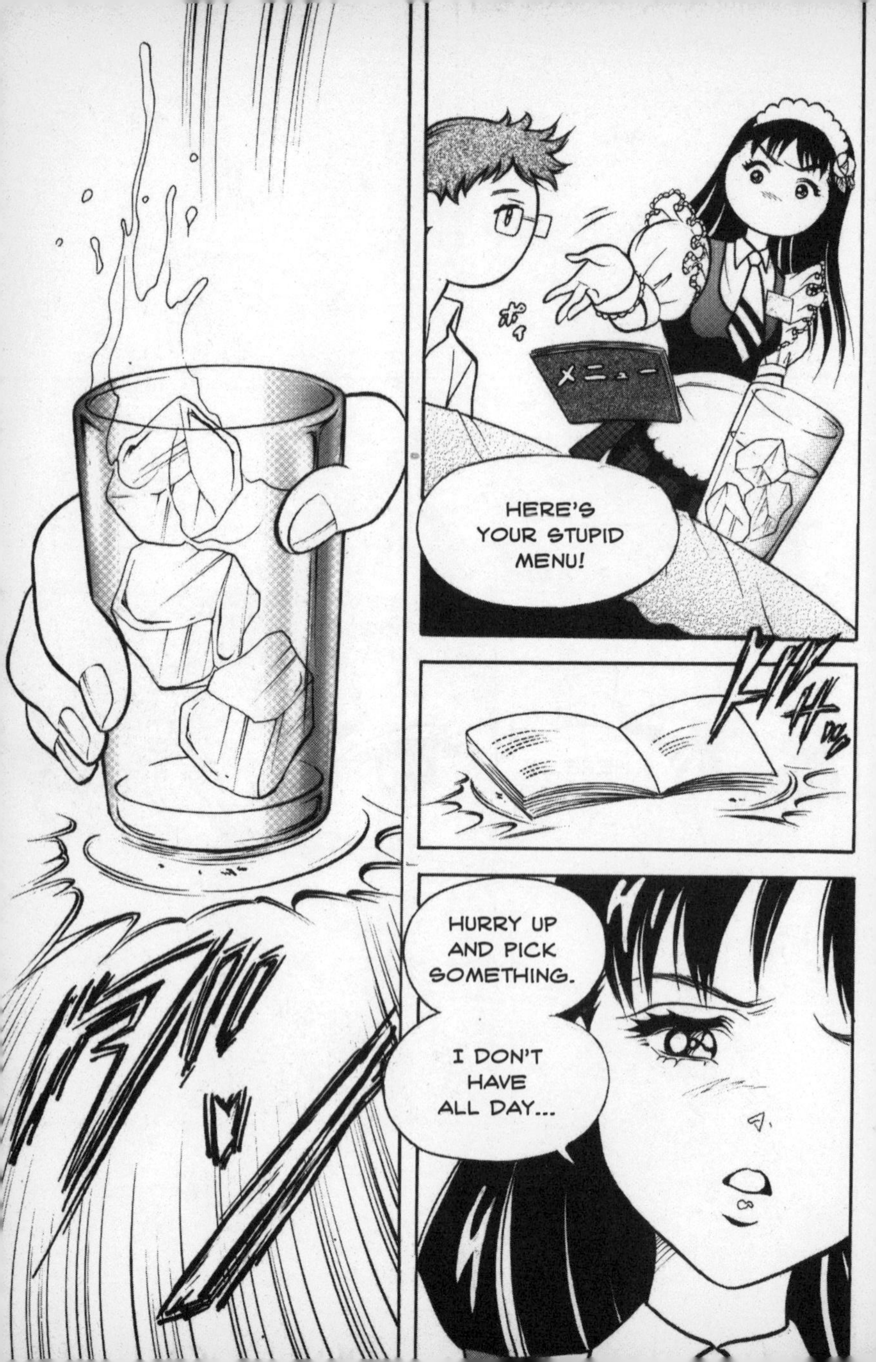
HERE'S YOUR STUPID MENU!
HURRY UP AND PICK SOMETHING.
I DON'T HAVE ALL DAY...

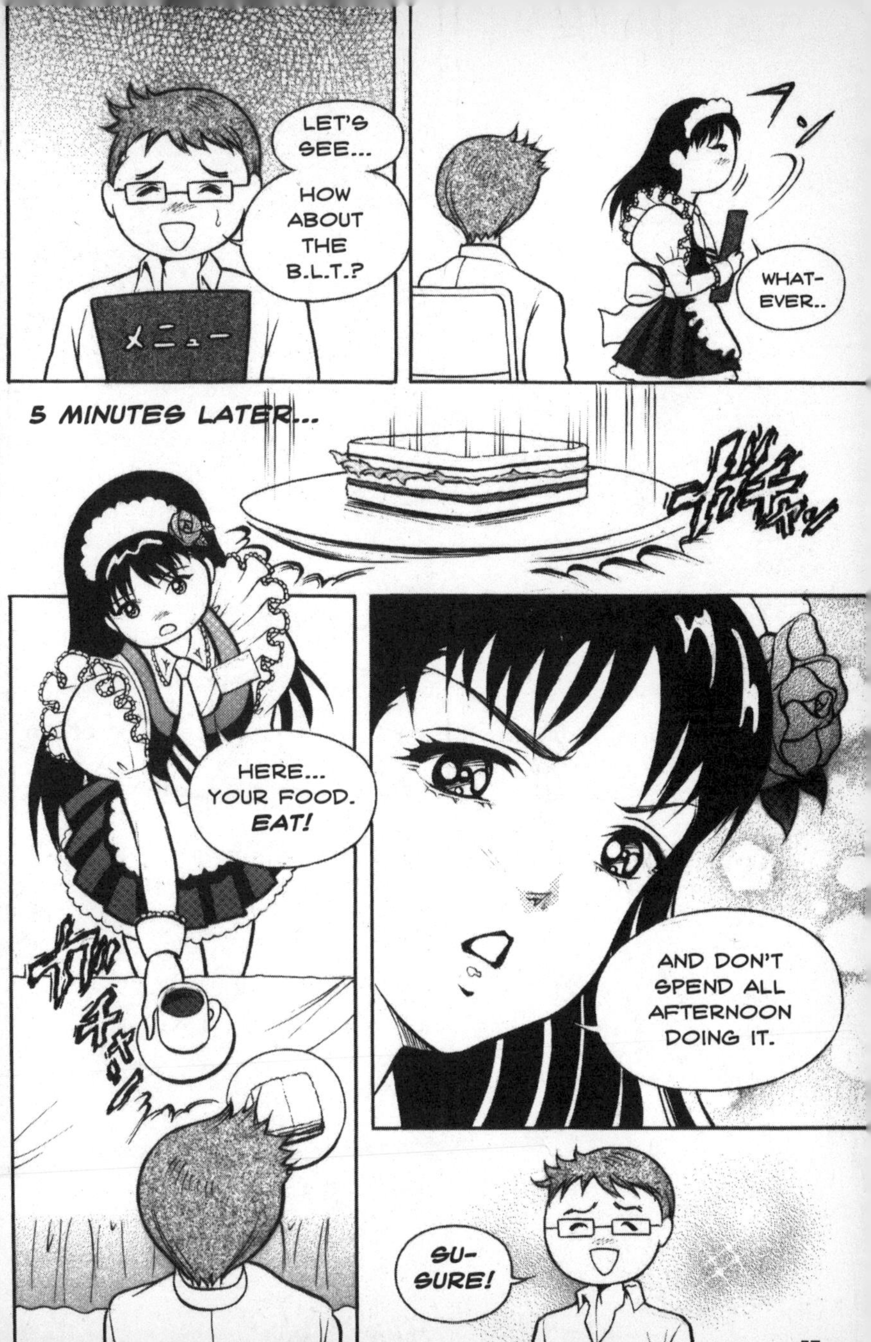
LET'S SEE...
HOW ABOUT THE B.L.T.?
メニュー
WHAT-EVER..
5 MINUTES LATER...
HERE... YOUR FOOD. EAT!
AND DON'T SPEND ALL AFTERNOON DOING IT.
SU-SURE!

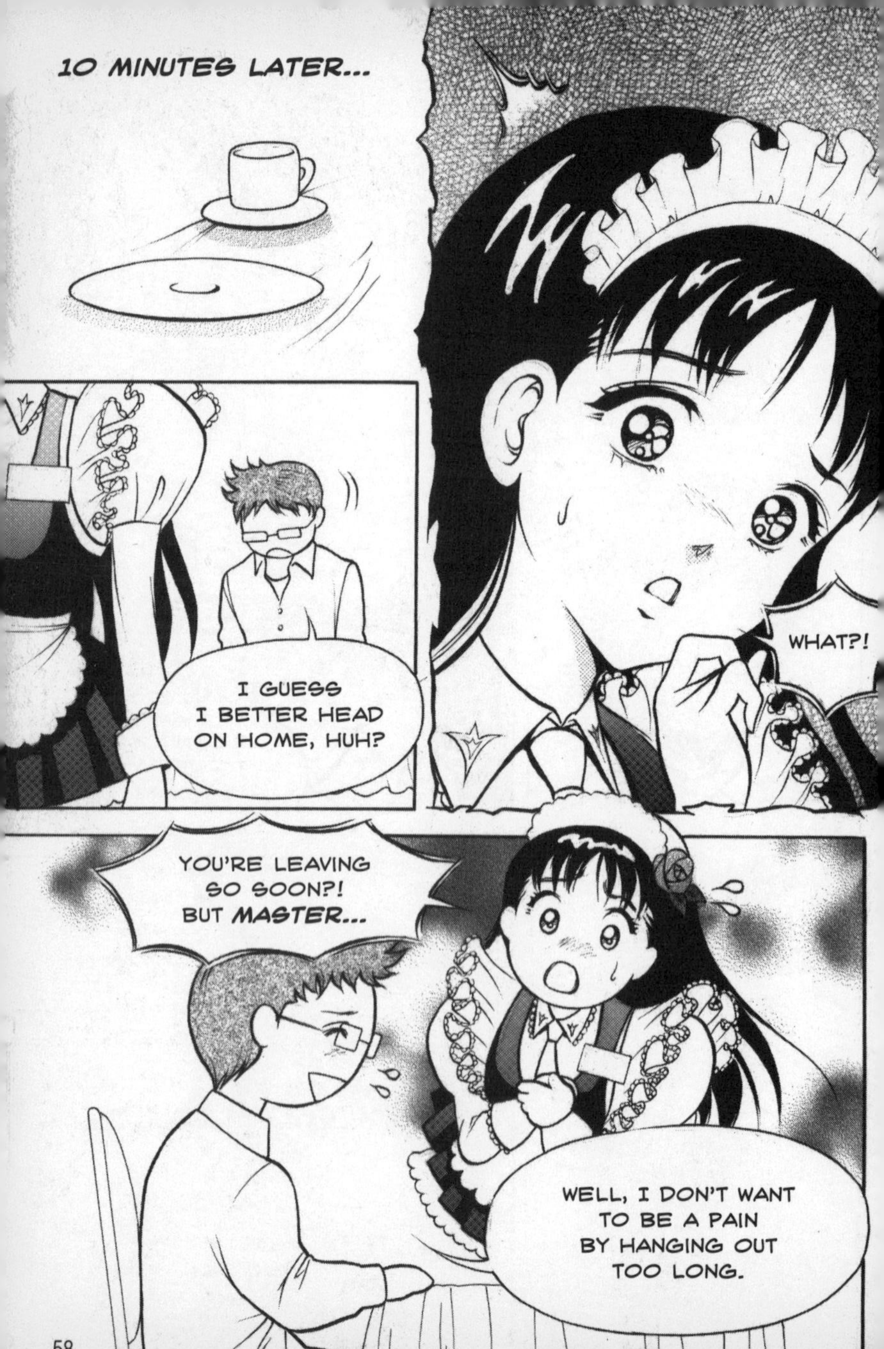
10 MINUTES LATER...
I GUESS I BETTER HEAD ON HOME, HUH?
WHAT?!
YOU'RE LEAVING SO SOON?! BUT MASTER...
WELL, I DON'T WANT TO BE A PAIN BY HANGING OUT TOO LONG.

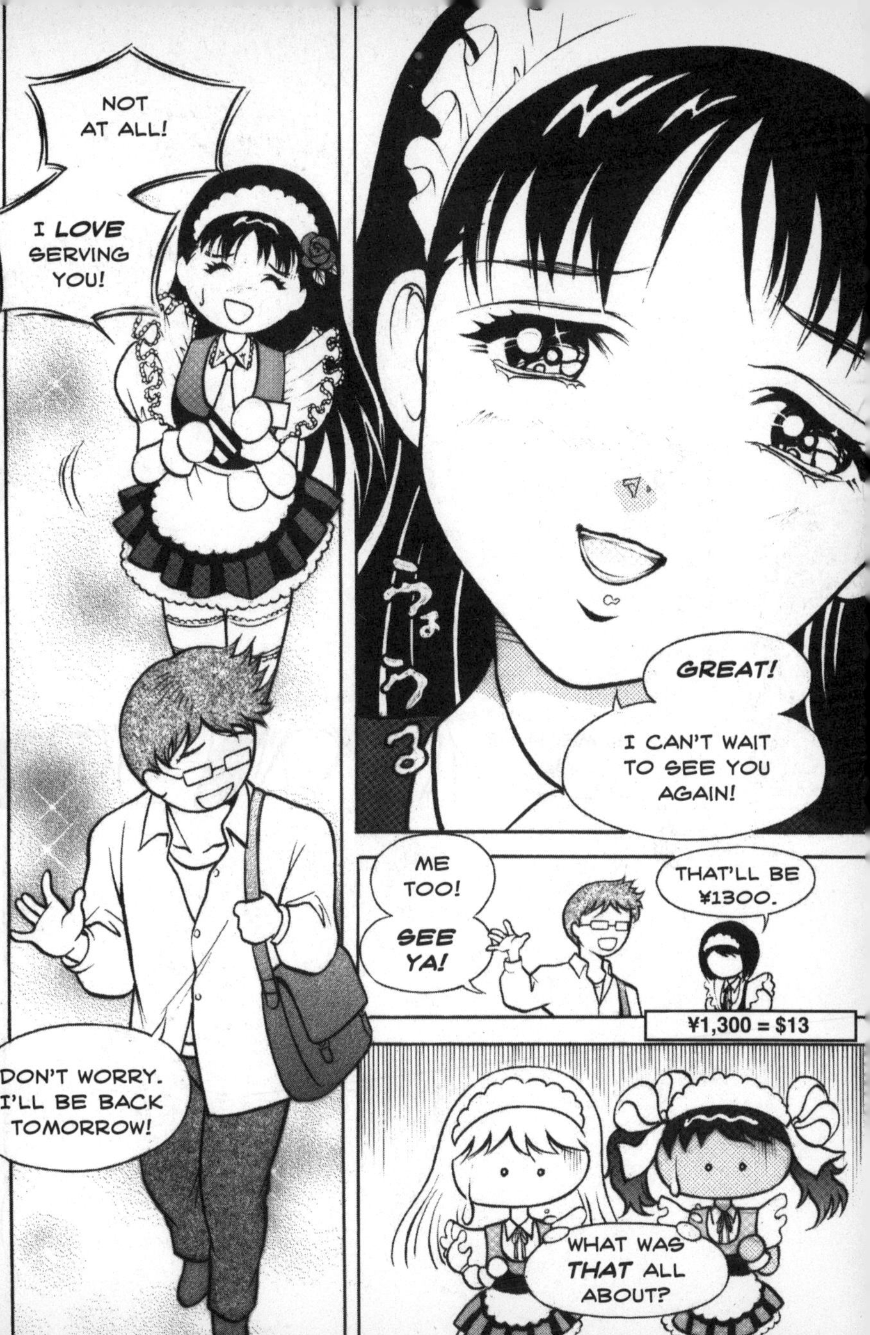
NOT AT ALL!
I *LOVE* SERVING YOU!
*GREAT!*
I CAN'T WAIT TO SEE YOU AGAIN!
DON'T WORRY. I'LL BE BACK TOMORROW!
ME TOO!
*SEE YA!*
THAT'LL BE ¥1300.
¥1,300 = $13
WHAT WAS *THAT* ALL ABOUT?

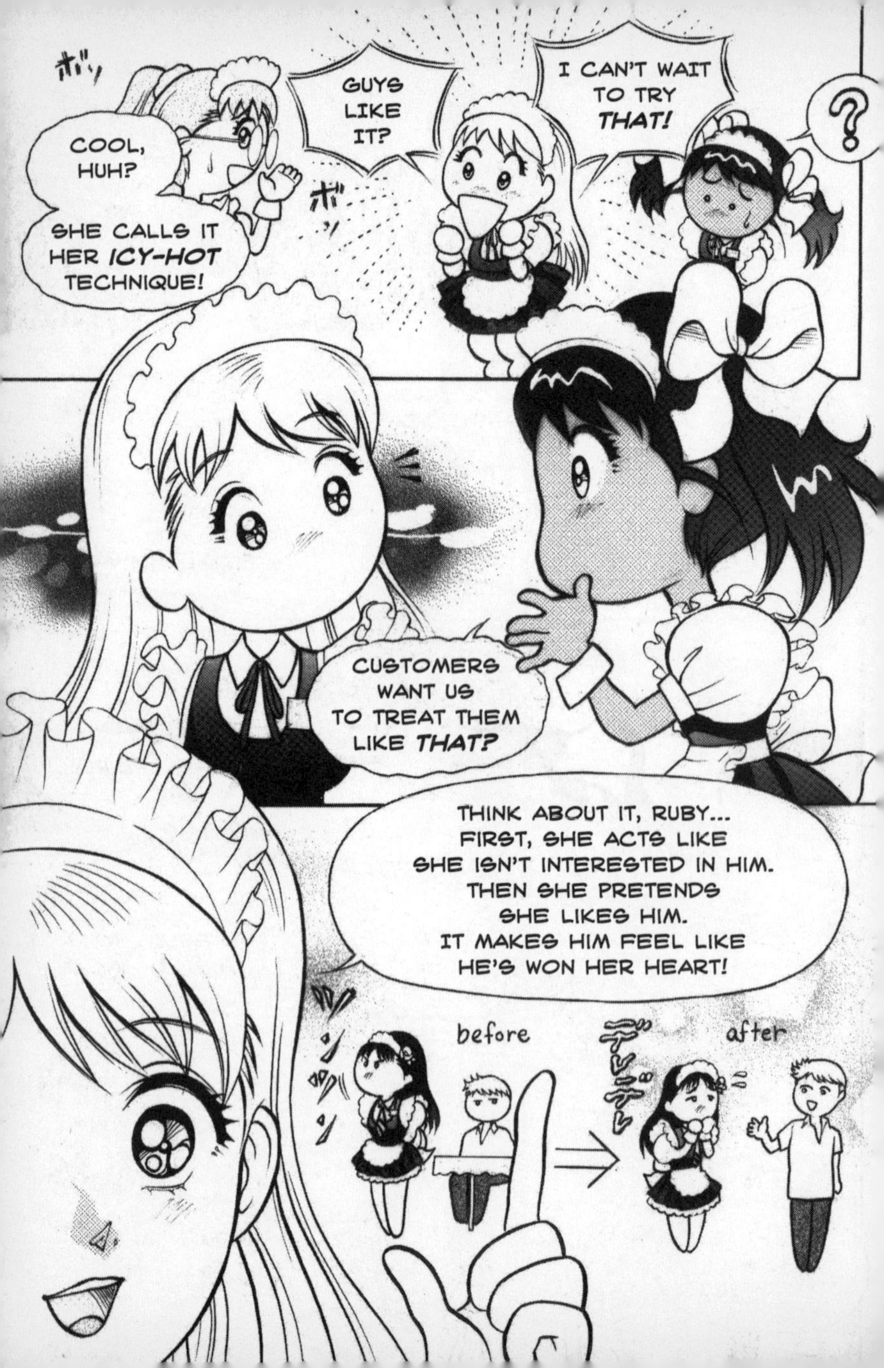
COOL, HUH?
SHE CALLS IT HER *ICY-HOT* TECHNIQUE!
GUYS LIKE IT?
I CAN'T WAIT TO TRY *THAT!*
?
CUSTOMERS WANT US TO TREAT THEM LIKE *THAT?*
THINK ABOUT IT, RUBY... FIRST, SHE ACTS LIKE SHE ISN'T INTERESTED IN HIM. THEN SHE PRETENDS SHE LIKES HIM. IT MAKES HIM FEEL LIKE HE'S WON HER HEART!
before
after

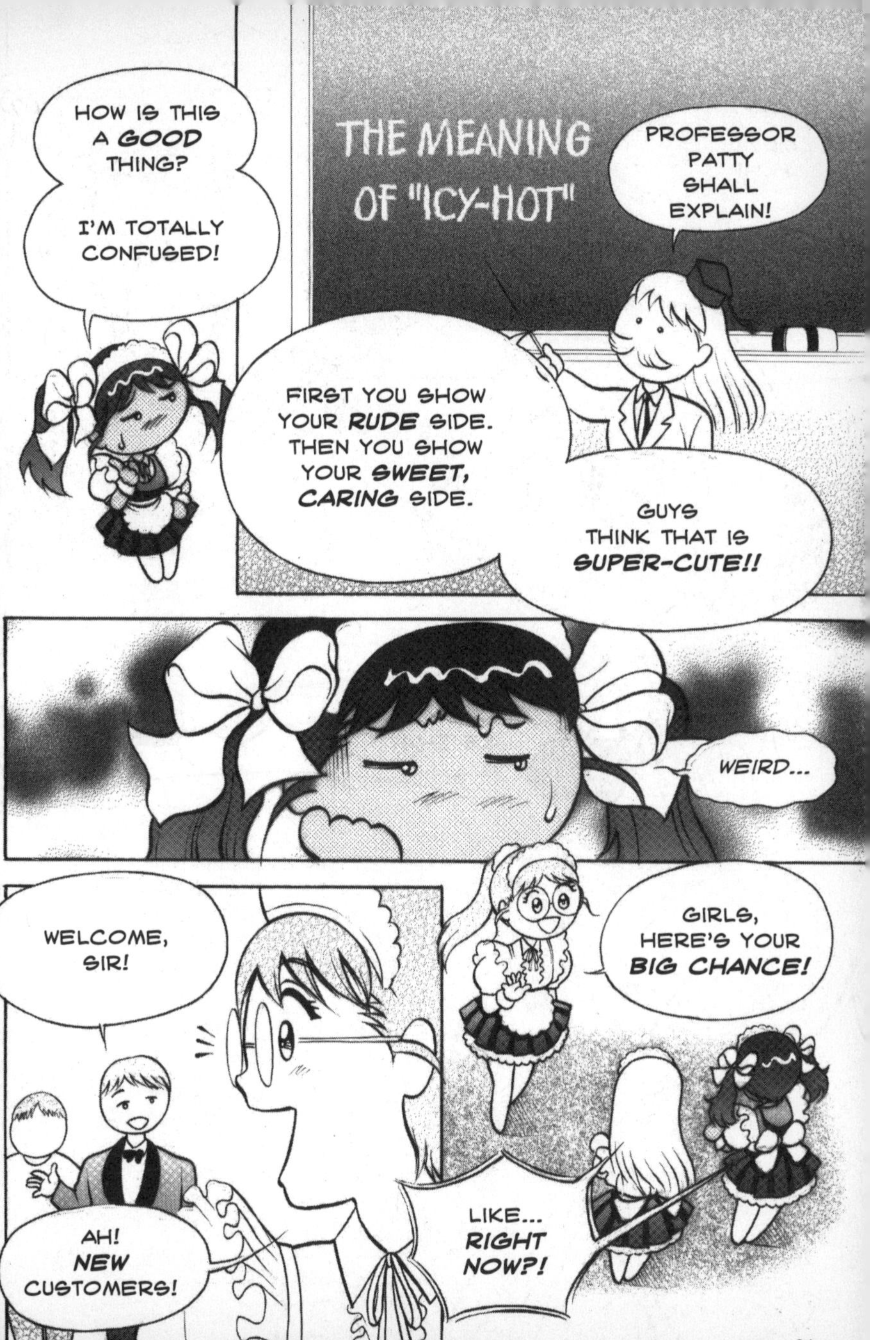
HOW IS THIS A GOOD THING?
I'M TOTALLY CONFUSED!
THE MEANING OF "ICY-HOT"
PROFESSOR PATTY SHALL EXPLAIN!
FIRST YOU SHOW YOUR RUDE SIDE. THEN YOU SHOW YOUR SWEET, CARING SIDE.
GUYS THINK THAT IS SUPER-CUTE!!
WEIRD...
GIRLS, HERE'S YOUR BIG CHANCE!
WELCOME, SIR!
AH! NEW CUSTOMERS!
LIKE... RIGHT NOW?!

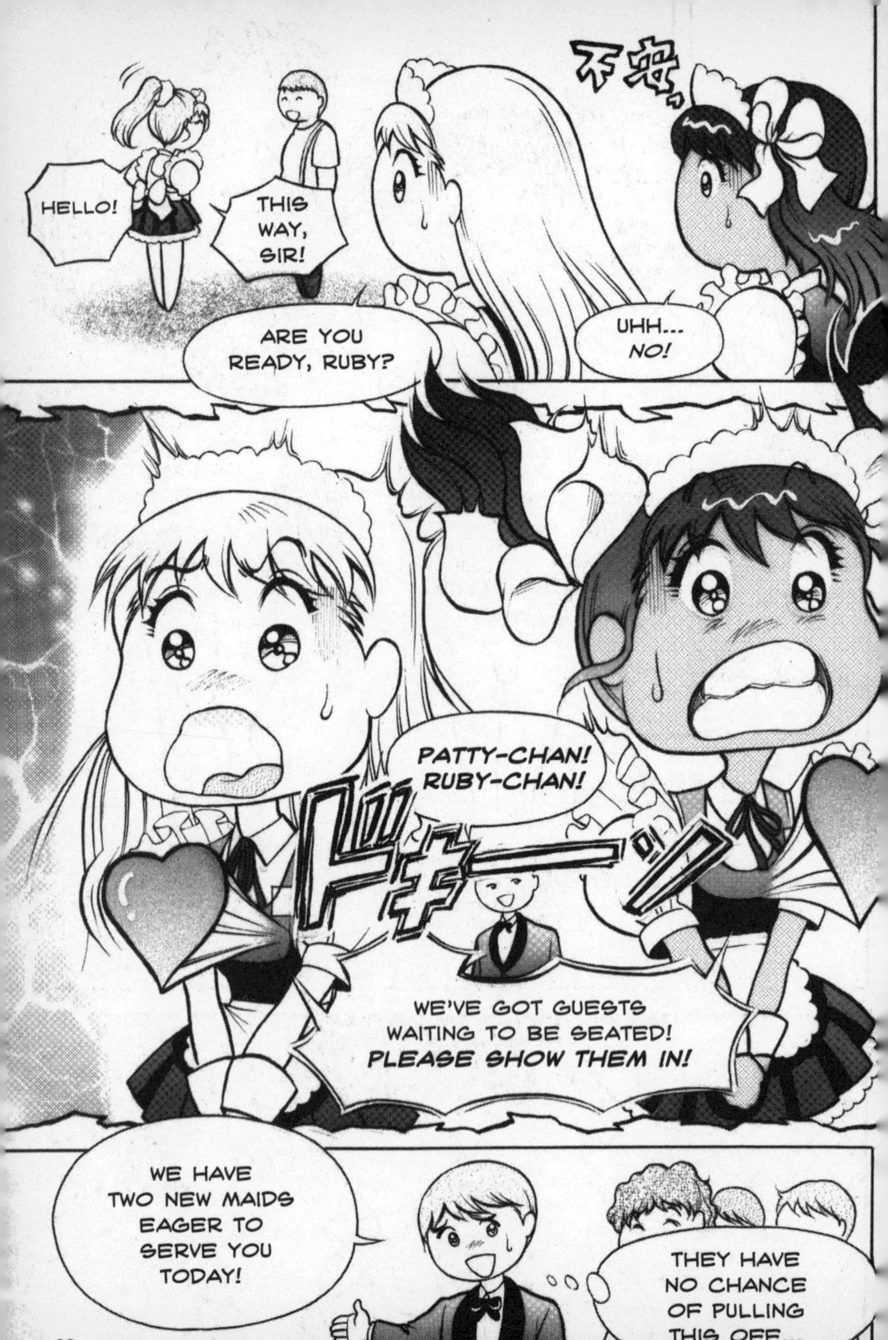

HELLO!
THIS WAY, SIR!
不安っ
ARE YOU READY, RUBY?
UHH... *NO!*
*PATTY-CHAN! RUBY-CHAN!*
ドッキーン
WE'VE GOT GUESTS WAITING TO BE SEATED! ***PLEASE SHOW THEM IN!***
WE HAVE TWO NEW MAIDS EAGER TO SERVE YOU TODAY!
THEY HAVE NO CHANCE OF PULLING THIS OFF...

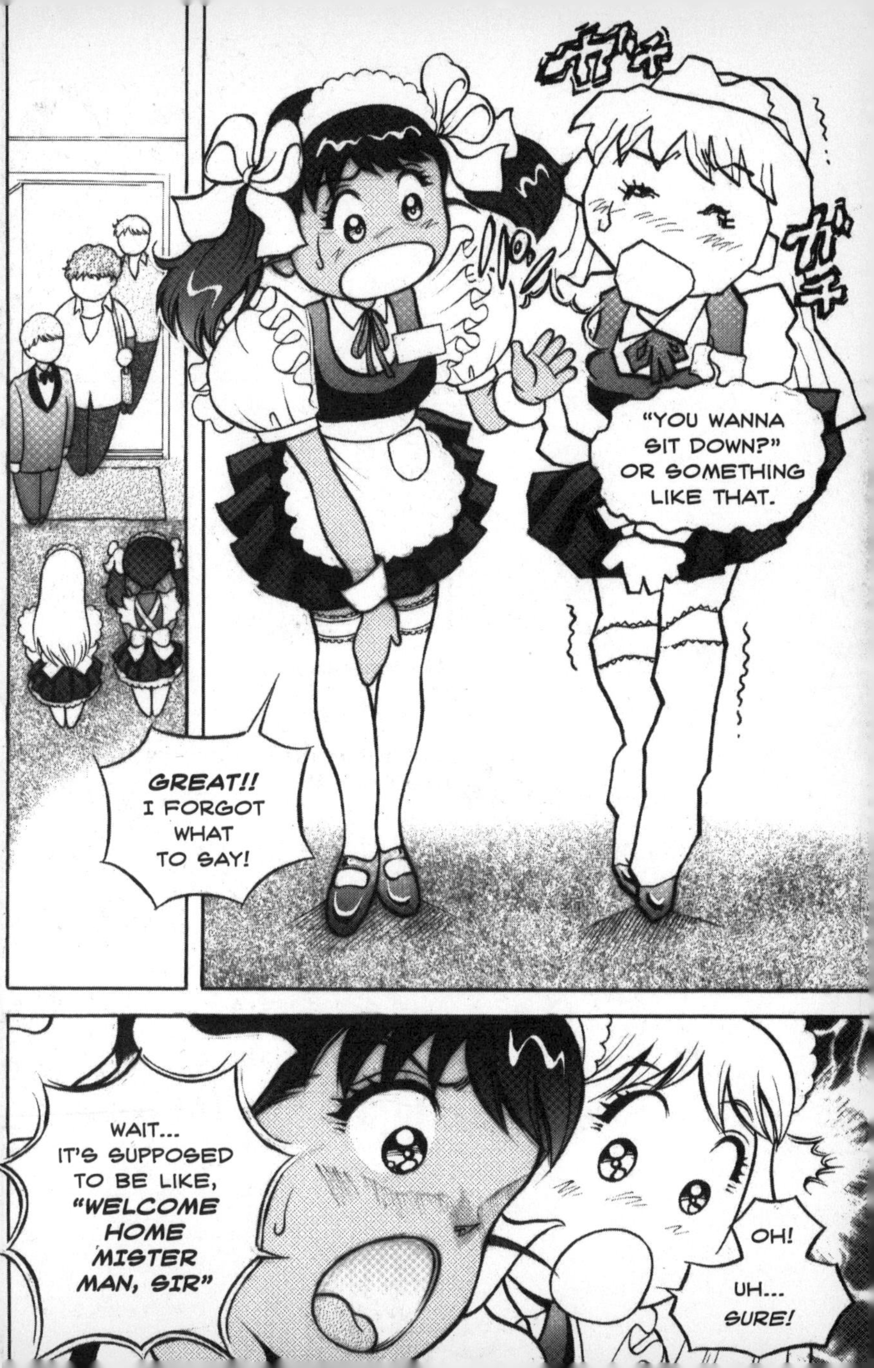
"YOU WANNA SIT DOWN?" OR SOMETHING LIKE THAT.
GREAT!! I FORGOT WHAT TO SAY!
WAIT... IT'S SUPPOSED TO BE LIKE, "WELCOME HOME MISTER MAN, SIR"
OH!
UH... SURE!

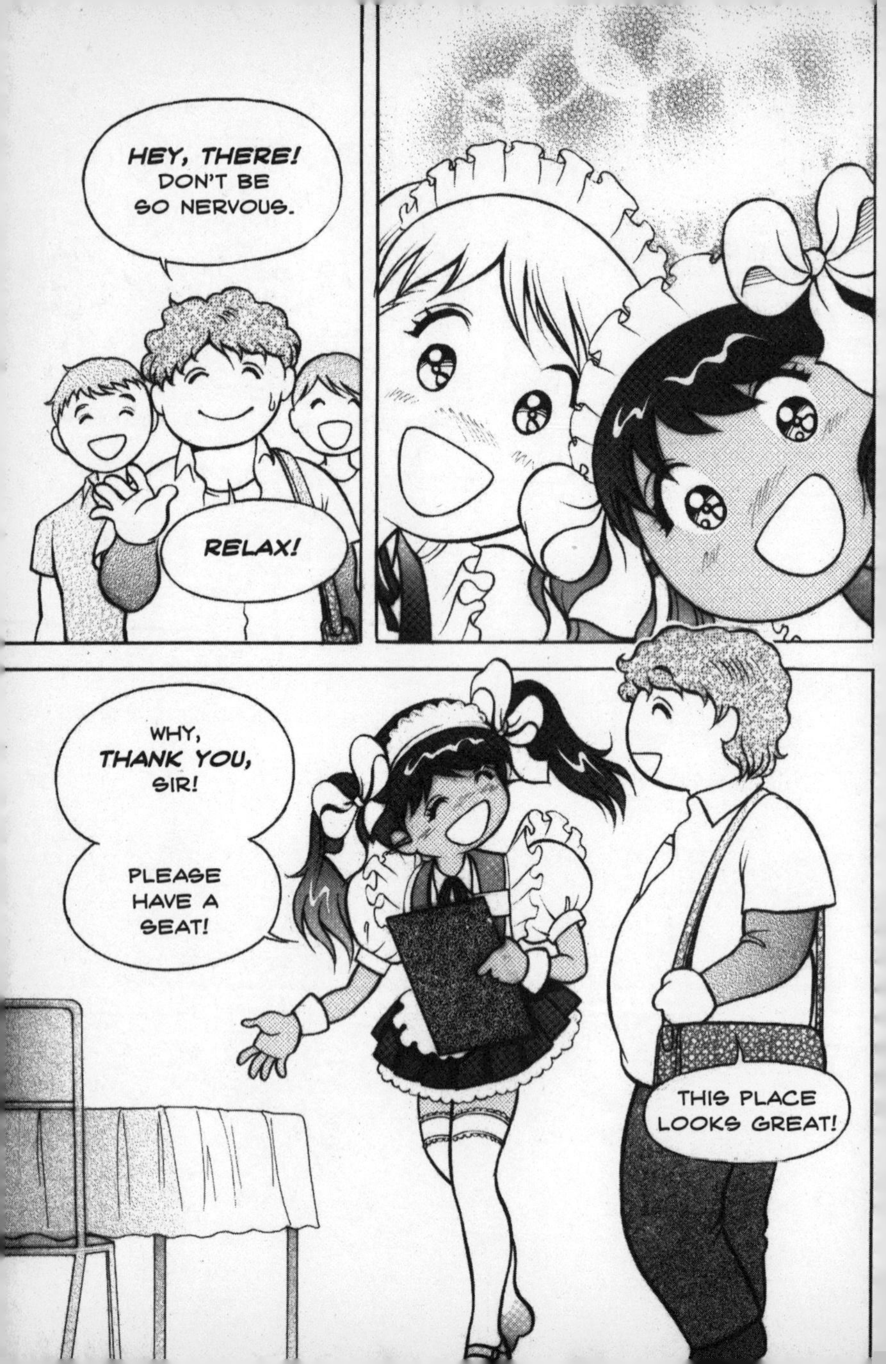
HEY, THERE! DON'T BE SO NERVOUS.
RELAX!
WHY, THANK YOU, SIR!
PLEASE HAVE A SEAT!
THIS PLACE LOOKS GREAT!

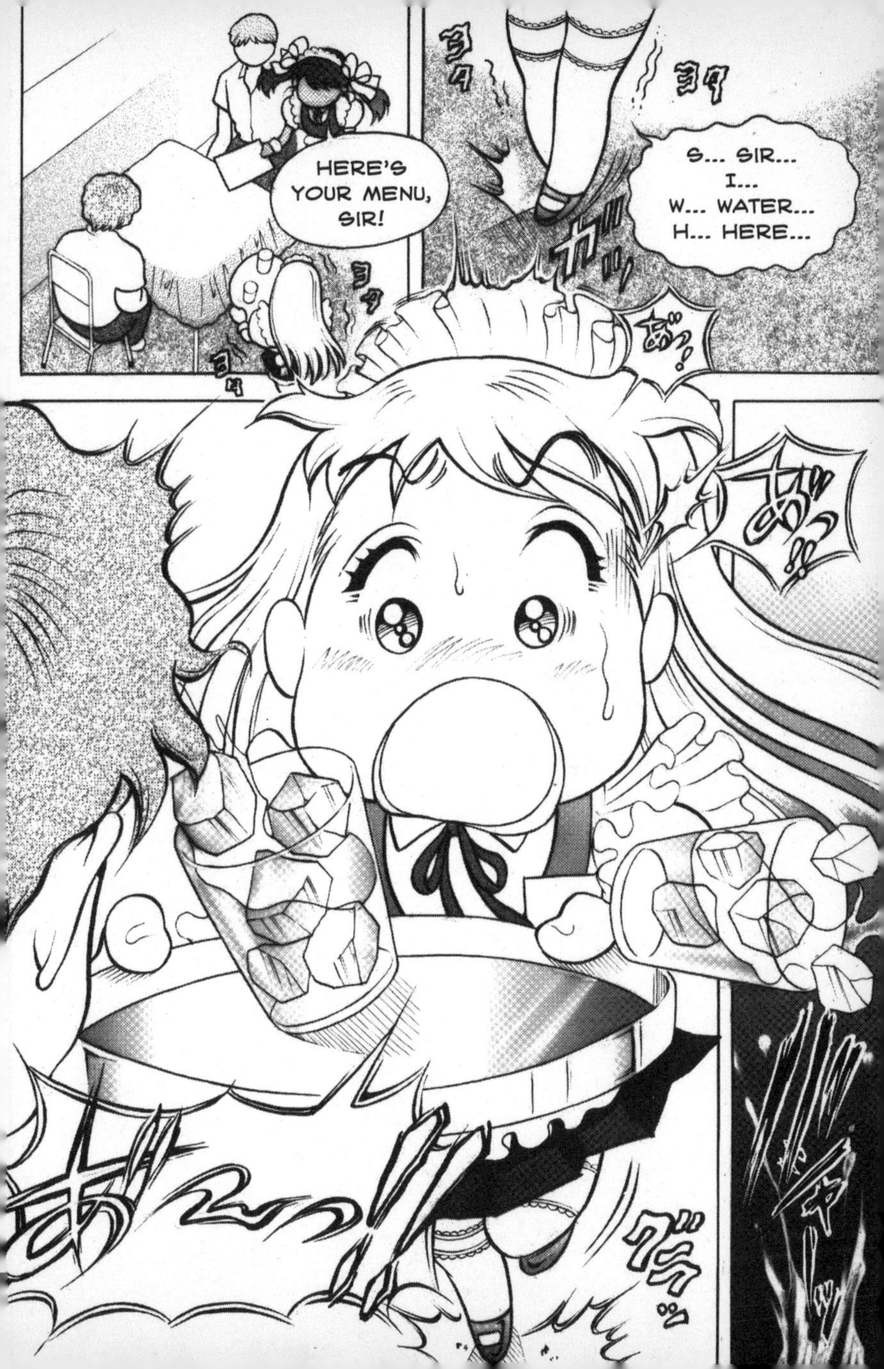

S... SIR...
I...
W... WATER...
H... HERE...
HERE'S YOUR MENU, SIR!

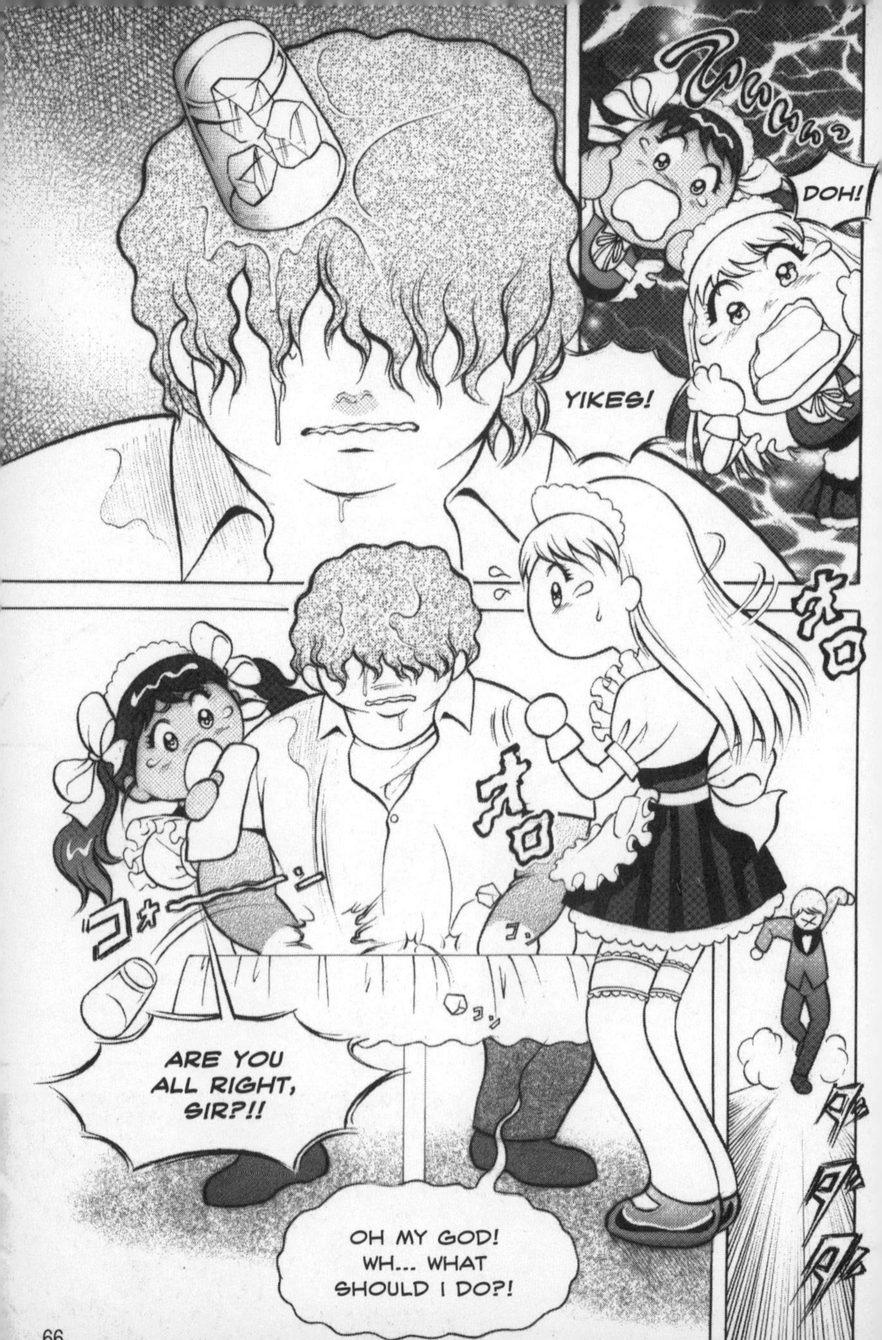
DOH!
YIKES!
ARE YOU ALL RIGHT, SIR?!!
OH MY GOD! WH... WHAT SHOULD I DO?!

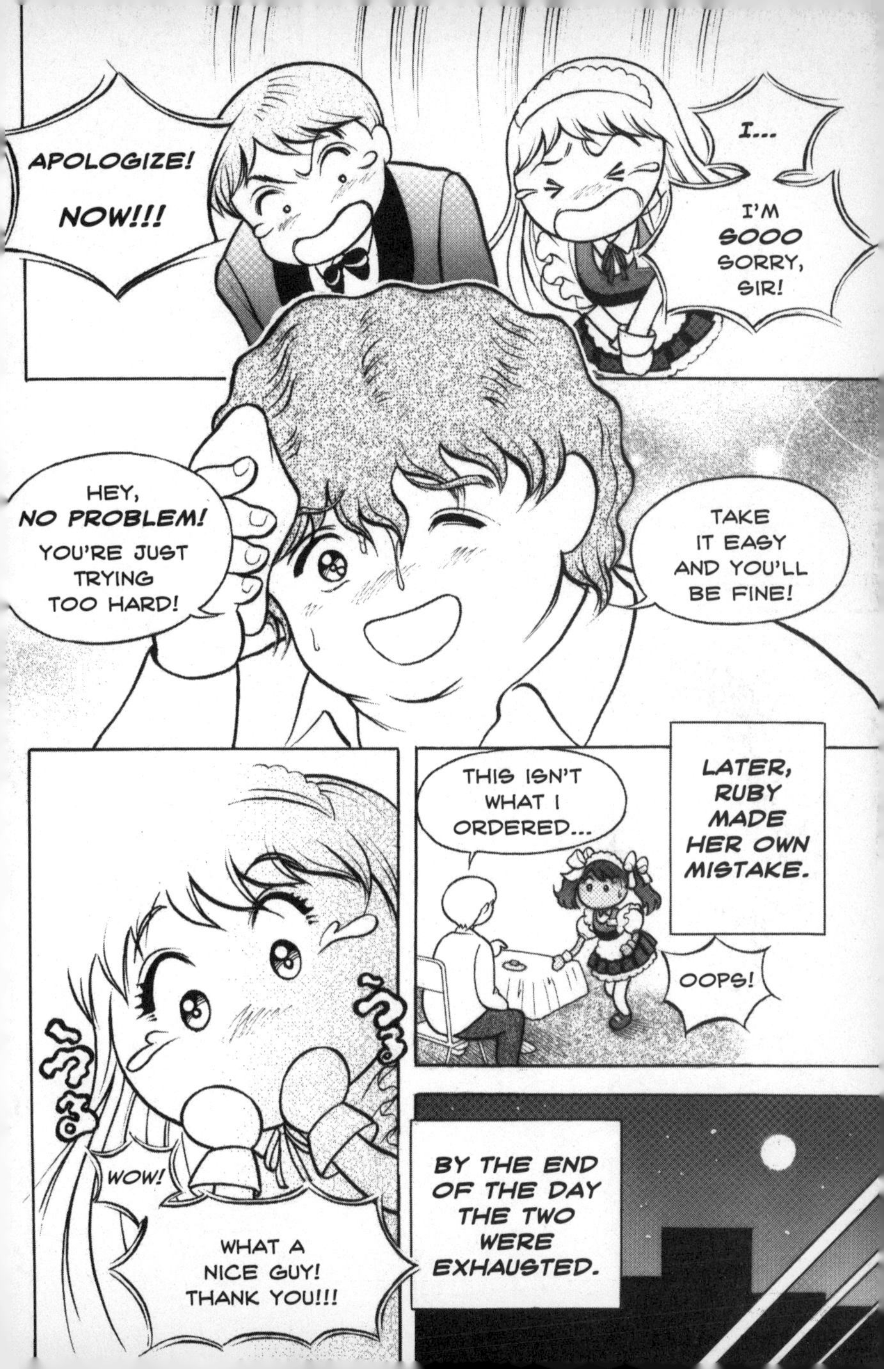
APOLOGIZE! NOW!!!
I... I'M SOOO SORRY, SIR!
HEY, NO PROBLEM! YOU'RE JUST TRYING TOO HARD!
TAKE IT EASY AND YOU'LL BE FINE!
WOW!
WHAT A NICE GUY! THANK YOU!!!
THIS ISN'T WHAT I ORDERED...
LATER, RUBY MADE HER OWN MISTAKE.
OOPS!
BY THE END OF THE DAY THE TWO WERE EXHAUSTED.

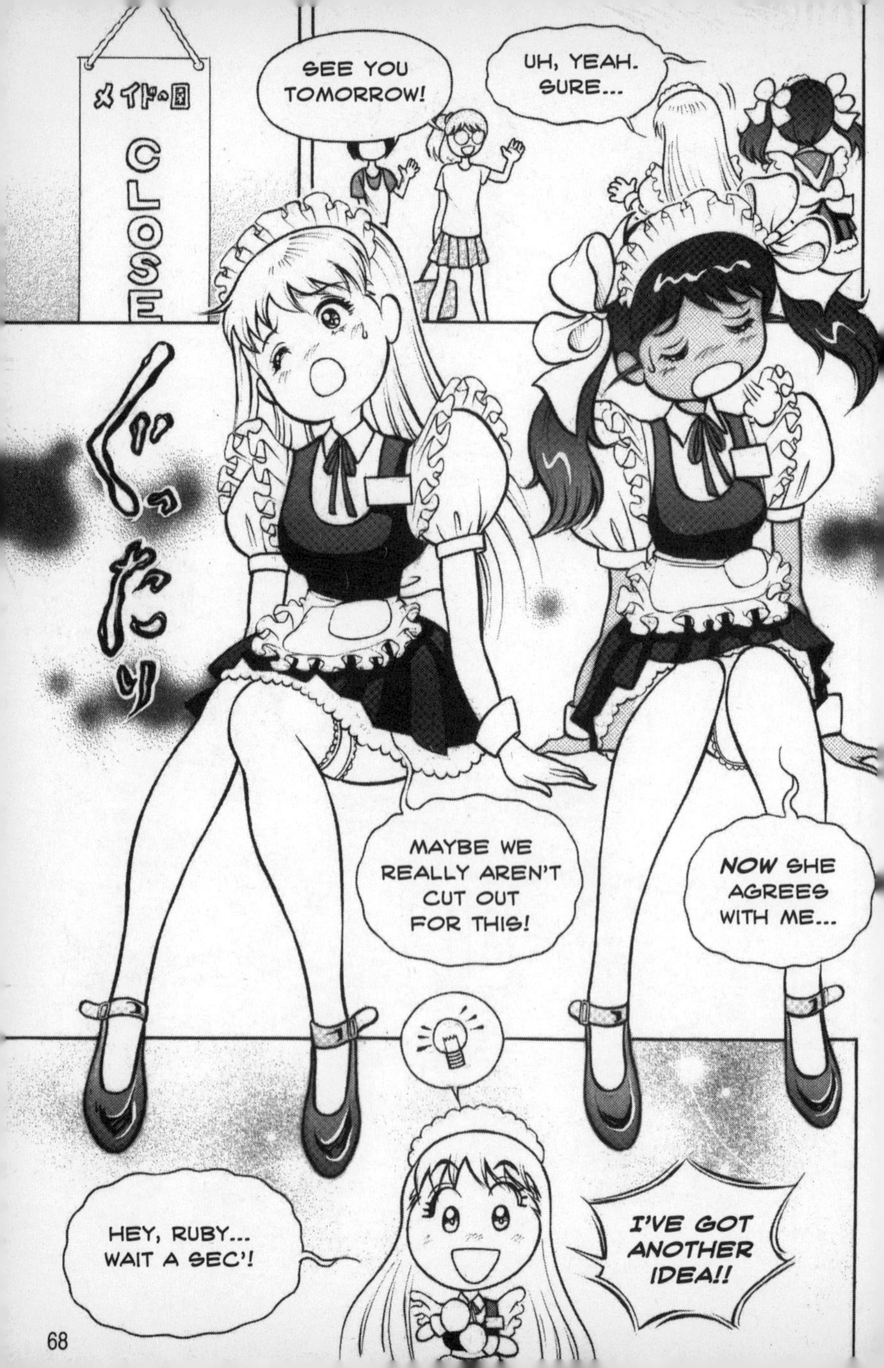
CLOSE
SEE YOU TOMORROW!
UH, YEAH. SURE...
ぐったり
MAYBE WE REALLY AREN'T CUT OUT FOR THIS!
NOW SHE AGREES WITH ME...
HEY, RUBY... WAIT A SEC'!
I'VE GOT ANOTHER IDEA!!

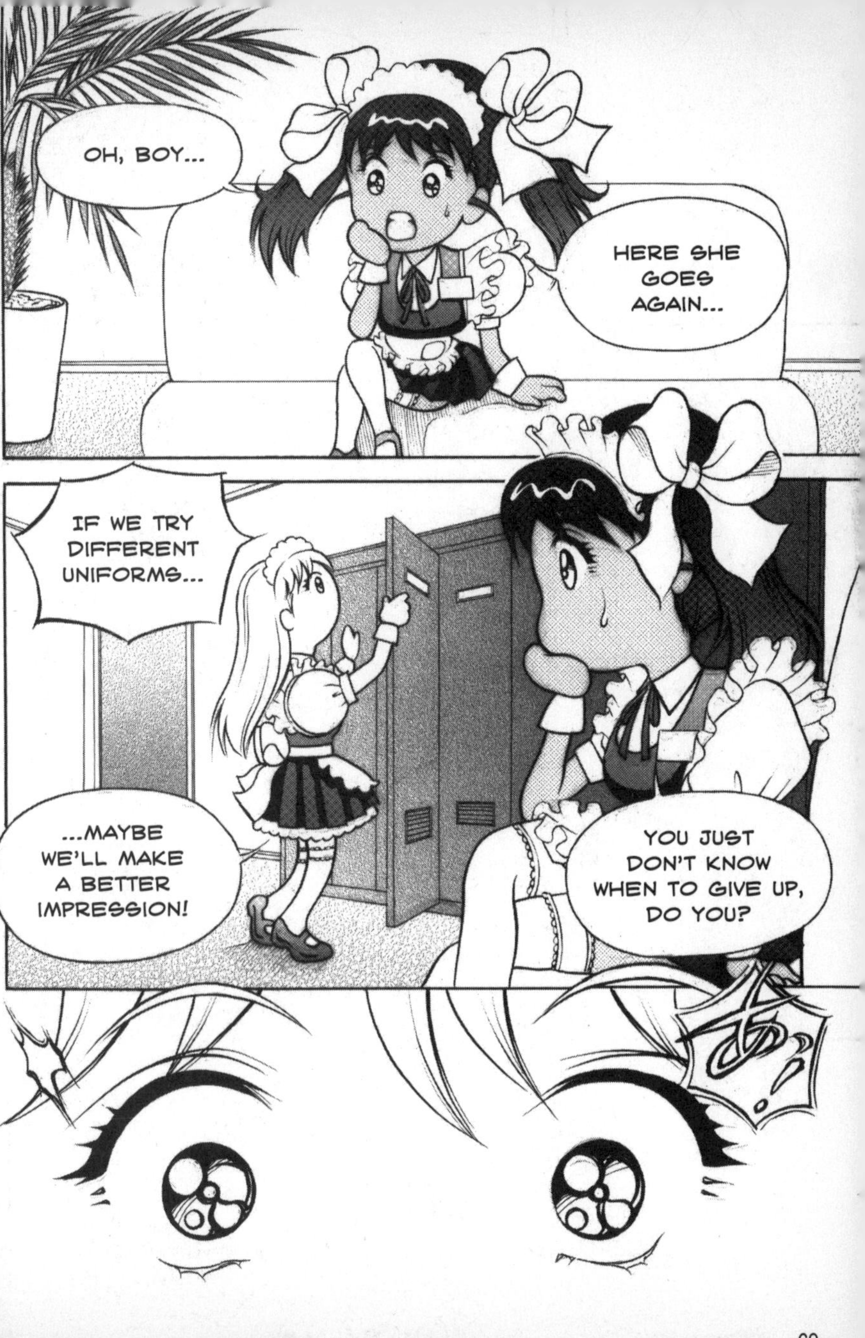
OH, BOY...
HERE SHE GOES AGAIN...
IF WE TRY DIFFERENT UNIFORMS...
...MAYBE WE'LL MAKE A BETTER IMPRESSION!
YOU JUST DON'T KNOW WHEN TO GIVE UP, DO YOU?

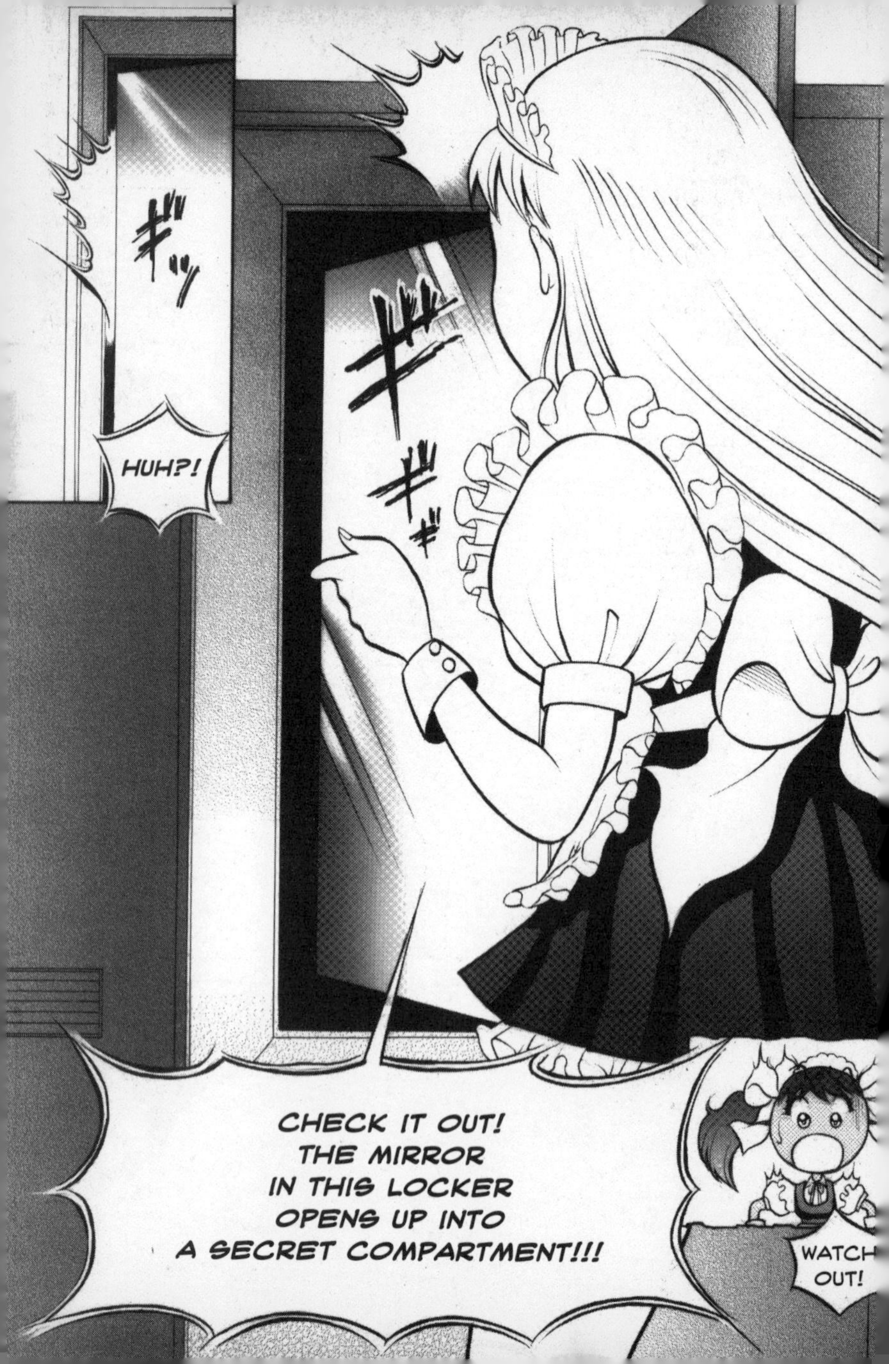
HUH?!
CHECK IT OUT! THE MIRROR IN THIS LOCKER OPENS UP INTO A SECRET COMPARTMENT!!!
WATCH OUT!

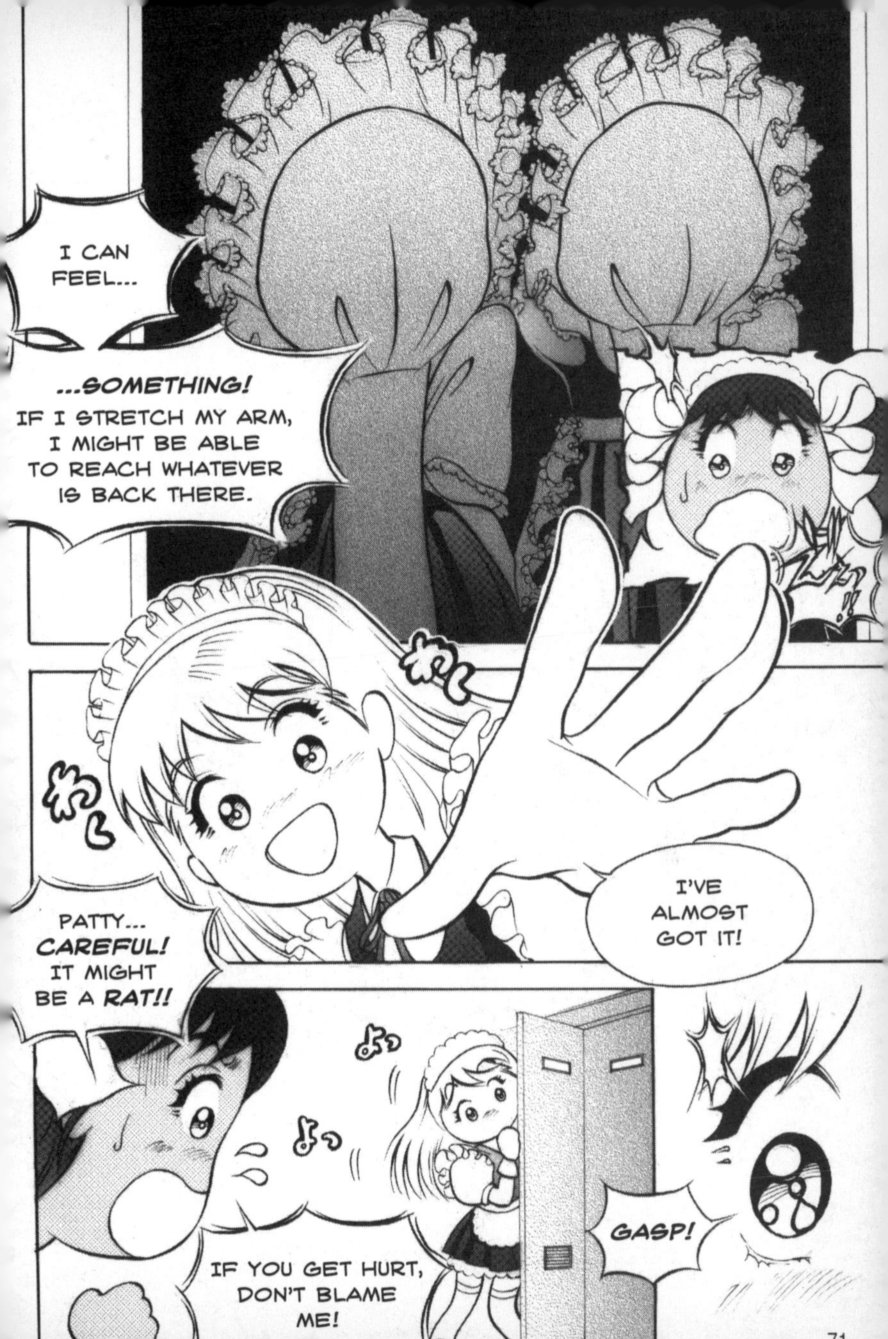
I CAN FEEL...
...SOMETHING! IF I STRETCH MY ARM, I MIGHT BE ABLE TO REACH WHATEVER IS BACK THERE.
I'VE ALMOST GOT IT!
PATTY... CAREFUL! IT MIGHT BE A RAT!!
よっ
よっ
IF YOU GET HURT, DON'T BLAME ME!
GASP!

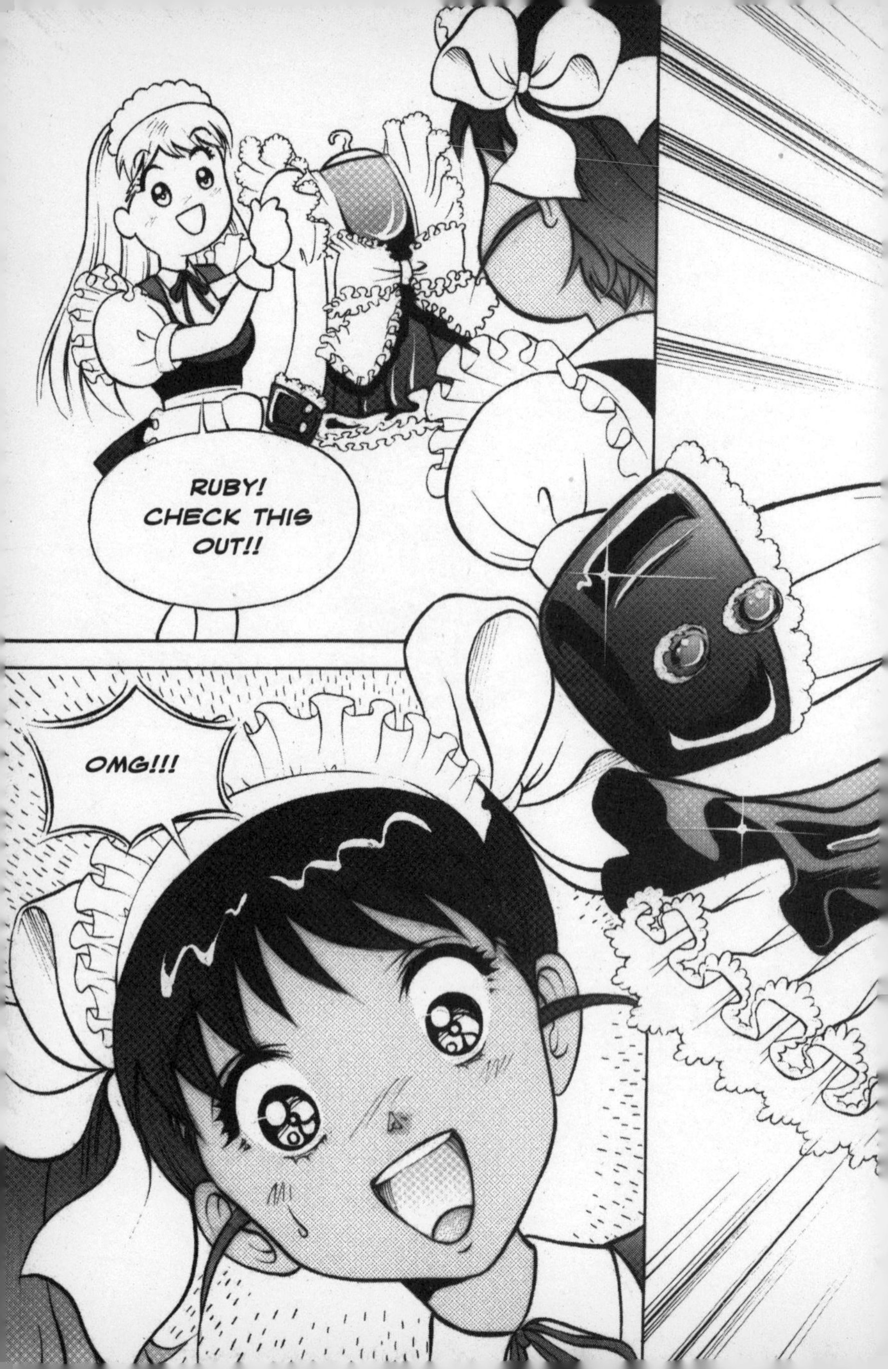
RUBY!
CHECK THIS
OUT!!
OMG!!!

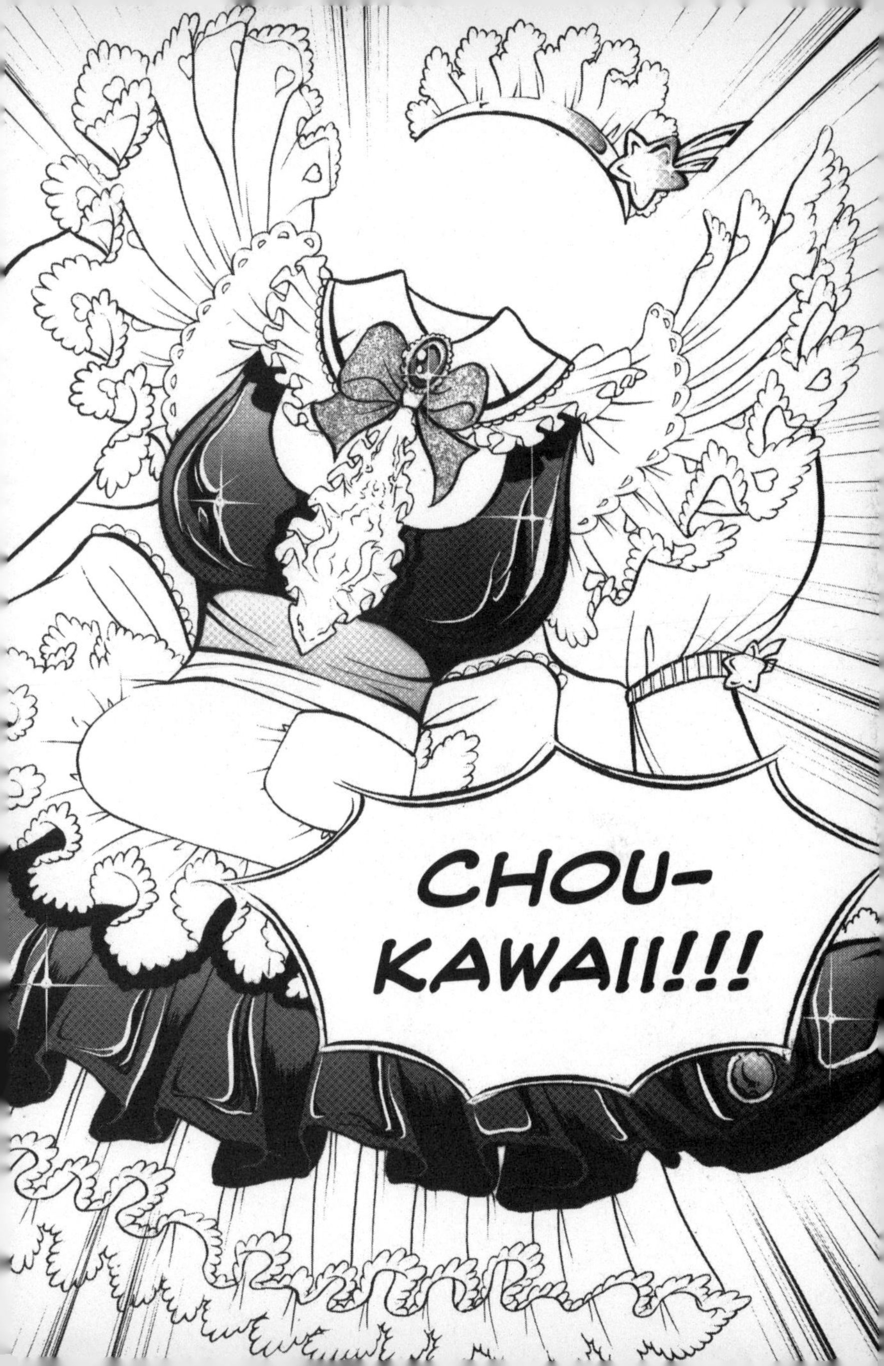
CHOU-
KAWAII!!!!

# ★★ moe ★★ USA

## chapter three
# ONLINE IDOLS

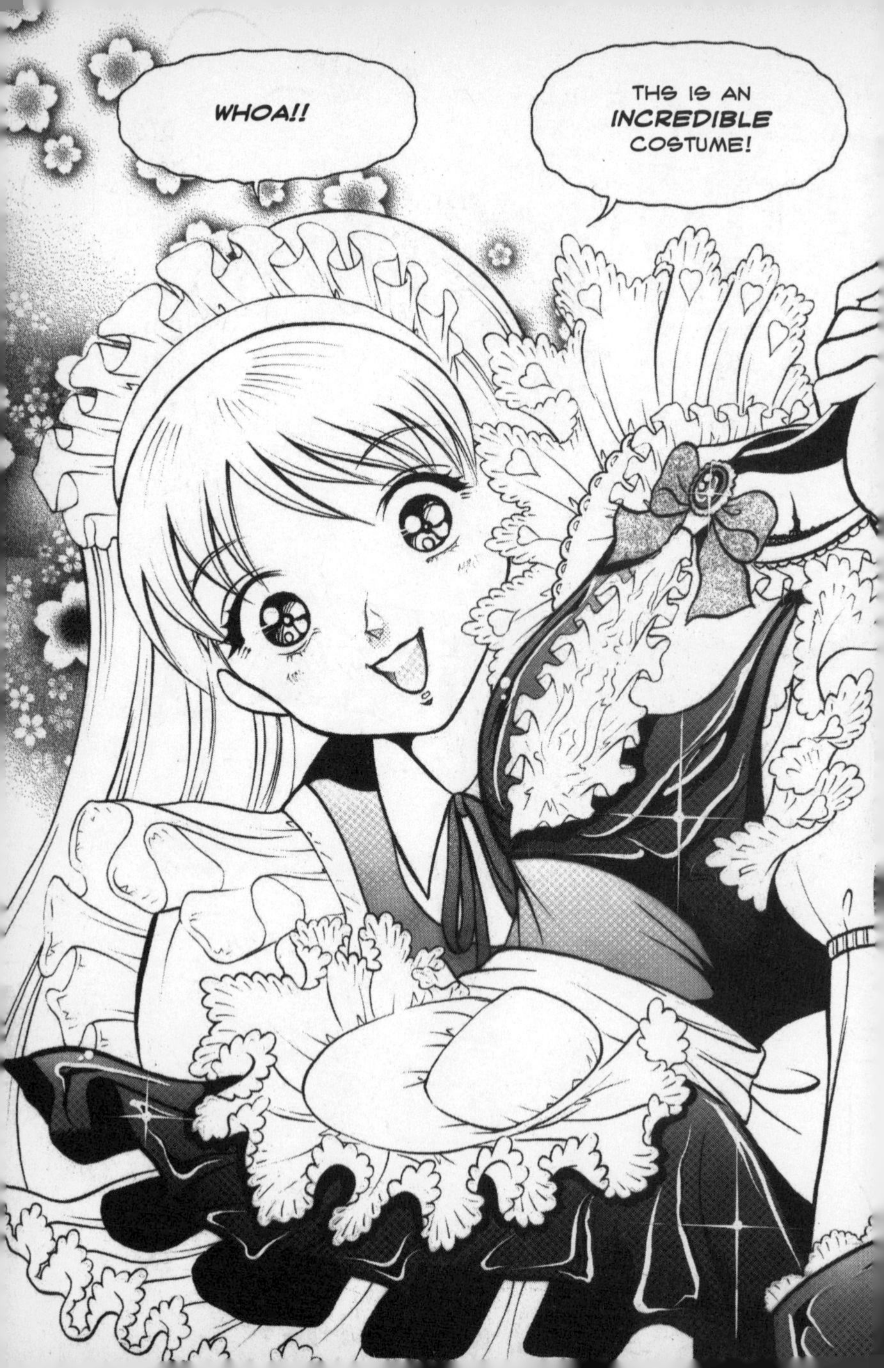
WHOA!!
THS IS AN INCREDIBLE COSTUME!

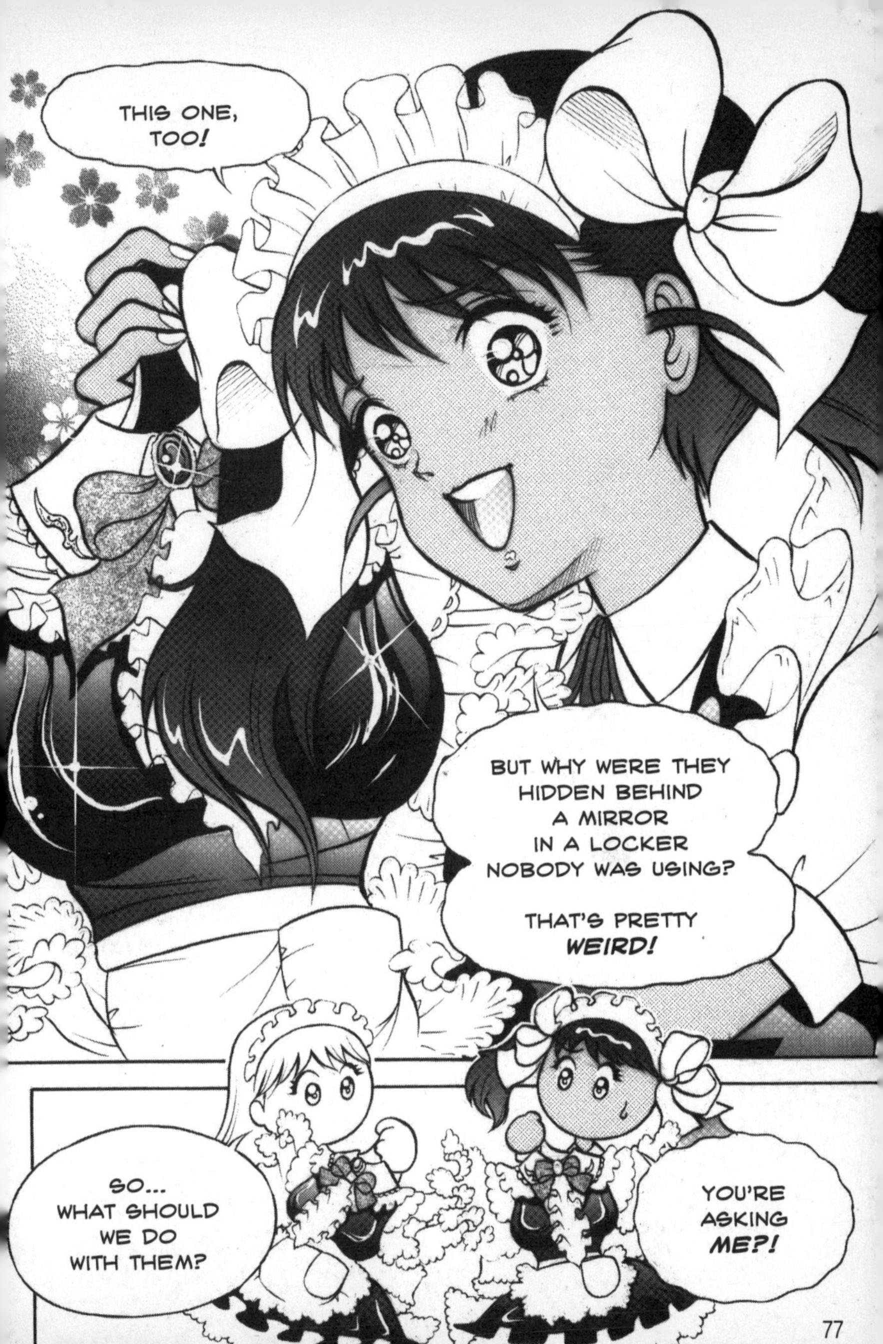
THIS ONE, TOO!
BUT WHY WERE THEY HIDDEN BEHIND A MIRROR IN A LOCKER NOBODY WAS USING?
THAT'S PRETTY WEIRD!
YOU'RE ASKING ME?!
SO... WHAT SHOULD WE DO WITH THEM?

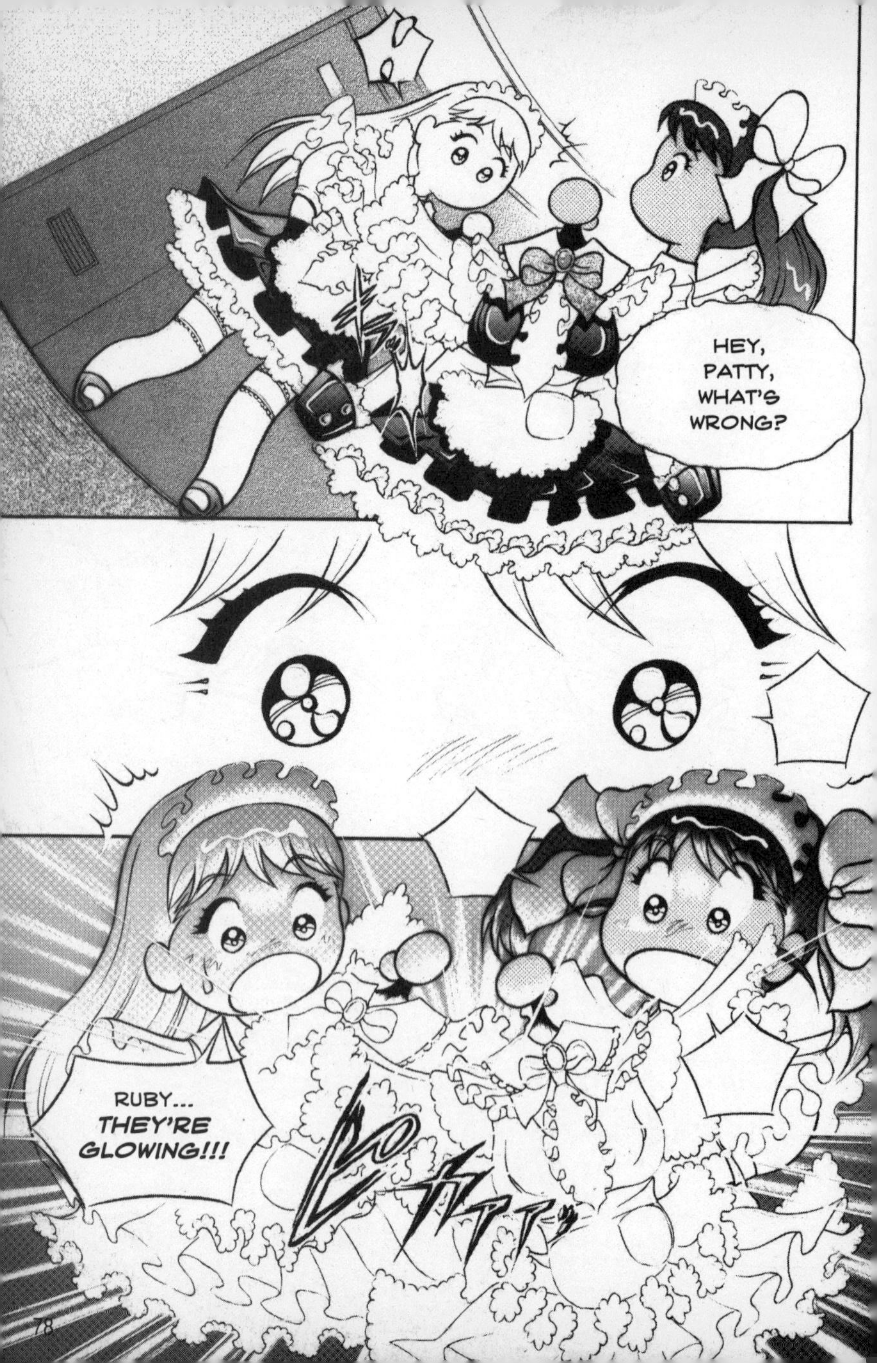
HEY, PATTY, WHAT'S WRONG?
RUBY... THEY'RE GLOWING!!!

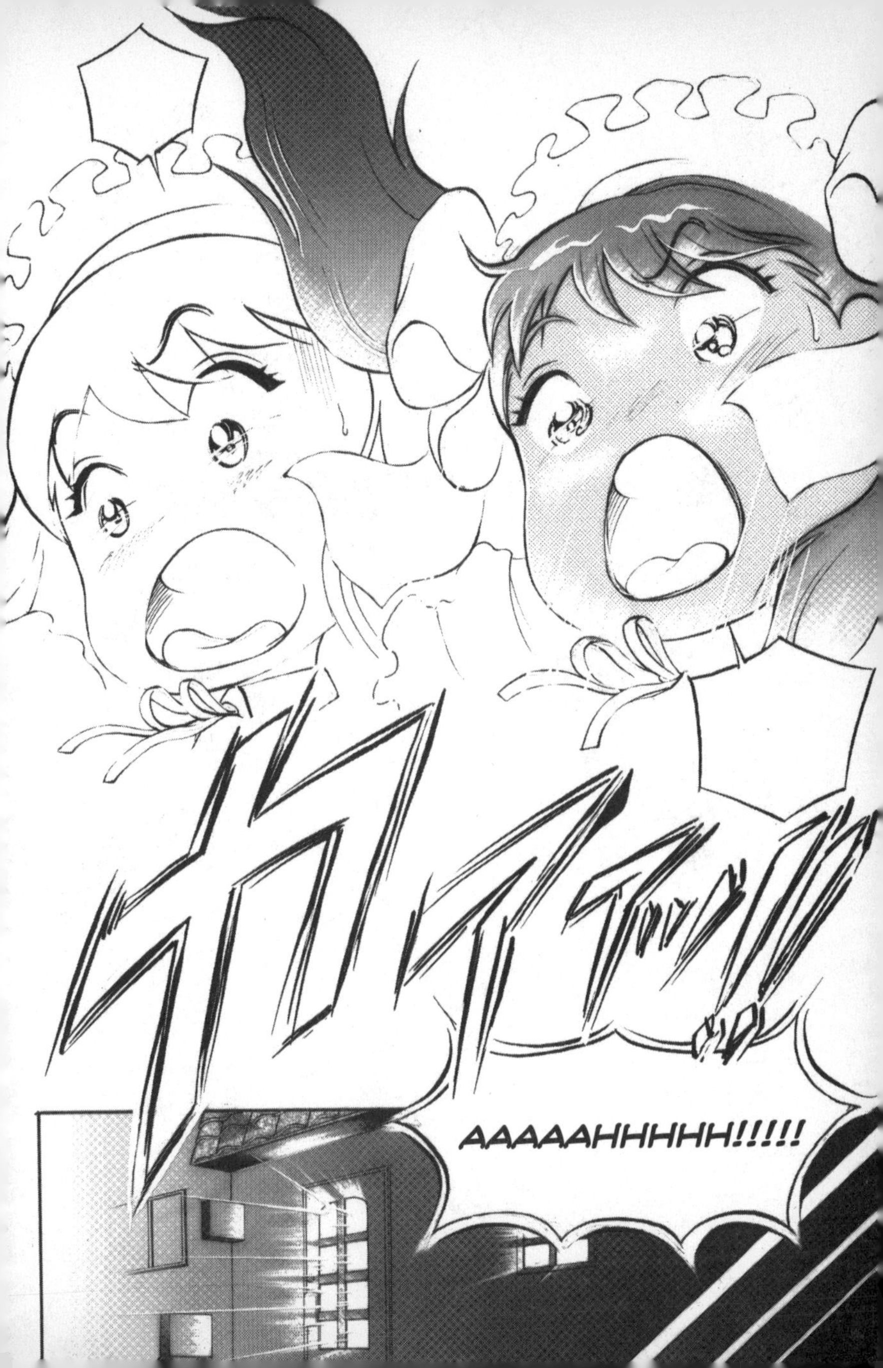
AAAAAHHHHH!!!!!

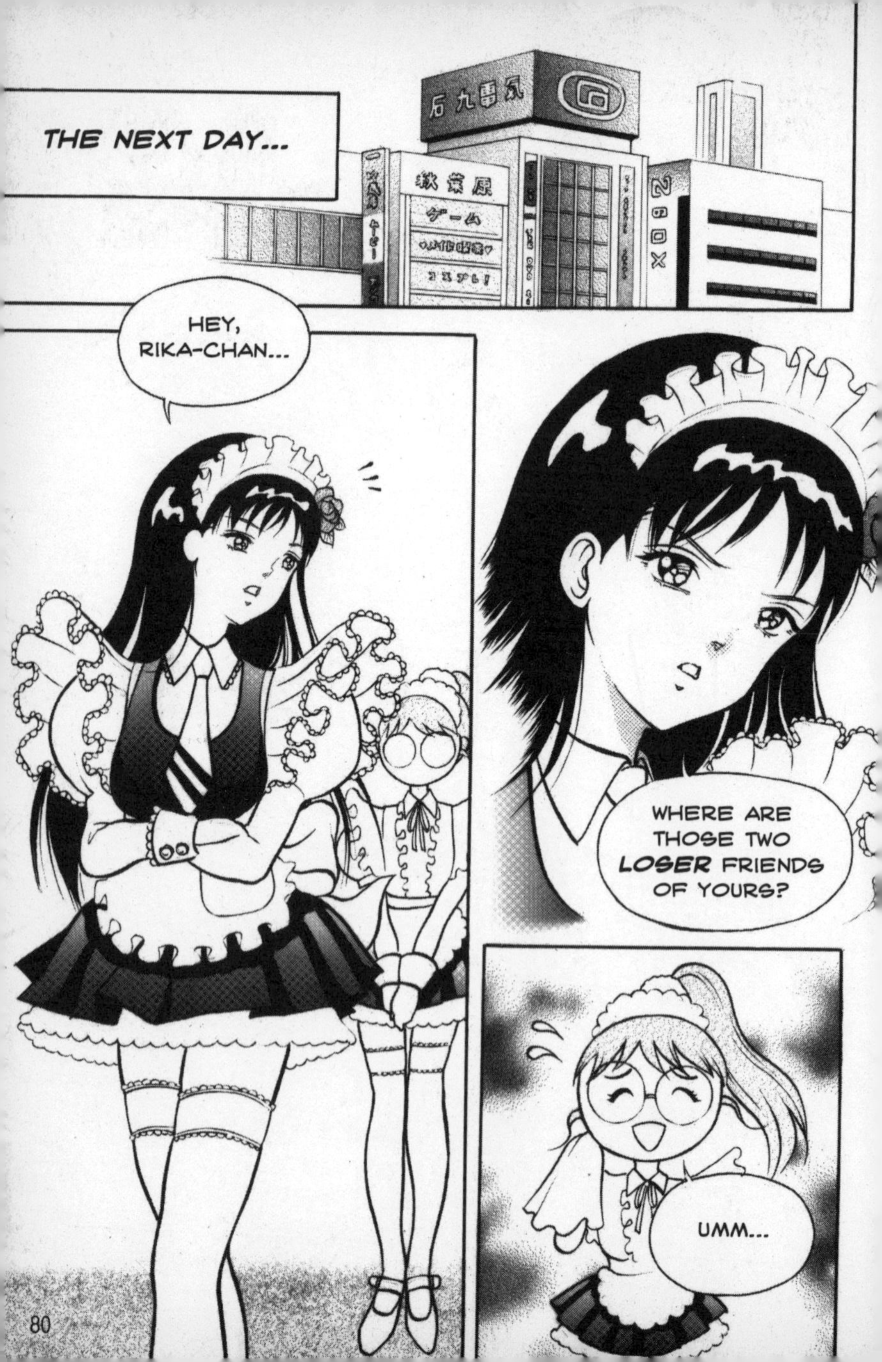
THE NEXT DAY...
HEY, RIKA-CHAN...
WHERE ARE THOSE TWO **LOSER** FRIENDS OF YOURS?
UMM...

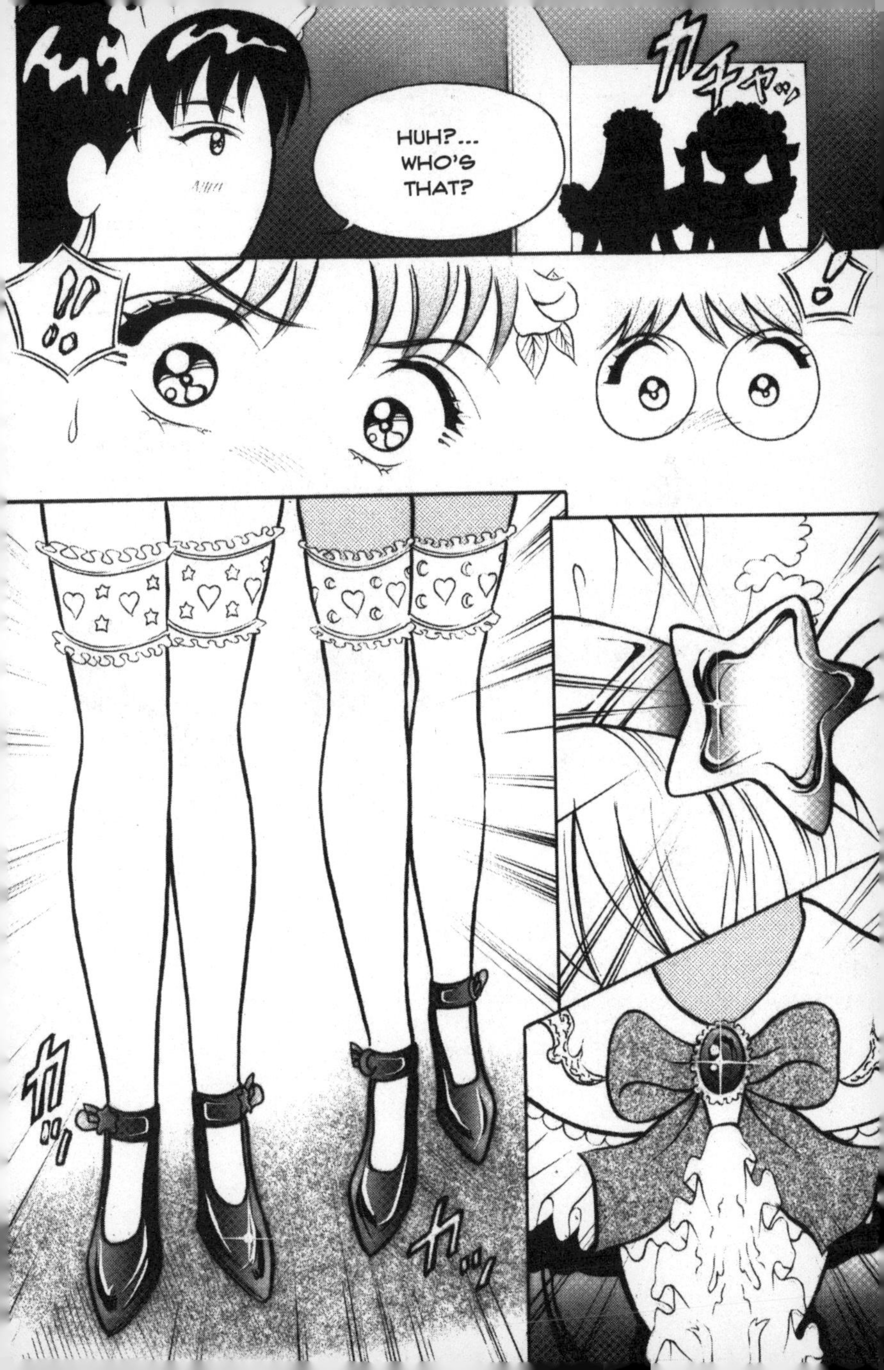
カチャッ
HUH?... WHO'S THAT?

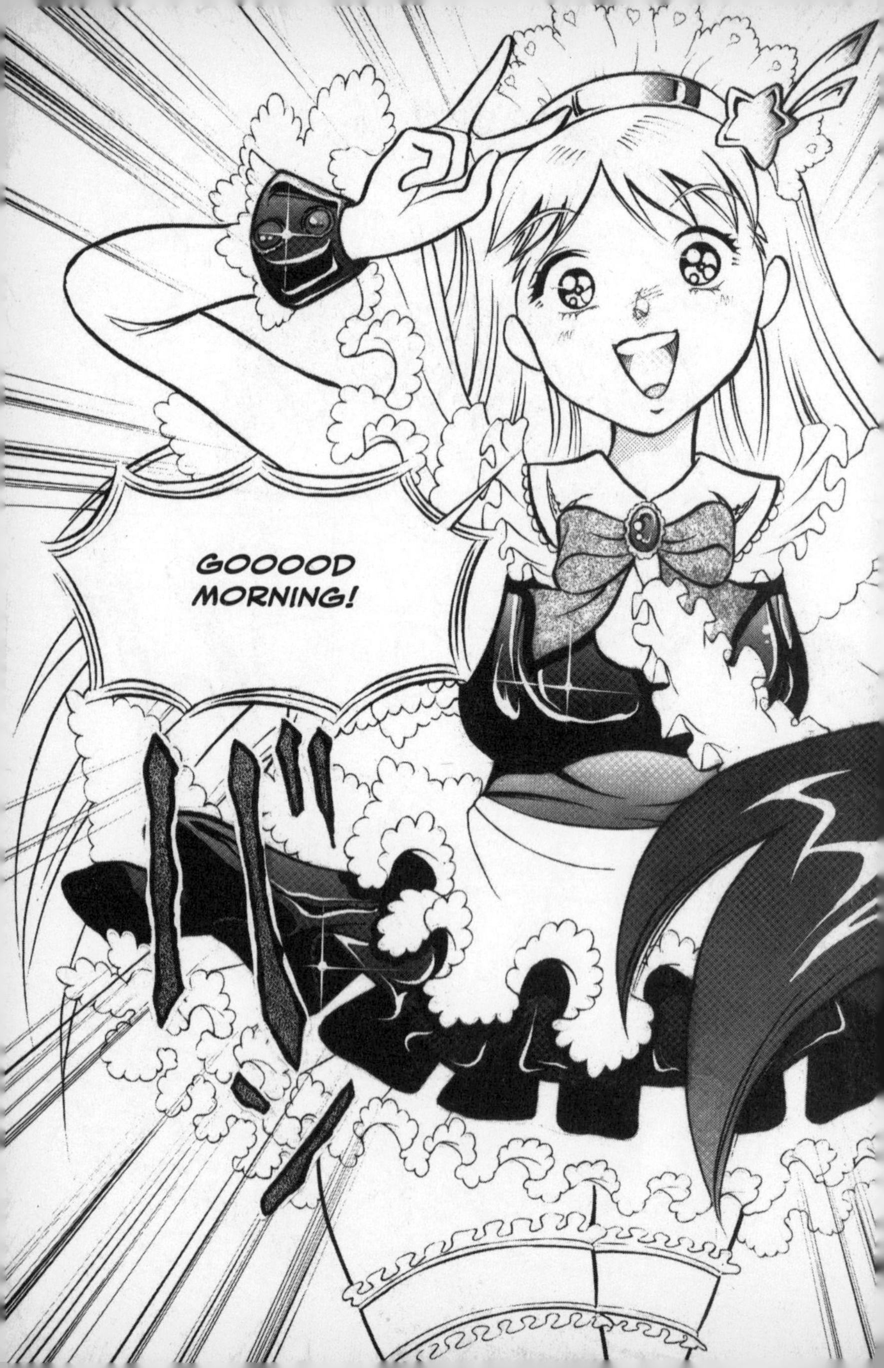
GOOOOD MORNING!

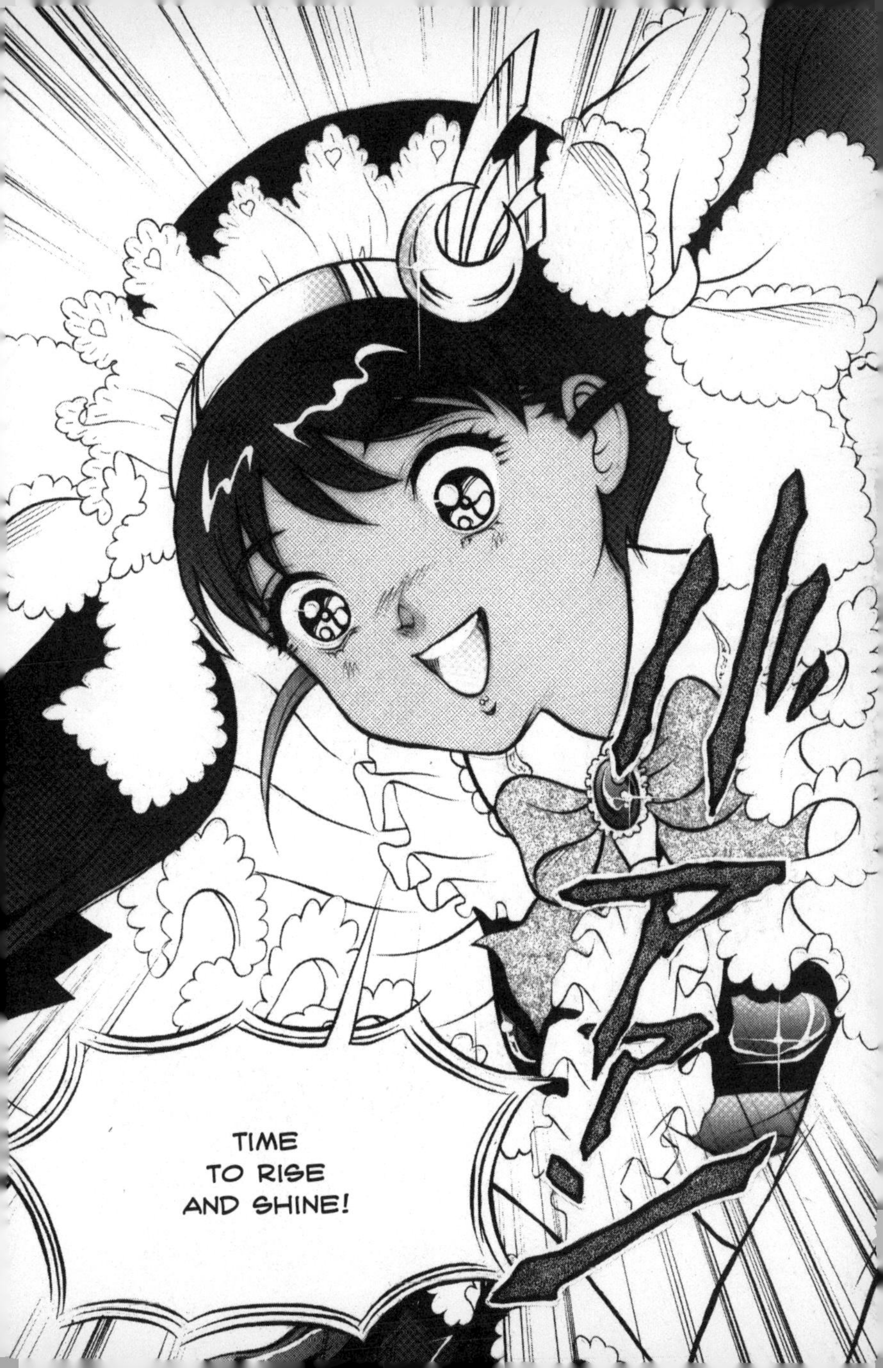
TIME TO RISE AND SHINE!

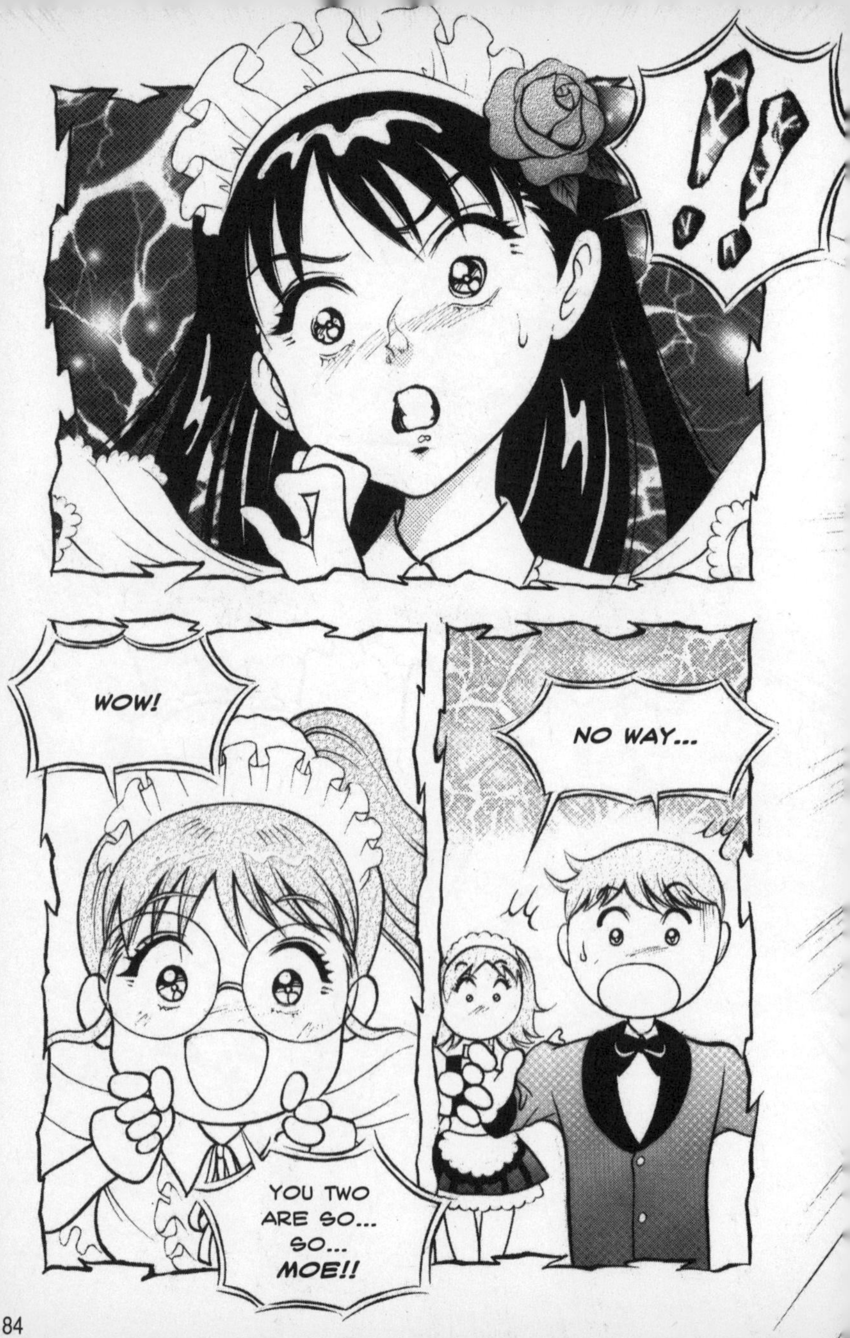
!!
NO WAY...
WOW!
YOU TWO ARE SO... SO... MOE!!

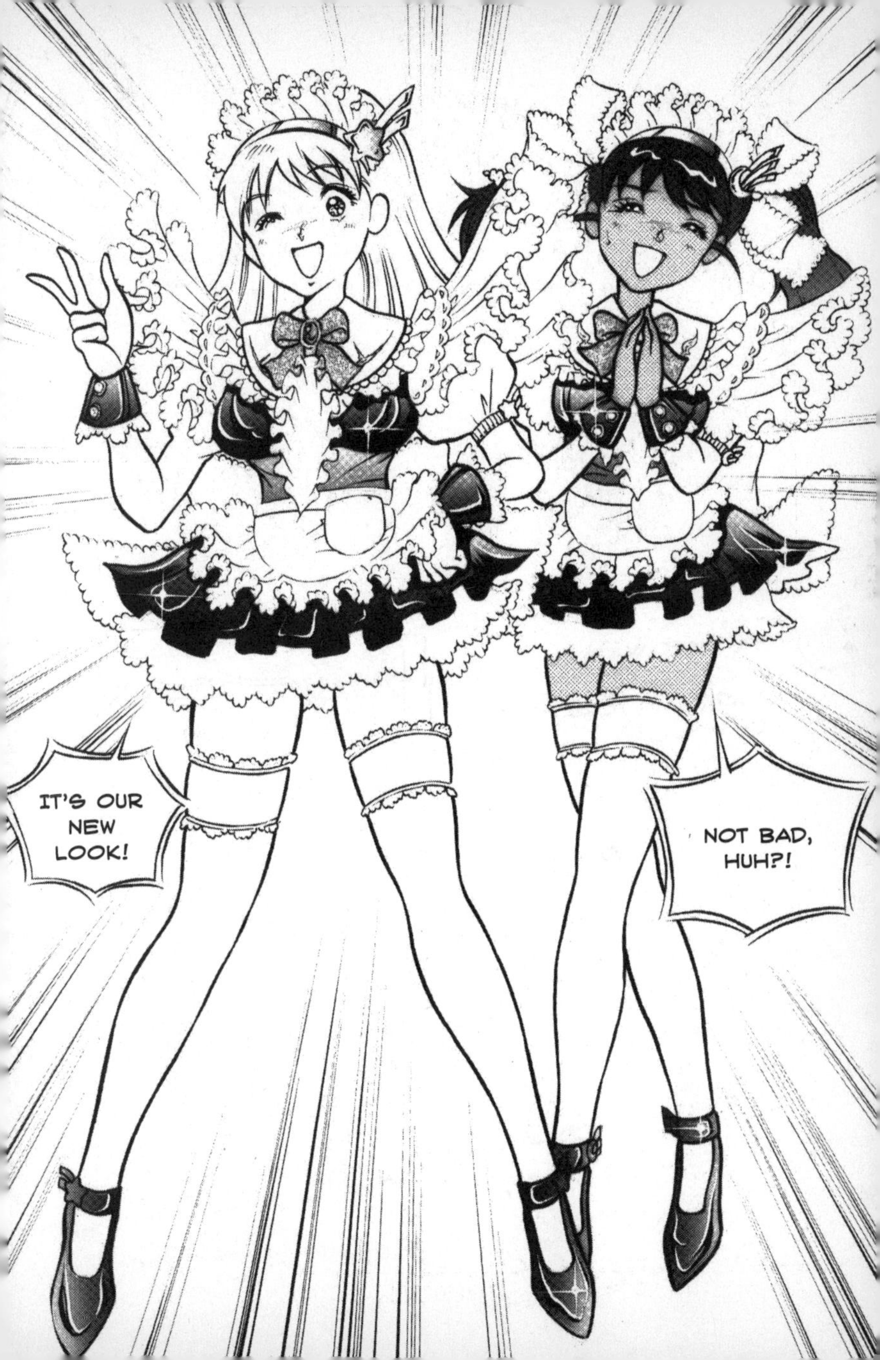
NOT BAD, HUH?!
IT'S OUR NEW LOOK!

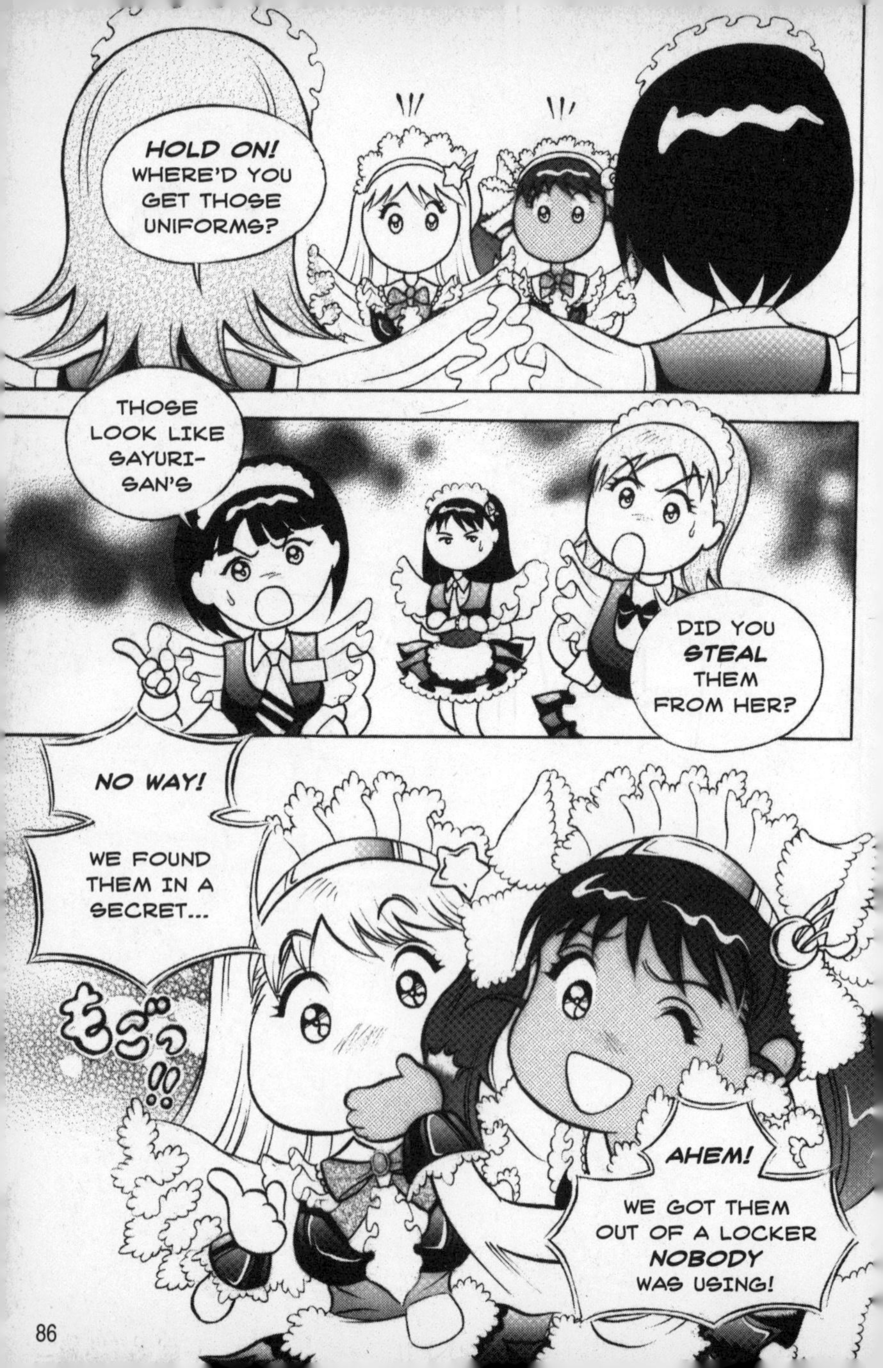
HOLD ON! WHERE'D YOU GET THOSE UNIFORMS?
THOSE LOOK LIKE SAYURI-SAN'S
DID YOU STEAL THEM FROM HER?
NO WAY!
WE FOUND THEM IN A SECRET...
もごっ!!
AHEM!
WE GOT THEM OUT OF A LOCKER NOBODY WAS USING!

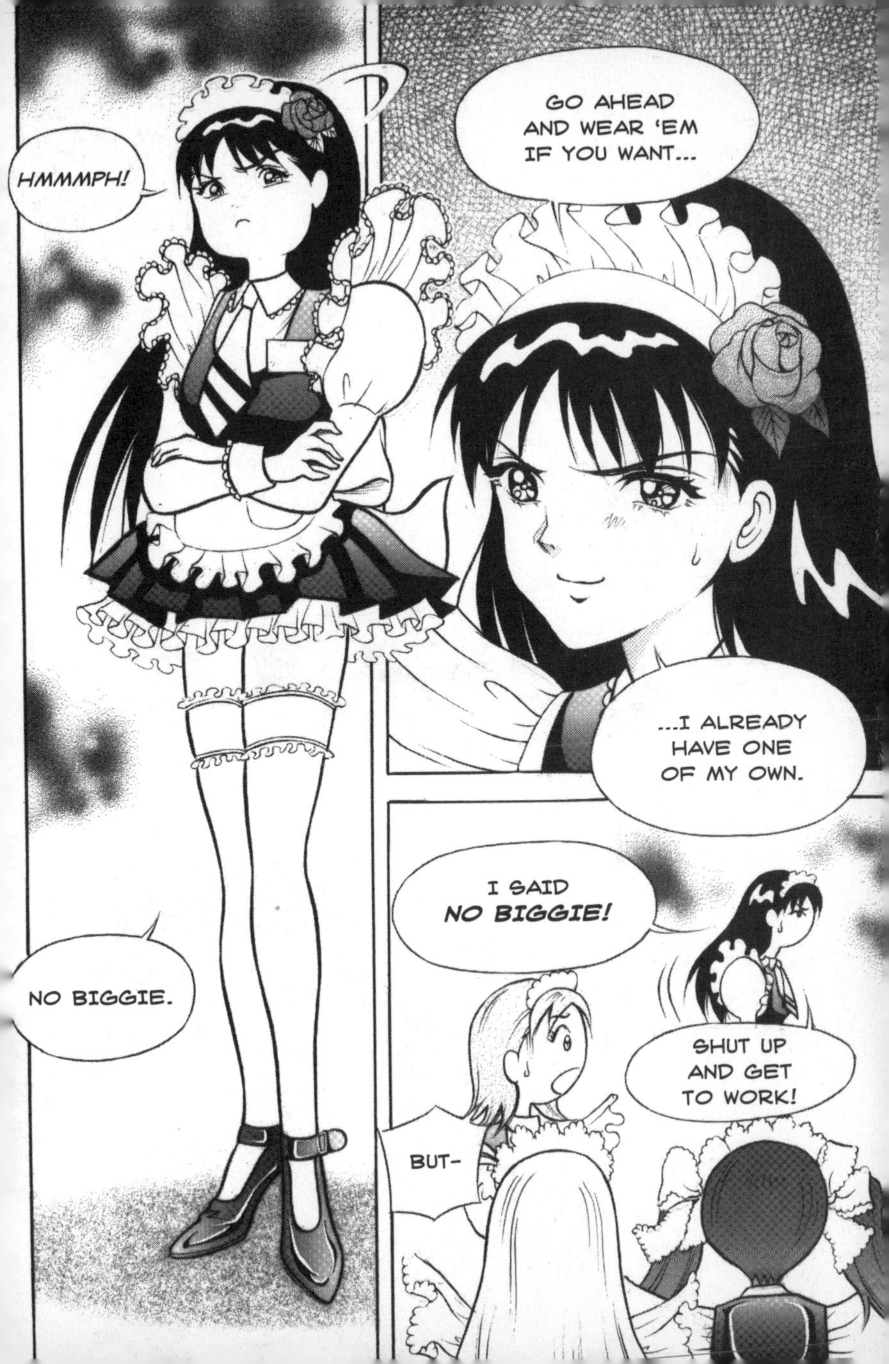
GO AHEAD AND WEAR 'EM IF YOU WANT...
...I ALREADY HAVE ONE OF MY OWN.
HMMMPH!
NO BIGGIE.
I SAID NO BIGGIE!
SHUT UP AND GET TO WORK!
BUT-

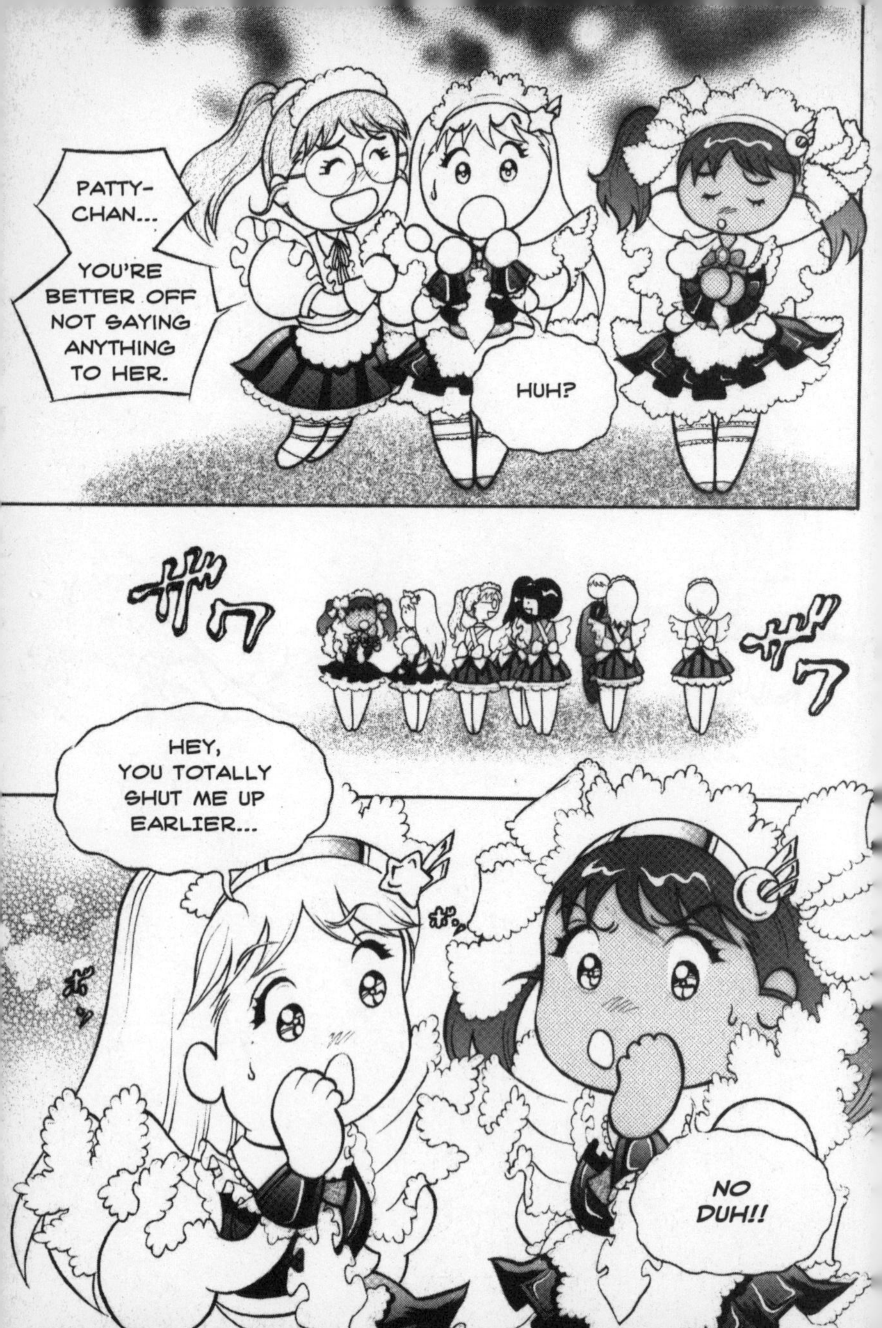
PATTY-CHAN... YOU'RE BETTER OFF NOT SAYING ANYTHING TO HER.
HUH?
ザワ
ザワ
HEY, YOU TOTALLY SHUT ME UP EARLIER...
NO DUH!!

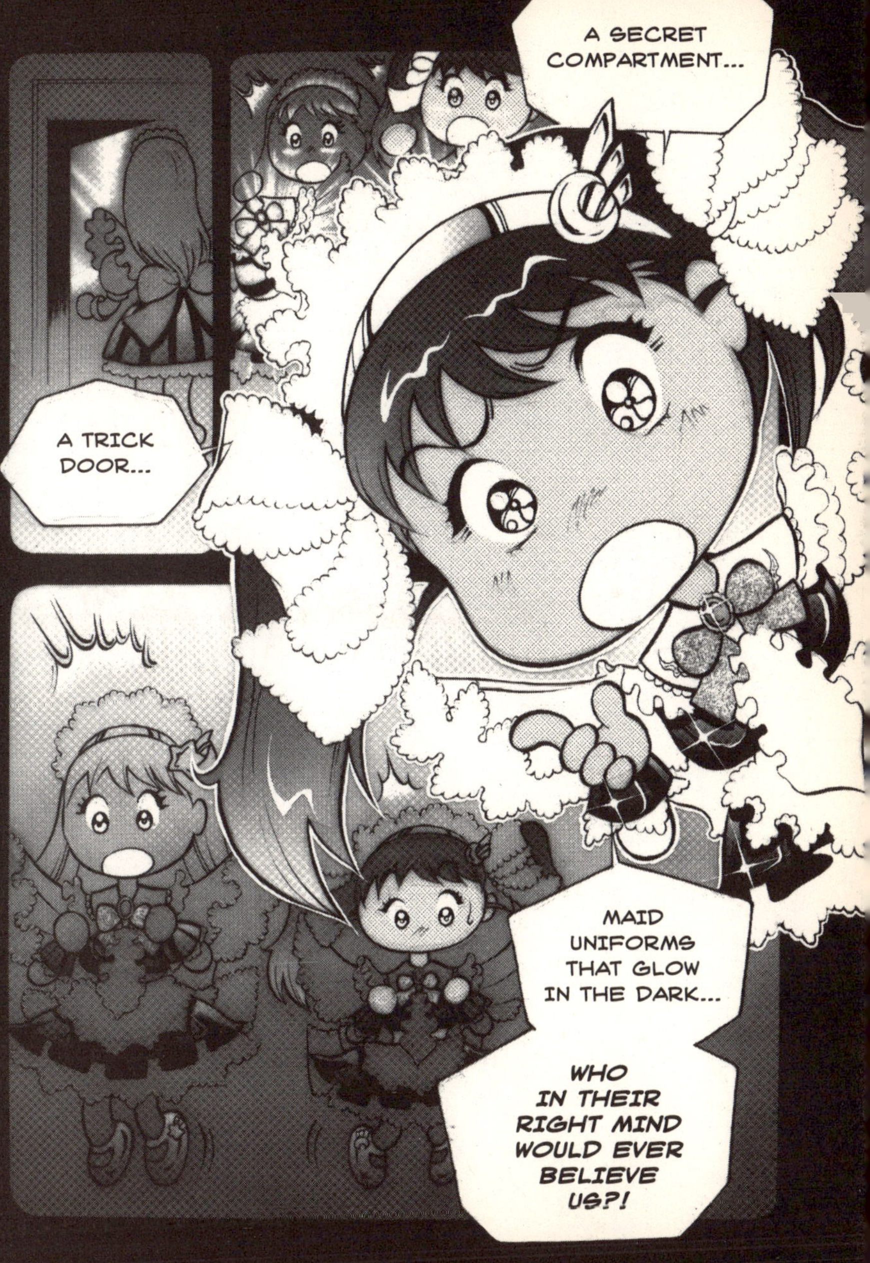

A SECRET COMPARTMENT...
A TRICK DOOR...
MAID UNIFORMS THAT GLOW IN THE DARK...
*WHO IN THEIR RIGHT MIND WOULD EVER BELIEVE US?!*

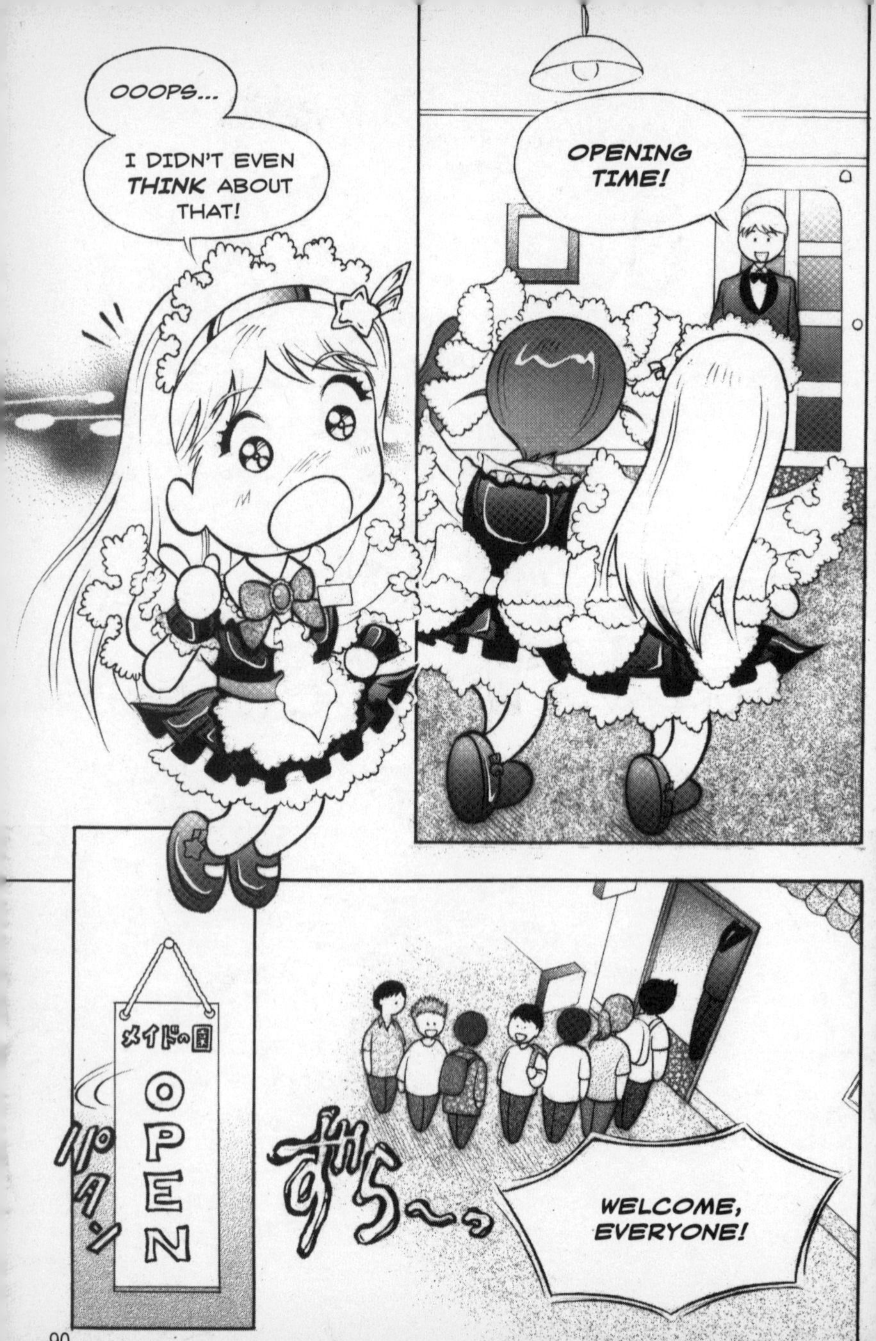
OPENING TIME!
OOOPS...
I DIDN'T EVEN THINK ABOUT THAT!
メイドの園
OPEN
WELCOME, EVERYONE!

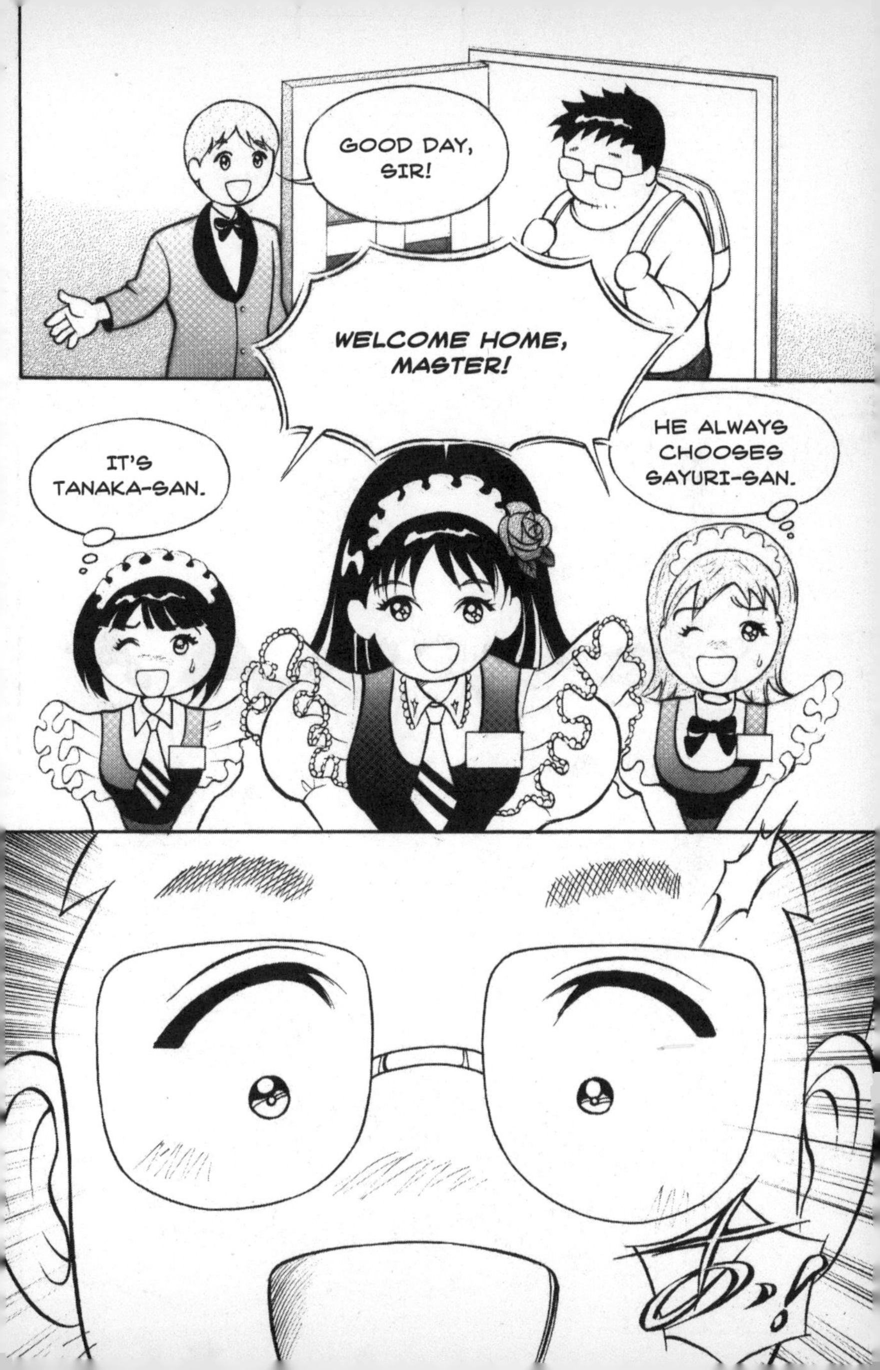
GOOD DAY, SIR!
WELCOME HOME, MASTER!
HE ALWAYS CHOOSES SAYURI-SAN.
IT'S TANAKA-SAN.

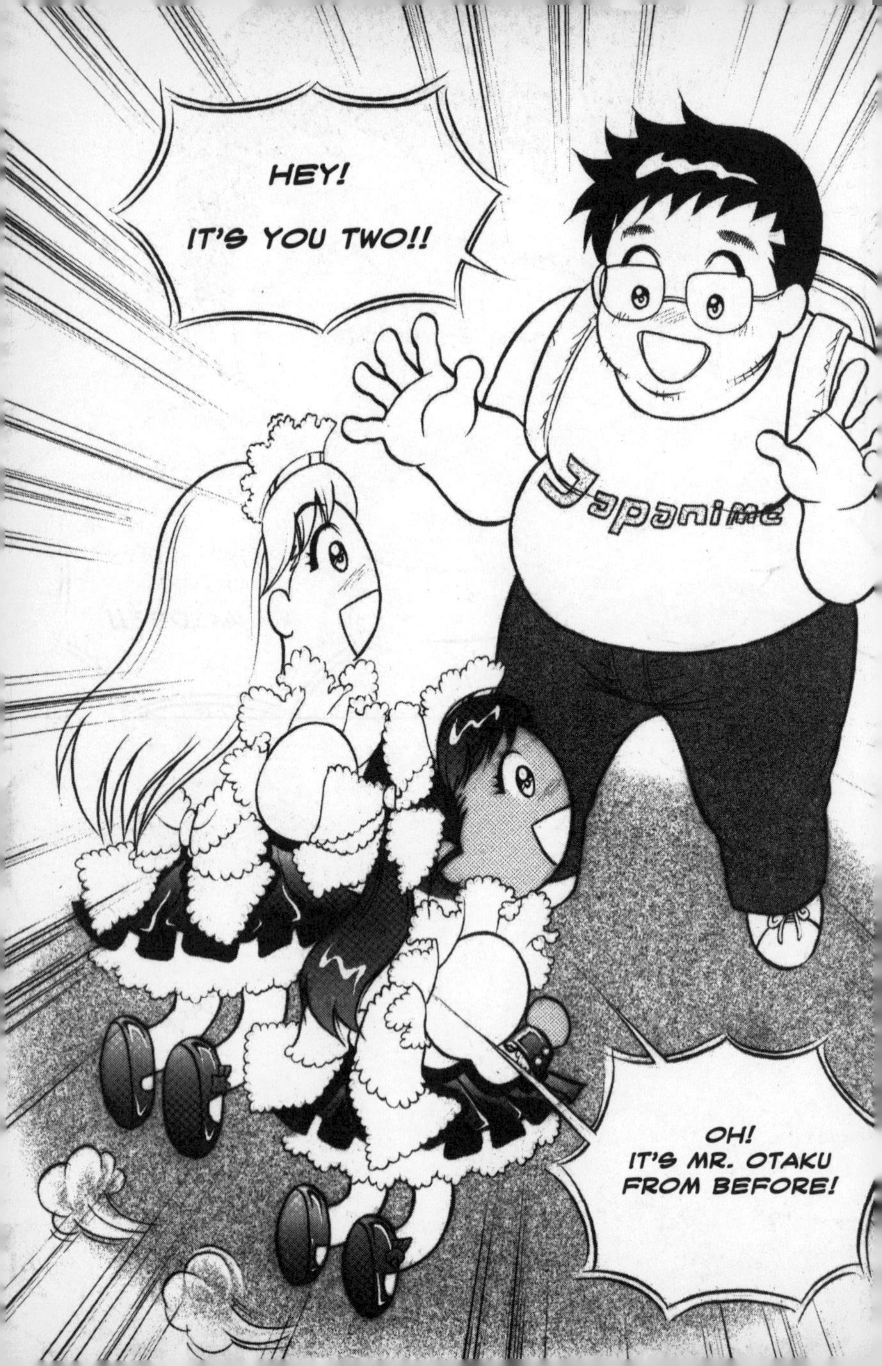
HEY!
IT'S YOU TWO!!
Japanime
OH!
IT'S MR. OTAKU
FROM BEFORE!

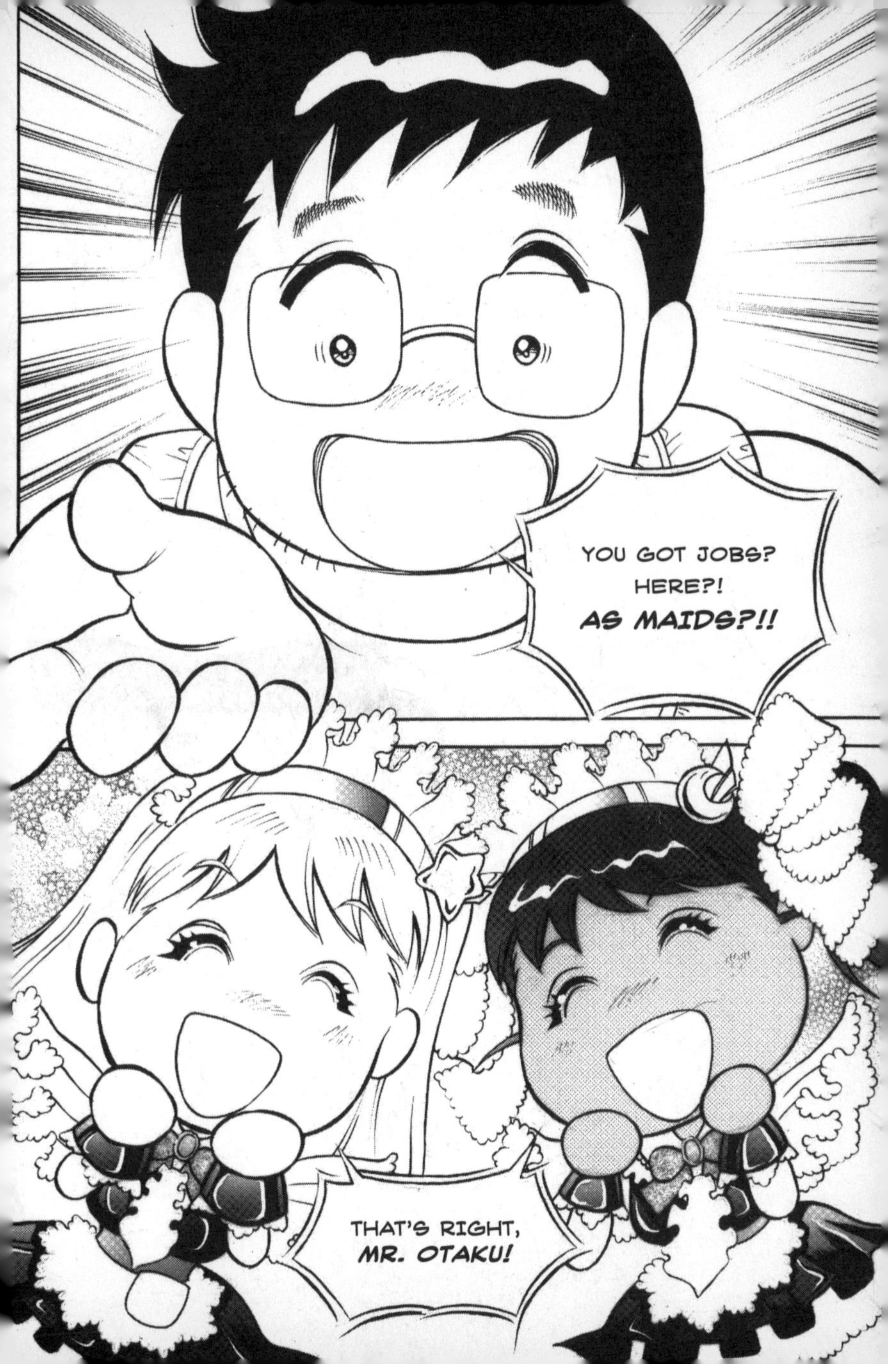
YOU GOT JOBS?
HERE?!
AS MAIDS?!!
THAT'S RIGHT,
MR. OTAKU!

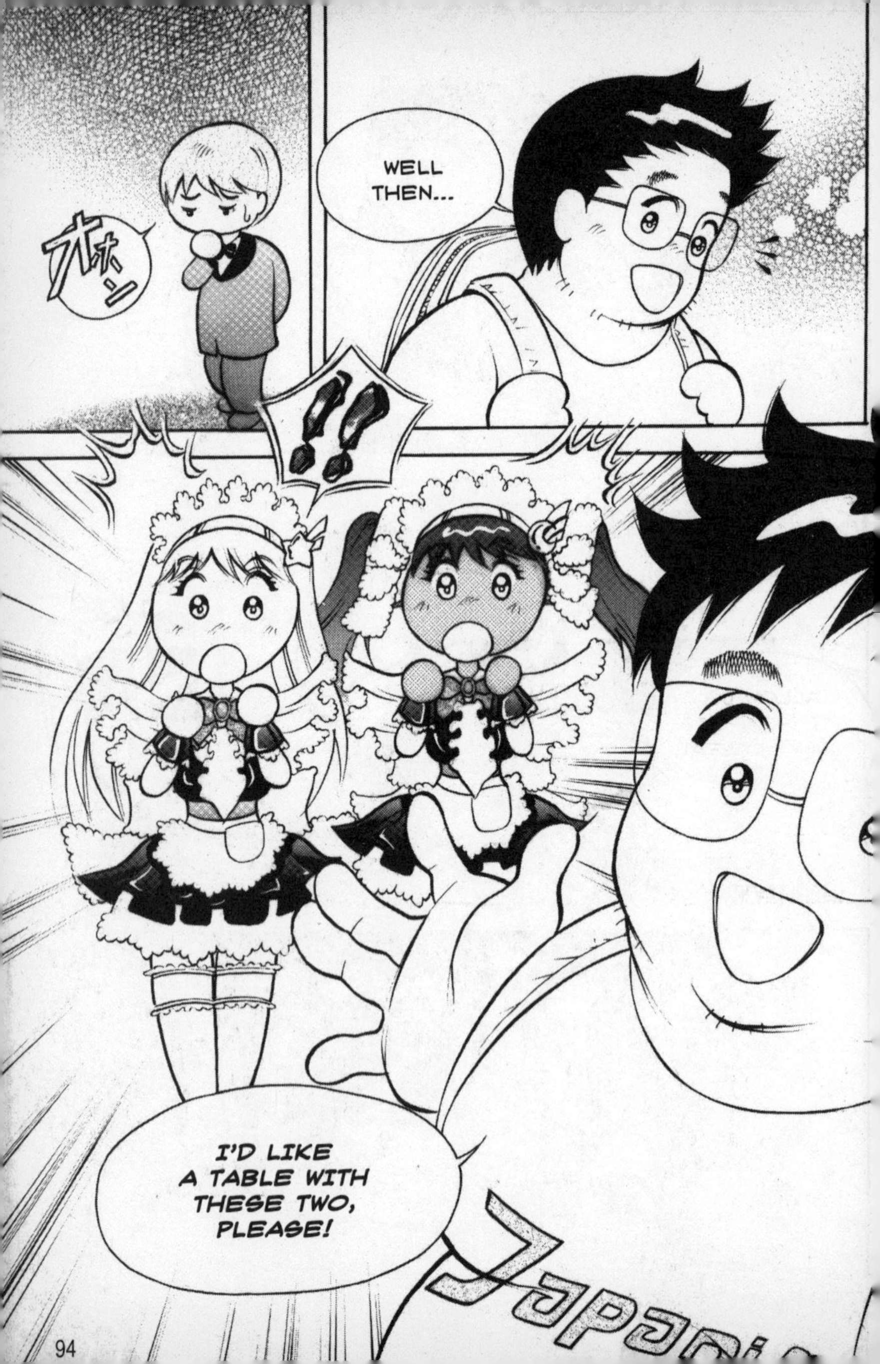
オホン
WELL THEN...
!!
I'D LIKE A TABLE WITH THESE TWO, PLEASE!
Japan!

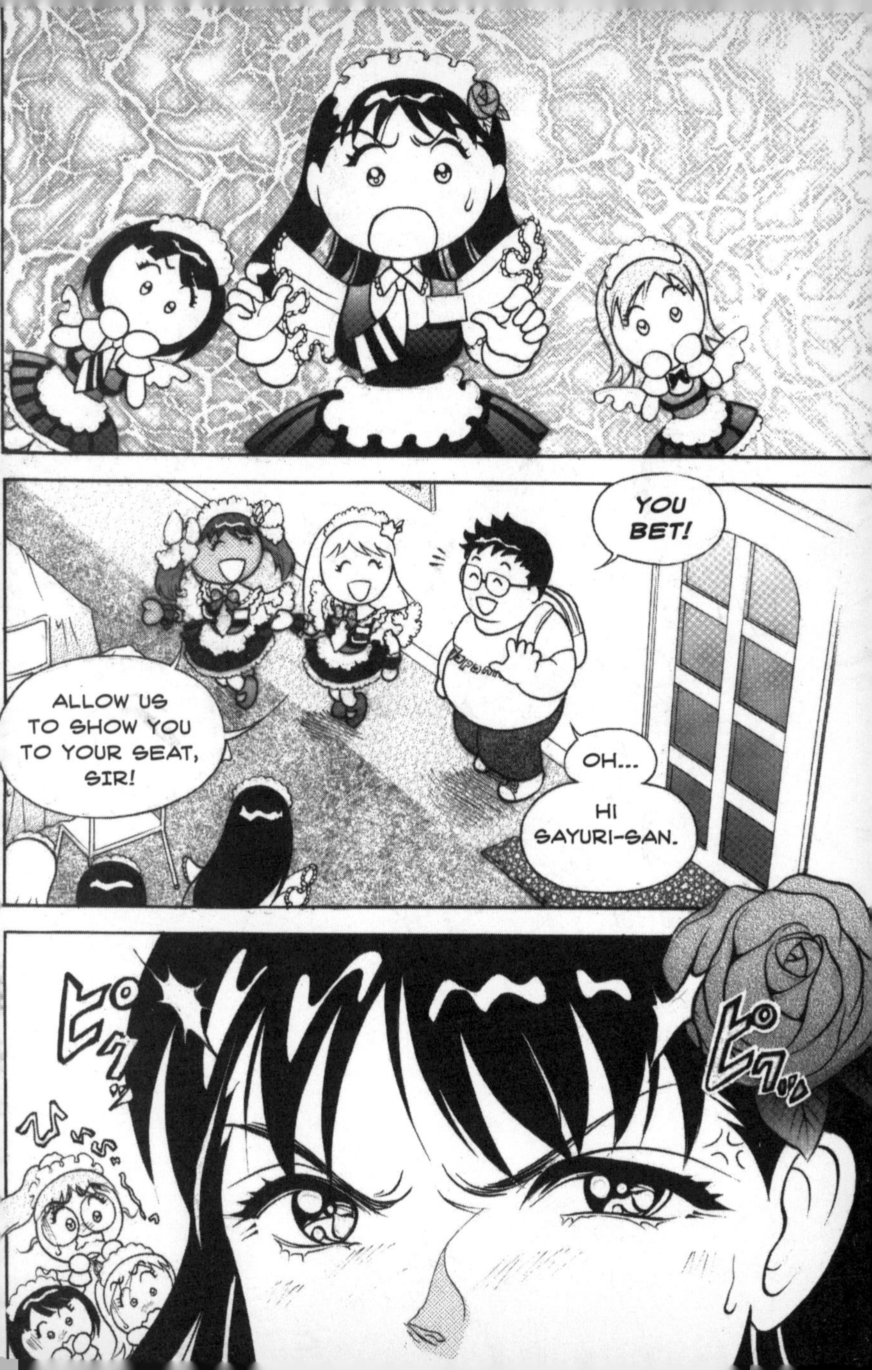

YOU BET!
ALLOW US TO SHOW YOU TO YOUR SEAT, SIR!
OH...
HI SAYURI-SAN.

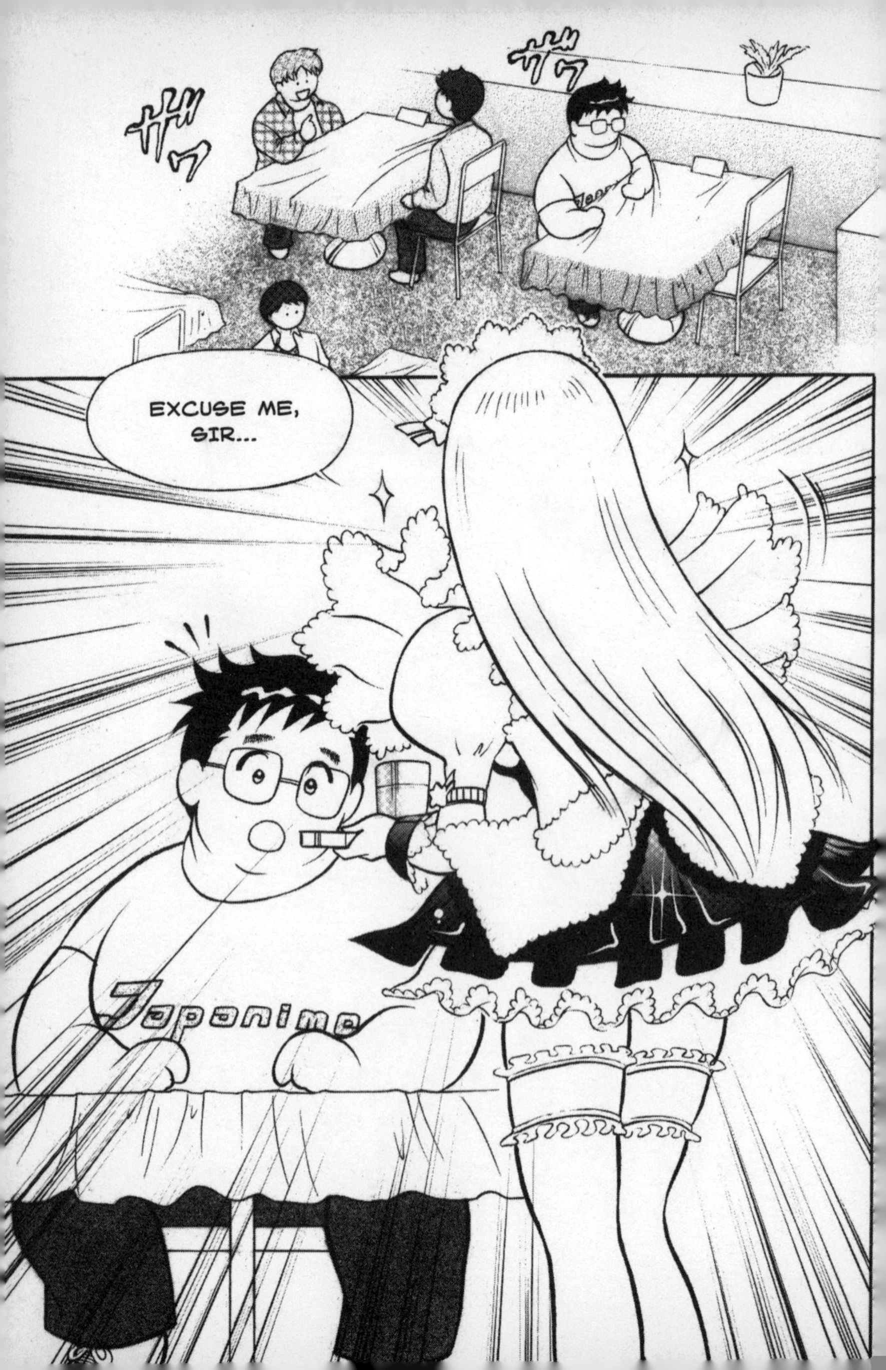
ザワ
ザワ
EXCUSE ME, SIR...

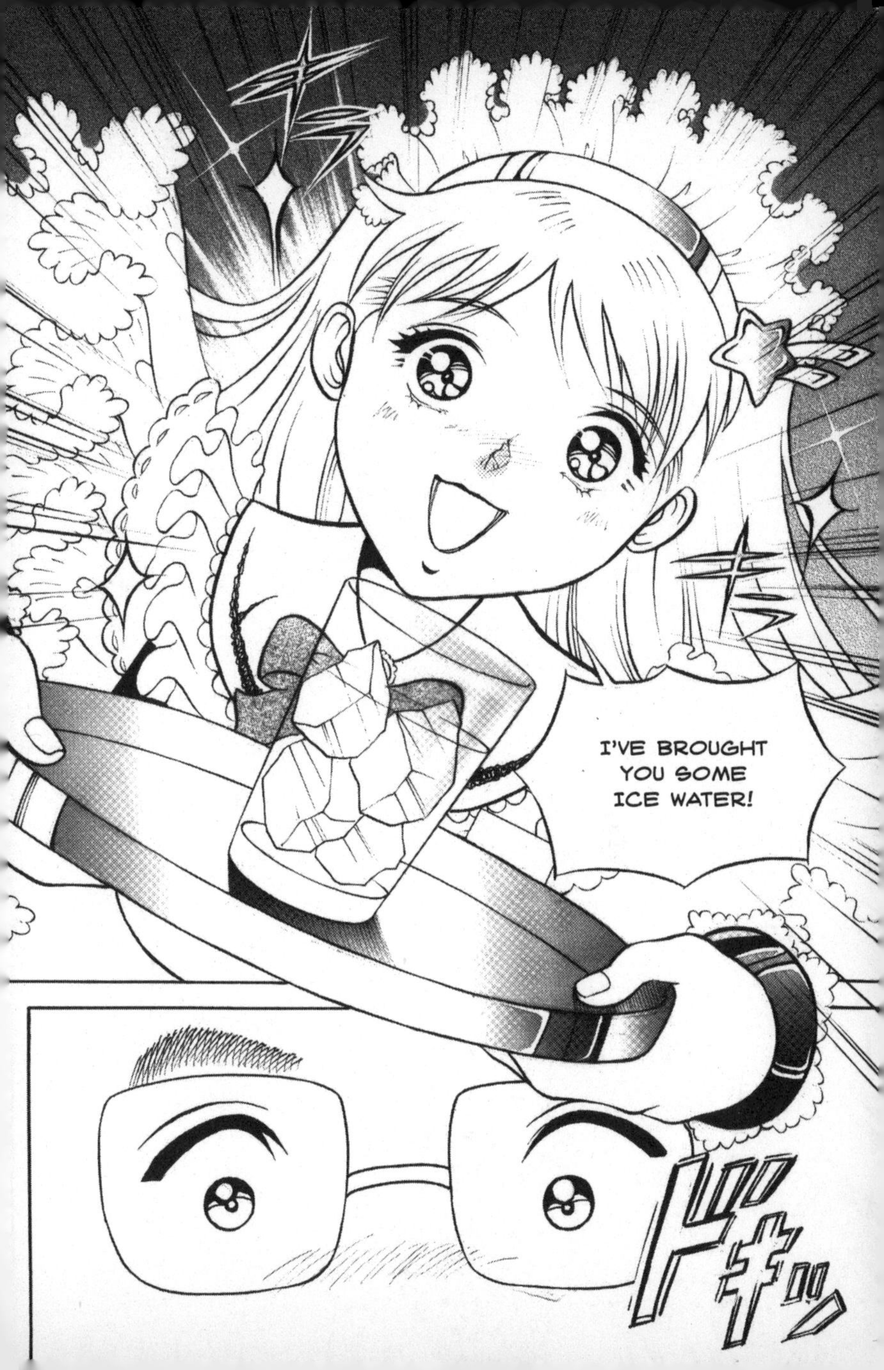
I'VE BROUGHT YOU SOME ICE WATER!

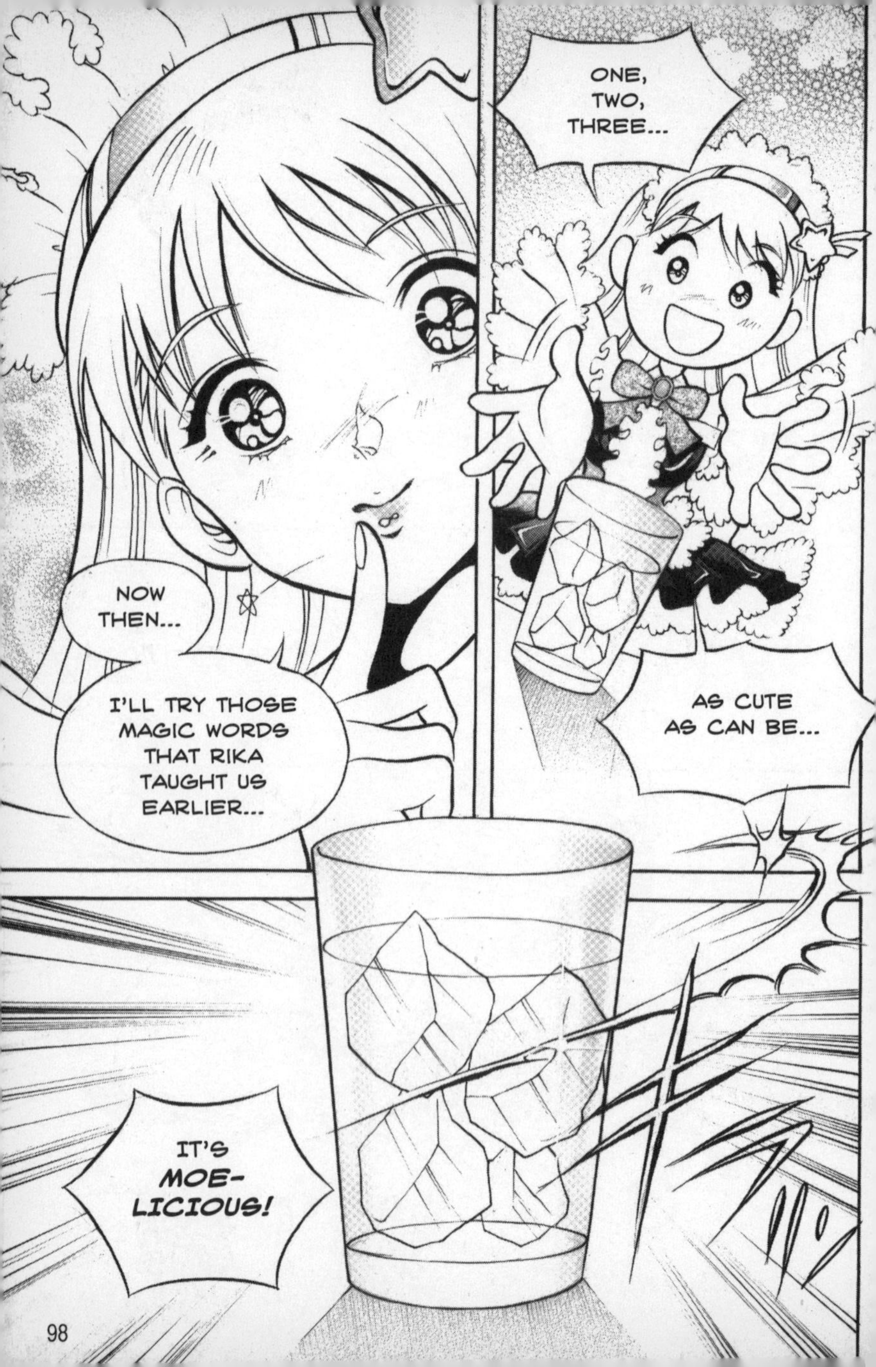
NOW THEN...
I'LL TRY THOSE MAGIC WORDS THAT RIKA TAUGHT US EARLIER...
ONE, TWO, THREE...
AS CUTE AS CAN BE...
IT'S *MOE-LICIOUS!*

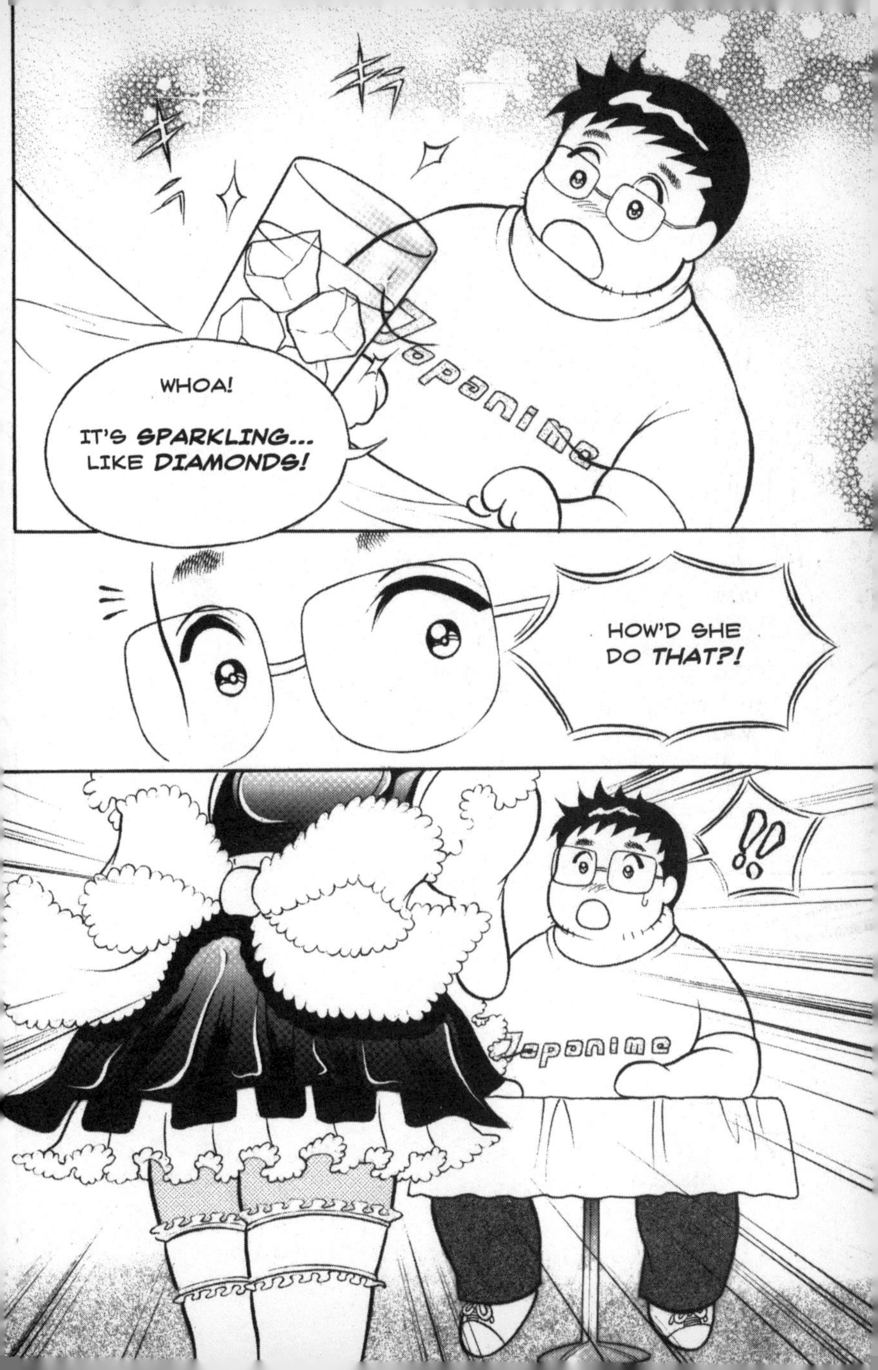
WHOA!
IT'S SPARKLING... LIKE DIAMONDS!
HOW'D SHE DO THAT?!
!!
Japanime

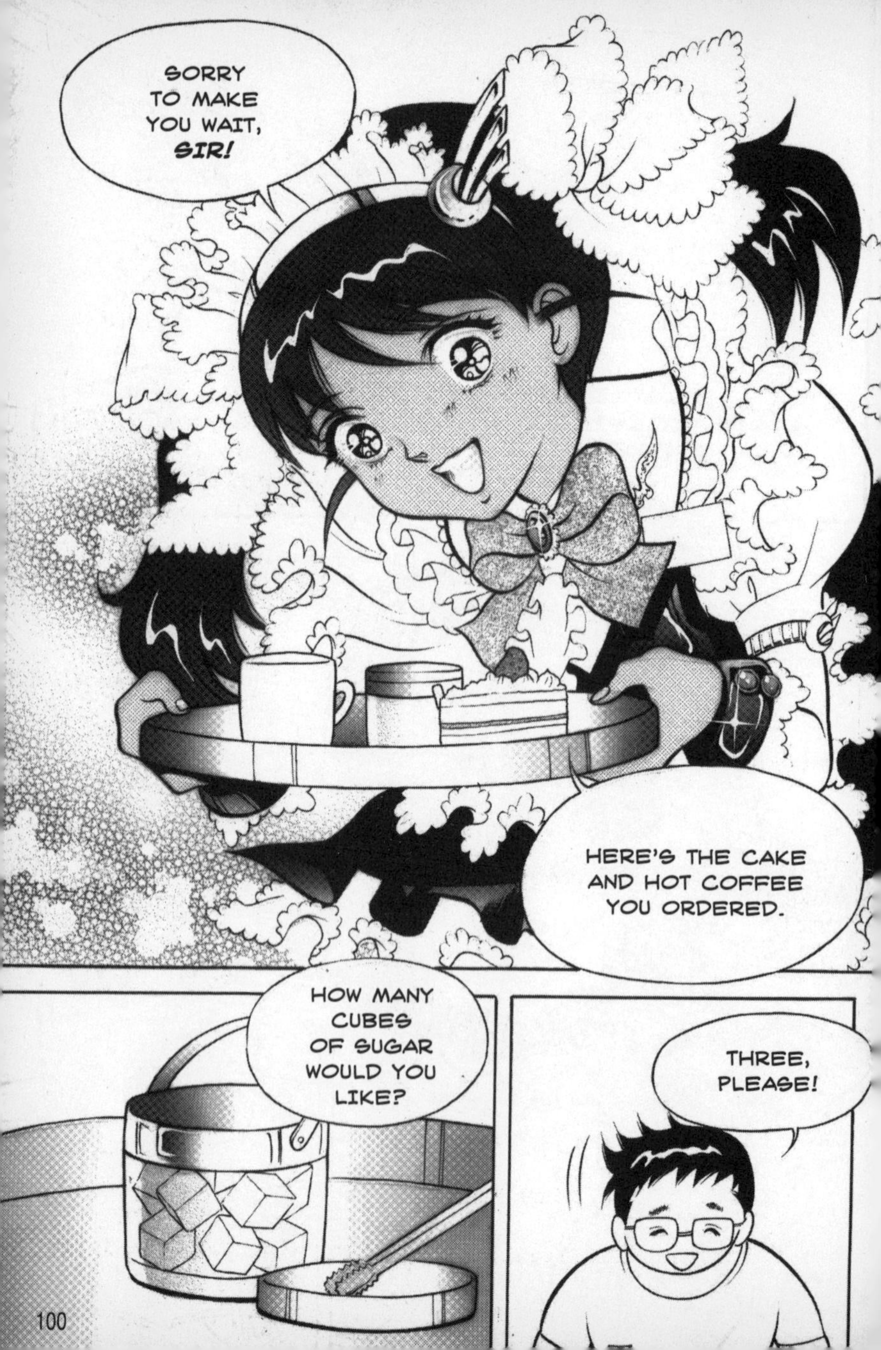
SORRY TO MAKE YOU WAIT, **SIR!**
HERE'S THE CAKE AND HOT COFFEE YOU ORDERED.
HOW MANY CUBES OF SUGAR WOULD YOU LIKE?
THREE, PLEASE!

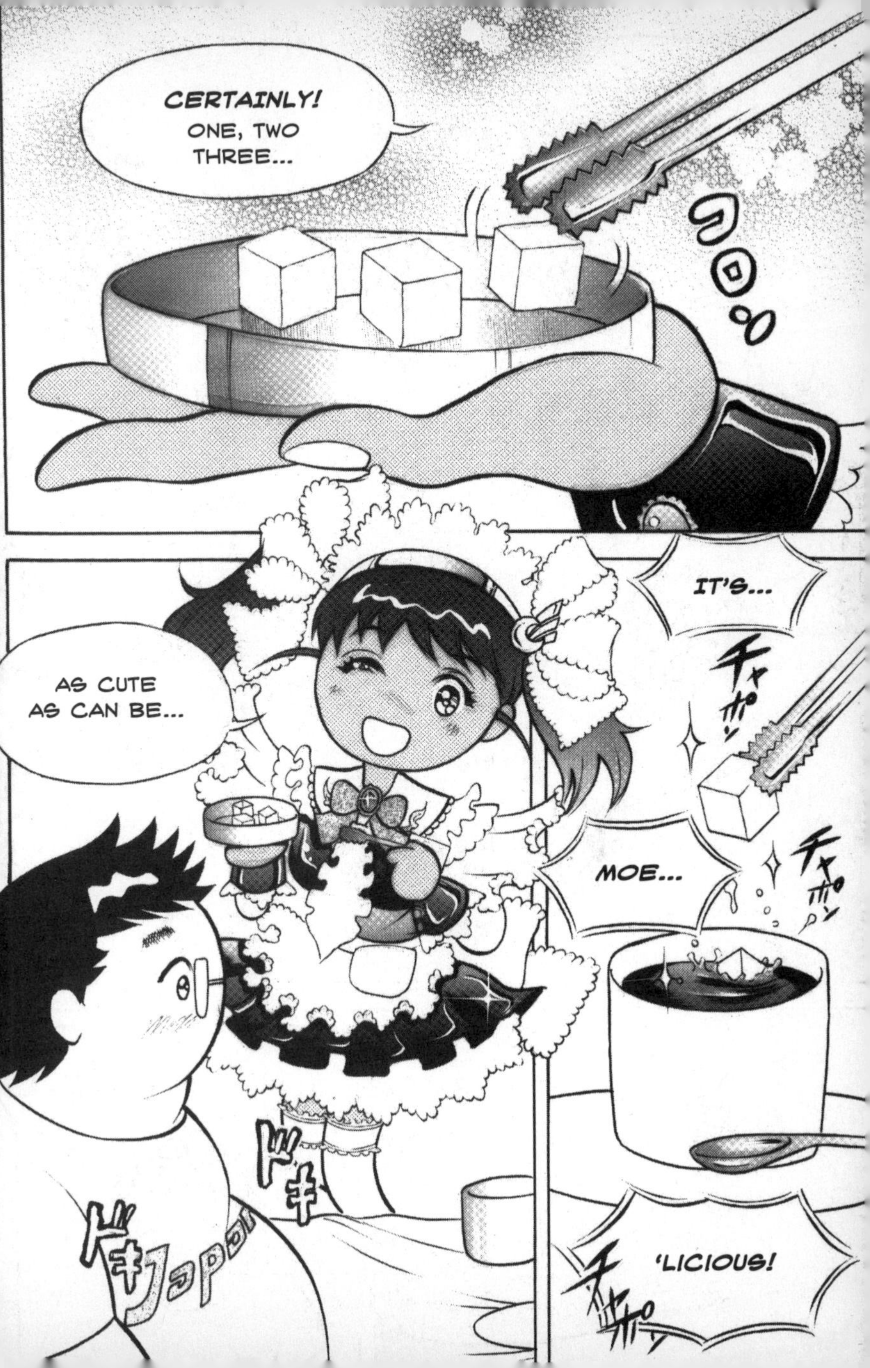
CERTAINLY!
ONE, TWO THREE...
コロ
IT'S...
AS CUTE AS CAN BE...
チャポン
MOE...
チャポン
ドキ
'LICIOUS!
チャポン

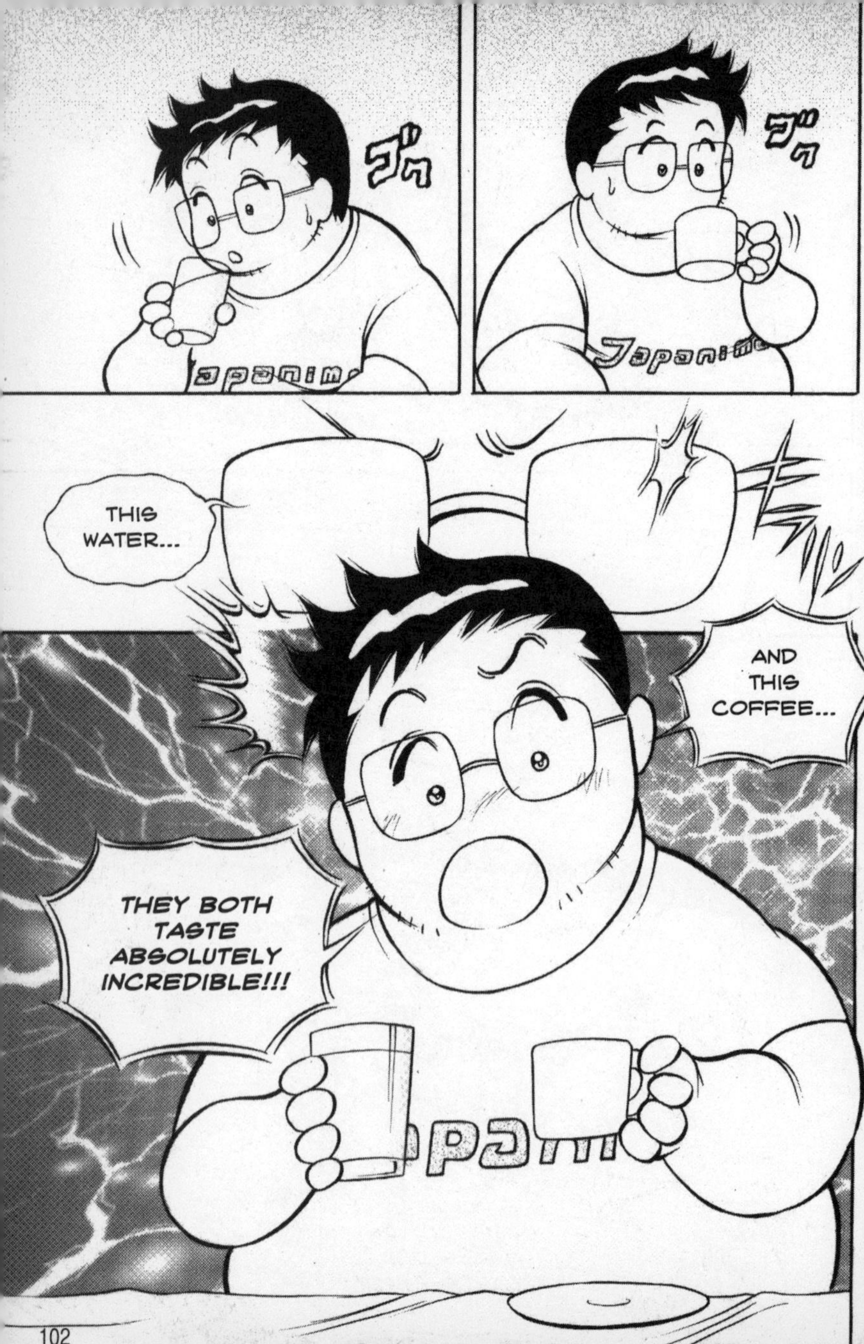
ゴク
ゴク
THIS WATER...
AND THIS COFFEE...
THEY BOTH TASTE ABSOLUTELY INCREDIBLE!!!

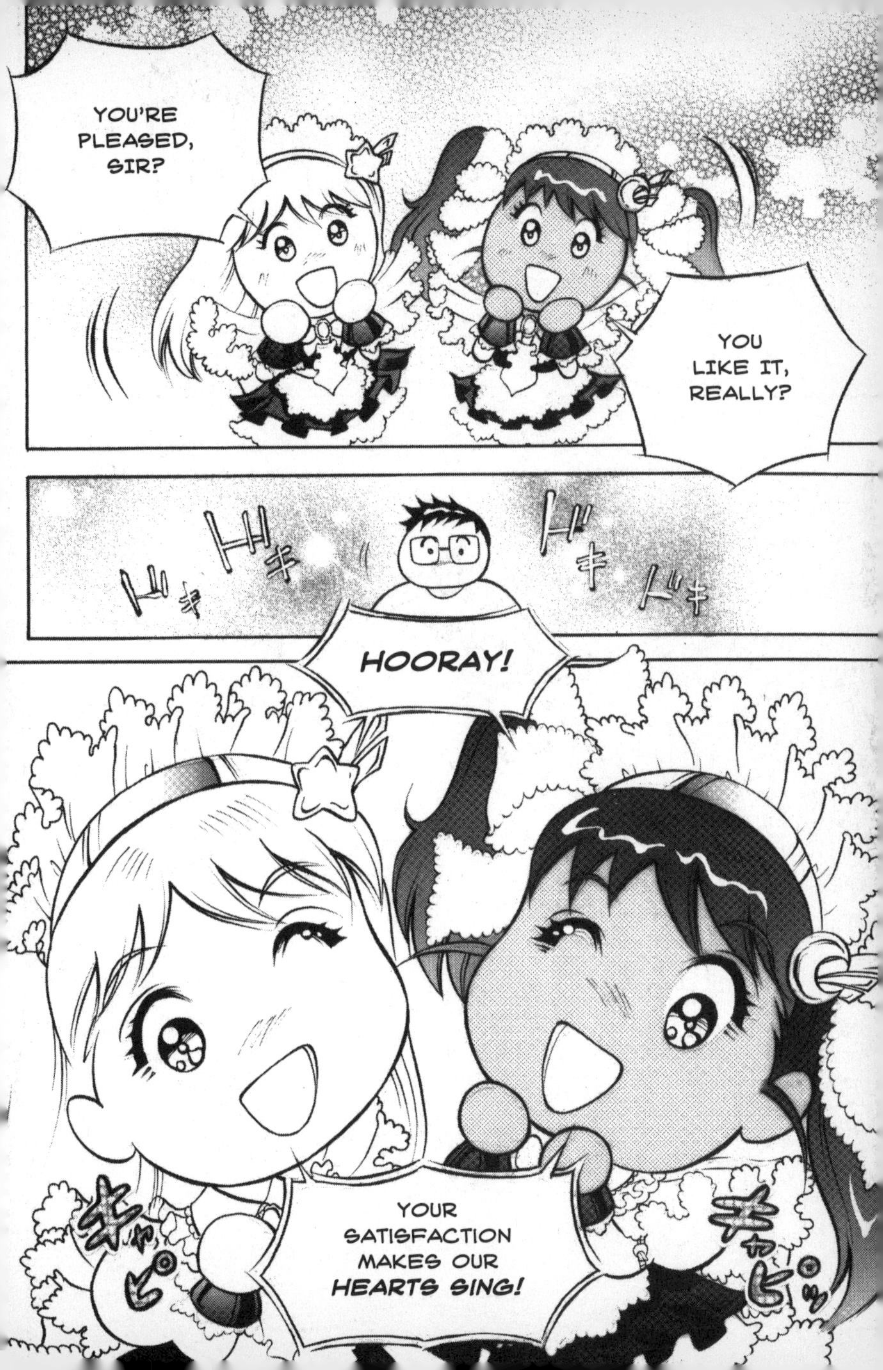
YOU'RE PLEASED, SIR?
YOU LIKE IT, REALLY?
ドキドキ
ドキドキ
HOORAY!
キャピ
キャピッ
YOUR SATISFACTION MAKES OUR HEARTS SING!

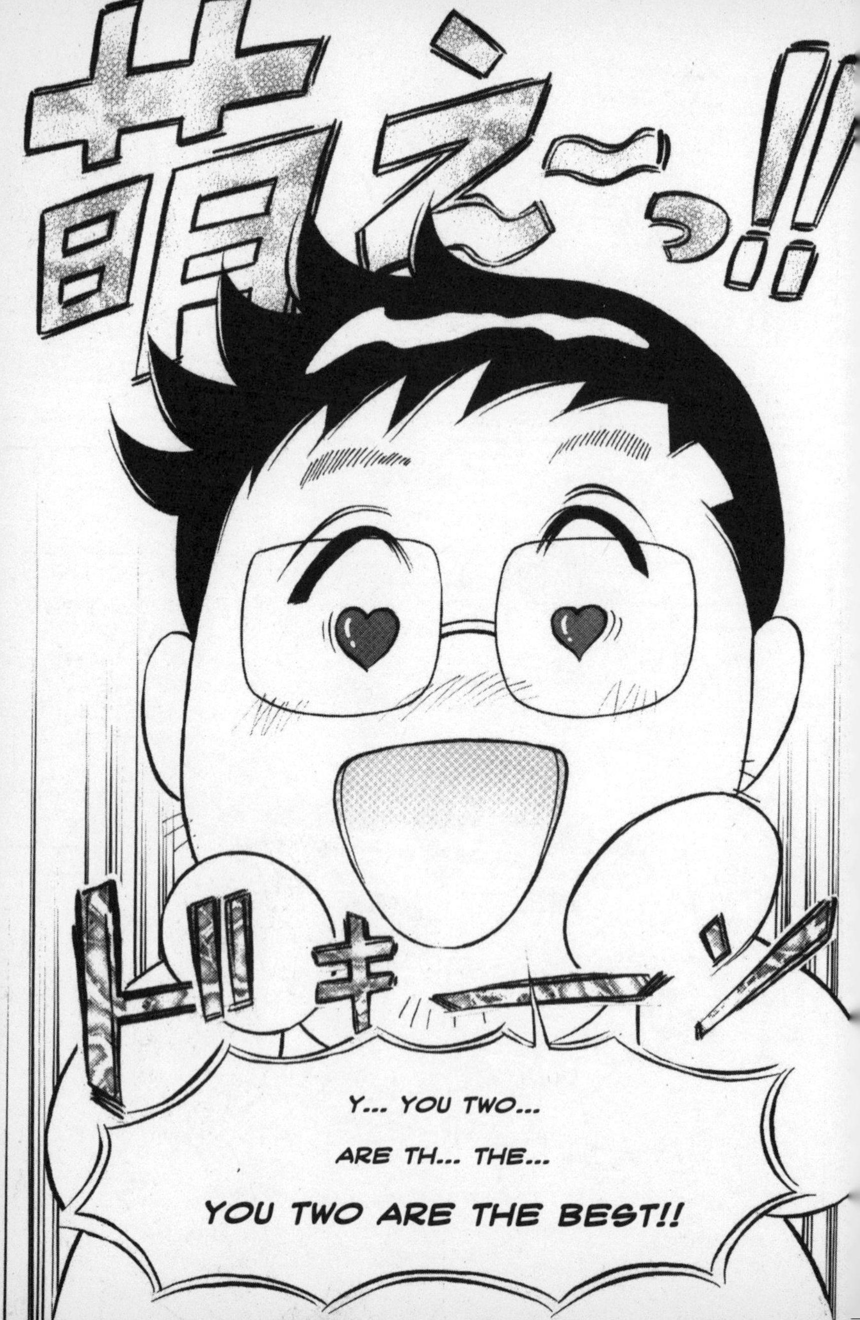
萌え〜っ!!
ドキーン
Y... YOU TWO...
ARE TH... THE...
YOU TWO ARE THE BEST!!

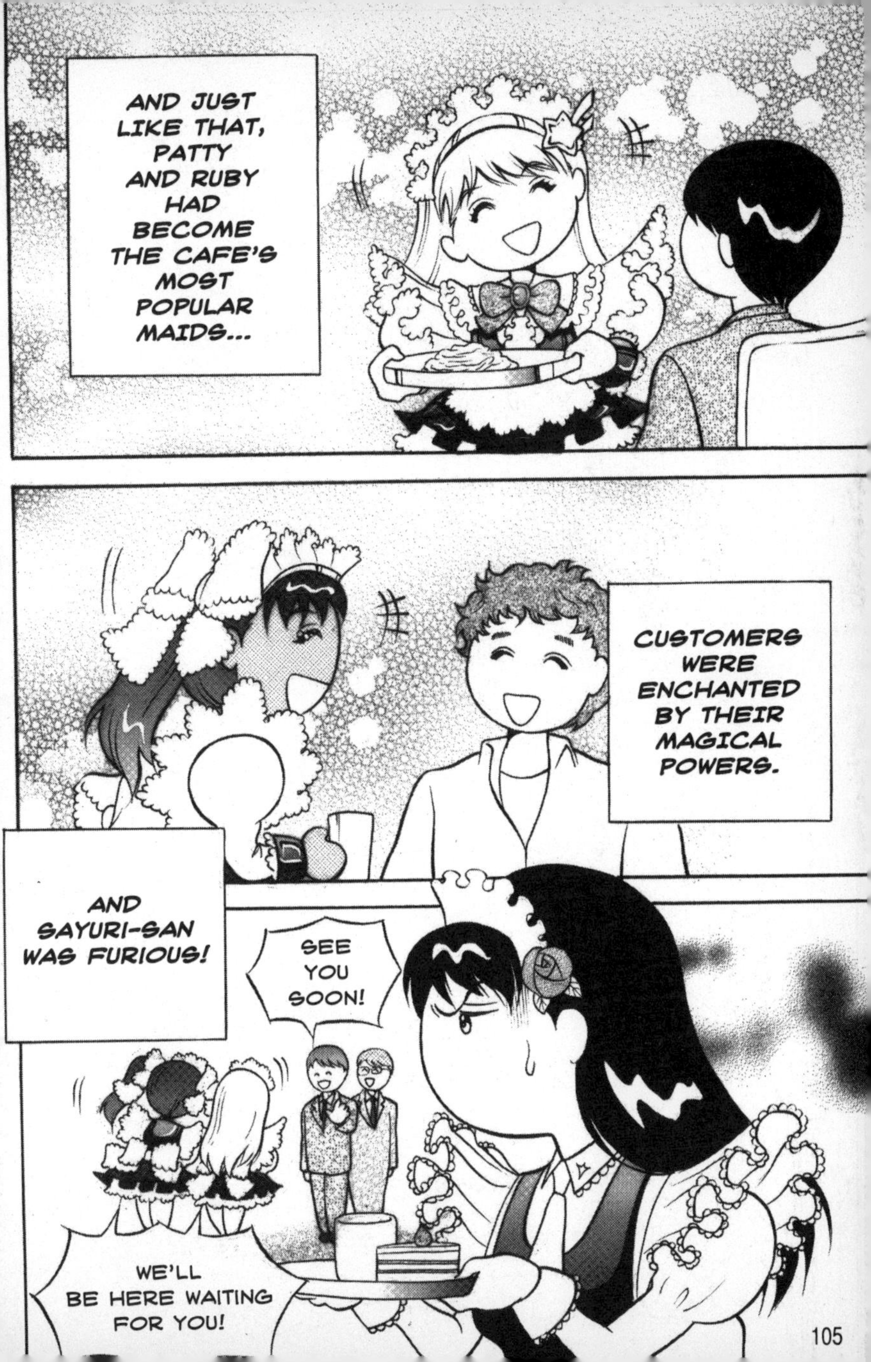
AND JUST LIKE THAT, PATTY AND RUBY HAD BECOME THE CAFE'S MOST POPULAR MAIDS...
CUSTOMERS WERE ENCHANTED BY THEIR MAGICAL POWERS.
AND SAYURI-SAN WAS FURIOUS!
SEE YOU SOON!
WE'LL BE HERE WAITING FOR YOU!

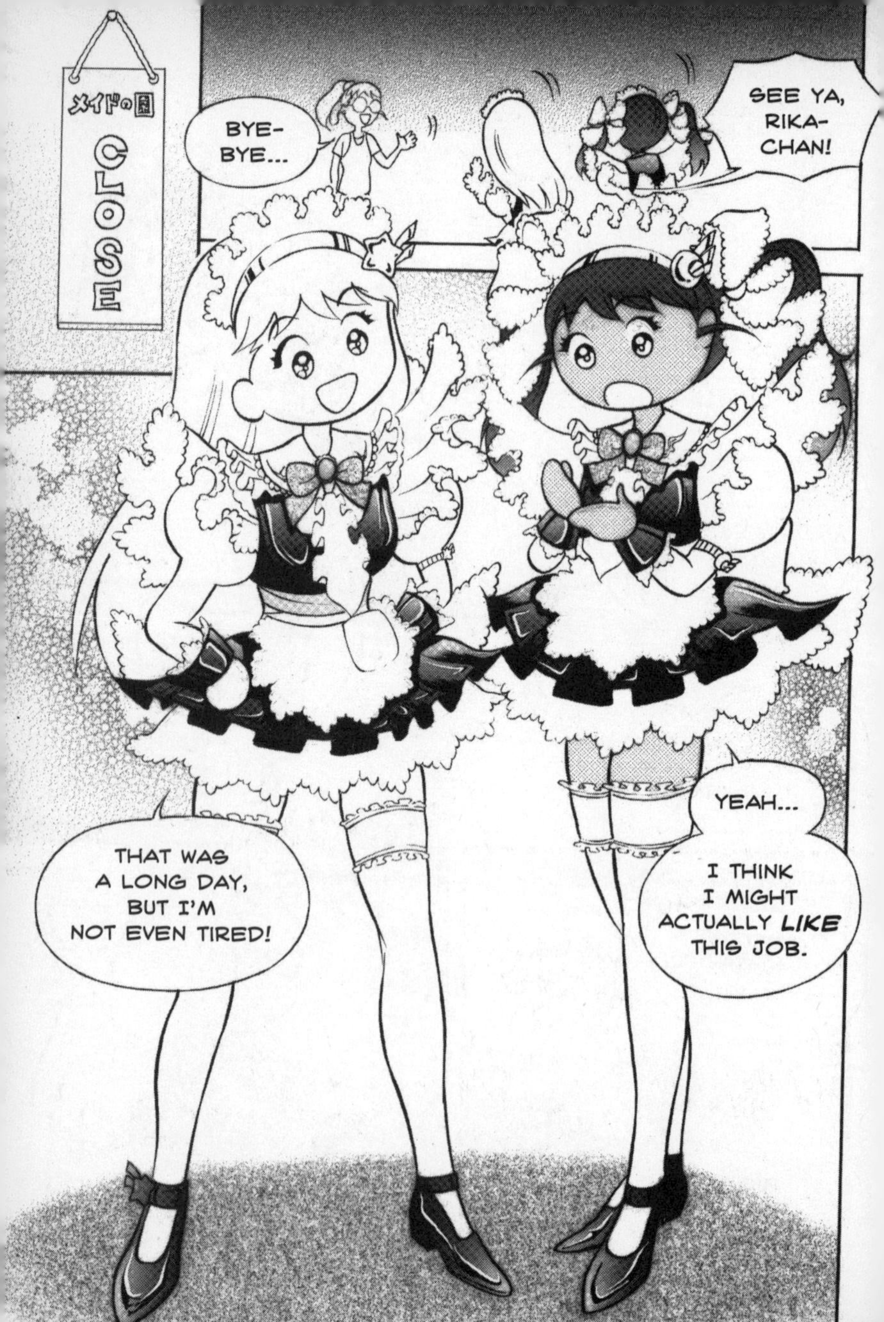
メイドの園
CLOSE
BYE-BYE...
SEE YA, RIKA-CHAN!
THAT WAS A LONG DAY, BUT I'M NOT EVEN TIRED!
YEAH...
I THINK I MIGHT ACTUALLY *LIKE* THIS JOB.

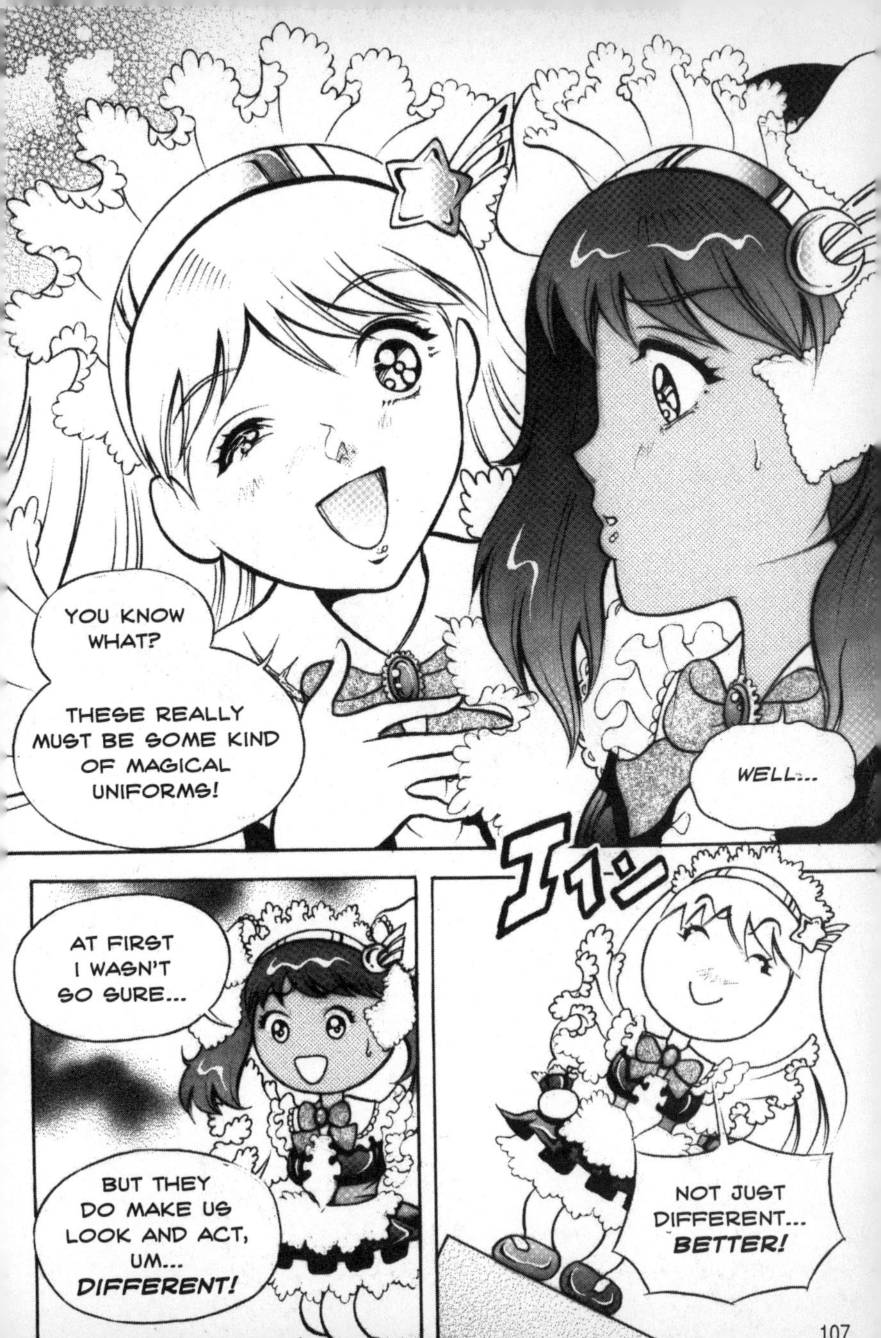
YOU KNOW WHAT?
THESE REALLY MUST BE SOME KIND OF MAGICAL UNIFORMS!
WELL...
AT FIRST I WASN'T SO SURE...
BUT THEY DO MAKE US LOOK AND ACT, UM... ***DIFFERENT!***
NOT JUST DIFFERENT... ***BETTER!***

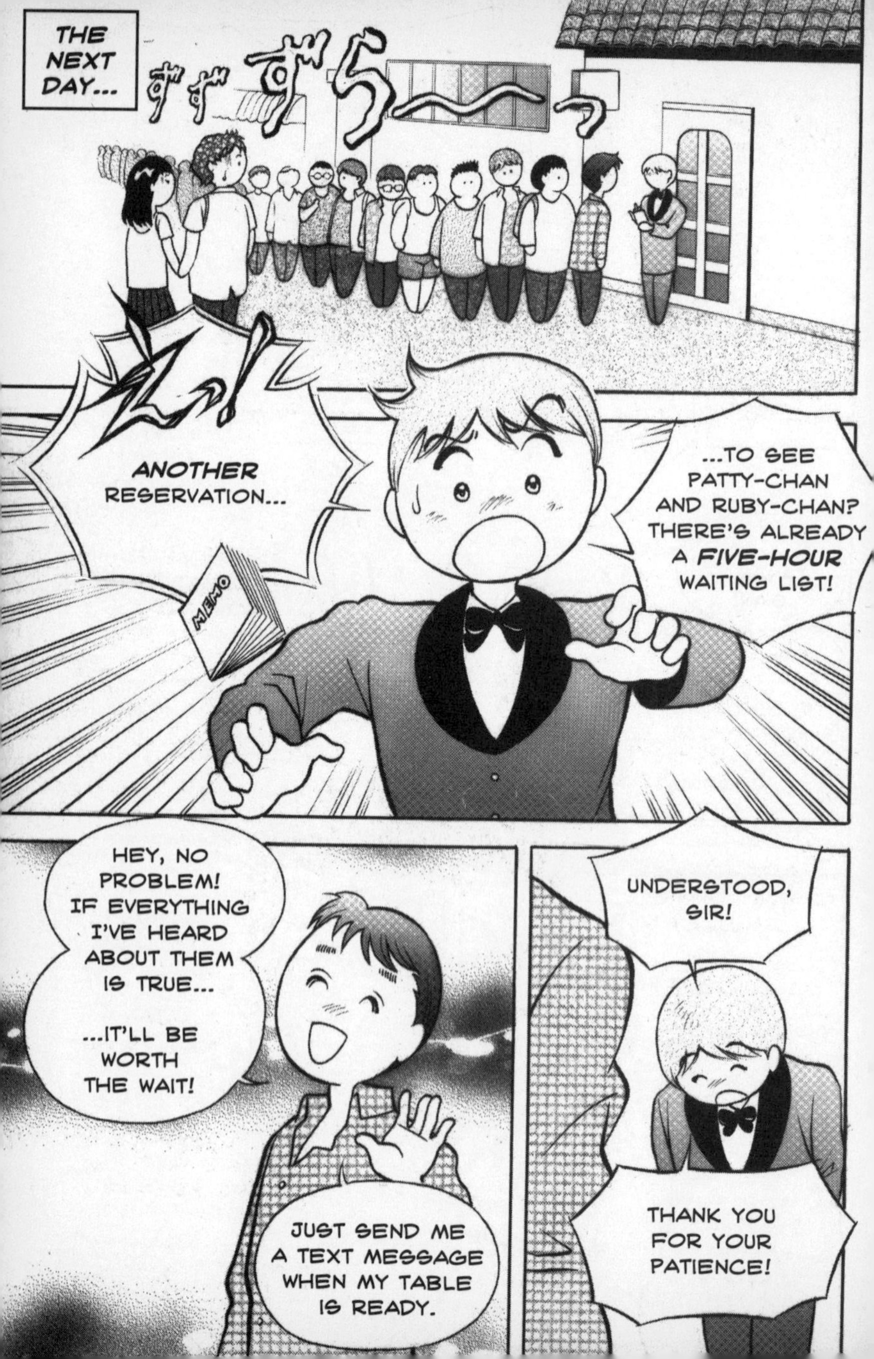
THE NEXT DAY...
ずず ずら〜〜っ
ANOTHER RESERVATION...
...TO SEE PATTY-CHAN AND RUBY-CHAN? THERE'S ALREADY A FIVE-HOUR WAITING LIST!
MEMO
HEY, NO PROBLEM! IF EVERYTHING I'VE HEARD ABOUT THEM IS TRUE...
...IT'LL BE WORTH THE WAIT!
JUST SEND ME A TEXT MESSAGE WHEN MY TABLE IS READY.
UNDERSTOOD, SIR!
THANK YOU FOR YOUR PATIENCE!

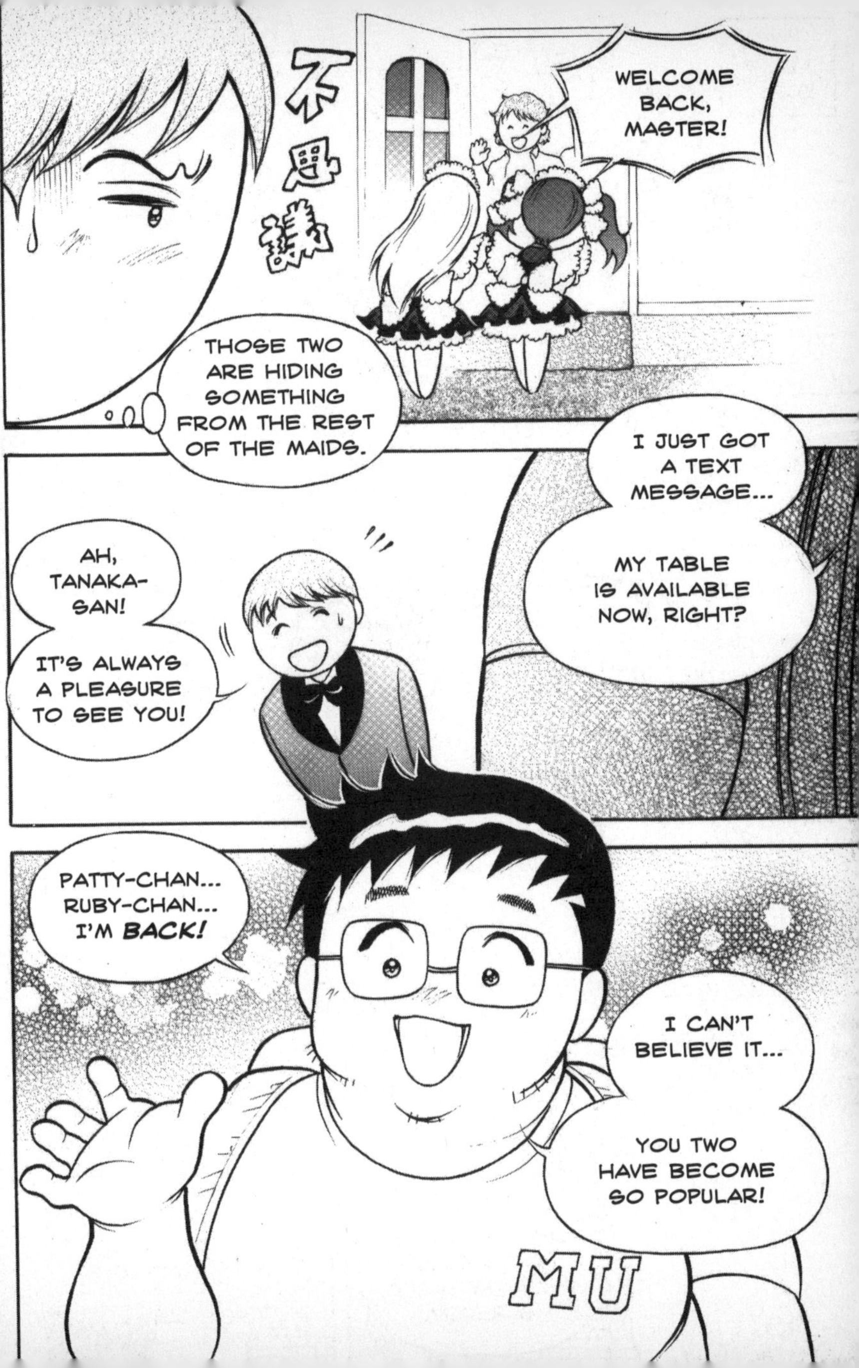
WELCOME BACK, MASTER!
不思議
THOSE TWO ARE HIDING SOMETHING FROM THE REST OF THE MAIDS.
I JUST GOT A TEXT MESSAGE...
MY TABLE IS AVAILABLE NOW, RIGHT?
AH, TANAKA-SAN!
IT'S ALWAYS A PLEASURE TO SEE YOU!
PATTY-CHAN... RUBY-CHAN... I'M BACK!
I CAN'T BELIEVE IT...
YOU TWO HAVE BECOME SO POPULAR!
MU

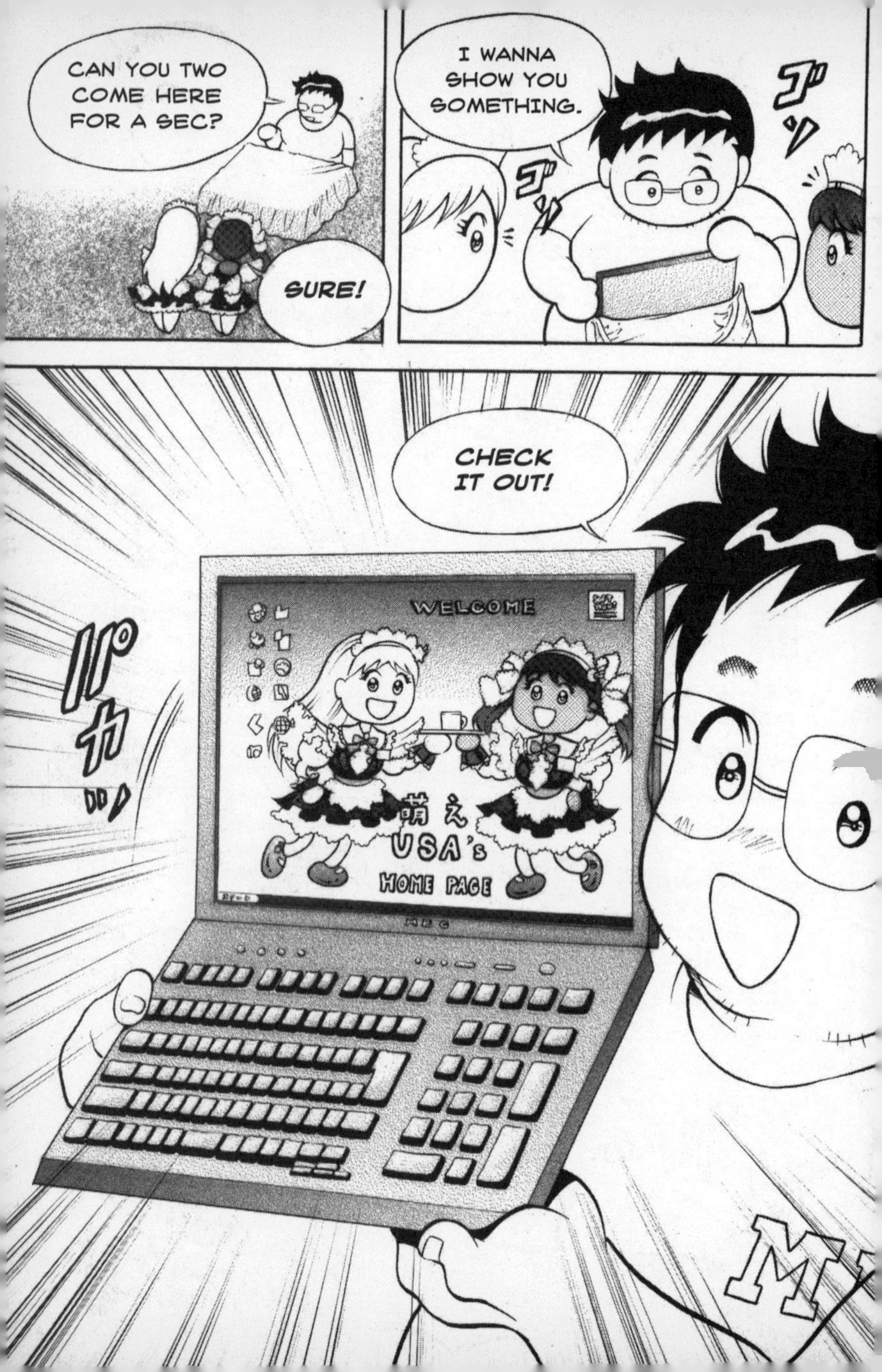
CAN YOU TWO COME HERE FOR A SEC?
SURE!
I WANNA SHOW YOU SOMETHING.
ゴッ
ゴッ
CHECK IT OUT!
パカッ
WELCOME
萌え USA's HOME PAGE

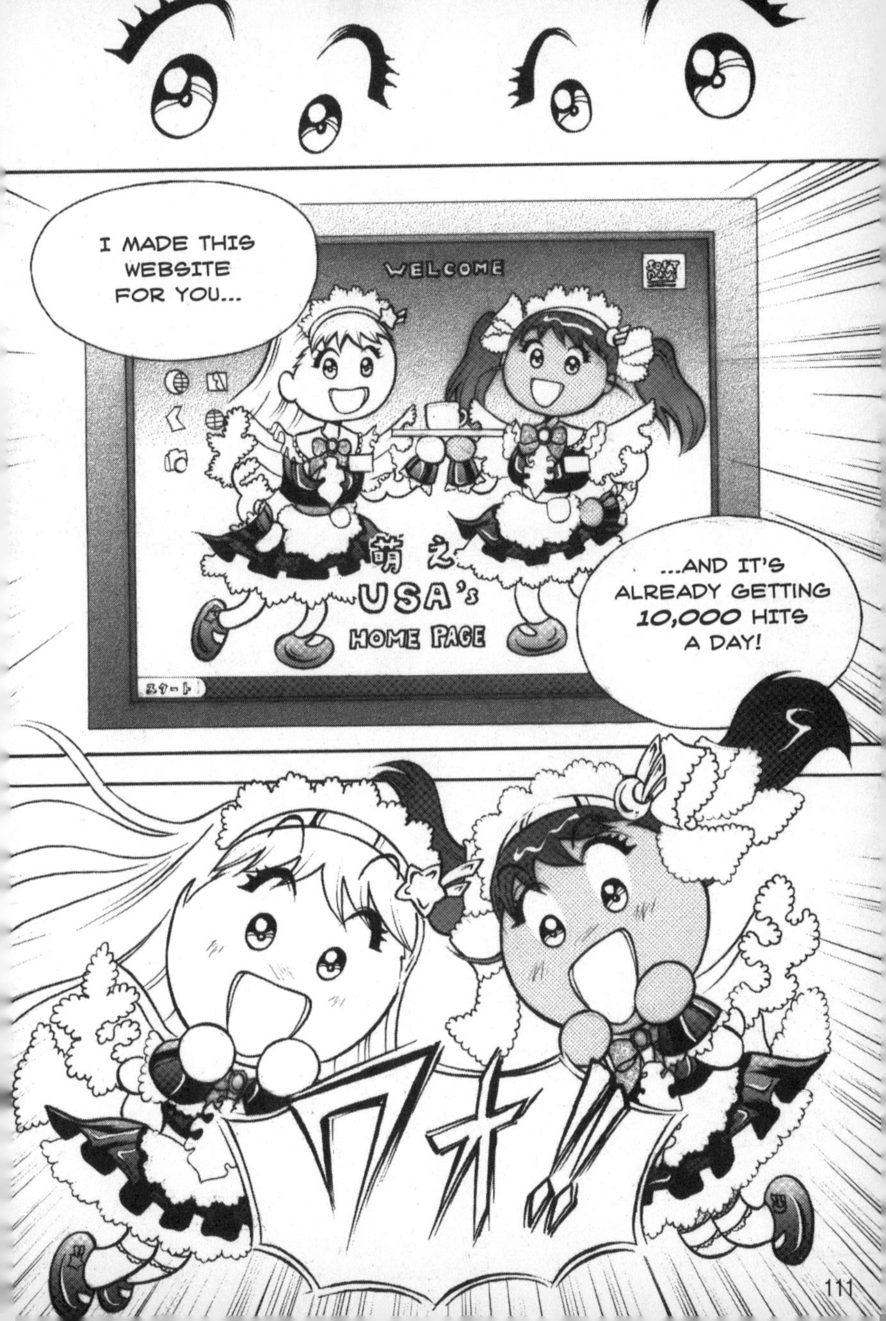
I MADE THIS WEBSITE FOR YOU...
WELCOME
萌之
USA's
HOME PAGE
スタート
...AND IT'S ALREADY GETTING 10,000 HITS A DAY!
ワオ!

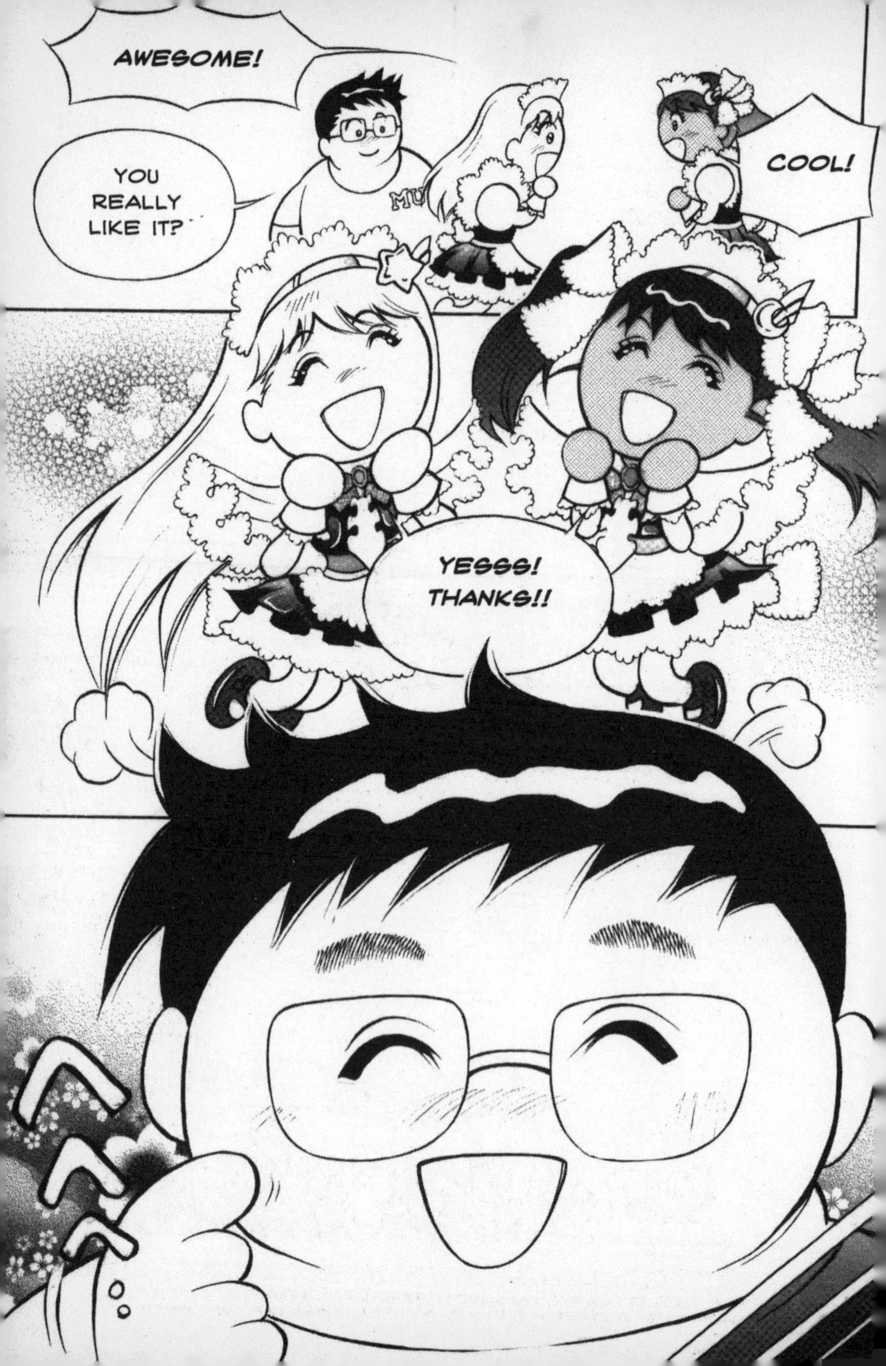
COOL!
AWESOME!
YOU REALLY LIKE IT?
YESSS! THANKS!!

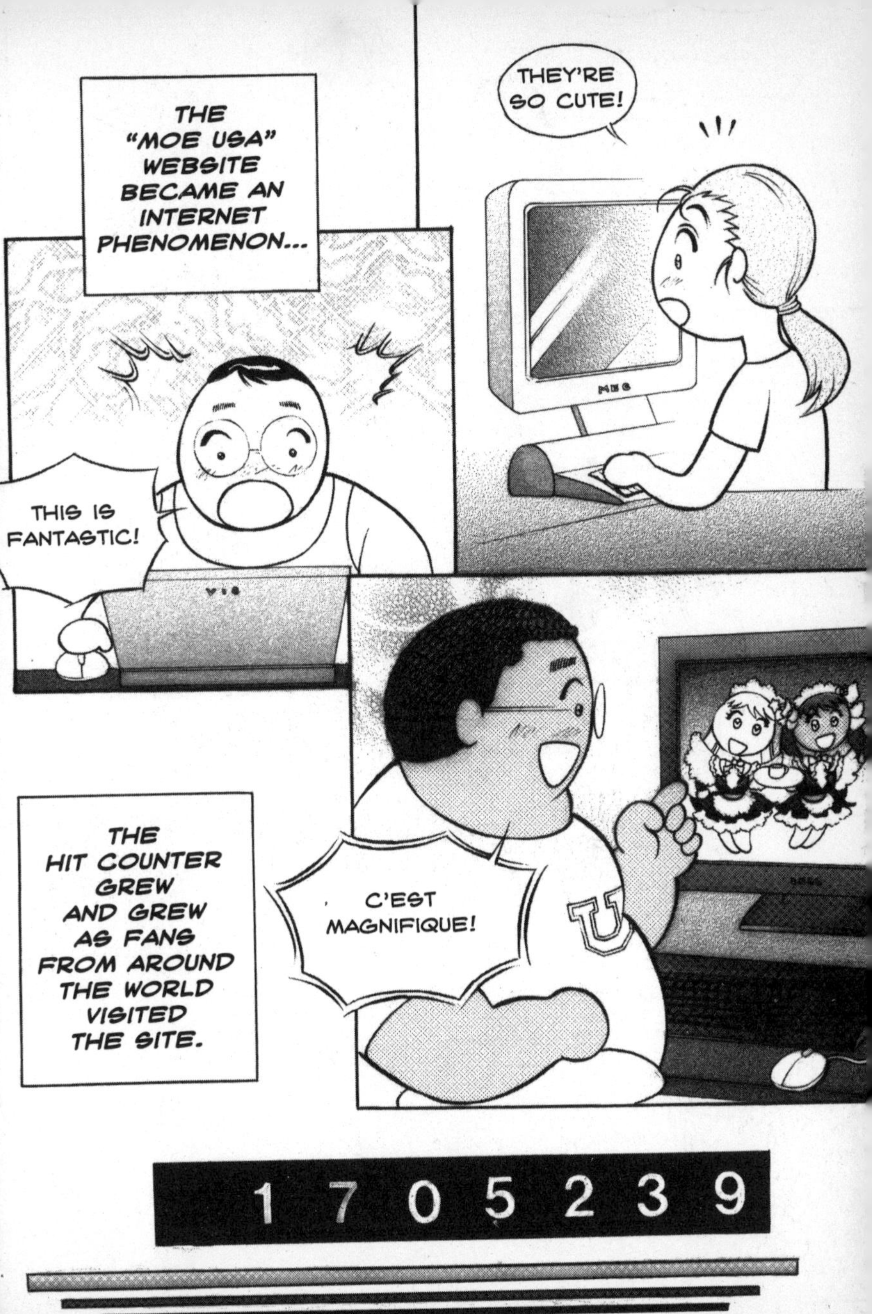
THE "MOE USA" WEBSITE BECAME AN INTERNET PHENOMENON...
THIS IS FANTASTIC!
THEY'RE SO CUTE!
THE HIT COUNTER GREW AND GREW AS FANS FROM AROUND THE WORLD VISITED THE SITE.
C'EST MAGNIFIQUE!
1705239

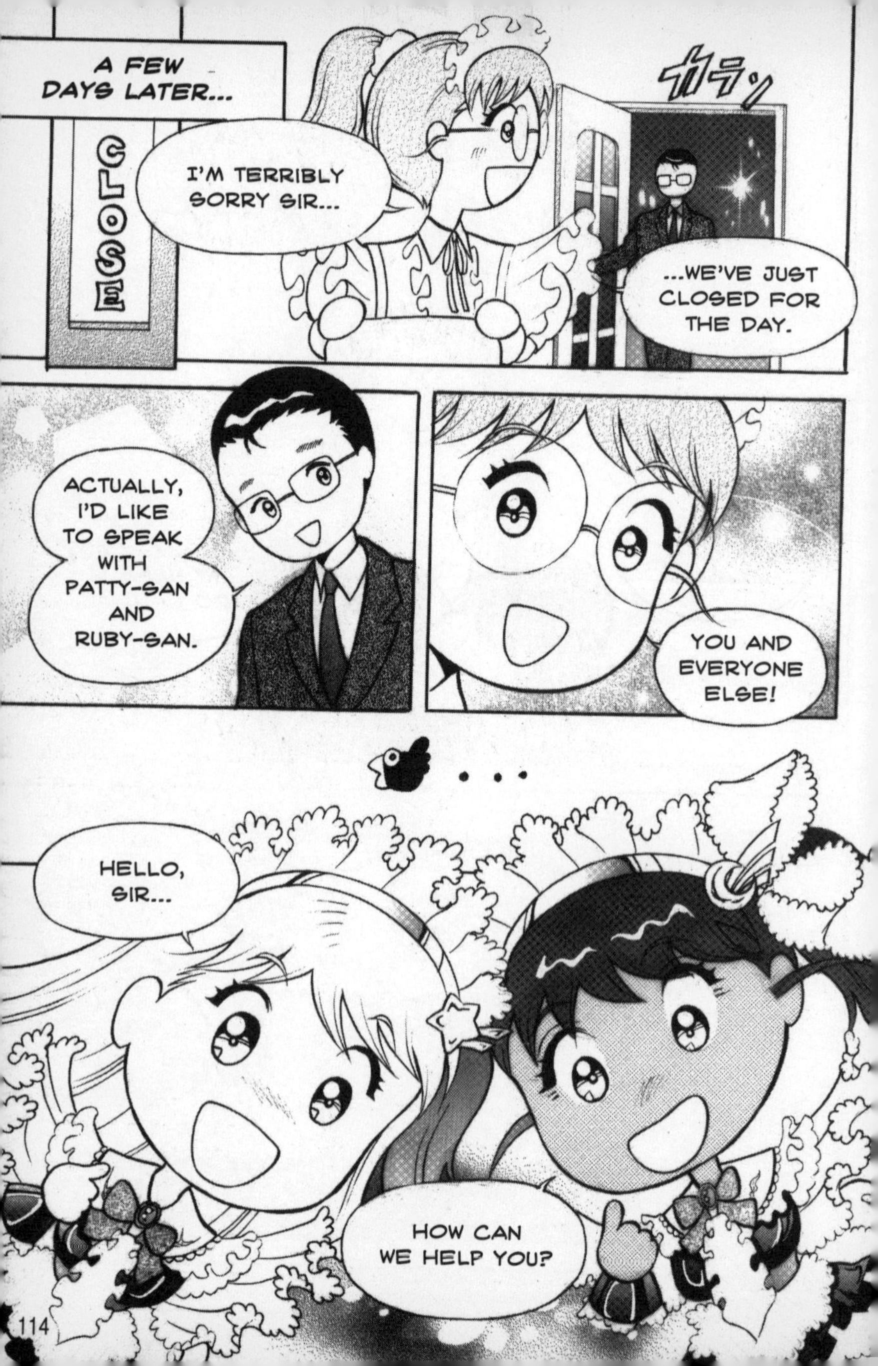
A FEW DAYS LATER...
カラン
I'M TERRIBLY SORRY SIR...
...WE'VE JUST CLOSED FOR THE DAY.
CLOSE
ACTUALLY, I'D LIKE TO SPEAK WITH PATTY-SAN AND RUBY-SAN.
YOU AND EVERYONE ELSE!
...
HELLO, SIR...
HOW CAN WE HELP YOU?

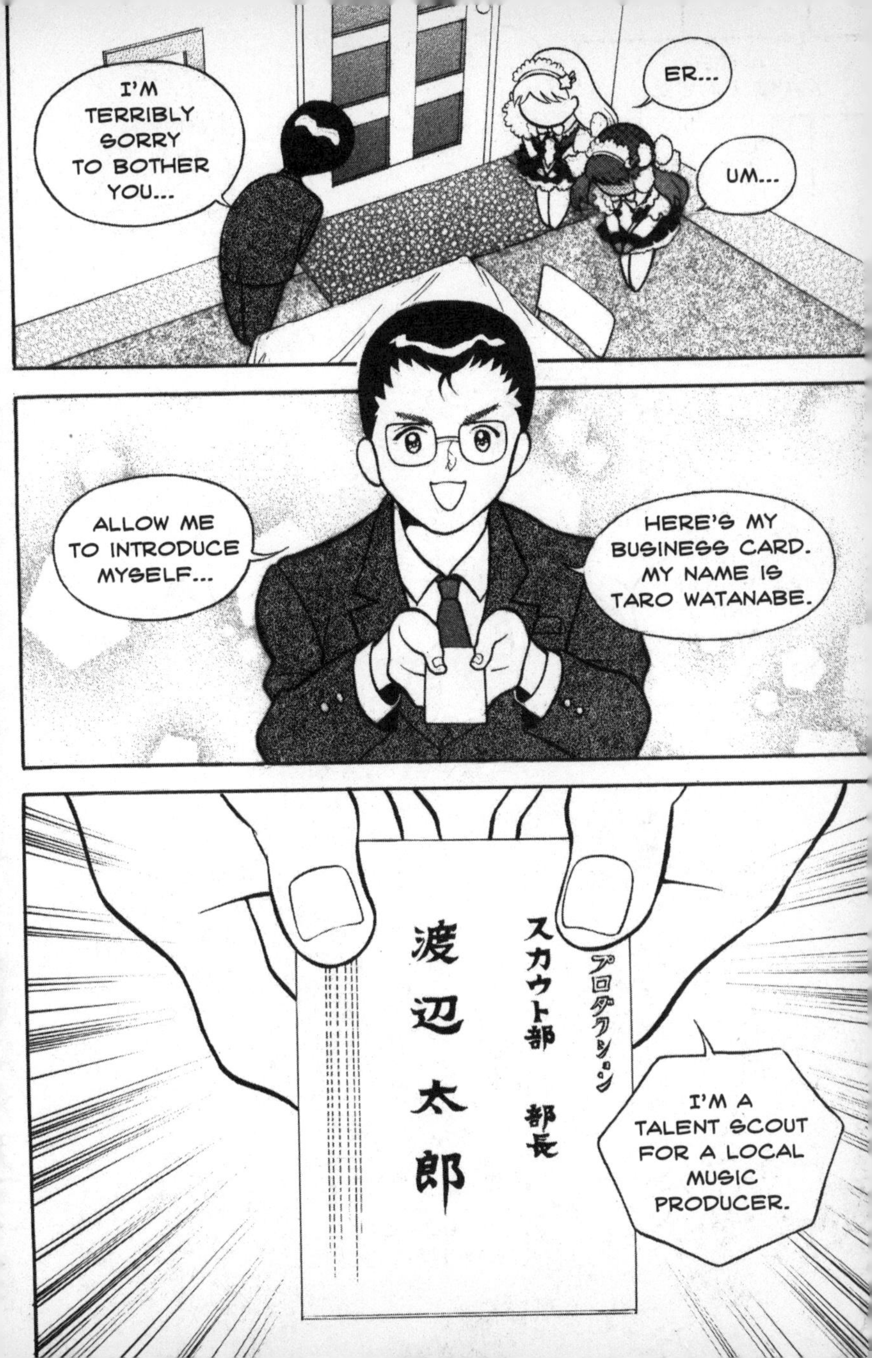
I'M TERRIBLY SORRY TO BOTHER YOU...
ER...
UM...
ALLOW ME TO INTRODUCE MYSELF...
HERE'S MY BUSINESS CARD. MY NAME IS TARO WATANABE.
プロダクション
スカウト部 部長
渡辺太郎
I'M A TALENT SCOUT FOR A LOCAL MUSIC PRODUCER.

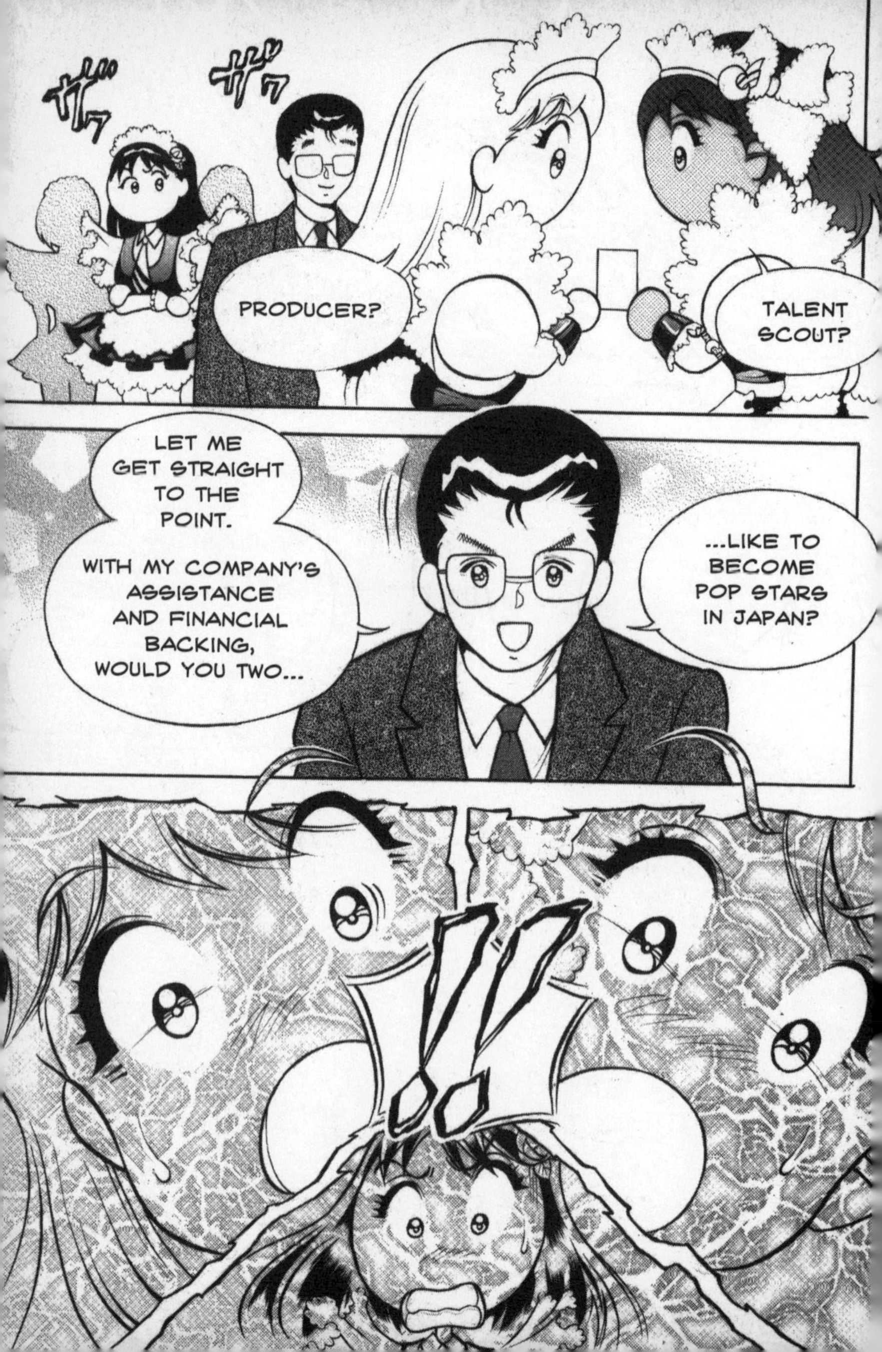
TALENT SCOUT?
PRODUCER?
LET ME GET STRAIGHT TO THE POINT.
WITH MY COMPANY'S ASSISTANCE AND FINANCIAL BACKING, WOULD YOU TWO...
...LIKE TO BECOME POP STARS IN JAPAN?

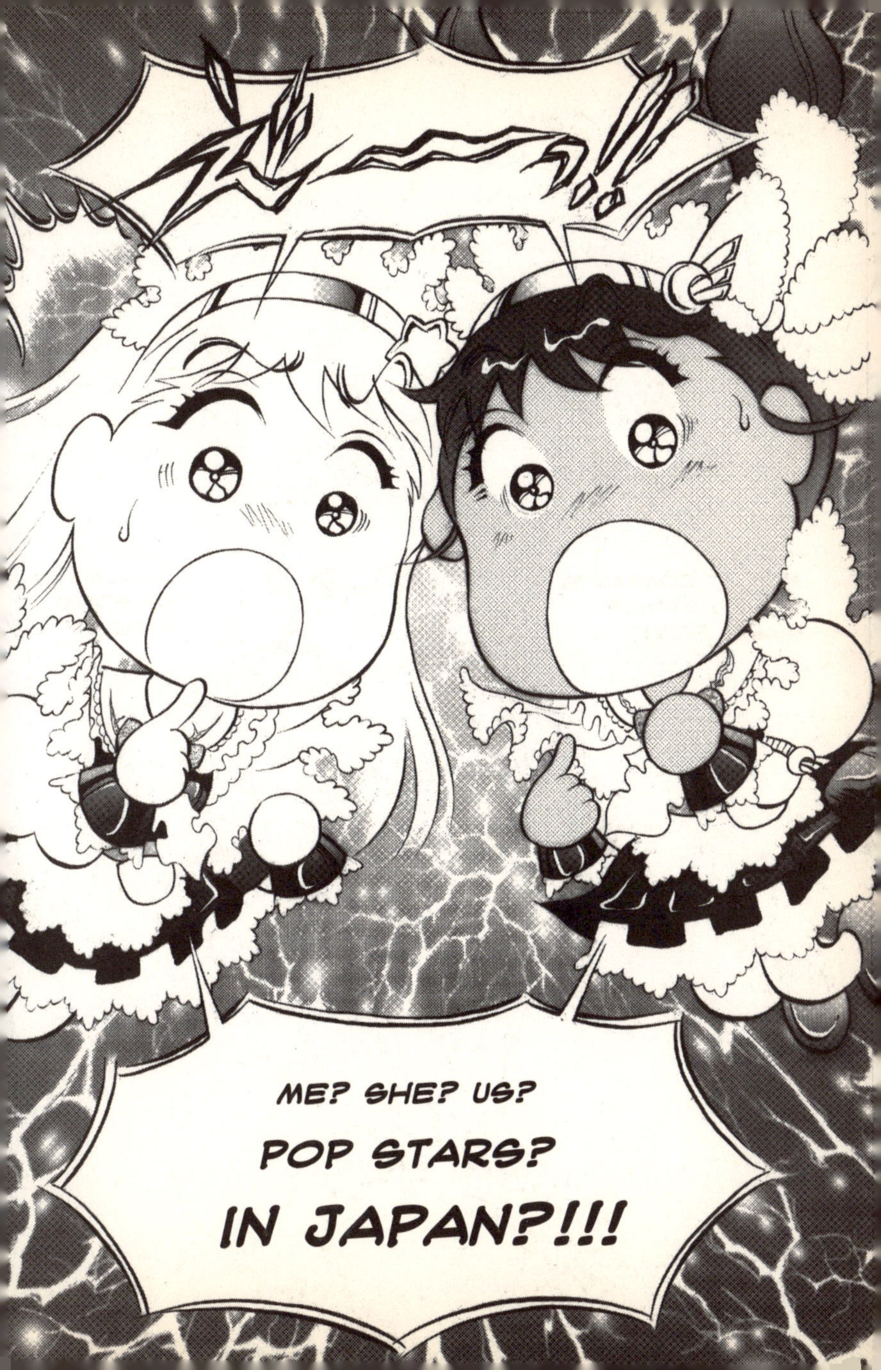
ME? SHE? US?
POP STARS?
IN JAPAN?!!!

# moe USA

## chapter four
## SCHOOL DAZE

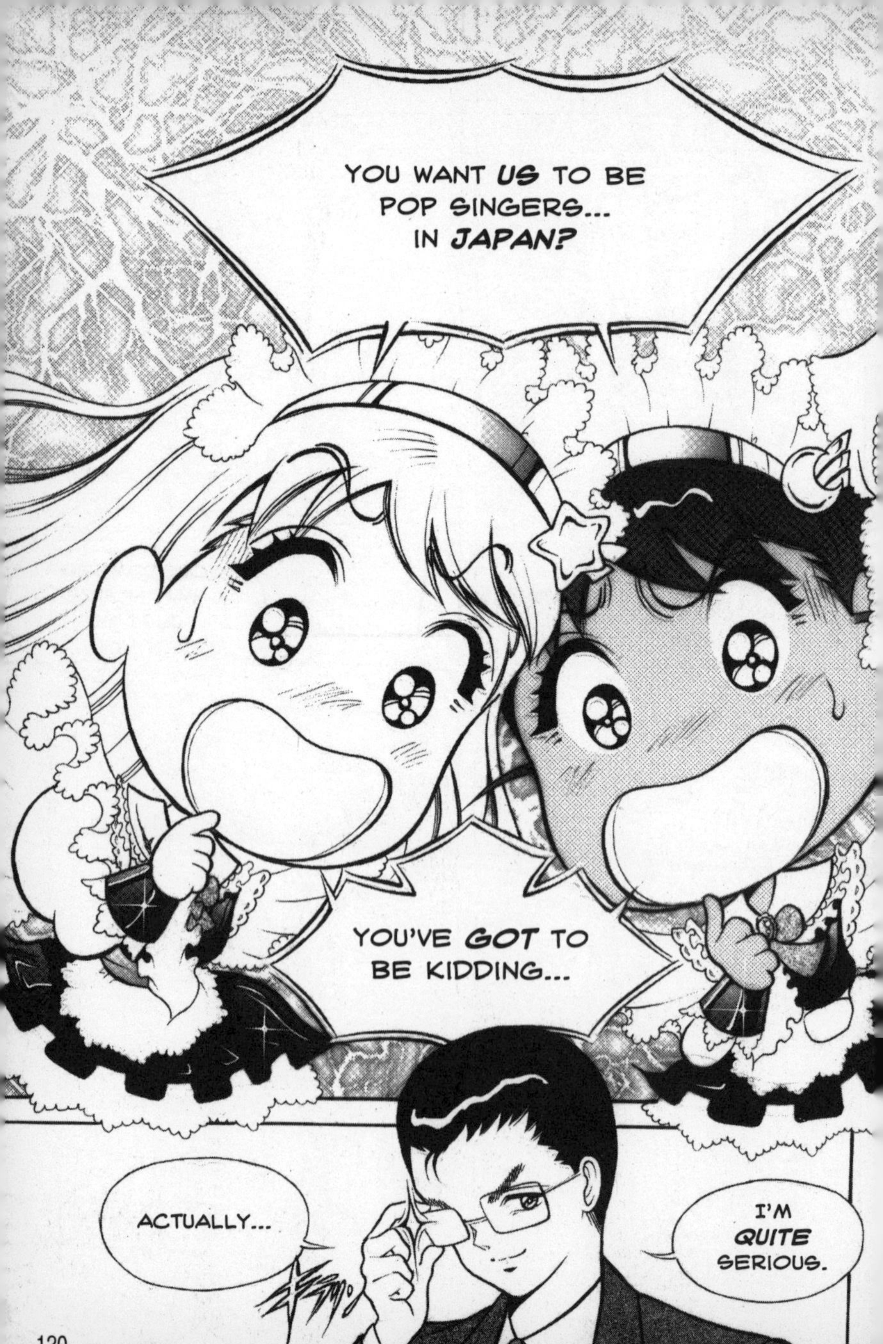
YOU WANT US TO BE POP SINGERS... IN JAPAN?
YOU'VE GOT TO BE KIDDING...
I'M QUITE SERIOUS.
ACTUALLY...

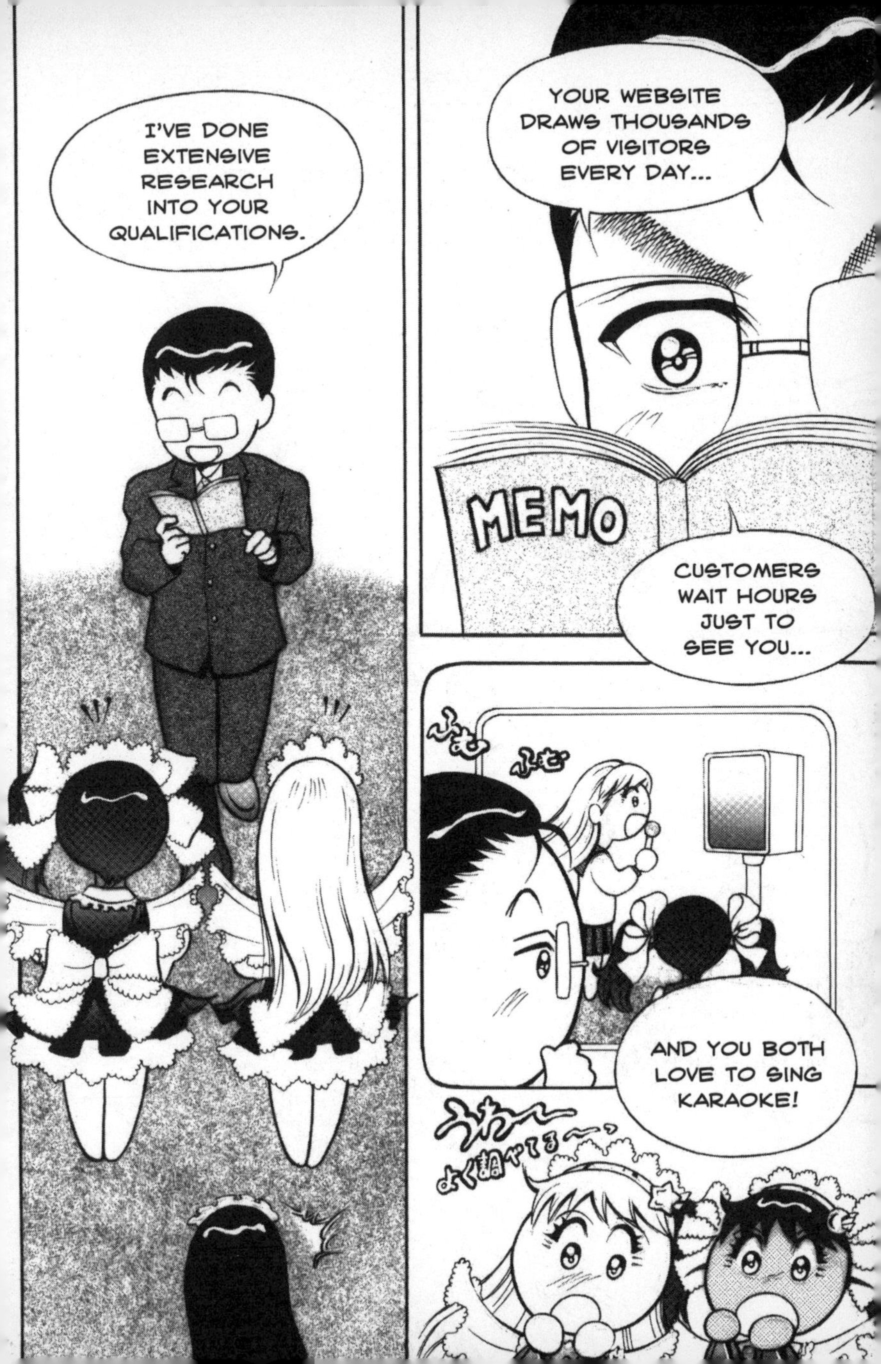
I'VE DONE EXTENSIVE RESEARCH INTO YOUR QUALIFICATIONS.
YOUR WEBSITE DRAWS THOUSANDS OF VISITORS EVERY DAY...
MEMO
CUSTOMERS WAIT HOURS JUST TO SEE YOU...
ふむ
ふむ
AND YOU BOTH LOVE TO SING KARAOKE!
うわ〜
よく調べてる〜っ

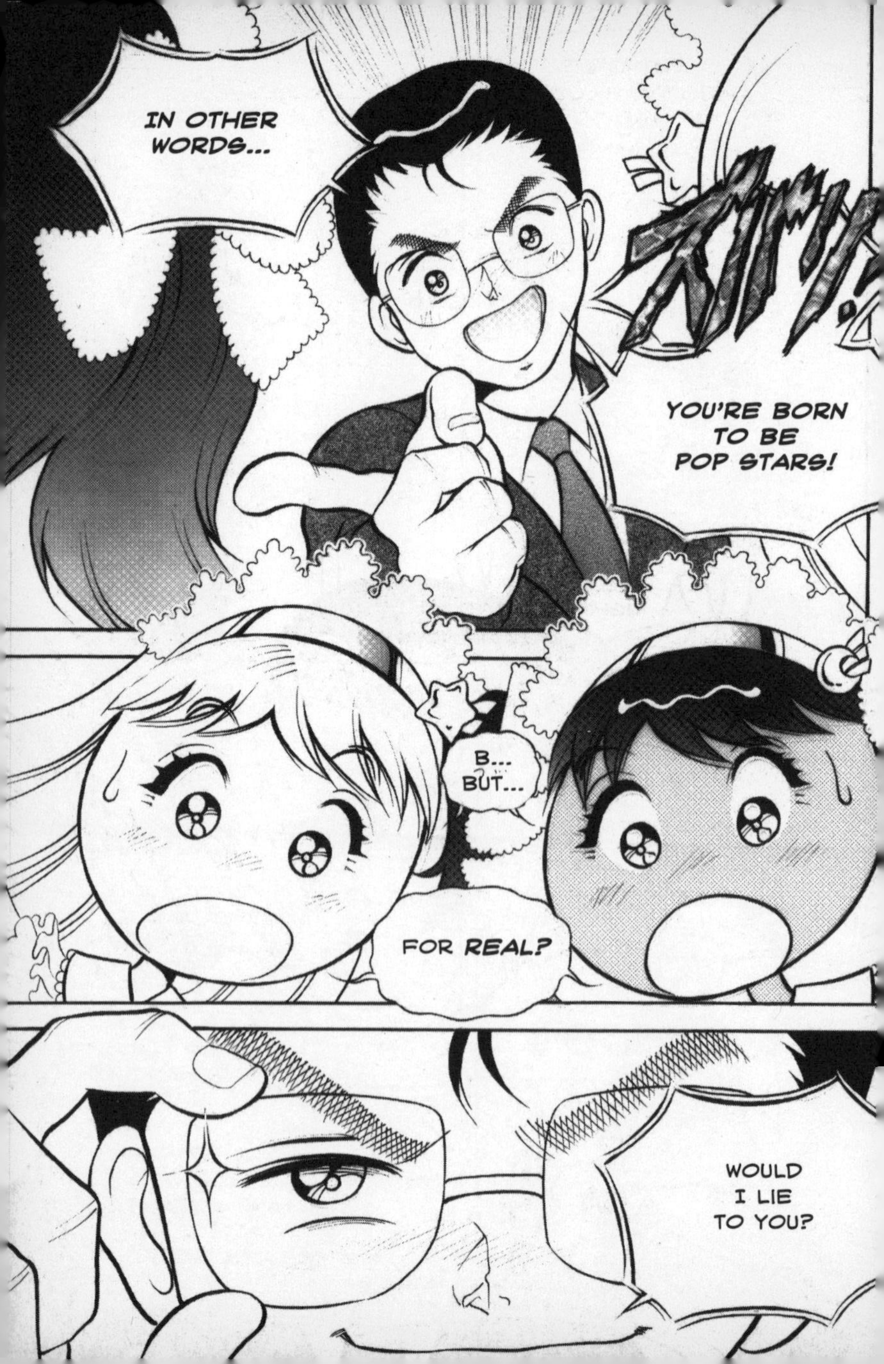
IN OTHER WORDS...
YOU'RE BORN TO BE POP STARS!
B... BUT...
FOR REAL?
WOULD I LIE TO YOU?

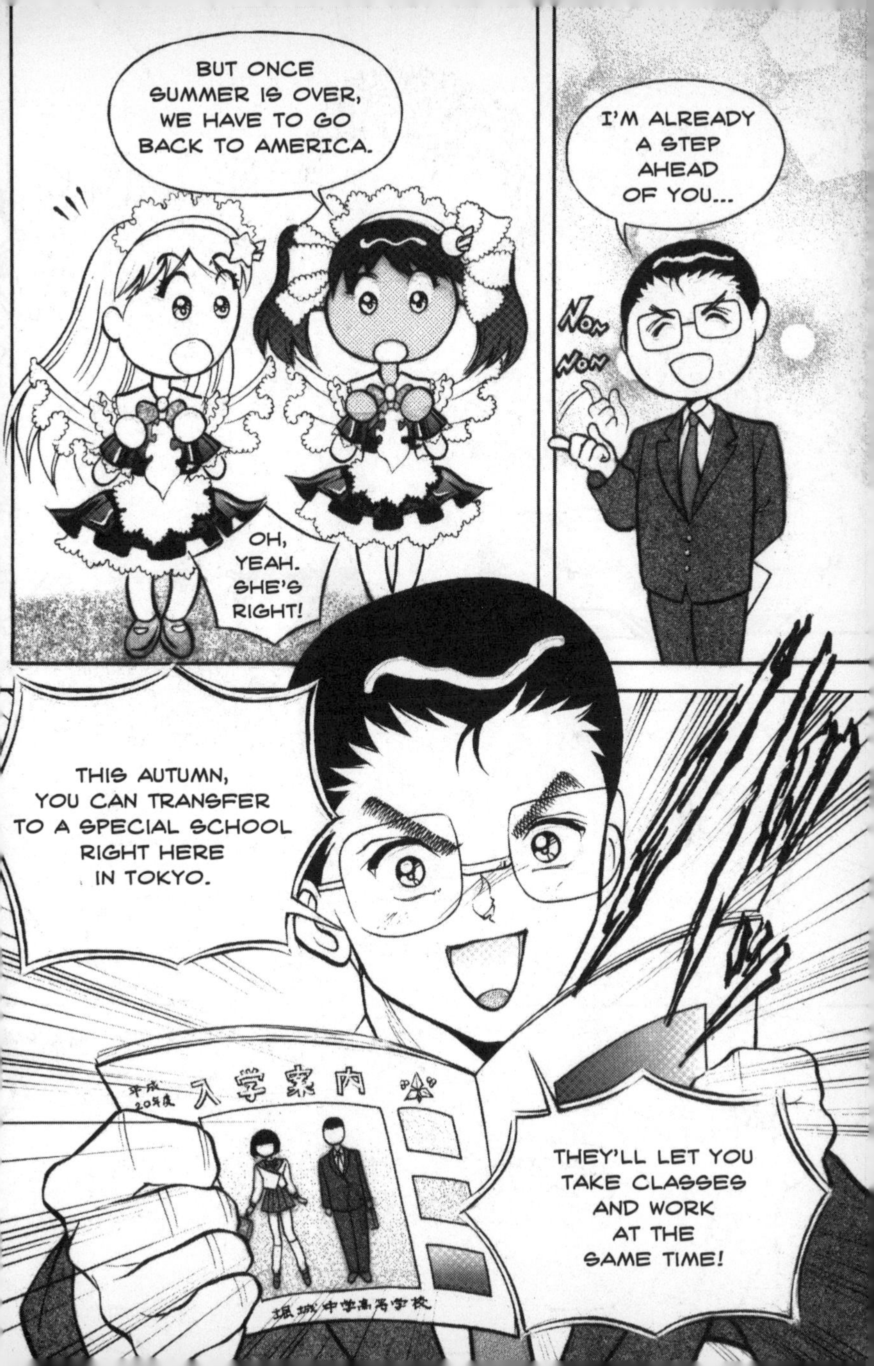
BUT ONCE SUMMER IS OVER, WE HAVE TO GO BACK TO AMERICA.
OH, YEAH. SHE'S RIGHT!
I'M ALREADY A STEP AHEAD OF YOU...
NON NON
THIS AUTUMN, YOU CAN TRANSFER TO A SPECIAL SCHOOL RIGHT HERE IN TOKYO.
入学案内
THEY'LL LET YOU TAKE CLASSES AND WORK AT THE SAME TIME!

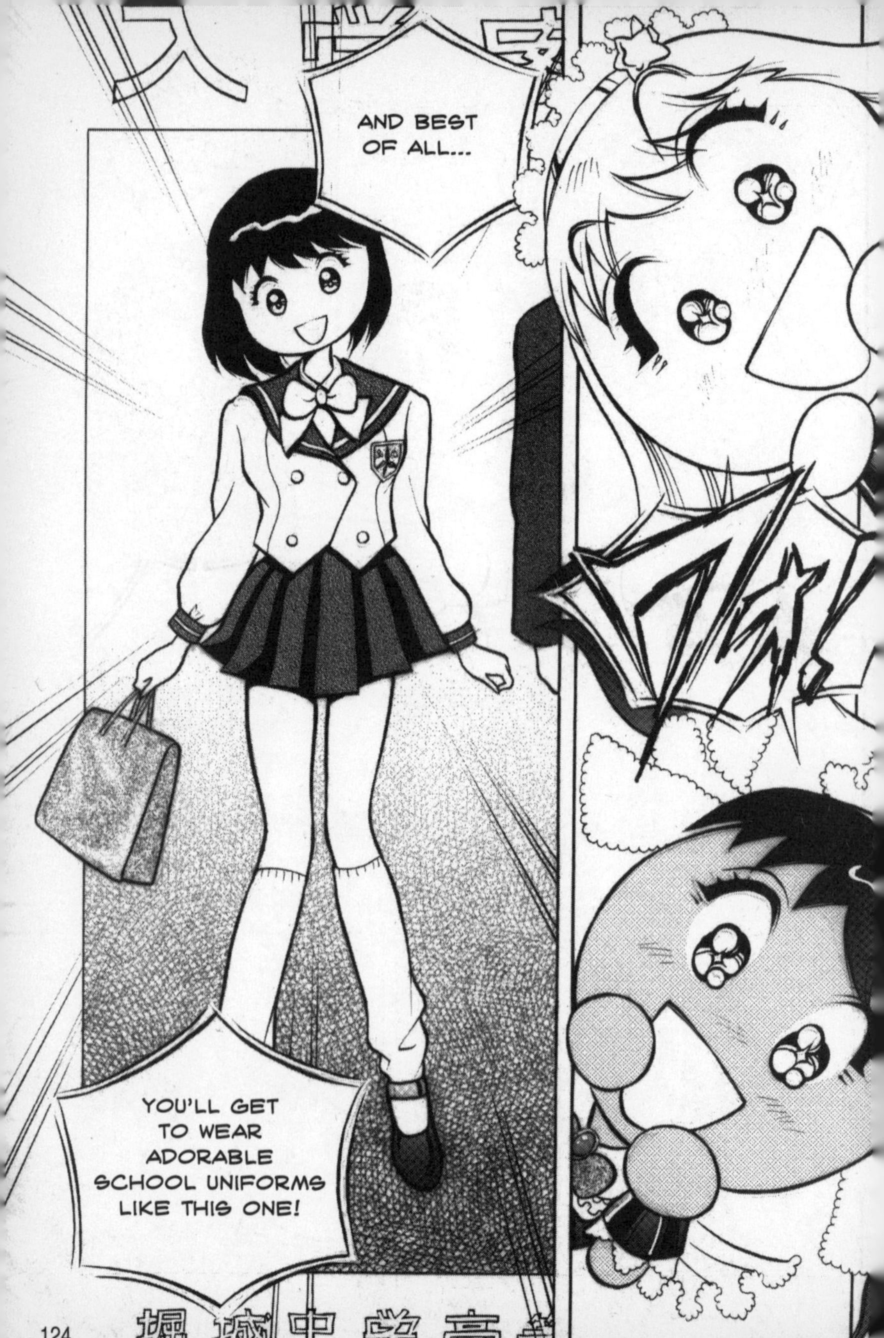
AND BEST OF ALL...
YOU'LL GET TO WEAR ADORABLE SCHOOL UNIFORMS LIKE THIS ONE!

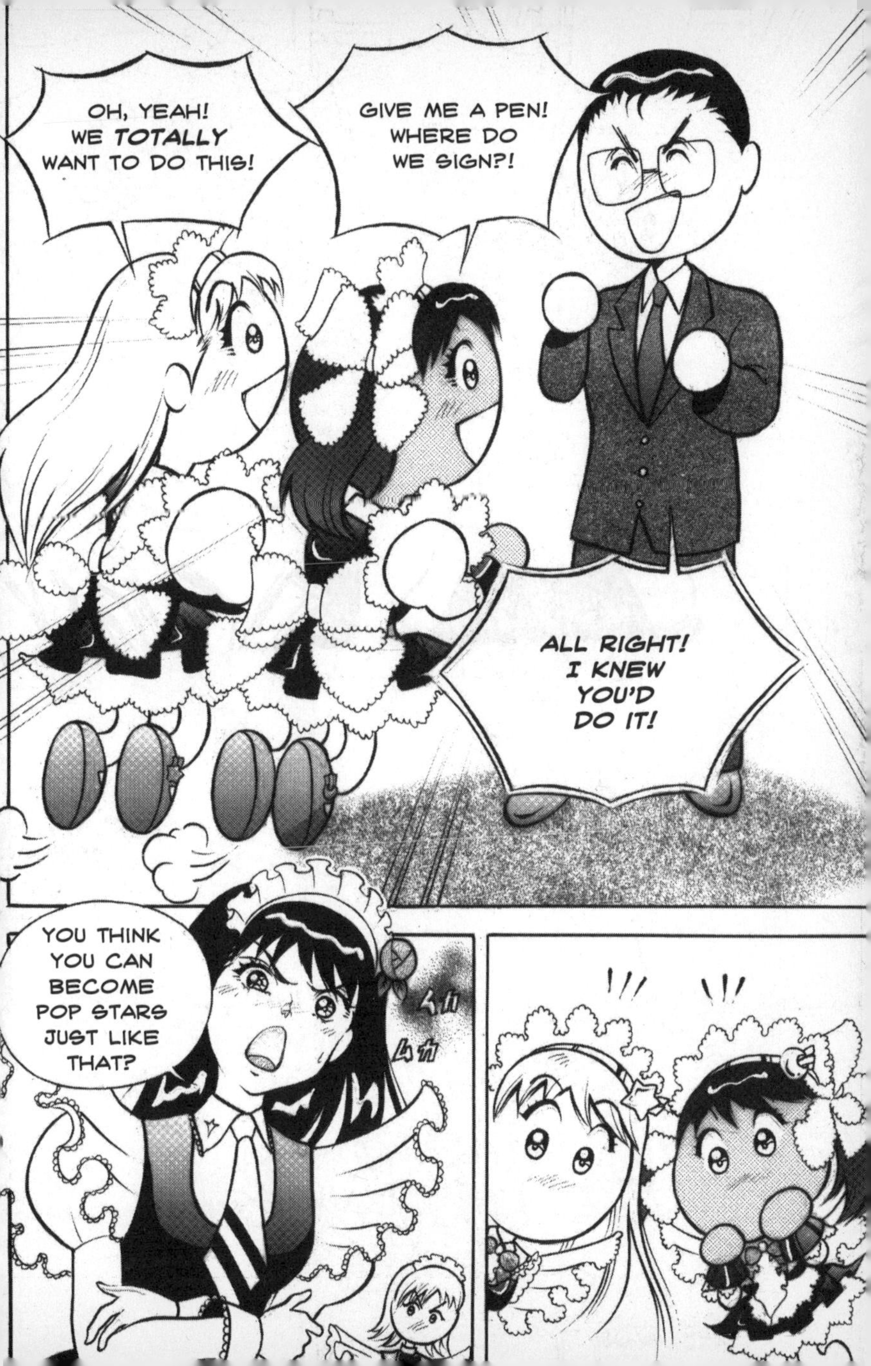

OH, YEAH! WE *TOTALLY* WANT TO DO THIS!
GIVE ME A PEN! WHERE DO WE SIGN?!
ALL RIGHT! I KNEW YOU'D DO IT!
YOU THINK YOU CAN BECOME POP STARS JUST LIKE THAT?
ムカ
ムカ
!!!
!!!

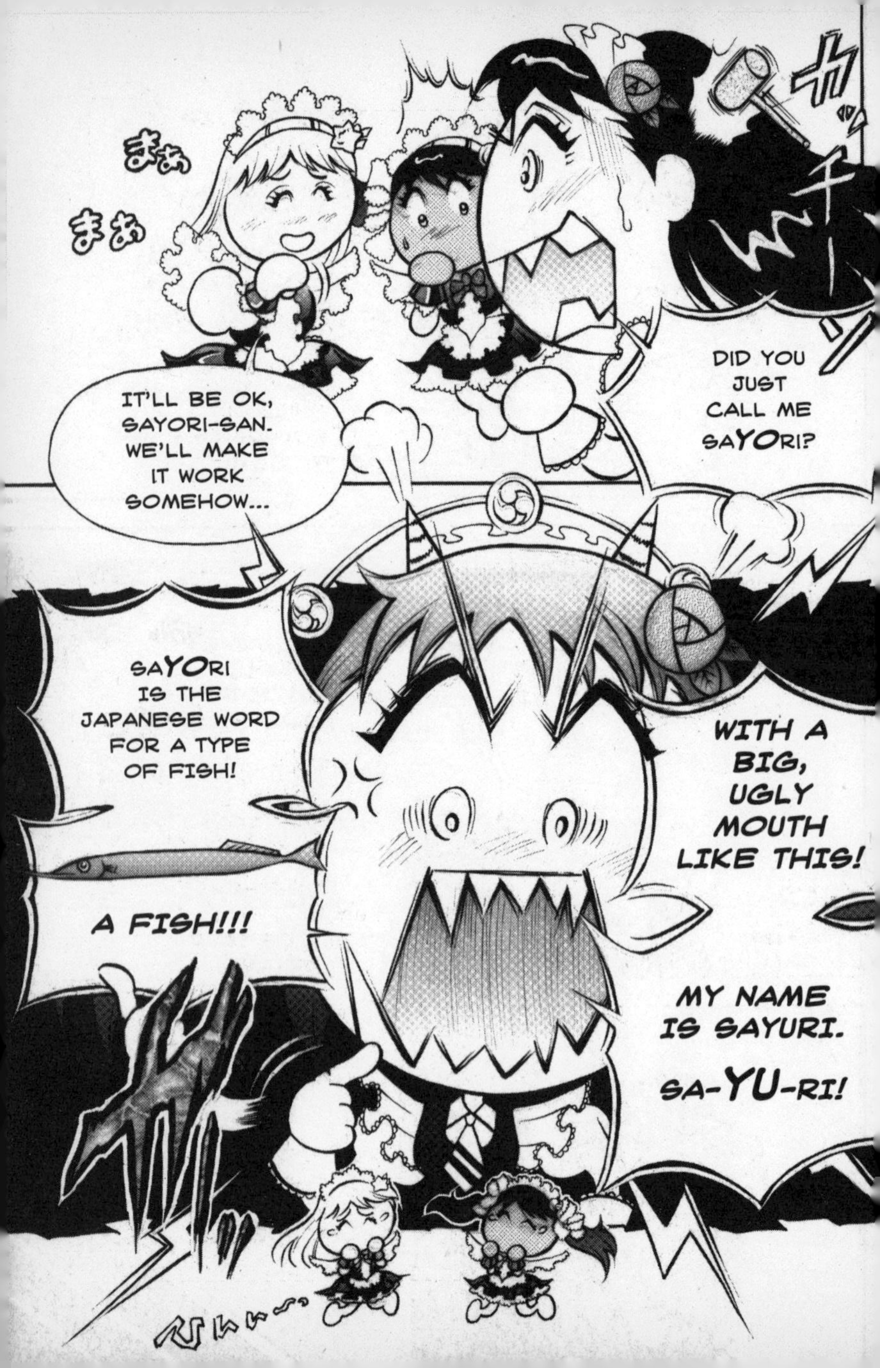

まぁ
まぁ
カッチーン
IT'LL BE OK, SAYORI-SAN. WE'LL MAKE IT WORK SOMEHOW...
DID YOU JUST CALL ME SaYOri?
SaYOri IS THE JAPANESE WORD FOR A TYPE OF FISH!
A FISH!!!
WITH A BIG, UGLY MOUTH LIKE THIS!
MY NAME IS SAYURI.
SA-YU-RI!
ぺしゃ〜

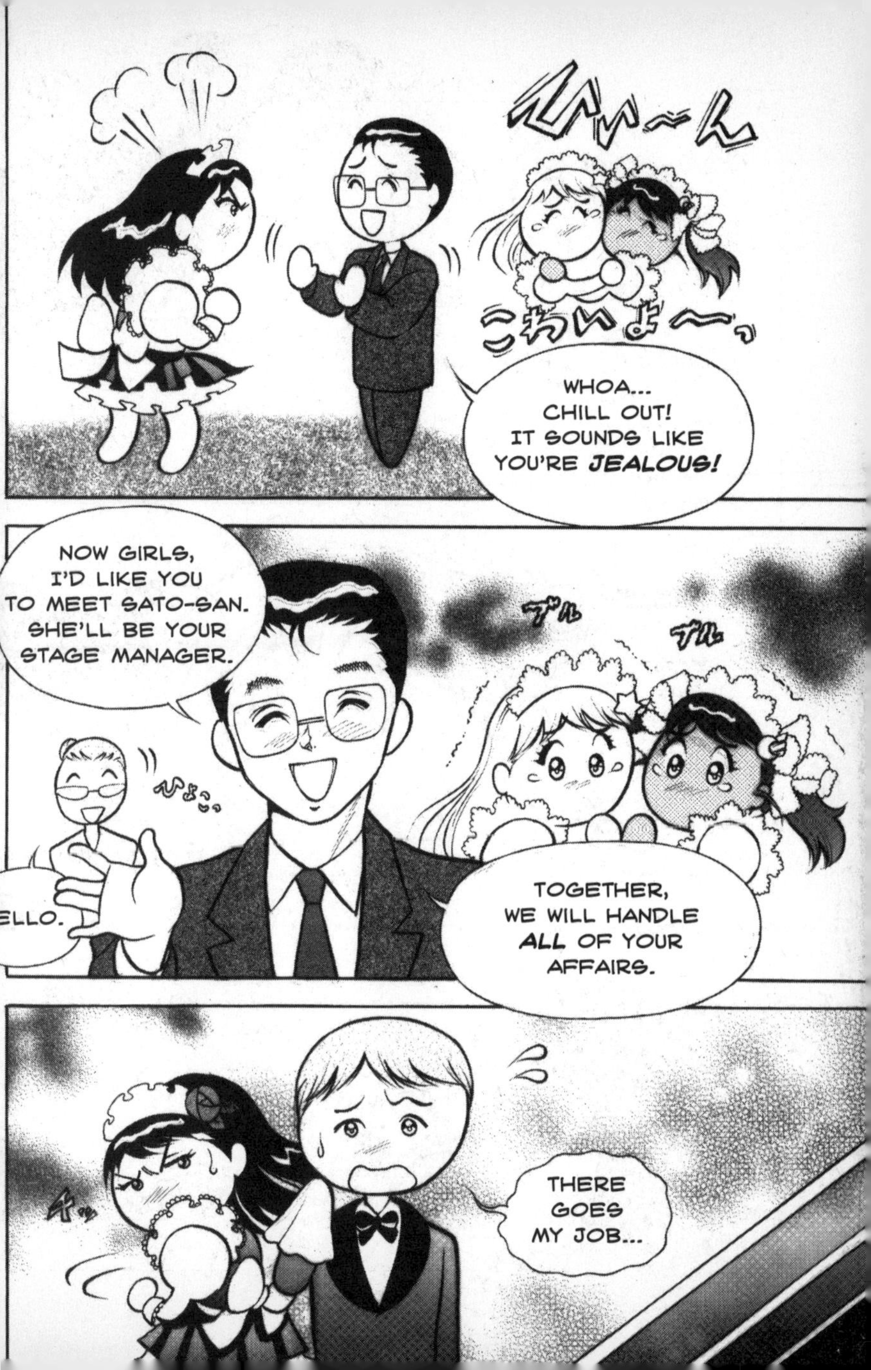
こわいよ〜っ
WHOA... CHILL OUT! IT SOUNDS LIKE YOU'RE ***JEALOUS!***
ブル
ブル
NOW GIRLS, I'D LIKE YOU TO MEET SATO-SAN. SHE'LL BE YOUR STAGE MANAGER.
ぴょこっ
ELLO.
TOGETHER, WE WILL HANDLE ***ALL*** OF YOUR AFFAIRS.
THERE GOES MY JOB...

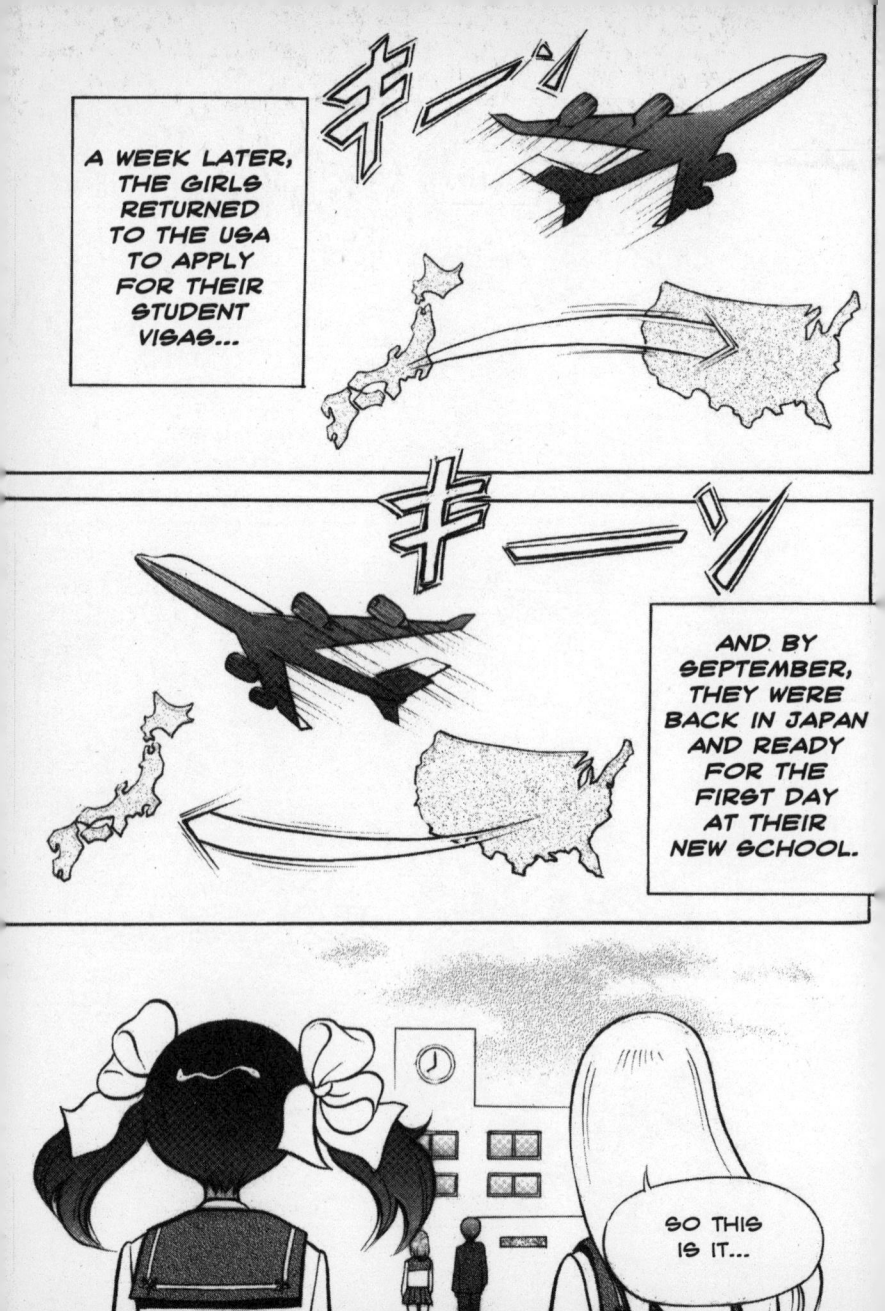

A WEEK LATER, THE GIRLS RETURNED TO THE USA TO APPLY FOR THEIR STUDENT VISAS...

AND BY SEPTEMBER, THEY WERE BACK IN JAPAN AND READY FOR THE FIRST DAY AT THEIR NEW SCHOOL.

SO THIS IS IT...

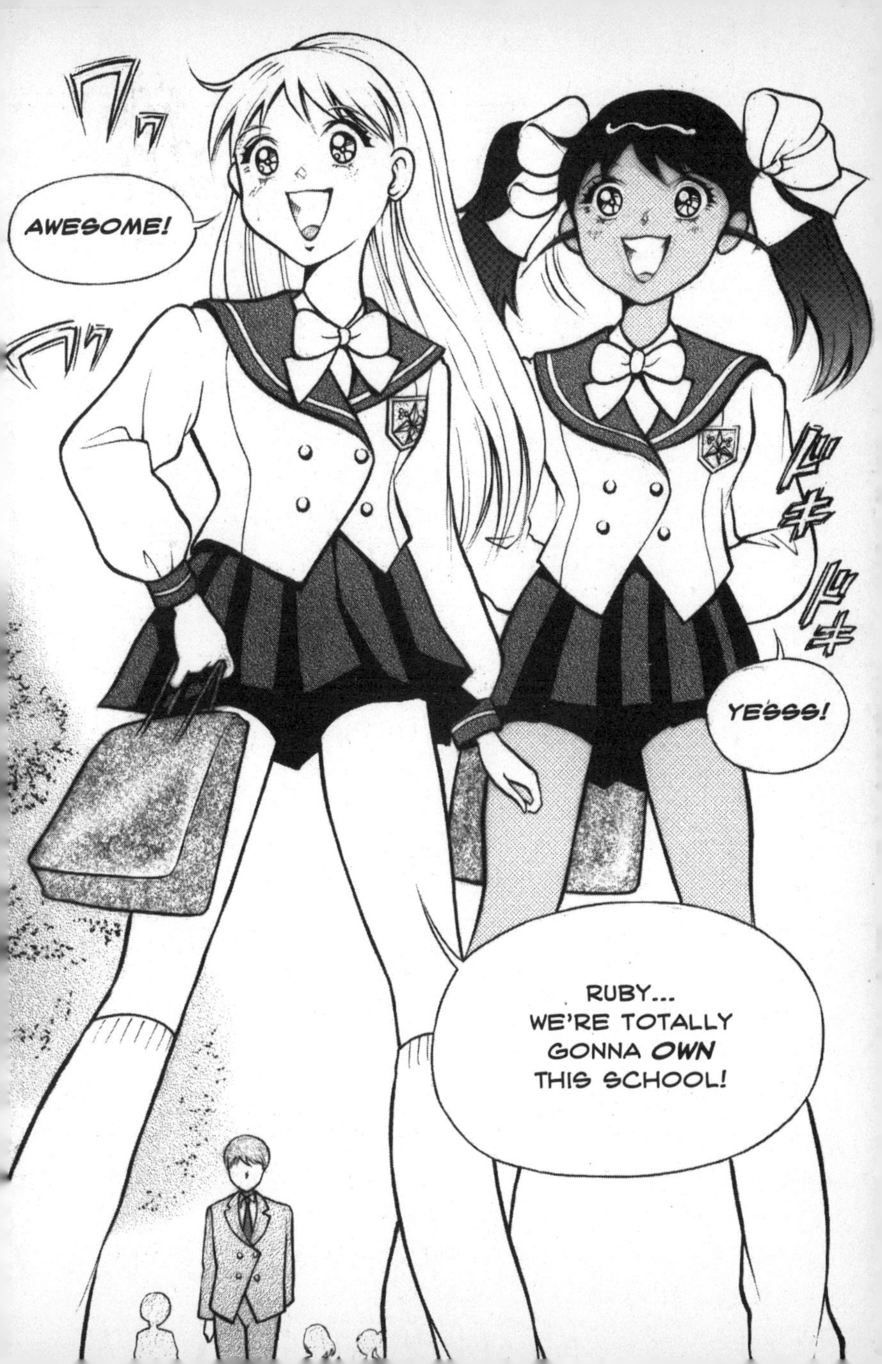
ワク
ワク
AWESOME!
ドキドキ
YESSS!
RUBY... WE'RE TOTALLY GONNA OWN THIS SCHOOL!

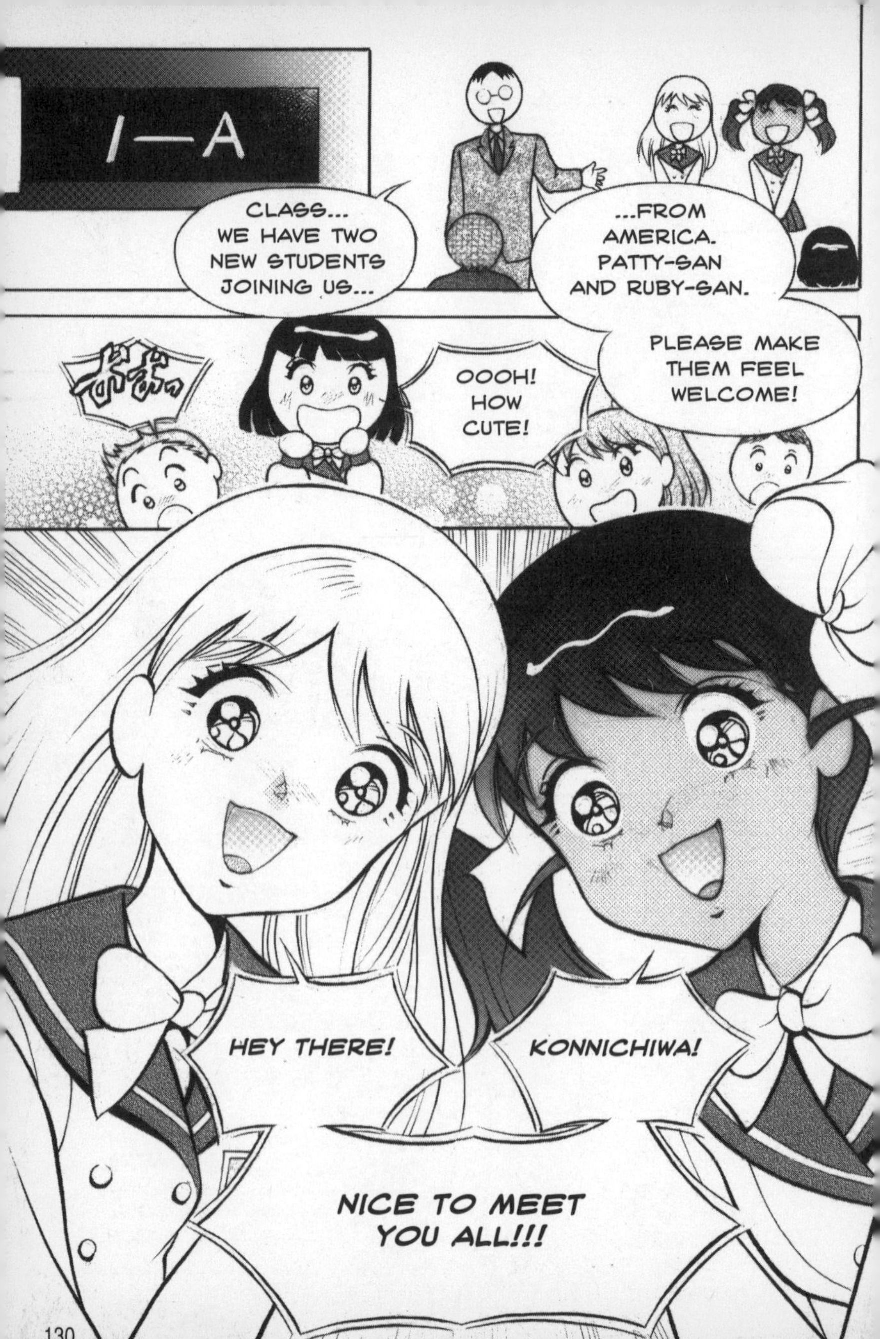
1—A
CLASS... WE HAVE TWO NEW STUDENTS JOINING US...
...FROM AMERICA. PATTY-SAN AND RUBY-SAN.
PLEASE MAKE THEM FEEL WELCOME!
OOOH! HOW CUTE!
HEY THERE!
KONNICHIWA!
NICE TO MEET YOU ALL!!!

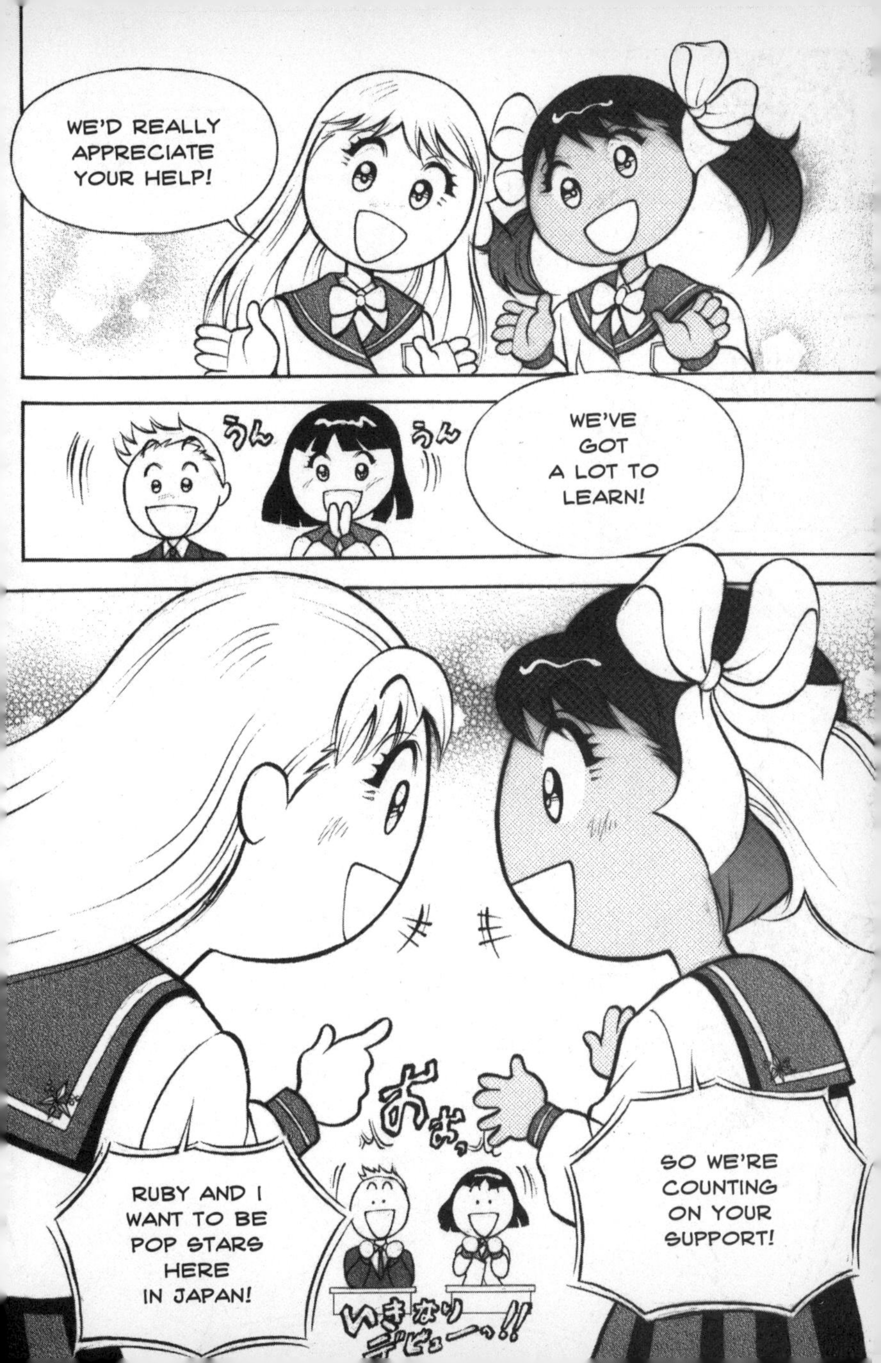
WE'D REALLY APPRECIATE YOUR HELP!
うん
うん
WE'VE GOT A LOT TO LEARN!
RUBY AND I WANT TO BE POP STARS HERE IN JAPAN!
SO WE'RE COUNTING ON YOUR SUPPORT!
おおっ
いきなりデビューっ!!

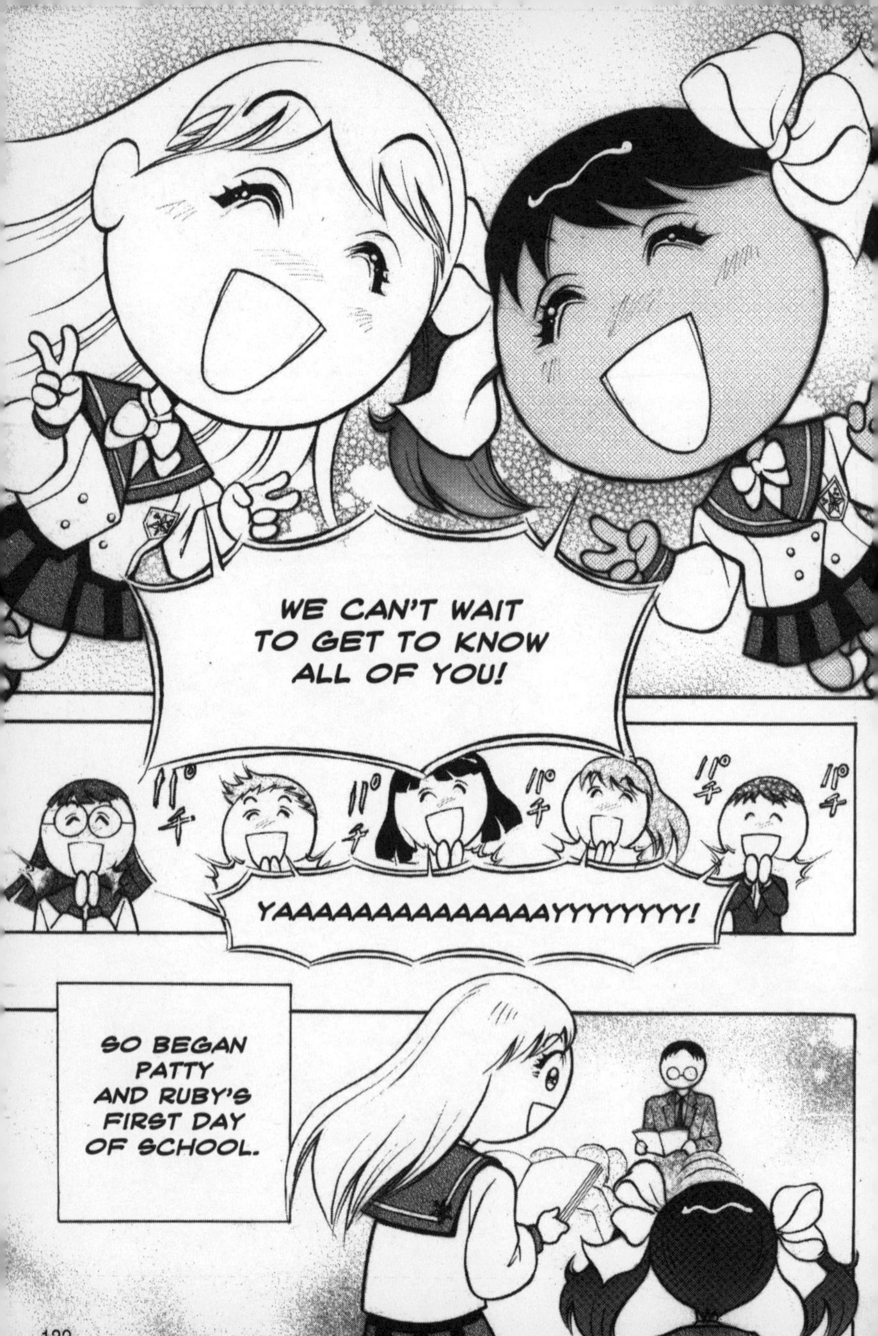
WE CAN'T WAIT TO GET TO KNOW ALL OF YOU!
パチ パチ パチ パチ パチ
YAAAAAAAAAAAAAAAYYYYYYYY!
SO BEGAN PATTY AND RUBY'S FIRST DAY OF SCHOOL.

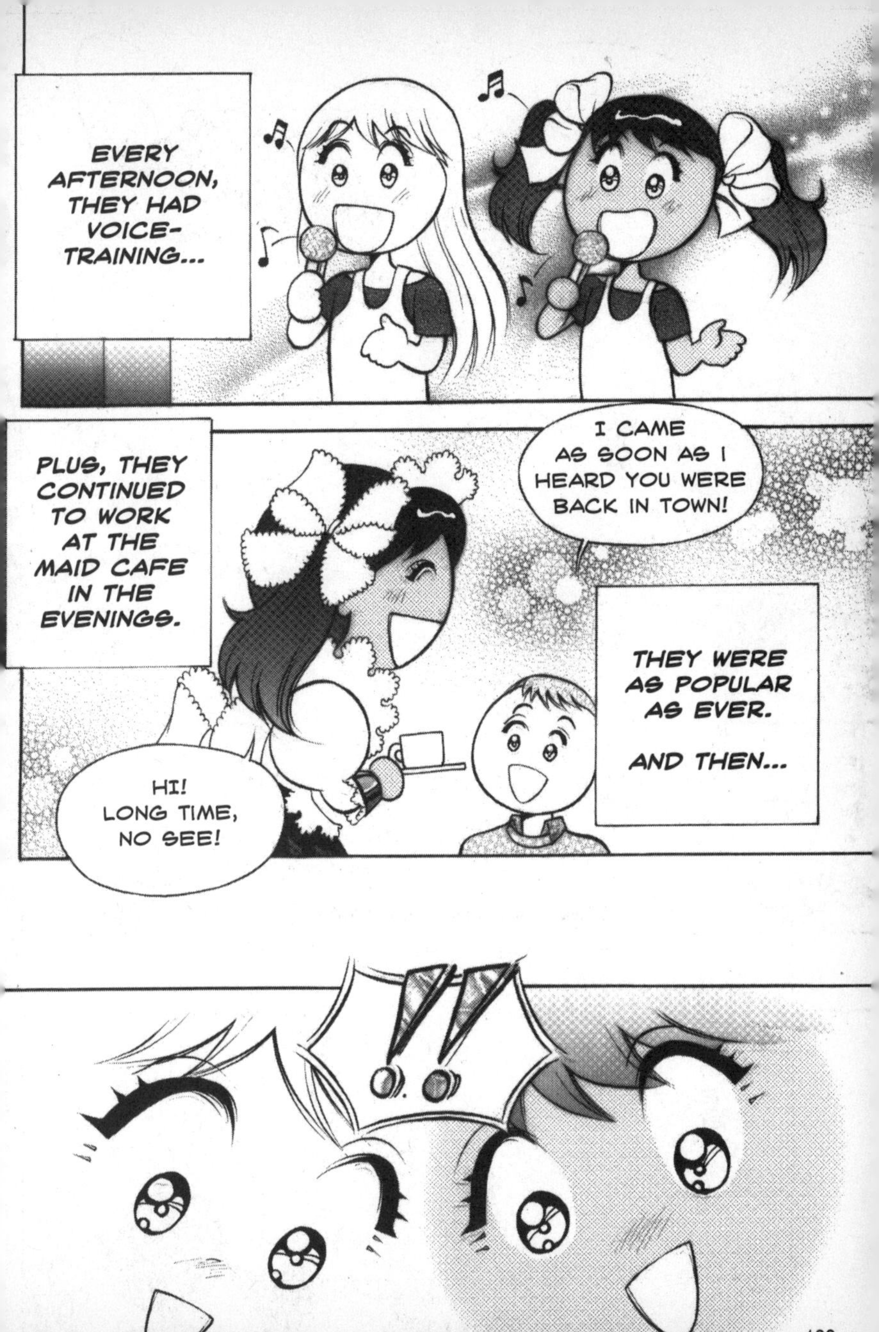
EVERY AFTERNOON, THEY HAD VOICE-TRAINING...
PLUS, THEY CONTINUED TO WORK AT THE MAID CAFE IN THE EVENINGS.
HI! LONG TIME, NO SEE!
I CAME AS SOON AS I HEARD YOU WERE BACK IN TOWN!
THEY WERE AS POPULAR AS EVER.
AND THEN...
!!

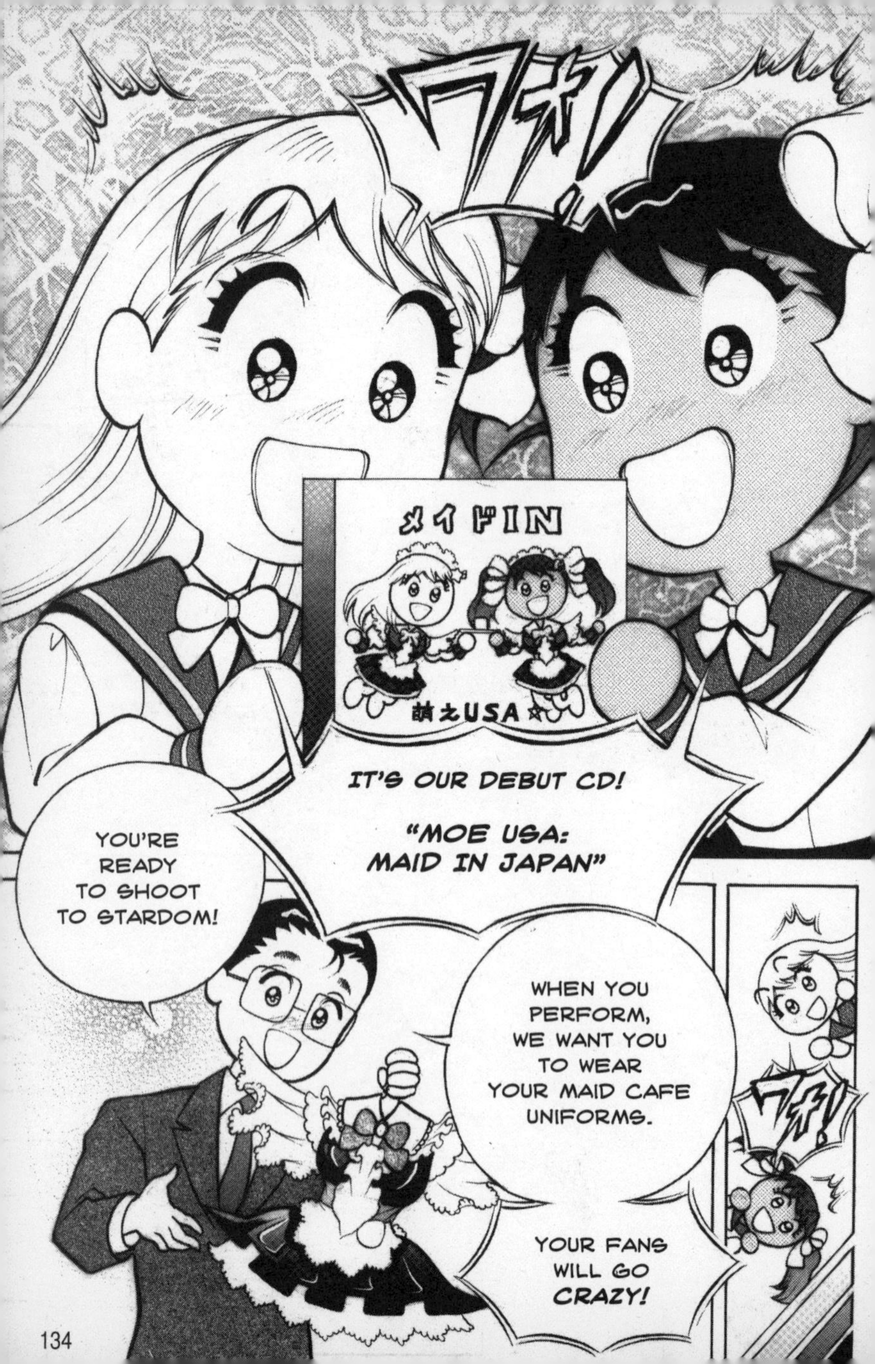
ワオ!
メイドIN
萌えUSA☆
IT'S OUR DEBUT CD!
"MOE USA: MAID IN JAPAN"
ワオ!
YOU'RE READY TO SHOOT TO STARDOM!
WHEN YOU PERFORM, WE WANT YOU TO WEAR YOUR MAID CAFE UNIFORMS.
YOUR FANS WILL GO CRAZY!

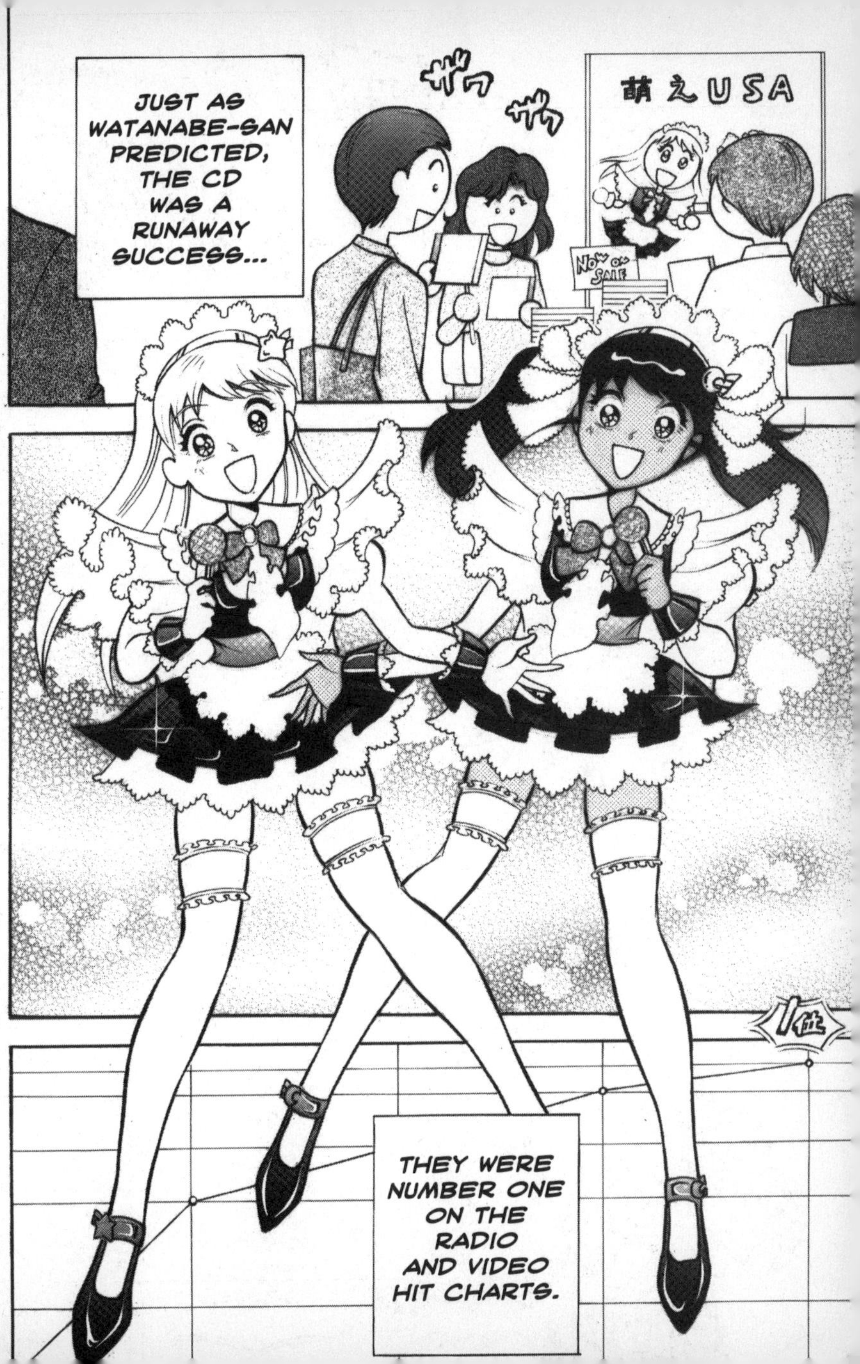
JUST AS WATANABE-SAN PREDICTED, THE CD WAS A RUNAWAY SUCCESS...
萌えUSA
NOW ON SALE
1位
THEY WERE NUMBER ONE ON THE RADIO AND VIDEO HIT CHARTS.

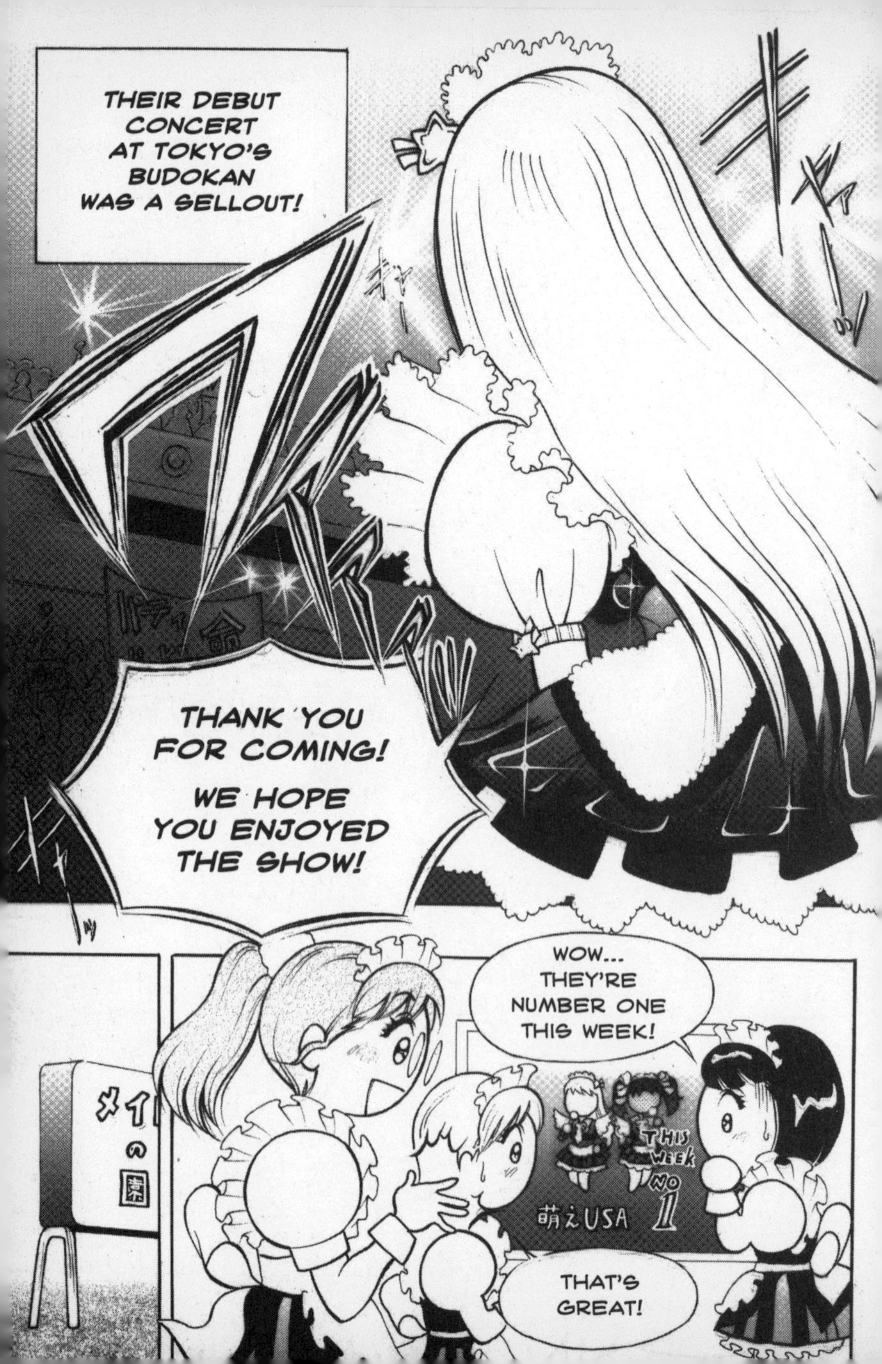
THEIR DEBUT CONCERT AT TOKYO'S BUDOKAN WAS A SELLOUT!
THANK YOU FOR COMING!
WE HOPE YOU ENJOYED THE SHOW!
WOW... THEY'RE NUMBER ONE THIS WEEK!
THIS WEEK NO 1
萌えUSA
THAT'S GREAT!

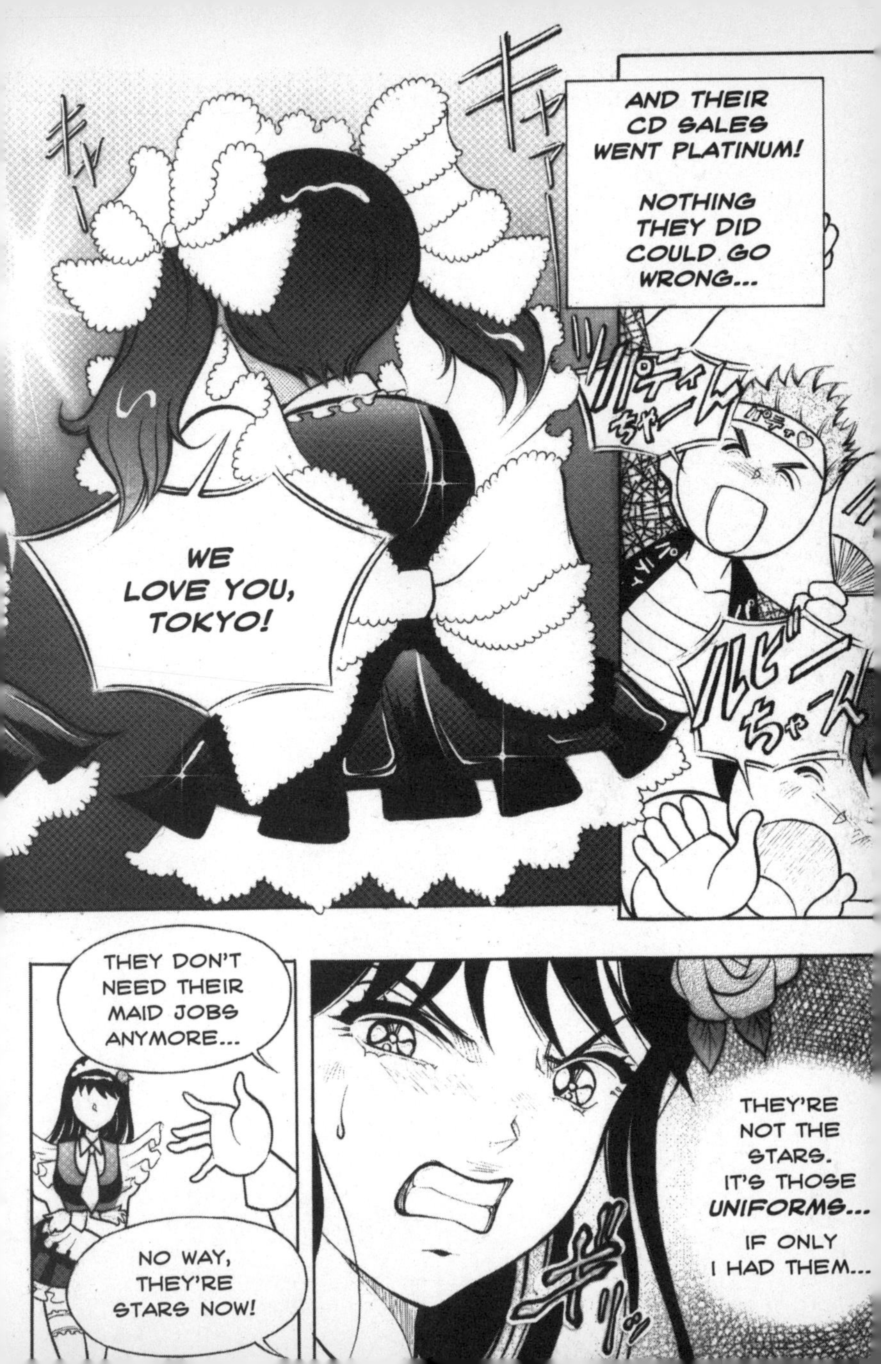
AND THEIR CD SALES WENT PLATINUM!
NOTHING THEY DID COULD GO WRONG...
パティちゃーん
ルビーちゃーん
WE LOVE YOU, TOKYO!
THEY DON'T NEED THEIR MAID JOBS ANYMORE...
NO WAY, THEY'RE STARS NOW!
THEY'RE NOT THE STARS. IT'S THOSE *UNIFORMS*...
IF ONLY I HAD THEM...

HAH! THAT'S IT!

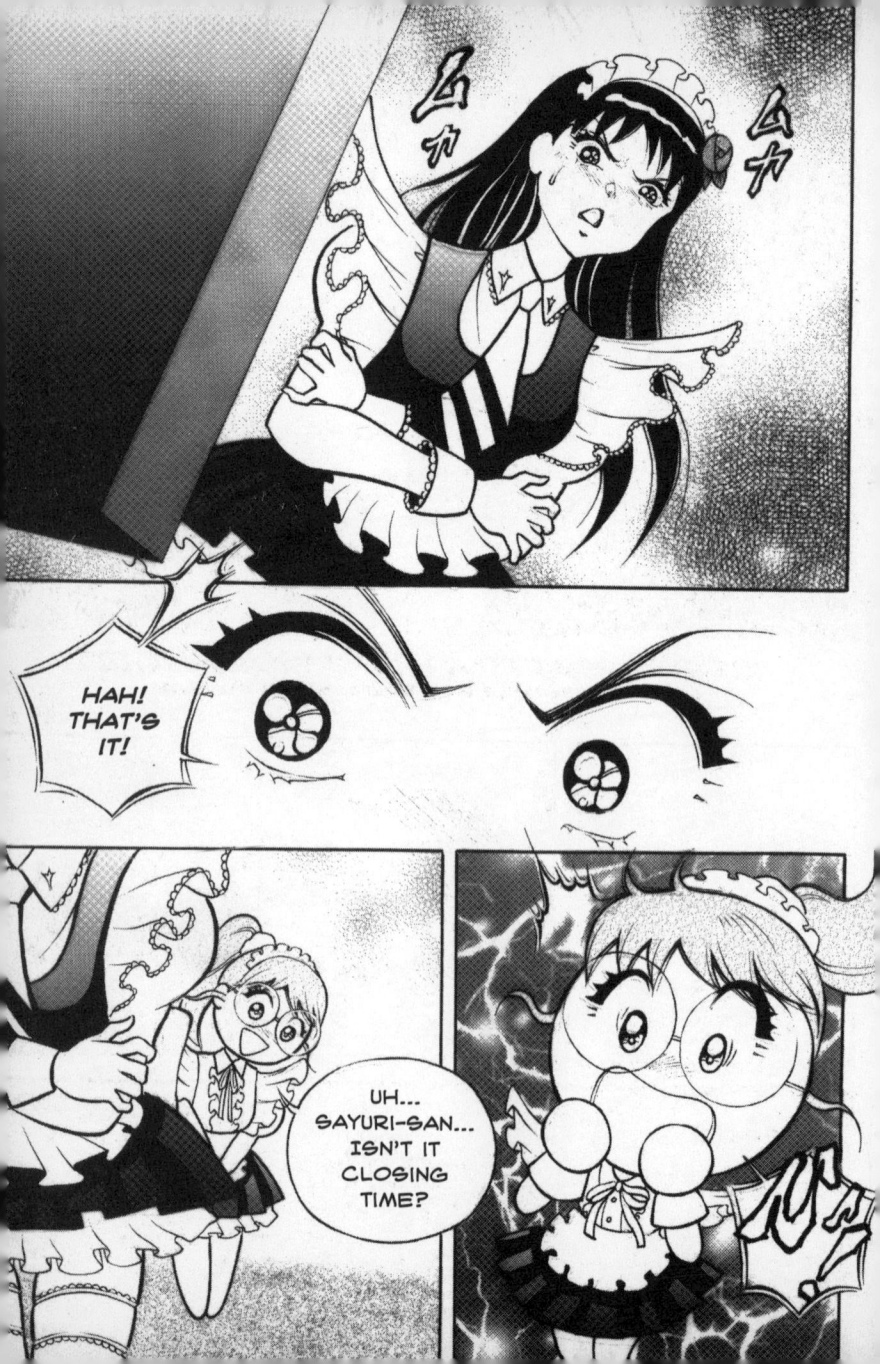

UH... SAYURI-SAN... ISN'T IT CLOSING TIME?

メイドの園

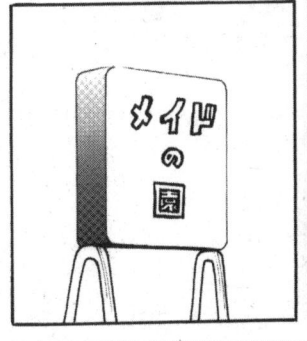

"WE'VE BEEN SO BUSY SINGING LATELY..."

"WE'D LIKE TO TAKE SOME TIME OFF FROM THE CAFE."

PATTY-CHAN... RUBY-CHAN...

Y... YE... YES?

I'VE GOT A SMALL FAVOR TO ASK...

WOULD YOU MIND...

WELL, YOU SEE...

WHA... WHAT?

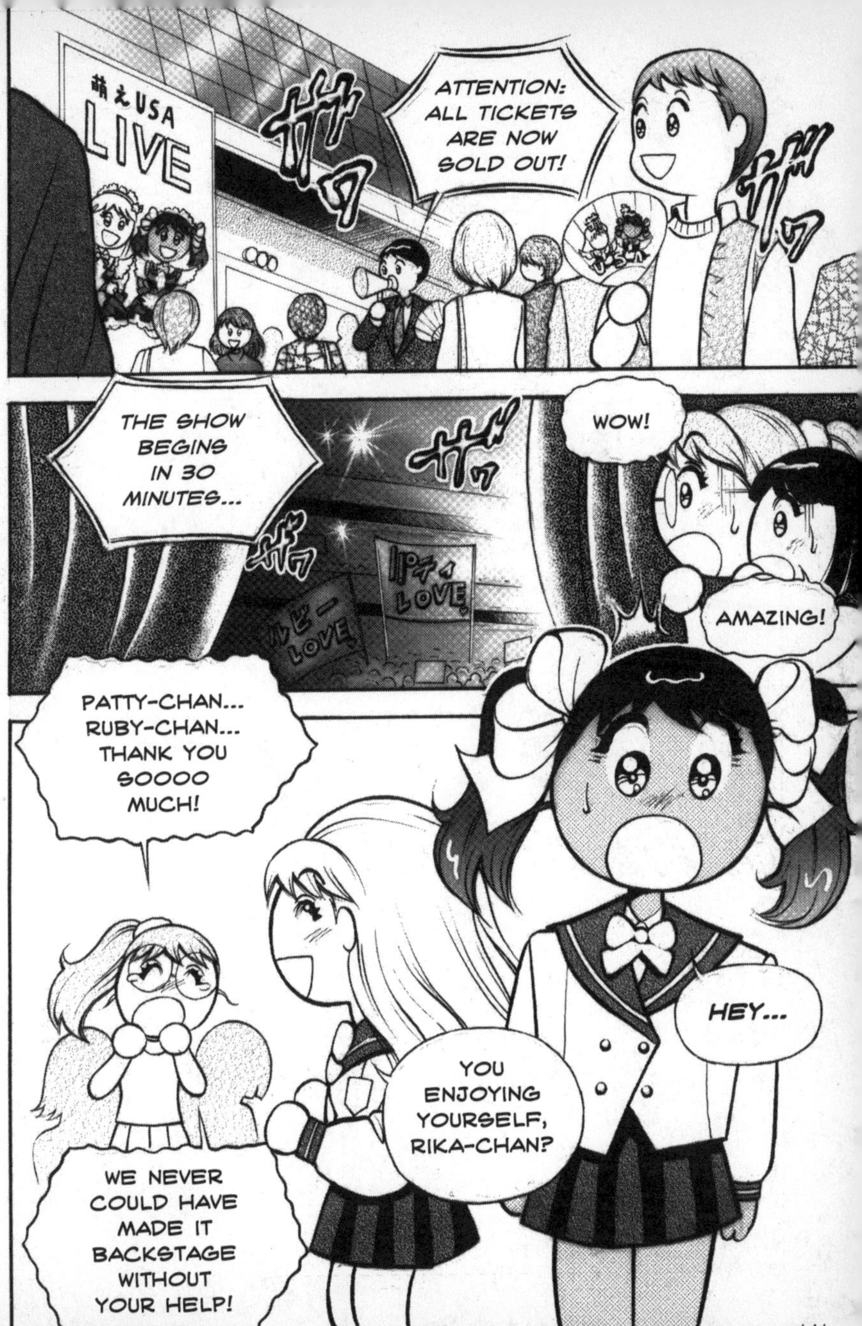
萌えUSA
LIVE
ザワ
ATTENTION: ALL TICKETS ARE NOW SOLD OUT!
ザワ
WOW!
AMAZING!
THE SHOW BEGINS IN 30 MINUTES...
ザワ
ザワ
パティ LOVE
ルビー LOVE
HEY...
YOU ENJOYING YOURSELF, RIKA-CHAN?
PATTY-CHAN... RUBY-CHAN... THANK YOU SOOOO MUCH!
WE NEVER COULD HAVE MADE IT BACKSTAGE WITHOUT YOUR HELP!

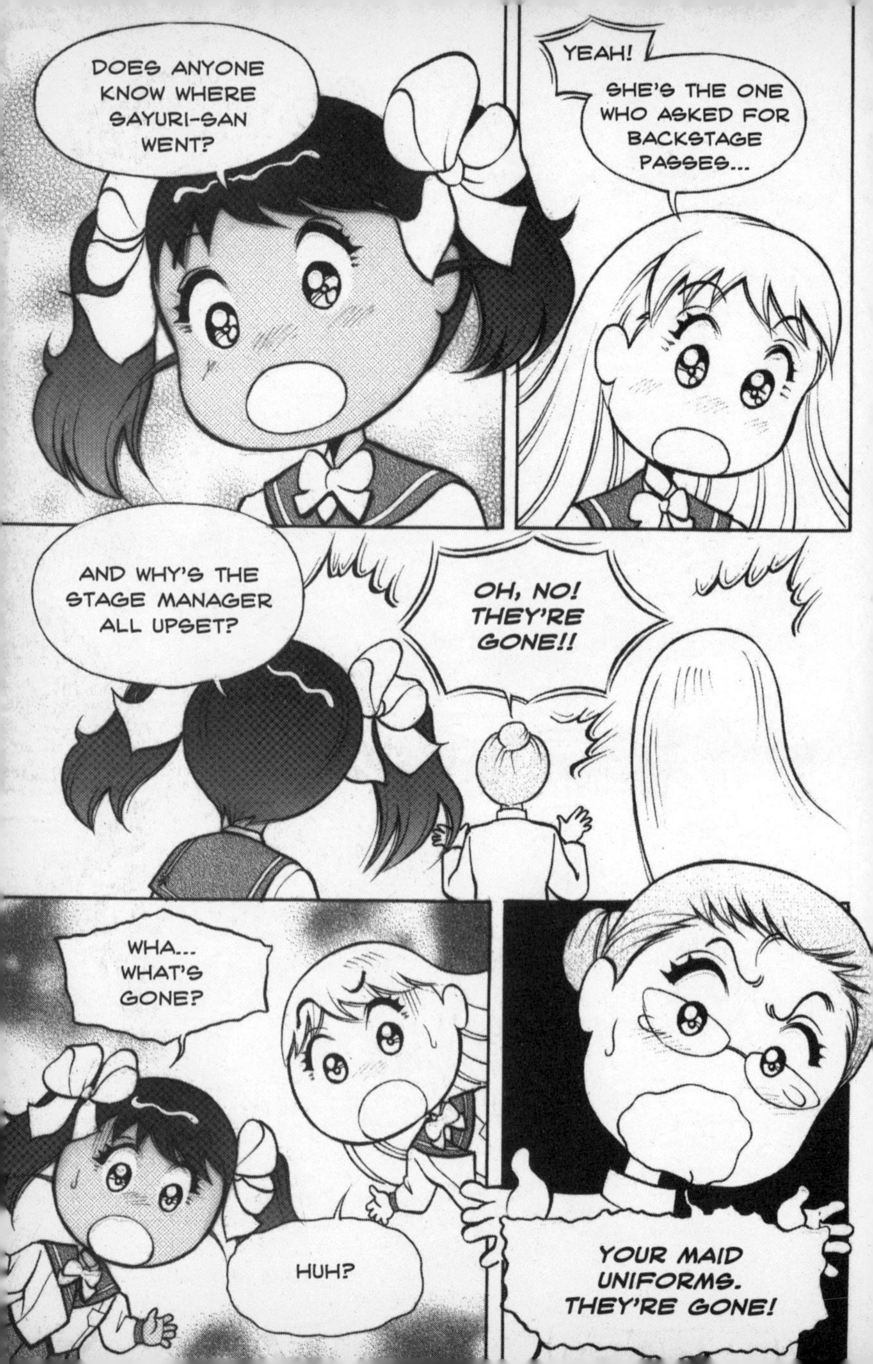
YEAH!
SHE'S THE ONE WHO ASKED FOR BACKSTAGE PASSES...
DOES ANYONE KNOW WHERE SAYURI-SAN WENT?
OH, NO! THEY'RE GONE!!
AND WHY'S THE STAGE MANAGER ALL UPSET?
YOUR MAID UNIFORMS. THEY'RE GONE!
WHA... WHAT'S GONE?
HUH?

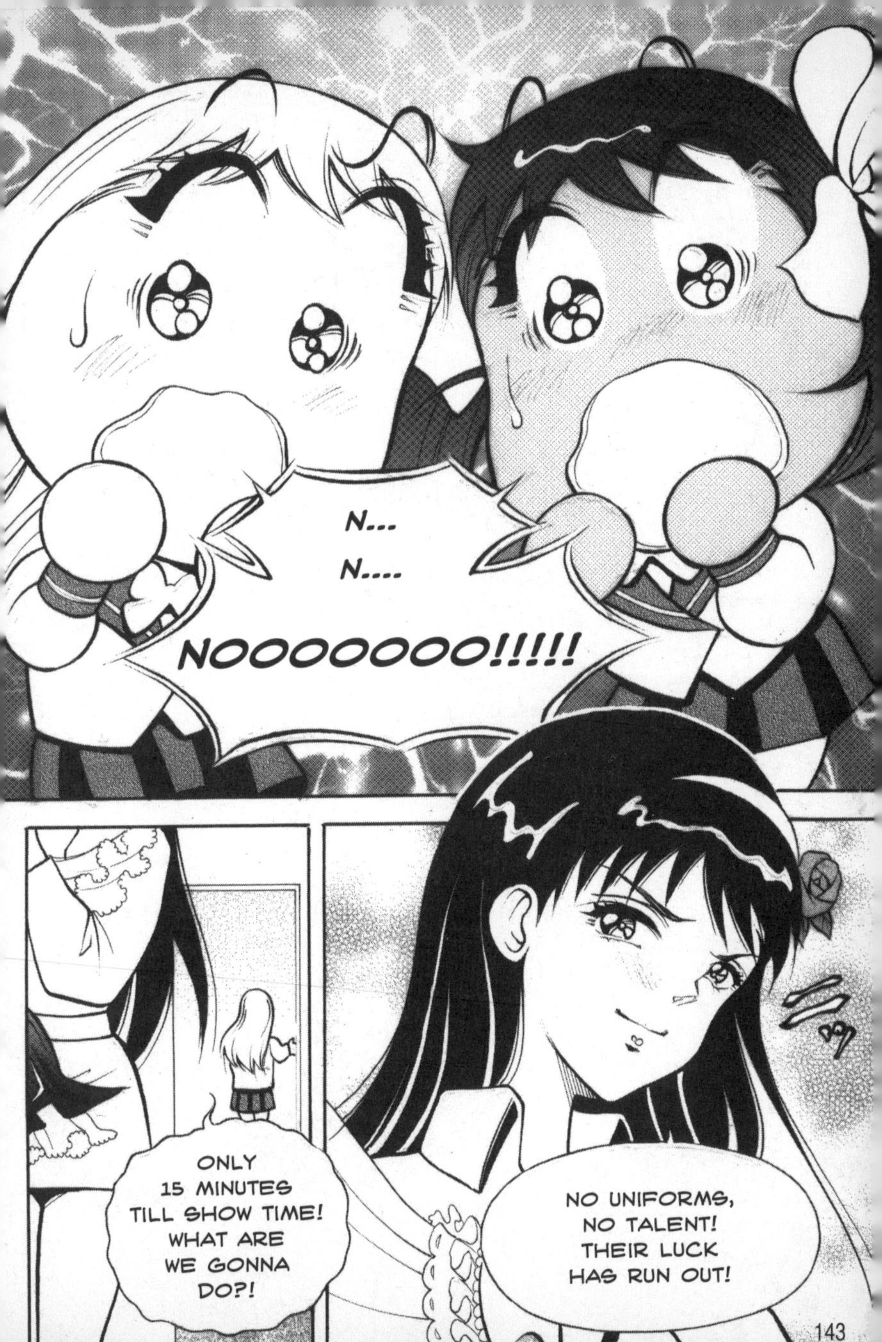
N...
N....
NOOOOOOO!!!!!
NO UNIFORMS, NO TALENT! THEIR LUCK HAS RUN OUT!
ONLY 15 MINUTES TILL SHOW TIME! WHAT ARE WE GONNA DO?!

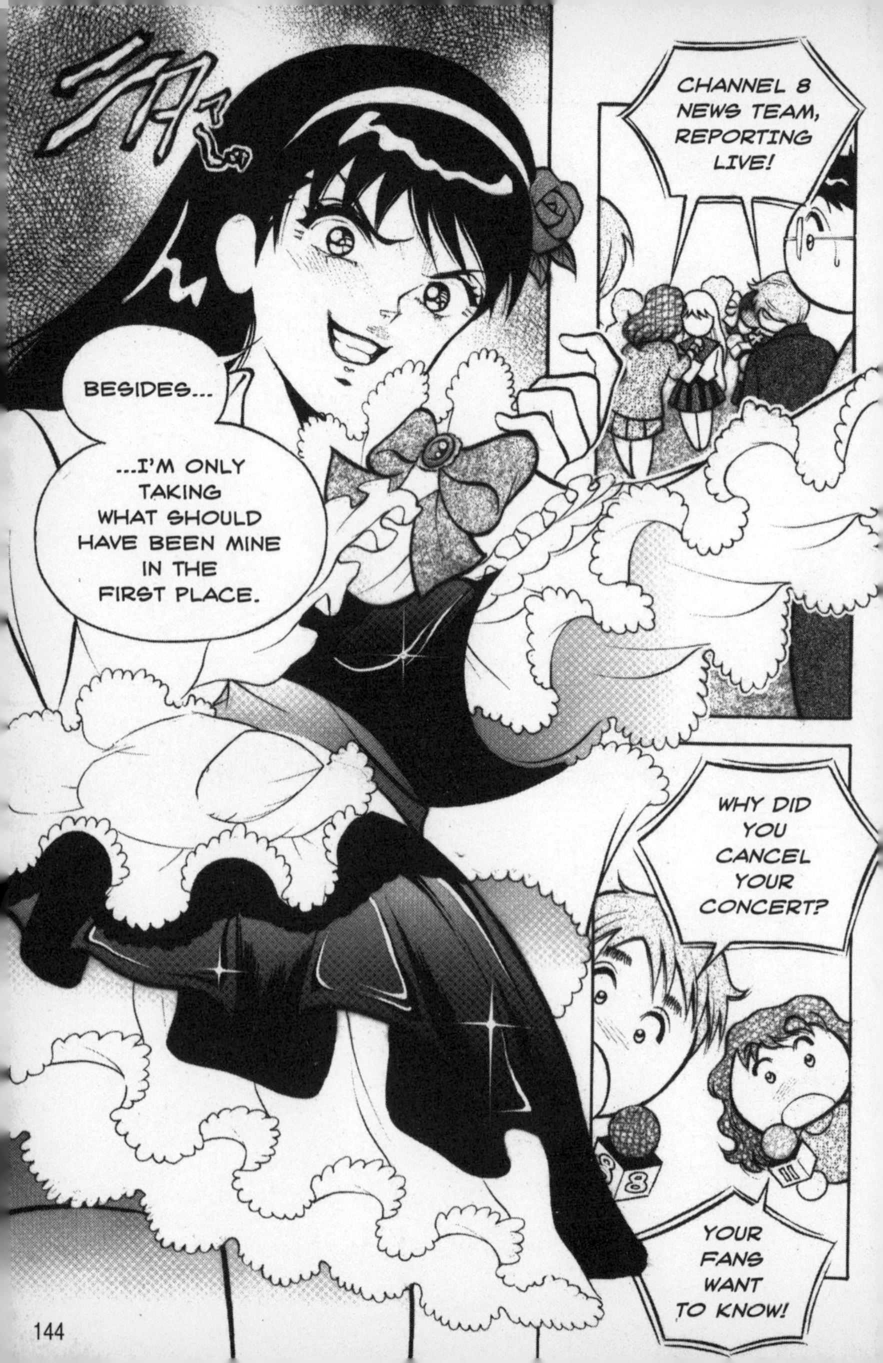
BESIDES...
...I'M ONLY TAKING WHAT SHOULD HAVE BEEN MINE IN THE FIRST PLACE.
CHANNEL 8 NEWS TEAM, REPORTING LIVE!
WHY DID YOU CANCEL YOUR CONCERT?
YOUR FANS WANT TO KNOW!

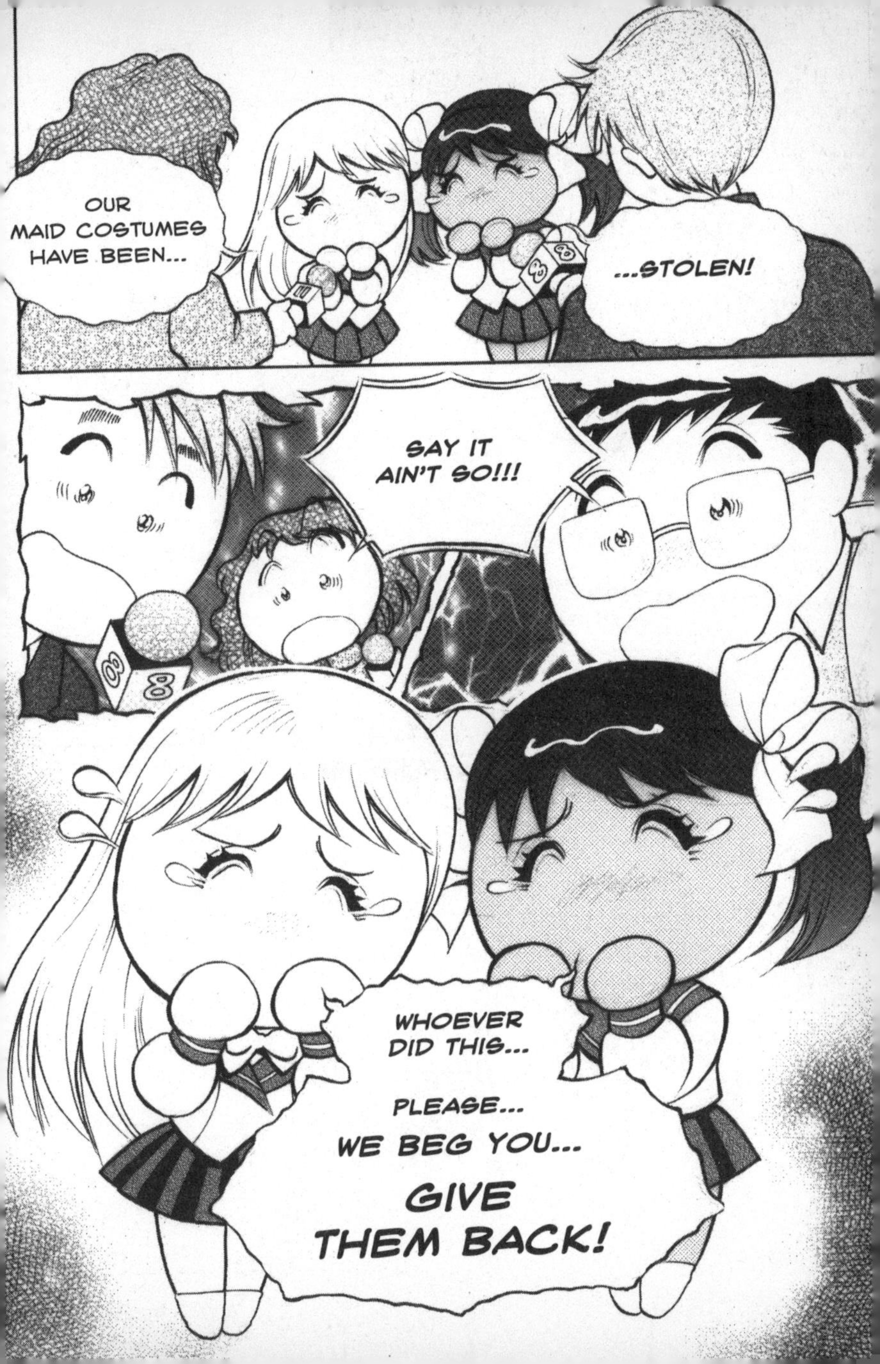
OUR MAID COSTUMES HAVE BEEN...
...STOLEN!
SAY IT AIN'T SO!!!
WHOEVER DID THIS...
PLEASE...
WE BEG YOU...
GIVE THEM BACK!

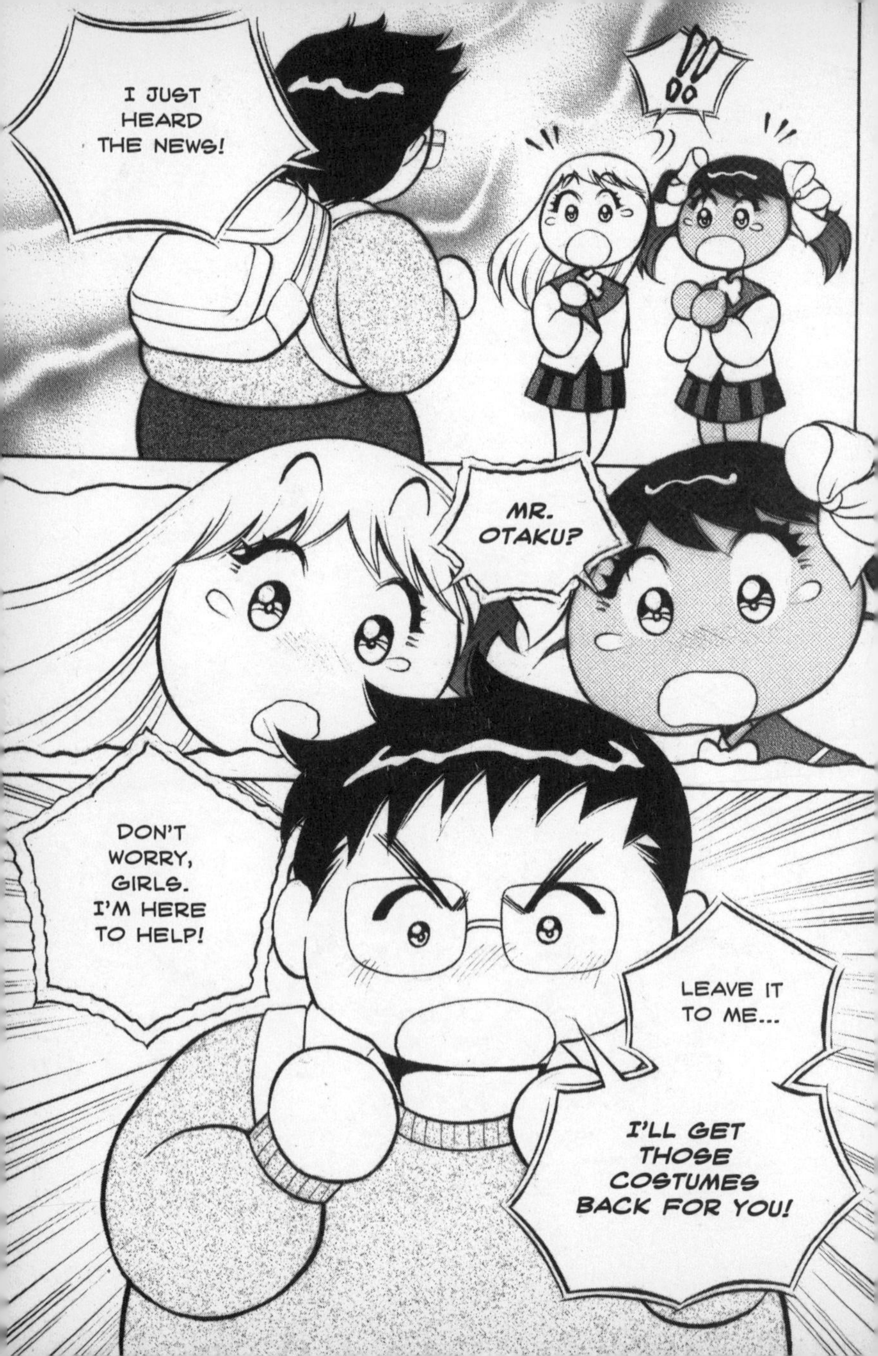
I JUST HEARD THE NEWS!
!!
MR. OTAKU?
DON'T WORRY, GIRLS. I'M HERE TO HELP!
LEAVE IT TO ME...
I'LL GET THOSE COSTUMES BACK FOR YOU!

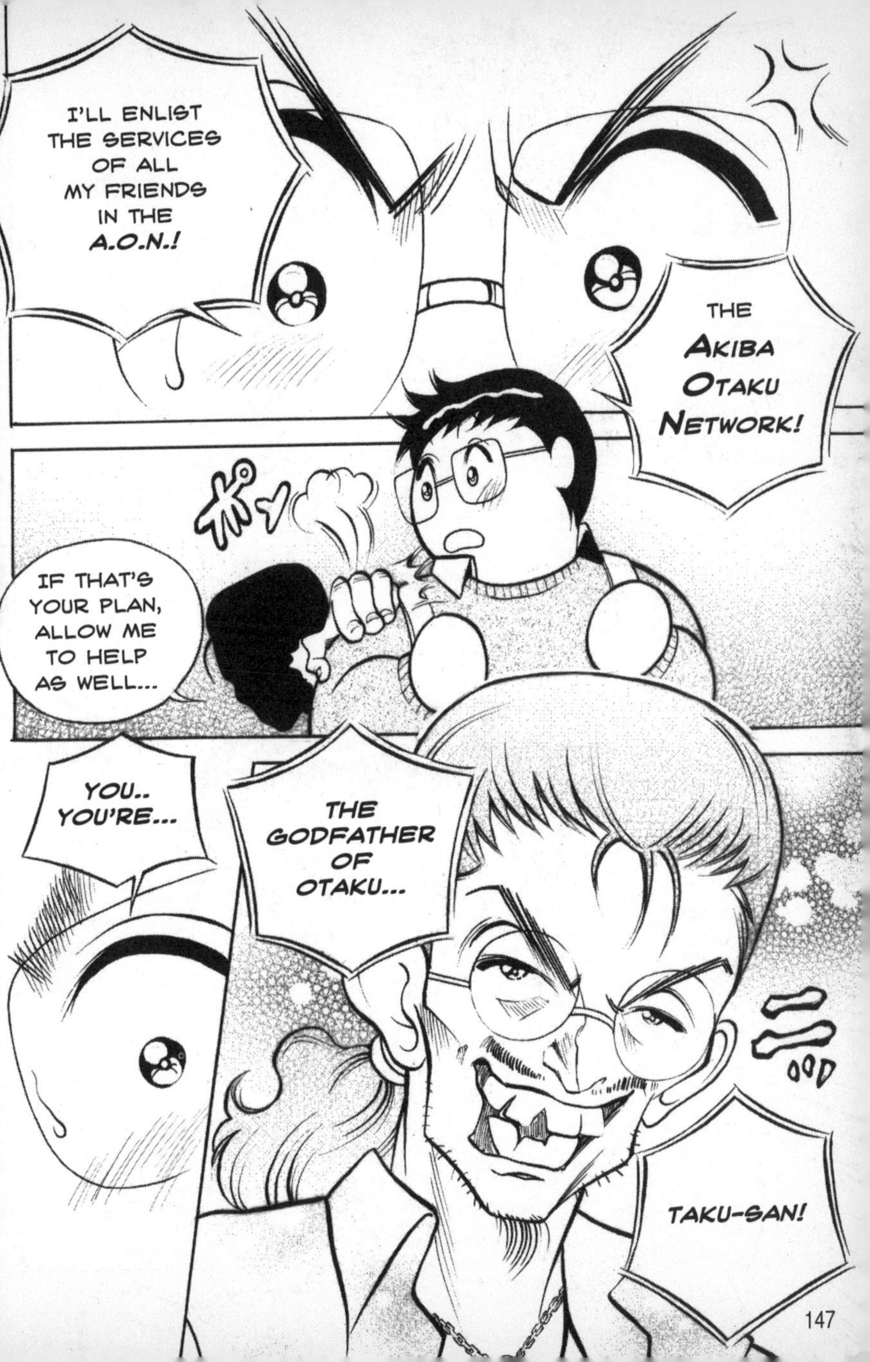
I'LL ENLIST THE SERVICES OF ALL MY FRIENDS IN THE A.O.N.!
THE AKIBA OTAKU NETWORK!
IF THAT'S YOUR PLAN, ALLOW ME TO HELP AS WELL...
YOU.. YOU'RE...
THE GODFATHER OF OTAKU...
TAKU-SAN!

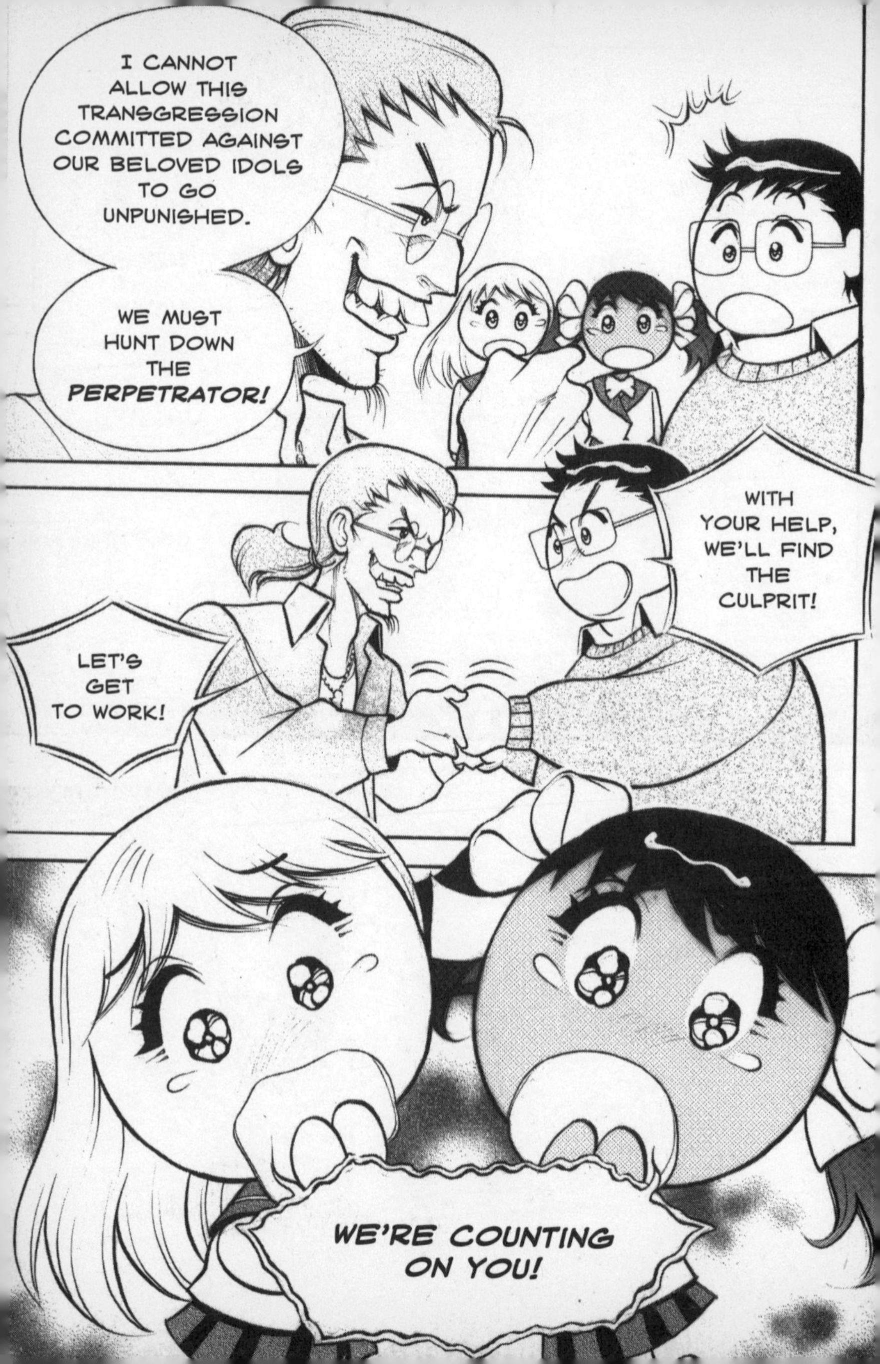
I CANNOT ALLOW THIS TRANSGRESSION COMMITTED AGAINST OUR BELOVED IDOLS TO GO UNPUNISHED.
WE MUST HUNT DOWN THE PERPETRATOR!
WITH YOUR HELP, WE'LL FIND THE CULPRIT!
LET'S GET TO WORK!
WE'RE COUNTING ON YOU!

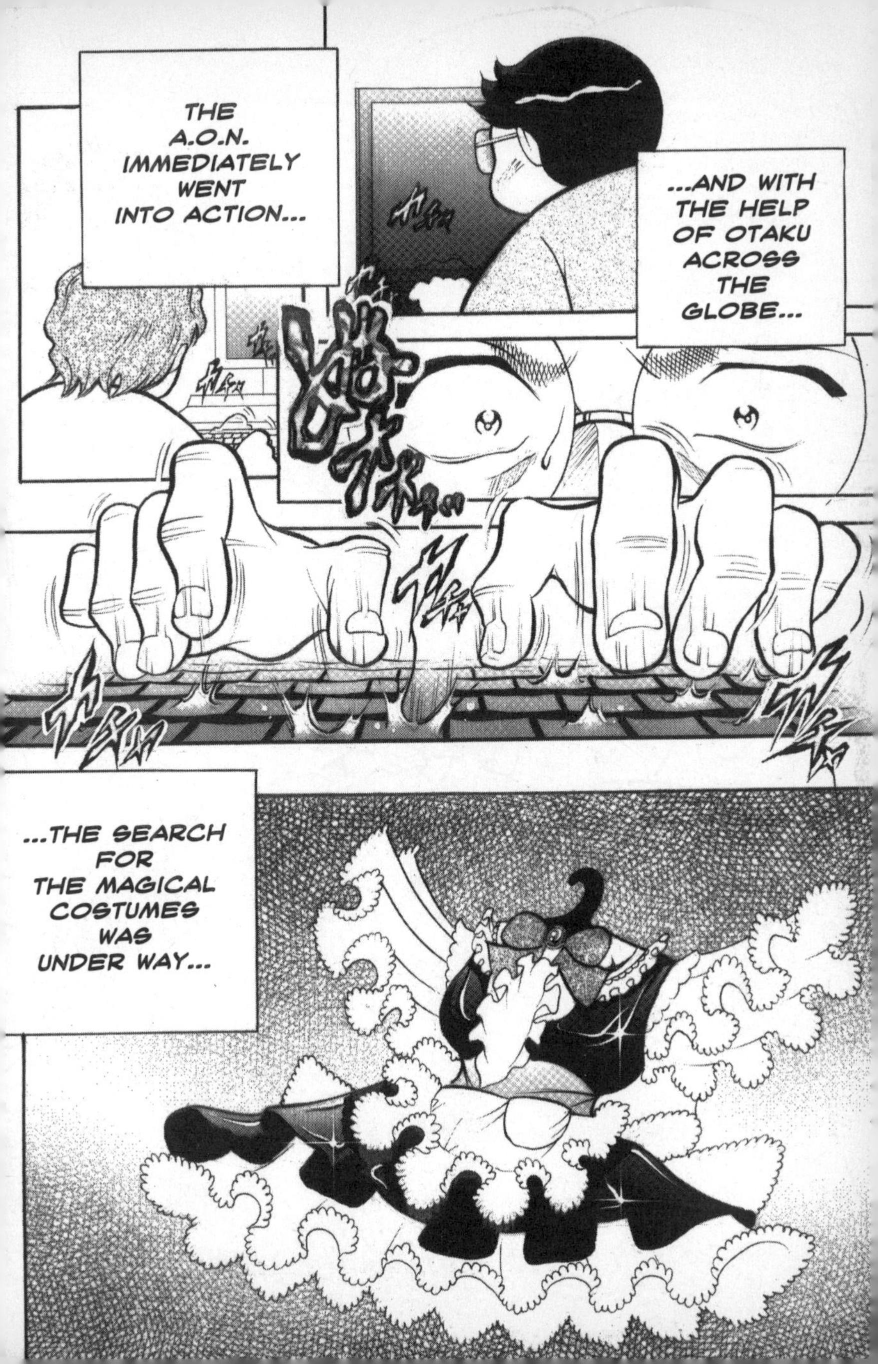
THE A.O.N. IMMEDIATELY WENT INTO ACTION...
...AND WITH THE HELP OF OTAKU ACROSS THE GLOBE...
...THE SEARCH FOR THE MAGICAL COSTUMES WAS UNDER WAY...

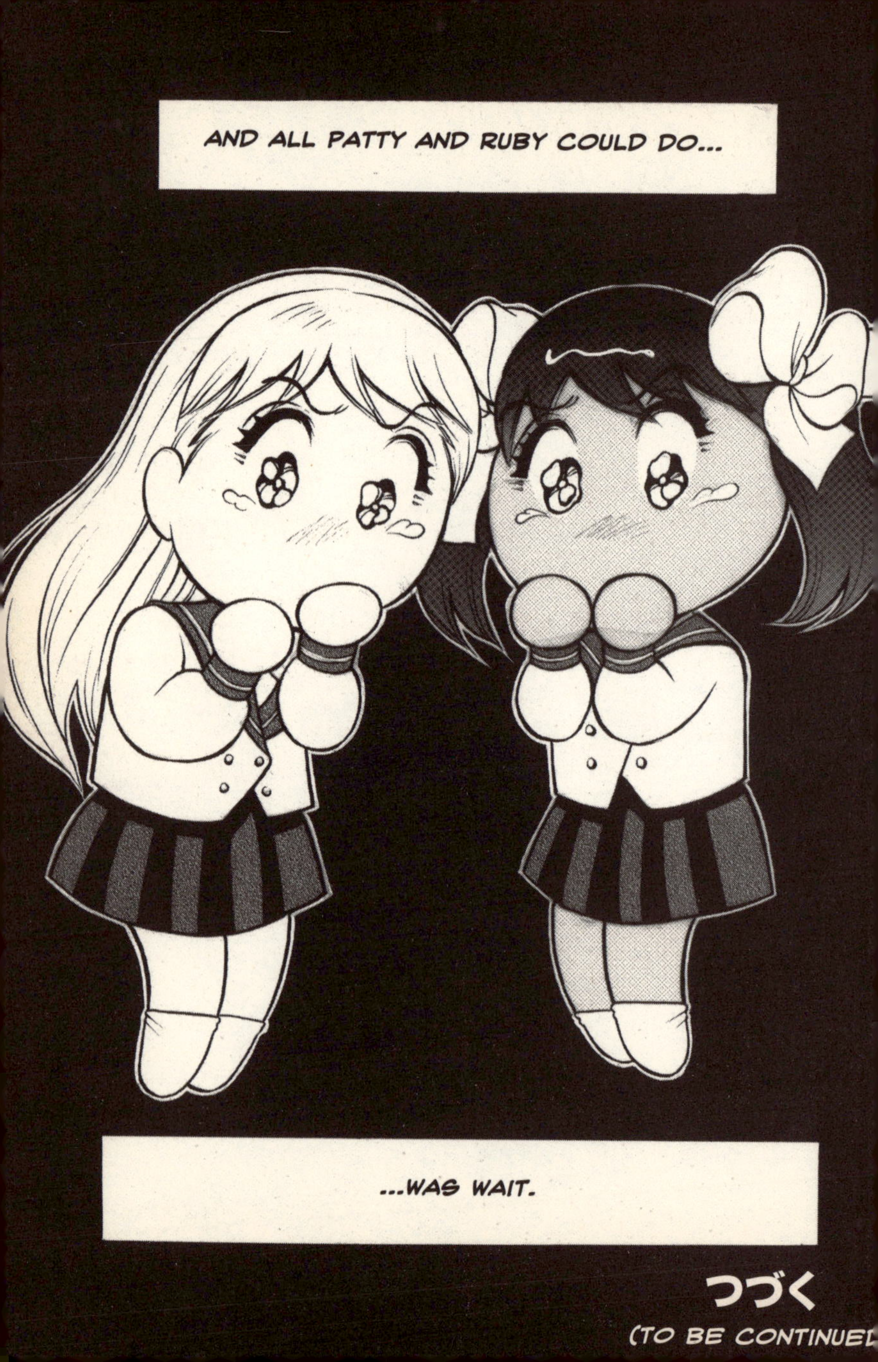
AND ALL PATTY AND RUBY COULD DO...
...WAS WAIT.
つづく
(TO BE CONTINUED

# moe USA

## index of SOUND FX

# ★ SOUND FX & TRANSLATIONS ★

| Page | Sound FX | Translation |
|---|---|---|
| ★ 07 ★ | ドキドキ (doki-doki) | Excited/rapid heartbeat |
| | ワクワク (waku-waku) | Excited |
| ★ 12 ★ | ドキドキ | Same as page 7 |
| | 萌え (moe) | “Moe” |
| ★ 13 ★ | ドキドキ (doki-doki) | Nervous/rapid heartbeat |
| ★ 14 ★ | ギクッ (giku) | Flustered |
| | ドキドキ | Same as page 13 |
| | セットセット (setto-setto) | Camera timer being set |
| | パシャッ (pasha) | Camera shutter |
| ★ 15 ★ | ザワザワ (zawa-zawa) | Crowd noise/murmur |
| ★ 16 ★ | ブソブソ (buso-buso) | Shaking hands |
| | ダーシュ (daashu) | Literally “dash” |
| | ガーッ (gaa) | Train speeding by |
| ★ 17 ★ | ドキッ (doki) | Single, strong heartbeat |
| | パシャッ | Same as page 14 |
| ★ 18 ★ | バッ (ba) | Sudden appearance |
| | パシャッ | Same as page 14 |
| ★ 19 ★ | ええっ (ee) | “Huh?” |
| | キラキラ (kira-kira) | Sparkling/twinkle twinkle |
| ★ 20 ★ | コスP (Cosu P) | Name of cosplay store |

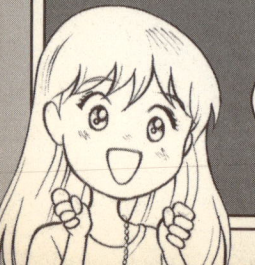

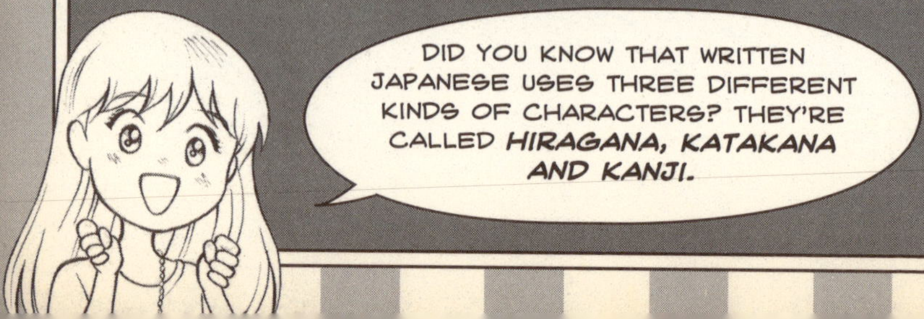

DID YOU KNOW THAT WRITTEN JAPANESE USES THREE DIFFERENT KINDS OF CHARACTERS? THEY'RE CALLED HIRAGANA, KATAKANA AND KANJI.

| | | |
|---|---|---|
| ★ 21 ★ | ぬオオオッ (nuooo) | Intimidated and afraid |
| ★ 22 ★ | シャッ (sha) | Curtain opening rapidly |
| ★ 23 ★ | バチバチッ (bachi-bachi) | Two rivals squaring off |
| | ピシャッ (pisha) | Curtain closing rapidly |
| ★ 24 ★ | シャッ | Same as page 22 |
| | メラッ (mera) | Rivals staring each other down |
| ★ 26 ★ | バチイッ (bachii) | Same as page 23 |
| ★ 28 ★ | オーマイ ガアーッ (oomai gaaa) | Literally "Oh, my god!" |
| ★ 30 ★ | ワナワナ (wana-wana) | Terrified |
| ★ 32 ★ | ダッダッダッ (daddadda) | Hard, rapid footsteps |
| ★ 37 ★ | カッ (ka) | Heels tapping |
| ★ 39 ★ | ひええ〜 (hieee) | A yelp in fear |
| ★ 40 ★ | ペコペコ (peko-peko) | Bowing to apologize |
| ★ 41 ★ | ドキッ | Same as page 17 |
| ★ 42 ★ | コクコク (koku-koku) | Nodding in agreement |
| ★ 44 ★ | ジャン (jyan) | Dramatic entrance ("Ta-da!") |
| ★ 45 ★ | ジャアァン (jyaaan) | Same as page 44 |
| ★ 47 ★ | へへっ (hehe) | Shy, awkward laugh |
| ★ 48 ★ | キター (kitaa) | Literally "This is it!" |

MOST SOUND EFFECTS ARE WRITTEN IN *KATAKANA*, BUT SOME SPOKEN SOUND EFFECTS ARE IN *HIRAGANA*, OR OCCASIONALLY *KANJI*.

| | | |
|---|---|---|
| ★ 49 ★ | ニコッ (niko) | Smile |
| | メニュー (menyuu) | Menu |
| | 納得っ (nattoku) | "I get it." |
| ★ 50 ★ | ふむふむ (fumu-fumu) | Nod of acknowledgement |
| | うふっ (ufu) | Shy, soft giggle |
| ★ 51 ★ | カチャッ (kacha) | A door opening |
| | ずらーっ (zuraa) | Indicates long length |
| ★ 52 ★ | ピンポーンパンポーン (pinpoon panpoon) | Clock chimes (The Westminster Chimes) |
| | メイドの国 (meido no kuni) | Maidland (the name of the cafe) |
| | バタン (patan) | Sign being flipped |
| | ゾロゾロ (zoro-zoro) | People moving in a group |
| | カランカラン (karan-karan) | A small bell ringing |
| ★ 54 ★ | ヒソヒソ (hiso-hiso) | Whispering |
| | ビシッ (bishi) | Pointing |
| ★ 55 ★ | ニッ (ni) | A treacherous smile |
| | ゾクッ (zoku) | Shock |
| ★ 56 ★ | ダン (dan) | Slam |
| | ポイ (poi) | Throwing something out |
| | ドサッ | Thump |
| ★ 57 ★ | フン (fun) | "Hmmph!" |
| | ガチャン (gachan) | Slam and rattle |
| ★ 59 ★ | うるうる (uru-uru) | Tears forming |
| ★ 60 ★ | ボソボソ (boso-boso) | Whispering |
| | ツンツン (tsun-tsun) | Impudent |
| | デレデレ (dere-dere) | Sweet (personality) |

| | | |
|---|---|---|
| ★ 62 ★ | 不安っ (fuan) | Uneasy |
| | ドキーン (dokiin) | A single, strong heartbeat |
| ★ 63 ★ | パン (pan) | A weak hand slap |
| | ガチガチ (gachi-gachi) | Shaking with nervousness |
| ★ 65 ★ | ヨタヨタ (yota-yota) | Shuffling nervously |
| | あっ/あ〜っ (a/aa) | "Aaah!" |
| | ガッ (ga) | Tripping on something |
| | グラッ (gura) | Almost falling down |
| | バシャッ (basha) | Sound of spilling water |
| ★ 66 ★ | ひいいいっ (hiiii) | Gasping |
| | オロオロ (oro-oro) | Flustered worrying |
| | コオーン (kooon) | A light object being hit |
| | コン (kon) | A tiny object bouncing |
| | ダダダ (dadada) | Rapid footsteps |
| ★ 67 ★ | うるうる | Same as page 59 |
| ★ 68 ★ | ぐったり (guttari) | Exhaustion |
| ★ 69 ★ | あっ (a) | Gasp |
| ★ 70 ★ | ギッ (gi) | Door opening up |
| | ギギギ (gigigi) | Creak of door hinges |
| ★ 71 ★ | えぇっ (ee) | "Huh!?" |
| | わくわく | Same as page 7 |
| | よっ (yo) | Straining to get something |

> A SMALL TSU (っ OR ッ) IS OFTEN PUT AT THE END OF A SOUND WORD TO ADD EMPHASIS, LIKE AN EXCLAMATION MARK IN ENGLISH. YOU DON'T ACTUALLY PRONOUNCE IT.

| | | |
|---|---|---|
| ★ 78 ★ | キラッ (kira) | Twinkle |
| | ピカアアッ (pikaaa) | Glowing brightly |
| ★ 79 ★ | カアアッ (kaaa) | Glowing even brighter |
| ★ 81 ★ | カチャッ | Same as page 51 |
| | カッ | Same as page 37 |
| ★ 82 ★ | バン (ban) | "Ta-da!" |
| ★ 83 ★ | バアアン (baaan) | Same as page 82 |
| ★ 86 ★ | もごっ (mogo) | Muffled speech |
| ★ 88 ★ | ザワザワ | Same as page 15 |
| | ボソボソ | Same as page 60 |
| ★ 90 ★ | バタン | Same as page 52 |
| | ずらーっ | Same as page 51 |
| ★ 91 ★ | あっ (a) | "Aaah!" |
| ★ 94 ★ | オホン (ohon) | A fake cough (like "Ahem!") |
| ★ 95 ★ | ピクッ (piku) | Shifty eyes |
| | ひいいいーっ (hiiiii) | Same as page 66 |
| ★ 96 ★ | ザワザワ | Same as page 15 |
| ★ 97 ★ | キラキラ | Same as page 19 |
| | ドキッ | Same as page 17 |
| ★ 98 ★ | キラリン (kirarin) | Shimmering |
| ★ 99 ★ | キラキラ | Same as page 19 |

THE JAPANESE LANGUAGE HAS **5 VOWELS**: A AS IN AH, I AS IN WE, U AS IN SOON, E AS IN GET, AND O AS IN OLD.

| | | |
|---|---|---|
| ★ 101 ★ | コロン (koron) | Small object dropping |
| | ドキドキ | Same as Page 13 |
| | チャポン (chapon) | Plop |
| ★ 102 ★ | ゴク (goku) | Gulp |
| | キラリン | Same as page 98 |
| ★ 103 ★ | ドキドキ | Same as page 13 |
| | キャピ (kyapi) | Childlike happiness |
| | キャピッ (kyapi) | Same as above |
| ★ 104 ★ | 萌え〜っ (moee) | "Moe!" |
| | ドキーン (dokiin) | Heartbeat |
| ★ 107 ★ | エヘン (ehen) | Gloating |
| ★ 108 ★ | ずずずらーっ (zuzuzuraa) | Same as page 51 (emphasized) |
| | えっ (e) | "Huh?" |
| ★ 109 ★ | 不思議 (fushigi) | "Mysterious..." |
| ★ 110 ★ | ゴソゴソ (goso-goso) | Searching for something |
| | パカッ (paka) | Something opening |
| ★ 111 ★ | ワォ (wao) | "Wow!" |
| ★ 112 ★ | へへへ (hehehe) | Shy laugh |
| ★ 114 ★ | カラン (karan) | Same as page 52 |
| ★ 116 ★ | ザワザワ | Same as page 15 |
| ★ 117 ★ | え゛〜っ (ee) | "Wha—?" |
| ★ 120 ★ | キラリン | Same as page 98 |
| ★ 121 ★ | ふむふむ | Same as page 50 |
| | うわ〜よく調べてる〜っ (uwaa yoku shirabeteruu) | "Wow, you really did your homework." |

| | | |
|---|---|---|
| ★ 122 ★ | ズバリ (zubari) | Pointing something out |
| ★ 123 ★ | バッ (ba) | Showing something suddenly |
| ★ 124 ★ | ワォ | Same as page 111 |
| ★ 125 ★ | ムカムカ (muka-muka) | Expression of anger |
| ★ 126 ★ | まあまあ (maa maa) | "Now, now..." |
| | カッチーン (kacchiin) | Suddenly affronted |
| | ガーッ (gaa) | Roar of anger |
| | ひいいいっ | Same as page 66 |
| ★ 127 ★ | ひい〜ん (hiin) | Same as page 66 |
| | こわいよ〜っ (kowai yoo) | "I'm scared!" |
| | ひょこっ (hyoko) | Someone suddenly appears |
| | ブルブル (buru-buru) | Trembling |
| | チッ (chi) | Annoyed (like "Tsk!") |
| ★ 128 ★ | キーン | Jets roaring |
| ★ 129 ★ | ワクワク | Same as page 7 |
| | ドキドキ | Same as page 7 |
| ★ 130 ★ | おおっ (oo) | Impressed (like "Whoa!") |
| ★ 131 ★ | うん (un) | Approval (like "Uh-huh.") |
| | おおっ | Same as page 130 |
| | いきなりデビューッ (ikinari debyuu) | Imminent debut |
| ★ 132 ★ | パチパチ (pachi-pachi) | Applause |
| ★ 134 ★ | ワォ | Same as page 111 |
| ★ 135 ★ | ザワザワ | Same as page 15 |
| | 1位 (ichi i) | Number one |
| ★ 136 ★ | ワアアアッ (waaaa) | Cheers from the audience |

| Page | Sound effect | Meaning |
|---|---|---|
| | キャアーッ (kyaaa) | Cheers from the audience |
| | キャーッ (kyaa) | Same as above |
| ★ 137 ★ | キャーッ | Same as page 136 |
| | キャアーッ | Same as page 136 |
| | パティーチャーン ルビーチャーン (Patii-chaan, Rubii-chaan) | Crowd calling out Patty's and Ruby's names |
| | ギリッ (giri) | Gritting of the teeth |
| ★ 138 ★ | ムカムカ | Same as page 125 |
| | ひぃ (hii) | Same as page 66 |
| ★ 139 ★ | ニターッ (nitaa) | Same as page 55 |
| ★ 140 ★ | ニコッ | Smiling |
| | いやな予感っ (iya na yokan) | "I've got a bad feeling about this." |
| | ドキドキ | Same as page 13 |
| ★ 141 ★ | ザワザワ | Same as page 15 |
| ★ 143 ★ | ニッ (ni) | Same as page 55 |
| ★ 144 ★ | ニタァーッ (nitaaa) | Same as page 55 |
| ★ 147 ★ | ポン (pon) | Patting someone's shoulder |
| | ニッ | Same as page 55 |
| ★ 149 ★ | カチャカチャ (kacha-kacha) | Typing on a computer keyboard |
| | ぬ゛オオオッ (nuooo) | Concentrated action |

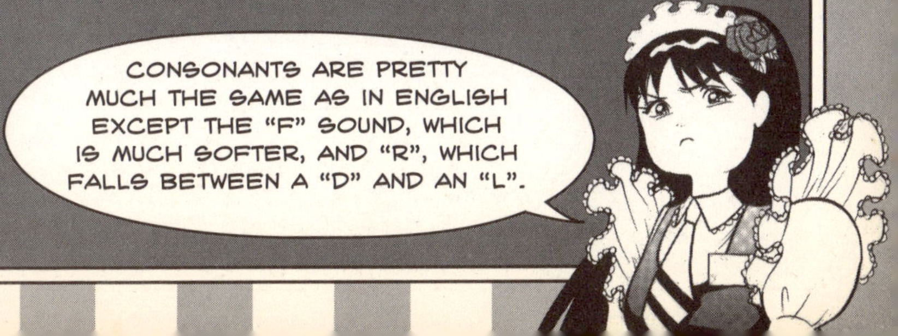

CONSONANTS ARE PRETTY MUCH THE SAME AS IN ENGLISH EXCEPT THE "F" SOUND, WHICH IS MUCH SOFTER, AND "R", WHICH FALLS BETWEEN A "D" AND AN "L".

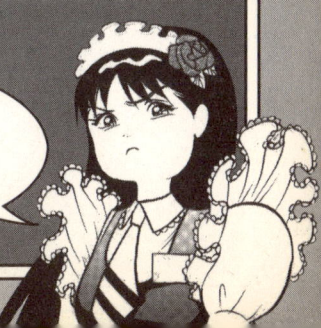

## ★ about the author ★

WHEN ATSUHISA OKURA ISN'T DRAWING MANGA, HE'S GROWING VEGETABLES.

ARMED WITH A COLLEGE DEGREE IN AGRICULTURE, HE GAINED CONSIDERABLE FAME AS A CONTESTANT ON TV TOKYO'S *TEREBI CHAMPION* (THINK "AMERICAN IDOL FOR GARDENERS"). ALAS, HE WAS THE RUNNER-UP, AND DECIDED TO TURN HIS ATTENTION FULL-TIME TO DRAWING COMICS. HIS STORIES HAVE APPEARED IN BUSINESS JUMP AND SHONEN MAGAZINE, AND HE IS A PAST RECIPIENT OF THE KODANSHA AND SHUEISHA PRIZES FOR BEST NEW MANGA ARTIST.

*MOE USA* IS HIS LATEST EFFORT FOR MANGA UNIVERSITY, FOLLOWING *50 THINGS WE LOVE ABOUT JAPAN*.